D1583013

THE CYCLOPS CONSPIRACY

THE CYCLOPS CONSPIRACY

DAVID PERRY

Pettigrew
ENTERPRISES

The Cyclops Conspiracy
Published by Pettigrew Enterprises, LLC
P.O. Box 1790
Grafton, Virginia 23692

For more information about our books, please write us or e-mail us at pettigrew enterprises@cox.net.

Library of Congress Control Number: 2011907703

ISBN-13: 978-0-9836375-0-9
ISBN-10: 0-9836375-0-4

10 9 8 7 6 5 4 3 2 1

To Alex,
the brightest star in my universe.
Set your sights on the heavens
and never stop going after your dreams.

"Courage does not always roar. Sometimes courage is the quiet voice at the end of the day saying, 'I will try again tomorrow.'"

—Mary Anne Radmacher—

"Happy are those who dream dreams and are ready to pay the price to make them come true."

—Leo Joseph Suenens—

ACKNOWLEDGMENTS

I had no idea where this literary journey would take me. I only knew that, someday, it would be complete. After four challenging, exciting, and occasionally frustrating years working before dawn and well into the wee hours, it's done.

No author successfully undertakes such a journey alone. Along the way I've dragged many generous souls into my adventure. Without their time and assistance you would not be holding this work.

First, I am deeply indebted to several law enforcement officers for their expertise: from the York County Sheriff's Office, Captain James Richardson; from the Newport News Police Department, Lou Thurston, Public Information Officer; Sergeant Rick Gaddis, Homicide Unit; Master Police Detective Linda Gaddis, Economic Crimes Unit; Master Police Detective Lorain Crain, Economic Crimes Unit and United States Secret Service Task Force; and from the Virginia State Police, Pamela Jewell, Public Relations Manager of the Insurance Fraud Program.

Thanks to all of you for your time and insight, as well as your dedicated service to our state and communities. At various points in the novel, I have taken literary license with some law enforcement procedures. Please forgive me.

I am also grateful for the assistance of Dr. Cheryl Lawson, Emergency Medical Services Medical Director and Clinical Operations

Section Chief at Riverside Regional Medical Center, and Dr. Wendy Gunther at the Office of the Chief Medical Examiner of Virginia. Their medical and forensic insights were invaluable.

To my editor, Frances Elliott, thanks for your careful reading of the manuscript, superb insights and suggestions.

I am indebted to Elaine Lattanzi and Shelley Sapyta for ensuring that this project saw the light of day.

To Carol Cipoletti and Ede Ashworth at Burke High School in Morgantown, West Virginia: Carol, thanks for being a good friend and an inspiration. Ede, thank you for the Latin translations. I'd like to also thank Rich "Sorry About Your Bad Luck" Stratton for allowing me to borrow a great catchphrase.

To my brother, Scott: words cannot express the love and gratitude I feel knowing you're only a speed dial away. Thanks for always having my back.

To Anne Wood: thanks for plowing through the manuscript. Your love and support keep me grounded and have taught me what generosity and true selflessness are. I hope I've been able to give them back to you in equal measure. Thanks for your patience and your understanding of my complex life, a life which is enormously richer with you in it.

PART ONE

CHAPTER 1

Tuesday, September 19

Jason waited for the door to his tortured past to swing open.

Having just rung the bell, he fidgeted on the stoop. His secret had haunted him for thirteen years. Separated from it now by only a thickness of wood and glass, he couldn't believe he was actually standing here, once again, after all these years.

The door opened, and a hunched old woman peered at him. "I'm Jason—Jason Rodgers," he said, the words catching in his throat.

"Chrissie warned me you might be coming by," croaked the elderly woman in a heavy Italian accent, pulling her shawl tighter around her frail shoulders. "Please come in." Her voice was filled with kindness, but her eyes penetrated Jason Rodgers as if she were already familiar with his history.

Over the years, the deep pain had faded, leaving only hollow regret. His secret had been confined to a dull ache in the recesses of his analytical mind. Every once in a while, though, a sight or a sound would trigger an agonizing flashback. He'd remember the pained look on Chrissie's face. Or the hangdog visage of his mentor, Thomas, Chrissie's father.

1

Those ghostly memories never really went away, and now they stirred as Jason stepped through the door into the Newport News, Virginia, colonial-style house. It had been Thomas Pettigrew's home for thirty-plus years and where he'd picked Chrissie up for their first date. His lungs seized, unable to push out air.

Though not responsible, Thomas had been at center stage in the episode that had nearly ended Jason's pharmacy career before it began and—at the same time—doomed his love affair with Chrissie. The man's tutelage had shaped Jason's pharmacy career. In the thirteen years since he'd left, Jason felt as if he'd failed both of them. The least he could do was attend the funeral of the man who'd given him his start.

He'd seen Chrissie graveside. It was an awkward reunion, one that Jason had both highly anticipated and deeply dreaded. Thomas was, after all, her father. She had every right to be pissed off at Jason. Her first reaction was a nervous smile and a stiff hug. They exchanged a few words, and then she made an offer that shocked him: to join her at her father's house for the funeral reception. His internal struggle was a monumental one, but in the end, Jason knew it was an invitation he would not decline. Nonetheless, he was daunted by the thought of actually setting foot in this house again; of actually talking for the first time in years to the only woman he'd ever really loved.

Long ago, his actions had blindsided her, in an excruciatingly painful way. Of course, he hadn't been around to see the pain he'd caused. But Jason knew how deeply Chrissie had loved him. He could deduce from the agony he himself had suffered that Chrissie's pain was magnified by unanswered questions. For many reasons, and for many years, he'd hoped and prayed for the opportunity to make her understand his actions.

The old woman said "warned." Despite the ominous implications of the word, a question nagged him. Had Chrissie been thinking about him after all these years?

"Did you find the house all right?" asked the old woman, her voice chalky and exhausted by life.

Jason nodded. "Yes, thank you," he replied, unable to force more than a whisper past the lump in his throat. *I've been here before!* he thought.

She offered him a hand spider-webbed with blue veins. "I've been Thomas's neighbor for five years. I've been helping Chrissie with the funeral. I'm experienced with this sort of thing—my Giuseppe passed last year."

Jason frowned, unable to muster any sympathy for the woman. "I'm sorry," he said mechanically, looking over her shoulder to the small gathering of mourners.

"You and Chrissie were lovers many years ago, weren't you?"

Jason's gut clenched, and she saw his reaction. "I see the pain in her eyes when she speaks of you. These eyes," she said, tapping her temple and then her chest, "and this heart have seen a lot." She leaned closer. "What happened?"

Jason stepped back, too stunned to answer her question.

"I know it's forward of me," she said, touching his arm as if keeping him from running away. "But I'm an old lady who doesn't have much time left. I speak my mind. No time for bullshit! And I see it in Chrissie's eyes—she truly loved you. Whatever you did wrong, you might still have a chance with her."

Jason felt his eyebrows lift at the audacity of the woman's words. What stung more was their accuracy. It had been more than a decade since Jason had dumped Christine. And only one other person on earth had known why. Thomas, Chrissie's father, had sworn Jason to secrecy. But Thomas was gone now. That left Jason holding the secret like a rucksack filled with the weight of a thousand universes.

Was he released from his obligation now that Thomas was gone? Jason had asked himself that question a hundred times in the last few days.

The old woman waved a hand. "But there are more pressing matters today, no?"

"Yes," said Jason, relieved the conversation was veering in another direction.

"Thomas's death was so tragic and so sudden," she said, placing a hand to her cheek. "He was *un uomo buono*."

"What?"

"A good man." She leaned in once more. "I'll tell Chrissie you're here. There's food and drink in the kitchen if you're hungry." She winked a paper-thin eyelid. "Good luck! Tread lightly!"

Jason shook his head slowly as he watched her shuffle through a klatch of mourners. He waited nervously in the foyer. Guests cast him sideways glances. He avoided them and studied the once-familiar surroundings.

The décor hadn't changed. This house had been his second home during their courtship. The familiar layout was thick with painful memories. The sparkle in Chrissie's eye as she descended the stairs on their first date. Bacon, lettuce, and tomato sandwiches at the kitchen table. Late-night movies on the television, ignored in the darkened living room as hands probed hungry flesh beneath blankets.

Outside, the house had not seen a fresh coat of paint in years, though Jason noticed a small satellite dish sloppily attached to a downstairs window. Apparently, Thomas had made a weak attempt to enter the new century.

The six-foot portrait of Thomas and his wife, Eleanor, still hung on the same wall in the foyer. No one who entered could miss it. Thomas stood regally behind his wife as she sat in an ornate chair, smiling stiffly. The gilded frame's tiny crevices were caked with dust. Surrounding the piece, the wallpaper's glow had faded to a dull, matte finish.

Jason overheard a woman whispering about the tragic circumstances of Pettigrew's death. The word "alcohol" reached his ear as if Satan himself had hissed it. Jason glared at the woman, ready to walk over to her and set her straight. But she was too engrossed in herself to notice him. His outrage rose another few degrees. There was no way he'd driven drunk! Not Thomas Pettigrew!

It was then that he spied Chrissie in the living room speaking with two older women. Probably acquaintances of Thomas. She was not facing him, but he studied her face from an angle. To say Christine was attractive was a gross understatement. She was drop-dead, you're-in-heaven-before-hitting-the-floor gorgeous. Her chestnut hair cascaded to her shoulders, curling gently behind petite ears. Sexy and understated, the style framed a perfect face and reminded you that a brain that crunched numbers like a supercomputer resided beneath. Her conservative dress, a tan blazer with matching skirt, low brown pumps, and an ivory blouse open at the neck, could never hide the firm curves of ample breasts and sleek hips. Then there were the eyes. The sweet caramel gaze would, Jason knew, still clench his soul the moment it was directed his way.

Her cherubic appearance and rambunctious, passionate nature had, most certainly, been tempered by the travails of life. Travails to which, he was certain, he had in no small part contributed. What had happened in her life? What had he given up? The sight of her told him one thing: she was not a frail, broken woman crushed by the weight of a failed love. Hers was a tested, demure confidence set in an unflappable foundation of femininity.

Christine caught his eye, excused herself from the women, and walked toward him. As she approached, Jason's stomach flipped as if he were on the first death-defying plunge of a roller coaster. *God, she's still gorgeous*, he thought.

Her lips formed a thin line. "Jason," she said. "I'm glad you could come." Her eyes were rimmed in red as she forced a smile and took his hands in hers.

Her voice sparked something in his chest. "I'm so sorry about your father, Chrissie. He was a great man, and a giant in pharmacy," he said softly. "He gave me my start."

"I remember, Jason. I was there," she replied, releasing his hands. "Come into the kitchen."

They faced each other from across a small island.

"How are you?" she asked stiffly. "Are you still over at Keller's?" Her eyes alternated uncomfortably between the counter and Jason.

"Actually," he replied. "I'm sort of between jobs right now." He didn't mention that, only three days ago, he'd resigned from his position as pharmacy manager at Keller's Food and Drug. The poor and potentially dangerous working conditions, which he'd tried so hard to redress, had finally defeated him.

"Really? Daddy told me a year or so ago that you seemed to love it over there."

"How would he know? I hadn't spoken to him in years."

"He had a lot of connections in pharmacy. He kept tabs on you, I'm sure. So, why the change?"

"Well," he said, ignoring the question, "I'm not completely out the door yet. They're trying to lure me back."

"Interesting." The word had an ominous tone. Unasked questions and issues floated beneath the surface like submerged icebergs.

"The question is, how are you?" asked Jason. "I know how hard all this is." He meant to sound solicitous. But after all this time and his lengthy absence, it sounded lame to his own ears.

"Thanks. It's easier than it looks."

"What do you mean?"

Christine waved the question away. The old woman returned with a glass of iced tea for Jason. "Would you like some swedish meatballs or finger sandwiches?" she asked Jason.

"No, thank you." Jason set the glass on the counter and ignored it.

The woman looked at them. "Christine, if you need anything I'll be in the living room."

"Thank you, Mrs. Liggieri."

"She seems like a big help," he said, when they were alone again. He thought about the woman's earlier comments and cringed.

"You have no idea. The night Daddy died—" She choked. "I came to the house looking for him. When I couldn't find him, I called the police. Mrs. Liggieri came over to make sure everything was all right. Later, after we found out he was—dead—she helped me with everything. I think she enjoys it. She knows how to bury someone properly." Moisture glistened in her eyes.

Jason smiled and said, "Old people always do."

Christine chuckled, blinking back tears. He wanted to reach out to her, to comfort her. But he was too far away, physically and emotionally, so he stood frozen in place.

Mrs. Liggieri reappeared. "Christine, honey," she said, "Ms. Zanns and her doctor friend have stopped by."

On the heels of the old woman strutted a small, elegant woman dressed in a navy business suit. She wore no expensive jewelry or rings, yet wealth and authority oozed from her. Her prim ensemble contrasted oddly with an ancient-looking amulet hanging from her neck. Wisps of gray dotted her temples, but her smooth skin gleamed like tan porcelain. The woman appeared irritated at the slow gait of Chrissie's neighbor, as if she were late for a meeting and did not have time to be held up.

Close behind the new woman followed a tall, lithe, and much younger woman. They were introduced to Jason as Lily Zanns and Dr. Jasmine Kader.

"Please," Zanns instructed Jason when he used their last names. "It's Lily and Jasmine." Zanns turned to Christine. "I apologize, Christine, but Sam couldn't be here. With your father's passing, we have a hole in our staffing. He's covering the pharmacy until we can find a suitable replacement. Of course, I don't think anyone could replace your father." Her thick Mediterranean-French accent was roughened by a guttural throatiness.

Christine forced another tight smile. "Thank you, Lily." Mrs. Liggieri motioned to her once again. "I'd better go see what my neighbor needs. Excuse me."

Kader, Zanns, and Jason smiled stiffly, enduring a pregnant awkwardness.

Jason broke the silence. "So you own the Colonial now?" It was more statement than question. Thomas Pettigrew had sold the Colonial

Pharmacy to this woman three or four years earlier. Pharmacists Jason had spoken to over the years had given her stewardship mixed reviews.

"Yes," replied Zanns. "For three and a half years now."

"And Thomas stayed on to work for you?"

"Yes, he said he wasn't quite ready to retire." She paused, then added, "His death was so…tragic."

Jason nodded solemnly. Jasmine Kader caught his eye. They shared an awkward smile.

"And how is it that you knew Thomas?" Zanns inquired.

"I was a pharmacy student of his."

"Of course. The pharmacy profession, like most, is a small community, isn't it?"

"Yes, it is. In fact, I work at Keller's, and I've filled many of the prescriptions your colleague Jasmine here has written."

Zanns's dark-brown eyes suddenly seemed to become alert with possibility. "I see," she said slowly. Then she quickly excused herself and moved off to speak with someone who was waving at her. Jasmine wandered in the direction of the food, leaving Jason alone.

The urge to bolt was formidable; he felt as if his sins against Chrissie were being broadcast on a moving teletype across his chest, like sports scores, for all these strangers to see. And naturally, Chrissie was distant, distracted and in mourning. *She just buried her father*, Jason thought. *Had you truly expected…?*

He ambled through the house, trying to shake off his uneasiness. The mere act of walking eased his anxiety slightly. The dining room table was covered with potluck platters, which were largely being ignored. He scanned faces, hoping for a friendly port in which to drop a conversational anchor. But he was miles from shore, and the seas were choppy. He circled twice.

On his final lap, he noticed a tall man who looked as out of place as he did, standing alone in a corner. With a gray, fuzzy ponytail, a fraying tweed jacket, and cratered skin, the man looked like a cross between a beardless Abe Lincoln and Willie Nelson. His eyes darted about, studying everyone, and locked on Jason's. They each nodded, kindred souls stuck in the abyss of social awkwardness.

Jason was about to drift over and strike up a conversation with the fellow misfit, when he spotted Christine, moving through the kitchen into the dining room. She was alone, trying to find some privacy. Tears lined her cheeks. She was overcome with emotion. Jason entered from the living room. Though it was not his to give, he wanted to offer understanding, support. A small voice inside him cautioned him to leave her alone, but he ignored it, intercepting her near the oak buffet.

Christine spotted him, wiped her eyes with the heel of her hand, and avoided his eyes. She let out an exasperated sigh, communicating with a wave of her hand what words could not. Jason reached for a paper napkin from a stack on the table and handed it to Chrissie. "Come with me," he said. He grasped her hand, and an electric jolt coursed through his body. He led her out the back door onto the porch, and sat on the top step. He patted the spot beside him. "Sit."

Chrissie complied. They stared out at the backyard in silence for a long moment as Jason tried to organize his thoughts. "I remember how hard it was burying my father five years ago," he began. "He had a massive heart attack. Died where he was standing and was gone before he hit the floor. I know how you feel, Chrissie."

Chrissie studied the steps and did not speak. Jason saw her lower lip quivering. "Jason, why did you come by today?"

"You invited me when I saw you at the funeral. Remember?"

"I know that. I didn't think you'd actually accept."

"I guess I owed it to your father…and you," Jason replied. He turned to look at her. "Why did you invite me?"

Christine sighed. "Seeing you at the funeral brought me back to happier times. At least, they were happier until you…" Her voice trailed off.

Jason scanned the backyard. The lawn was dying, yellow, and overgrown, sprouting weeds. He wanted to crawl into it and die himself.

"Maybe someday I could explain it all to you. But I know now's not a good time." He removed a Keller's business card from his suit and scribbled his cell number. "When you're ready, let me know."

Christine accepted the card and turned it in her hands. "We'll see," she whispered.

Jason cleared his throat and changed the topic. "I hadn't spoken to Thomas in years, but I think about him every so often. Was he in good spirits before the accident?"

"I wouldn't know," she replied. "Daddy and I weren't close in the last few years."

"Really? Why not?" Jason remembered how Chrissie had adored her father and hung on every word he uttered.

"Daddy changed. It got worse with each month that passed."

"I know it's none of my business, Chrissie, but I have a hard time believing what I read in the papers. The article said he was drunk and ran off the road. Is that what you're talking about? Because that's not the man I knew."

"Tell me about it. I grew up with him. I got all the Southern Baptist lectures." Christine squeezed her nose with the napkin. "I'm not talking about drinking. There were other things about Daddy that were strange." She placed her hand on Jason's arm. Her touch was magnetic through the sleeve of his suit. "I'm talking about his obsession."

"What obsession? What are you talking about? Your father wasn't the obsessive type."

"Daddy changed. It's complicated—and somewhat embarrassing. I can't get into it here, I have to get back to my guests," she said.

"I understand." Jason studied her swollen eyes. "Chrissie, if there's anything I can do…"

Christine held up the card he'd just given her. "Maybe we'll have that conversation and we can talk about…the past. And I could tell you about Daddy's transformation, as disconcerting as it was. But it would be much easier if I showed you."

CHAPTER 2

As Lily Zanns smoothed her bulky sweater in the mirror, she heard Oliver, her powerful jack-of-all-trades, moving about above her in the yacht's command center. She knew that he was watching the weather radar and the electronic jamming equipment like a nervous mother. *Vengeance* shuddered as the keel scraped the bottom of the hidden cove. They were well beyond the Coleman Bridge, miles into the York River.

Her stomach tensed. After she'd made the appropriate, polite appearance at Thomas Pettigrew's house after the funeral, she'd raced back to the mansion with Jasmine Kader. They'd changed clothes and hopped on the waiting yacht. This was their seventh cruise up the river to discuss the details of their plan. If all went well, there would be only one more before the fateful day.

The intercom crackled with Oliver's rich voice. "We are in position, Ms. Lily."

Sam Fairing and Jasmine Kader waited, sitting on the cushioned seats lining the main salon inside Zanns's sixty-eight-foot motor yacht.

The sun had descended behind the treetops, and the moonlit water sparkled through the large windows.

Zanns scuffed her leather deck shoes into the thick carpet and regarded herself in the mirror a moment longer. Rather than evaluating her appearance, though, her thoughts wandered to the secret faction led by the mysterious man with only one name. Hammon. The word was of Greek derivation and meant "hidden one." It was an apt description. The only portal through which Zanns could contact Hammon was the weasel, Steven Cooper. Cooper was Hammon's eyes, ears, and mouthpiece. Through him, Hammon had expressed his deep concern over Pettigrew's discovery of the drop site and the archaic delivery method they were employing. Of course, Pettigrew hadn't known what he'd stumbled upon, thinking it merely a prescription scam. Their plans were put on hold while steps were taken to bury the nosy bastard. Several tense days of dialogue with Hammon through his intermediary had ensued. She'd finally managed to convince both of them that all was in order.

They had come too far and sacrificed too much to turn back now. Her lover, the man for whom she was carrying out this mission, had been executed nearly three years ago. Their plan had been hatched before he was gone. The time of reckoning was nearly at hand. Three long years of work and worry would be rewarded in a mere nineteen days.

On the table in the center of the room rested a map and a package. Moving from the mirror, Zanns checked the coordinates she'd given Oliver an hour earlier. It was time to take the next step. She faced her two illegitimate children, studying them with analytical aloofness.

Jasmine Kader broke the trance and walked to the table beside Zanns. She was taller and younger than her brother, floating with the graceful, long-legged stride of a prima ballerina. Long black hair hung down to her perfectly formed breasts, framing a face that rarely smiled, and black eyes that devoured weakness.

Sam Fairing, on the other hand, was shorter and seemed to be constructed of rigid, inflexible fibers. Every part of him was exact, never out of place. Zanns studied his eyes as he took a spot beside his sister. Both of them possessed the black, soulless eyes of their dead father. She had grand plans for her son. Their mission would vault him onto the world stage and catapult him into the vacuum created by his father's death.

Zanns's gaze was not that of a loving, nurturing mother. She did not recall with fondness bygone days of birthday parties, graduations, and recitals. No, Zanns analyzed and evaluated her children as perfect killing machines. They were weapons that would deliver fatal blows and bring—as the yacht's name so succinctly described—vengeance for all the world to witness.

"This is the second-to-last delivery," she said, running her hand over the torn plastic of the package. "The information has been confirmed and is finalized. The words and diagrams on these pages will allow us to seal the fate of the two cowardly infidels and leave our mark on history."

A cardboard shipper wrapped in black plastic sat open on the polished oak table beside the map, its contents—two simple pages—resting beside it. An overhead lamp illuminated the documents in the otherwise-dark cabin. Zanns continued, "Pettigrew's death, though necessary, has put a crimp in our plans. Now that he is gone, we have no one on whom we can hang the blame. Fortunately, someone to take his place has fallen into our laps."

"Who?" Fairing shifted nervously in his tall swivel chair. He drummed the armrest with his fingers and expelled a breath.

Zanns explained about her earlier encounter with Jason Rodgers. "He has no idea at the moment, but he will soon be joining our team at the Colonial."

"He hasn't been offered a position with us yet, Mother," Fairing observed.

"Oh, he will be. And when he accepts, Jason Rodgers will provide us with the needed diversion in the aftermath of our decisive blow.'

Zanns studied her bastard son. *He's holding something back,* she thought.

"How will you frame Rodgers? We had a plan for Pettigrew. There is no time to develop a new one now," said Sam.

"You're wrong. I've devised one as we sailed. It will be crude, but it can work," she said. "Come, and we'll review what our colleague from the north has sent us." Zanns turned back to the table.

She lifted the first document, an eight-by-ten, hand-drawn map. The package had been delivered by a mole Zanns's team had recruited years ago with Hammon's help. Without the information provided in the packages, their mission would not have been possible.

"This is the seating chart," she said. "Note the positions of our targets. Your shots will be taken while Torpedo is at the podium. Thunderbolt will be seated—here. After he has introduced his father." Her index finger tapped the penciled X. Zanns glanced at Kader, her unflappable—and also bastard—daughter.

Kader leaned over the drawing. "I will eliminate Thunderbolt. Sam will kill Torpedo, correct? Two shots, two kills!"

"Yes," replied Zanns. She picked up the second page, a typed list of names. "This is the agenda for the event. The numbers beside each name represent the length of time they are expected to speak. This will give us an idea of when Torpedo will be in place."

Fairing leaned in, placing his face inside the cone of light. A bead of sweat had formed above his upper lip. "And Cyclops will be ready? These shots are difficult enough. Without Cyclops, they're impossible."

"Cooper assures me it will be ready," said Zanns.

"This would be an excellent chance to inflict maximum casualties—" said Kader.

"The mission is Torpedo and Thunderbolt. Do not forget that!" interrupted Zanns.

Fairing cleared his throat and dabbed the sweat from his lip with a napkin.

Zanns crossed her arms in front of her chest. "What is it, child?"

Fairing and Kader exchanged nervous glances.

"What are you not telling me?" insisted Zanns. She was answered with silence. Zanns leaned on the table, placing her weight on her knuckles, which whitened under the burden. Suddenly, her hand sliced through the air and connected with Fairing's cheek. "Now! Sam!"

Fairing did not flinch. His eyes remained locked on the shiny wood in front of him. "Thomas Pettigrew kept a box of files," he whispered.

"And you learned of these files when you tortured him? Before he was killed?"

Fairing dipped his head in a slow, single nod.

"Why did you not mention this before?"

"We didn't think it important. After all, the man is dead." Fairing lifted his eyes once again, pleading with his mother.

"What is in these files?"

Kader jumped to her brother's aid. "He had a sketch"—she pulled up the sleeve of her sweater, revealing a small, quarter-sized tattoo on her left forearm—"of this."

"He saw our tattoo? He knew about the Simoon?"

"He saw the tattoo," said Fairing. "He did not know what it meant, nor anything of our true plans. We're done with Pettigrew. It's over."

"It is not a good idea to pursue the matter, Mother," added Jasmine, braving her mother's icy stare. "It might draw additional scrutiny. The box is of no value with Pettigrew dead. There are only weeks left before we complete our task."

"I want no loose ends. Oliver will go there when the time is right, find the box, and remove it. Then we will have—as they say in American baseball—all our bases covered. There must be no connection to our organization." She turned to Fairing. "And nothing is over until I say it is."

Zanns sucked in a lungful of air and expelled it. She waved away the remnants of her frustration with a flick of her wrist. It was time to plan for the coming days. "Both of you will increase your trips to the Camp. You must continue to hone your skills," she said. Her children were top shots. But the difficulty of this mission would challenge even their skills. "Oliver will shuttle you down to the site, alternating your visits so you are run out of town together. We must not draw attention." She motioned toward the papers. "Have you memorized these?" she asked.

They nodded in unison. Zanns folded the documents and placed them in her pants pocket.

"Don't you want me to burn those, Mother?" Jasmine offered. "We always destroy the documents."

"Not this time. These will be useful later for what I have planned for Jason Rodgers."

CHAPTER 3

Christine plunged her hands into the scalding water. The pain felt good. It reminded her she was still alive. She had been numb for the last week, the last few years in fact. The last seven days seemed like seven decades.

The last guest had departed thirty minutes ago. Mrs. Liggieri had wanted to stay and help her tidy up, but Christine, needing the solitude, had practically shoved her out the door.

It had been the most challenging week in her life. Her relationship with her father had been strained, distant for some time. But his death still turned her world upside down and shook it violently. She had driven to the morgue in a trancelike fugue to identify the body. The attendant had peeled back the plastic sheet just long enough for her to nod. The bluish-white face, striped with lacerations, eyes closed. The mangy shock of white hair. Yes, it was him. Then, the attendant pulled the sheet back up and Thomas Pettigrew, the living, breathing man, was gone. Thomas Pettigrew, the father, had vanished years ago.

The meeting with the pastor about the service, the readings, and the eulogy was full of slow, painful jabs. She'd been asked if she wanted

17

to say a few words at the funeral. She'd declined. They had not been close. She wouldn't know what to say. Christine spent the entire funeral service with her head bowed, unable to make eye contact with anyone. Hands patted her shoulder, gentle voices offered condolences. The pastor's voice was nothing more than background noise.

She hadn't experienced grief this excruciating in over a decade. It was not so much that her father was gone. No, the grief was over lost opportunities. She would never make him a doting grandfather. He would never give her away on her wedding day. He would never marvel at the success she was gaining in her career. She'd always held out a sliver of hope that their relationship would be repaired. But even that had vanished. Her tears were splattered reminders of the forever-lost milestones of her life. The only torment she'd felt that even came close to this had been over her doomed relationship with Jason.

What remained was to deal with the microscopic pittance of her father's estate. His bank statements showed a little more than a thousand dollars in his checking account. Even less in savings. He'd had no retirement plan that she could find. The only real asset was the decaying house. All his money had been sunk into his foolish, quixotic quests.

She was his sole heir, his only offspring and only living relative. Her mother was dead, eaten away by cancer. Daddy's only brother, Clyde, had died years ago, after being shot in a holdup. He'd never married nor had children. Christine brushed a tear from her cheek with a forearm as soap dripped from her hands. She puffed a cleansing sigh that was only partially effective. Her chest lightened, but the relief was measured in milligrams.

Like most people, her father had had a public face. The one nonfamily saw. He had served on the board of the Boys and Girls Club for eight years, on that of the Arts Commission for five, and had consulted for the Peninsula Agency on Aging for three. Elected president of the Peninsula Pharmacists Association, he'd negotiated with and convinced state legislators to fund the recruitment of pharmacists to the area. As the president of the Virginia Pharmacists Association, Pettigrew had lobbied hard for the benefit of pharmacists throughout the state. He'd helped kill detrimental legislation and pushed beneficial bills. They were going to honor him with a lifetime achievement award of some kind at Lily Zanns's mansion soon. They wanted Christine to attend. She'd declined.

The private face, his naked face, was different. The real Thomas Pettigrew was a deluded man whose peccadilloes, which had reared their heads in the last ten years, were disguised and glossed over by those closest to him. Christine and her mother, naturally, had protected the public image, speaking of his shortcomings only in hushed whispers. On her deathbed, Christine's mother had pleaded with her to make amends with her father.

Pettigrew's unhealthy obsession crept from its cave in the years after he'd shunned his political and professional duties. After Jason had left, Christine had often listened to him like a parent listening to a child's rants about monsters under the bed. She'd had a hard time taking him seriously. Americans never landed on the moon; Kennedy had been killed by a constantly changing consortium of killers that wavered depending on which week it was or what web site he'd come across; the Zionists were responsible for 9/11. Thomas had saved mountains of documents about alien encounters in Roswell, New Mexico, and many others.

Thomas believed lunatic conspiracies polluted every level of political life. His crusade was to tilt at the windmills, exposing the festering flesh of corruption. That he should die due to drunk driving had shocked her initially. Alcohol had been forbidden in their house growing up. But considering his other failings, perhaps that end was not that far-fetched. Though it didn't seem to fit, perhaps he'd simply managed to hide it from her.

His singular obsession had slowly chiseled a wide chasm between them. It had ruined his business and personal finances and ultimately resulted in the sale of the Colonial to Lily Zanns, the self-made millionaire.

She had swooped in, saving the enterprise and allowing Daddy to keep his job. Christine held a soft spot in her heart for the woman.

She scrubbed a plate with the sponge, gliding it absent-mindedly over the ceramic disk. She rinsed it in the adjacent sink and placed it on the drying rack. No dishwasher tonight. The manual labor, however slight, was therapeutic.

Then, without warning, Jason's face appeared in her mind. He had surfaced at the funeral like a prodigal son to pay his respects. She wondered if she'd invited him back to the house out of courtesy, or something deeper. Jason had mentioned that they might talk about the reason he'd left. It was what she had wanted for all these years, wasn't it? To know what had happened. To know the reason he'd bolted so unexpectedly. A cold shiver enveloped her.

The old, deep wounds he had inflicted still hurt. As she rinsed a pot in the cold water, the memories resurfaced. Their love affair had been wild, passionate, and all-consuming.

Over the years, she had made him into an evil monster in her mind. His absence and the lack of closure caused her to fill in the blanks with malicious and heinous motives. They lived in the same area, and she often wondered why they never ran into each other, even by accident. It was as if Jason had vanished. Christine had learned to hate him. Then, with time, the hate had softened to contempt and was followed more recently, by reluctant acceptance. She had almost gotten past the pain when he'd showed at the funeral, and she surprised herself and invited him to her father's place.

He'd managed to salvage some honor, saving her in the dining room from her swelling sadness. For a fleeting instant, Christine had glimpsed the Jason Rodgers she'd once known. The caring, affectionate young man with whom she'd fallen in love.

One word described Jason in those days: fun. When he wasn't working for Daddy or managing his fledgling nest egg of investments, they enjoyed day-trips and weekend jaunts around Virginia, North Carolina, and DC. He tolerated her corny jokes and playfulness with aplomb and patience. During the drives, they discussed every topic: politics, sex, the thorny issues of male-female relationships, or situations that arose in the pharmacy. Christine expressed her thoughts and feelings, and he'd never made her feel stupid or insignificant.

To this day, that year had been the best of her life.

Then it had all changed in a white-hot flash. First, it was the hushed, closed-door meetings with men in suits in Daddy's tiny office. She never remembered another time when Daddy had closed his door. In the days that followed, both Jason and Daddy became withdrawn and irritable, walking around with shocked, stunned expressions like refugees from a war-torn country, casting a black pall over the Colonial. Christine caught snippets of conversation. Something serious had happened. And it involved her boyfriend. Her questions were sharply rebuffed. "I can't talk about it, honey," her father would say, his voice trailing off impatiently.

Jason's said, "It's bad. Don't ask me again!" She reluctantly complied. But not knowing ate at her. She worried for and about him. Sleep became a memory.

The last afternoon they were together was burned into her mind. It'd been a sunny Thursday afternoon. Jason hadn't worked in three days. She hadn't laid eyes on him in those seventy-two hours, and he wouldn't return her calls. Technically, they were still dating, but connected only by the thinnest of tendrils. He called and said they needed to talk. A spark of hope surged in her as she waited for him to pick her up. He looked worn and tattered. Puffy circles darkened his eyes. The fun, the spontaneity, the passion—the life—had been sucked out of him.

They drove to Huntington Beach, near the entrance to the James River Bridge. His mood was sullen, her attempts to engage him, shunned. Her fear tripled with each minute they drove. Jason took her hand as they'd walked, refusing to look at her. It was the first time he'd touched her in two weeks. The sensation sent a cold shiver down her spine. They trudged to the escarpment overlooking the river and sat on a hard, cold bench. He faced her, but wouldn't meet her eyes.

He spoke with head bowed. When he did raise his head to look at the water, a hint of moisture welled in his eyes.

Christine began to weep, afraid of the unknown and at the same time knowing what he was going to say. She clutched his hand in hers. Her words pierced the silence, hoping to plug the hole in the disintegrating dam that was their love. "Jason, honey, I know it's bad. But I love you. We can get through this. Please talk to me," she said, running a hand over his cheek.

He blurted out the words. "Chrissie, I...don't want to see you anymore. I'm leaving the Colonial too. I can't stay. I'm...sorry."

Carving her heart out with a butter knife would have hurt less. The air became thin, poisonous. Christine gasped audibly, forcing herself to breathe. She pleaded with him to open up to her, hoping that words would reveal a solution. They sat hand in hand. She squeezed with all her might, not wanting to let go. It would be the last time they would ever touch each other in a loving way.

Jason tried to give back to her the polished, heart-shaped stone she'd given him the first time she told him she loved him. Christine refused and wrapped his fingers around it. "You keep it," she whispered through her tears.

When they pulled into the driveway, Christine climbed out of the car, every fiber in her body screaming in protest. With every inch she moved away from him, her heart plunged lower. She leaned into the passenger-side window. The words were choked through tears: "Don't do this. I love you!"

"I'm sorry, Chrissie. I really am." He backed out of the driveway and sped off.

Now, the pain in her gut felt as it had that day so many years ago. Christine finished washing the silverware, running the utensils under the water. A heavy ache dragged on her chest. Tears fell into the dishwater. She braced herself on the edge of the sink. The room began to spin. That sunny, awful day seemed like it was thirteen minutes ago.

She recovered and wiped her hands on a towel. Her father's house was large and empty now. Every light was on, and the air seemed to have been sucked out of the space. She robotically poured herself a cup of coffee and sat at the kitchen table, sipping the strong, bitter brew. Its harsh taste mirrored her mood.

Why now, after all these years?

She had hinted that she would reveal to Jason the object of her father's obsession. Could she trust herself to meet with him? Could she avoid dragging herself down into the cesspool of self-pity again? Christine sat pondering these questions when the phone rang. She looked at the caller ID and saw it was him. She poised her thumb over the talk button.

* * *

Jason had been working on his Tae Kwon Do forms for the last forty-five minutes in the spare room he'd set up as a dojang. He'd spent most of the time on the nineteen movements of the Chon-ji, followed by the thirty-nine movements of the Kwang-gae. His frustration mounted with every thrust and block. His technique tonight was sloppy, uninspired. The kihaps were loud, as if he were trying to cast out the demons of his past. Finally he quit, knowing full well the source of his annoyance. He walked quickly to his bedroom.

Before starting his workout, he had tried to call her house twice; he didn't have her cell number. Both calls had gone unanswered. So Jason had begun his session already vexed.

He picked up the phone and looked at it for a moment. A small drop of perspiration settled on the tip of his nose. His gray T-shirt was darkened with an inverted triangle of sweat above a pair of white ha'i. A brown dhee was knotted at his waist.

The gathering had been at her father's house; perhaps she was still there. His hand shook as if he had Parkinson's as he clutched the handset.

Jason had avoided her at every turn over the years. He never went to any of the places he thought he might run into her. On a few occasions, he'd spied her from a distance and turned around or ducked into a store to keep from coming face to face with her. As it turned out, it was easier than he'd imagined. They traveled in different circles. He could hardly believe he was calling her after more than a decade.

Jason rolled the stone around his palm. Christine had given it to him on their trip to Myrtle Beach. They'd stayed at the Sands Resort, playing and sunbathing during the day, partying and dancing at Ocean Annie's by night. In between, they'd snuck back to the room to make lung-busting, toe-curling love.

Jason held up the stone to the light of the bedside lamp.

It was nothing more than a rock. He didn't know what kind it was. But it had been carved into a traditional, plump heart, painted a Valentine's Day red, and polished to a glossy shine. The stone swirled with stormy striations beneath the red paint. The sum total of the rock, paint, and lacquer wouldn't amount to fifty cents. But to Jason, it held all the feelings and memories of their year together, making it priceless. Jason had given it a name. He called it the Heart Stone.

After he left Chrissie, Jason kept it in his pocket constantly, hoping that somehow circumstances would fall into place that would allow them to be reunited. But when his own heart finally realized this would not happen, Jason had placed it on the tall dresser where he could see it every day. Then he began dating Jenny, and the Heart Stone was relegated to a back corner of his private drawer, which he kept locked. Even after Jenny became his wife and the mother of his child, Jason never told her about it. Eventually, it was buried deep beneath photographs in a box in a corner of his closet.

Standing in his bedroom, Jason closed his eyes and was transported back to that night. He remembered the way the breeze on the beach moved Chrissie's hair, the briny smell of the waves pounding the combed sand. They had stopped to embrace, kissing deeply. Chrissie's face and skin had glowed in the moonlight.

She pulled back and said, "I bought you a present."

"Really? Is it X-rated?" asked Jason.

"No, silly boy! Close your eyes," she commanded gently.

Jason shut his eyes. Chrissie placed the polished stone in his hand, put her mouth near his ear, and said, "I love you, Jason Rodgers."

Jason opened his eyes as he had that night thirteen years ago. Lost in the memory, he half expected to see Chrissie standing before him. He could almost smell her flowery scent. What had he done?

He shook the feeling away. Now that Thomas was dead, Jason wondered how far he should take the promise he'd made to keep the secret. Leaving her had been heart-rending, but it was also the least damaging choice for everyone involved. What could it hurt to reveal it now?

Maybe she would find it in her heart to hear him out. *Just let me say the words!* he thought.

On the other hand, he wasn't sure he could stand such a meeting himself, given his present, tumultuous circumstances. Two weeks ago, he'd ended his stormy relationship with Sheila Boquist, an often-selfish and impulsive bitch who felt threatened by his son, Michael. Jason had left his job at Keller's. Then there was Pettigrew's strange and untimely death. The man never drank, and Jason refused to believe he'd changed. Now, Christine was saying he was a man obsessed.

In the hours since he'd left her, he'd struggled with the thought that she might not call. Perhaps she would just let the past lie undisturbed. That was unacceptable. He looked for an excuse to call her. Her statement replayed in his mind endlessly, gnawing at him.

There are other things about Daddy that were strange.

He punched in Pettigrew's number. It rang five...six...seven times. An eternity yawned between each ring. Jason lowered his thumb to end the call when the ringing stopped and he heard her say, "Hello?"

* * *

"Chrissie, it's me, Jason," he said quickly. "I'm sorry to bother you again."

"What is it?" she asked softly. Her tone, however, screamed, *This better be good.*

"Do you need any help?" Jason paused. "I mean, I know how hard it was when my father died. It's a lot to handle. I just thought you might need…"

Christine chuckled. "Jason, is that really why you called?"

"Yes…and no. My offer to help stands. Really, if you need anything?"

"That's sweet and I appreciate it. I promise if I need something, I'll call you. Now, what's the *other* reason?"

"You always could read me, Chrissie—"

"Like a dime-store novel."

His voice was nervous, hesitant. "I know…this hasn't been the best week for you. But your father's death bothers me. And I think it bothers you, too. You said I could maybe see whatever it was your father was obsessing about. I'd really like to do that as soon as possible. I didn't want it to be forgotten in all the other things. It's important—"

"Jason," she began heavily. "I've reconsidered. I don't know if that's a good idea. I haven't seen or spoken to you in years. There's still a huge, unresolved issue between us."

Silence hung on the line.

"Are you there?" she asked.

"Yeah, I'm here."

"You do admit there's still the eight-hundred-pound gorilla sitting out there?"

"Yeah, I do. And I know it's been way too long in coming. But I'm not sure this is the best time to talk to you about it. You just buried your father." He paused, his voice suddenly thicker. "I want to explain what went on. But I want to respect what you're going through. I'd like to see whatever it is you wanted to show me. Thomas was very important to me. He had a tremendous effect on me professionally. Now they're dragging his reputation through the mud, and I just can't believe that. No way he got drunk and drove his car into a tree. It wasn't who he was. If you want to talk about the past—our past—we can do that when you feel the time is right."

"Would you be calling me right now if Daddy hadn't died?" Her voice was hard, cold steel.

"To be honest, probably not. Maybe it's fate. It's a long and... complicated story. I was a jerk for ending it the way I did. But I was asked to make a very difficult decision—"

"Jason, if you're just trying to ease your own conscience, I'll let you off the hook. You don't need to do this. This is how our lives turned out. It can't be changed now, after all these years. You don't owe me an explanation." *Yeah, you do, damn it. Please don't hang up!*

"Maybe I don't," he said. "But I want to explain. Please, give me an hour. I had to make a choice that had miserable consequences for everyone involved. I chose the one that had the least impact."

Christine screwed her mouth into a tight circle. *The least impact! What other choices could have been worse?*

"Are you there?"

"Yeah, I'm here," she whispered.

"Let me buy you a cup of coffee. If you're up to it, I'll say what I have to say, and then I'll leave you alone. You just tell me where and when."

If curiosity was an illness, Christine's would have been diagnosed as terminal. Here he was, ready to give her the explanation she'd so long deserved and—she had to admit—wanted. But she didn't trust herself to be alone with him. This would need to be a calm, professional meeting.

Yeah, right!

She wanted to tell him to meet her right now, before he changed his mind. But she was tired. It had been a long seven days. She wanted to be at her best when she sat across from Jason Rodgers and looked him square in the eye. It would be show and tell. The "tell" belonged to him. If groveling was involved, so be it. The "show" was on her. She would show him she was a strong, independent woman. What happened had been ancient history—until he'd reappeared last night at the funeral home. She had survived. It had waited all these years, she told herself. It could wait one more day.

"I have to go to the Colonial tomorrow to pick up Daddy's belongings from Lily. Meet me there at nine."

CHAPTER 4

Wednesday, September 20

Jason waited impatiently on the sidewalk for Christine to appear from inside the pharmacy. She was probably in there right now. His memories were thick and miserable. He trudged to the double doors, holding his breath. He checked his watch. Fifteen minutes had passed.

The Colonial Pharmacy anchored a strip of businesses, including two restaurants, a sports bar, a video store, and a hobby shop. It sat at the intersection of Jefferson Avenue and Denbigh Boulevard. The huge neon sign hummed like a high-voltage transformer. *Colonial Pharmacy* was scrawled in a handsome cursive. The *h* blinked on and off intermittently. For years, it been referred to as merely "the Colonial." Jason tried to peer through the tinted windows. He saw only his haggard, worried expression reflected in the glass.

Jason tugged the door open with a clammy hand.

The twenty-thousand-square-foot space had the appeal of an old-time pharmacy. The faces were different. But the walls, fixtures, and aisles all looked as they had thirty years ago. Its antique charm made people feel as if they had stepped back into the fifties and Ike was still in the White House. The aisles were tight, crammed full of candies, health and beauty aids, school supplies, and nonprescription medications. A phalanx of slow-winding ceiling fans silently churned air.

Jason's mind reverted back to his first day on the job as a newly licensed pharmacist. An angry seventy-something woman had cussed him up and down because he wouldn't refill her prescription for Premarin. He spied the exact spot where she'd stood, looking up at him over the counter. An electric jolt ran through his body.

The rear of the building, the centerpiece of the business, was the two-tier prescription department. *Prescriptions* was also spelled in a handsome, gold cursive against a sky-blue façade. The first level, one step up behind the counter, was roamed by a blue-smocked, gum-chomping teenager whose blond hair was streaked with purple. Behind her, shelves were chock-full of condoms, diabetic testing supplies, meters, blood-pressure machines, and various over-the-counter drugs.

Up two more steps was the pharmacy department itself. Its shoulder-high counter was bisected by an opening to the land of medicated plenty. On a high, thin ledge in front of frosted glass, an assortment of antique pharmacy paraphernalia was displayed. There were mortars and pestles of polished ceramic, marble, and brass. Short, stout porcelain apothecary jars were labeled with Latin words like *Lactucarium, Paeonia Albiflora,* and *Pro Dolore.* Thick copies of yellow-paged tomes silently attested to bygone days of tinctures, elixirs, and compounds. *The United States Dispensatory, United States Pharmacopoeia,* stood next to a more modern, bound version entitled *An Illustrated History of Pharmacy.* Pharmacists and technicians peered down over the glass at impatient patients waiting for much-anticipated remedies.

Set against the far wall were four identical rectangular bays of shelves, laden with stock bottles of various shapes, colors, and sizes. Mounted on the narrow walls between bays were three multiline phones and an assortment of official certificates and regal-looking diplomas. The back wall of the far-right bay was missing. In its place was a shadowy doorway leading to a tiny office. It was in that cramped office that Jason had first met Thomas Pettigrew. A physical ache clawed his gut. It had also been the first time he'd laid eyes on Christine.

A small man with dark skin and darker hair was manning one of the phones behind the partition. He was neither white nor black. Indian, perhaps. The phone cord stretched from his ear across the department like a suspension bridge. His unseen hands, Jason was certain, were scribbling furiously, taking a prescription from a nurse in a doctor's office. A younger, black man appeared beside the pharmacist. The movement of his shoulders and upper arms told Jason he was scraping clusters of pills along a plastic counting tray with a spatula into the cylindrical chamber running along the side of the tray. Then, with a flick of his wrist, the pills were transferred from the chamber into a prescription vial. It was a task Jason and his technicians performed hundreds of times daily.

Jason walked slowly up one of the aisles. The store seemed especially crowded. Perhaps curiosity seekers had come to walk the same aisles the now-dead Pettigrew once had. He was a local icon, whose death had been carried on the newscasts and drew the interest of the locals.

Every step pushed him deeper into the swarming ghosts whispering from the walls. Christine was nowhere to be seen. The young, purple-blond cashier didn't acknowledge him at first. She rummaged under the cash register and then looked up, snapping her gum. "Can I help you?"

He asked for Christine Pettigrew, and the young woman turned and disappeared into the shadowy doorway. A few moments later, Christine appeared, followed by Lily Zanns, the proper, starched businesswoman. Zanns motioned for Jason to join them.

"Mr. Jason. Come in, come in."

Zanns squeezed his hand with a strong, yet feminine grip. The acrid odor of tobacco hovered. Her business suit, a pinkish red that women would call mauve, was similar in design to the one she'd worn to the funeral. Its only accessory was arrogance.

Jason looked past Zanns to Christine, who cradled in her arms a brown cardboard box stuffed with her father's professional possessions.

"Excuse me," he said to Zanns, "I was here to meet Christine for coffee."

Zanns turned Jason by placing a hand on his elbow. "Just a moment. First, I want you to meet Sam Fairing, our staff pharmacist. Sam, Jason Rodgers." The small, dark-skinned pharmacist had ended his phone call, and now turned to meet Jason.

Fairing stood as if his spine was rigid steel. On closer view, Jason could see his dark brown hair was trimmed tight to his scalp, while the cuffs of his navy pants were creased expertly with a medium break over polished black wingtips. Intelligent dark eyes devoid of emotion blinked slowly. Fairing forced a smile and extended a less-than-enthusiastic hand. "Ms. Lily is a very difficult woman to refuse," he said.

Jason cast a sideways glance at Zanns. "What are you talking about?" he asked. Behind the millionaire, Jason saw Christine's eyebrows hop. She shrugged. Zanns waved off the confusion as if it was a gnat.

Jason heard a cell phone chirp. Christine placed the box on a counter, pulled her phone from her purse, and turned away for privacy. Lily took the opportunity to introduce Jason to the young black pharmacy technician.

Christine returned to the group and looked directly at Jason. "I'm afraid we're going to have to reschedule. I'm needed at work right away, it can't be helped. Sorry."

"You and Ms. Christine," Zanns interjected, "can meet another time, then. Since you are here, Jason, there is something very important I would like to discuss with you."

CHAPTER 5

"You are divorced from your ex-wife, Jenny Johnson, who remarried four years ago. Her new husband is an architect. Your son's name is Michael. He is eleven, plays baseball and the drums. You see him about four times a week." Lily closed the dossier on Jason, from which she'd been regaling him with precise, disconcerting details about his professional and personal life. She placed a dark, slender cigarette to her lips and took a long draw.

"How did you get that information?" he demanded for the second time.

Lily held up a hand, asking for his patience as smoke was ejected from her nostrils. "Jason, in my business, which is buying distressed businesses and making them profitable, it is very important that we have timely and accurate information. My business partner and I have put together a network of resources that allows me access to information quickly, before anyone else."

"My personal life is none of your damned business!"

"It's my business to know if the people I'm hiring are up to the job. I need to know what their distractions and weaknesses are."

33

"Did you say 'hiring'?"

Zanns simply nodded.

"I assume your resources for gathering this information are very nontraditional."

"You mean illegal?"

"I didn't say that." Jason paused.

She stood. Her perfume cut through the smoke and tobacco. "No, but that's what you meant. You see, I couldn't rely on you or anyone else to fill out an application accurately. My system is much more dependable."

"I'm not sure I like your system," Jason muttered. Did she know why he'd been forced to leave the Colonial? Did she know about the one-night stand that had ended his marriage to Jenny?

"Let me assuage your fears. You are a good father. You do not have any major vices, like drinking or gambling. That tells me you are a good risk."

"You managed to gather all this in twelve hours?"

"As I said, it is important to get information quickly." Zanns leaned closer, lowering her voice. "Would you like to get in on the ground floor of a new venture and help me build it?" She did not pause for a response. "We will be expanding the Colonial Pharmacy brand into a chain of stores across the Peninsula, the Southside, and the entire state. After that, who knows? I call it the 'Colonial concept.' We will restore the soda fountain which Thomas removed years ago. The design will attract patients and customers, give us a corner drugstore feel. We will also provide delivery service, which patients crave desperately and the big chains refuse to provide. Is this something that would interest you?"

She walked to one of the filing cabinets, pulled out a bound report, and handed it to him. As she sat back on the edge of the desk, Jason noticed the heavy amulet hanging around her neck. It was of old silver that had been smoothed by years of handling. The round, kneaded design gave Jason the impression it was European and from another century.

"This is an outline of the project. Schematics, financials, and a business plan. Review it when you have a chance today," she said.

He accepted the booklet and shifted in his seat. "Aren't you trying to replace Thomas Pettigrew?"

"Yes and no. I do not want your talents wasted in one pharmacy department. I need someone who can get out and find suitable locations, hire staff, prepare budgets, and oversee construction of stores. I want to open four new stores in the next year. And six more the year after. I don't want it getting out yet that we are expanding. We will purchase the land through a series of holding companies. Thereafter, we will announce our intentions."

"Sounds aggressive," he declared. "Where will the money come from?"

"I have substantial assets, and as I said, I have a business partner."

"How much will all this cost?"

"Real estate, construction, and inventory for the first four pharmacies will cost anywhere from thirty to fifty million, we estimate. It's all outlined in the report."

He let out a long, slow whistle.

"It is aggressive, and I want you to be my new vice-president of operations for this new venture." Lily looked Jason dead in the eye.

He peered back at her, shocked, but did not flinch.

Zanns grinned. She walked back around the desk and sat down. Opening the small drawer in front of her, she withdrew a large desktop checkbook and flipped it open. As she scribbled, she said, "To show you I'm serious, I am giving you earnest money on this position." She tore off the check and handed it to him along with her business card, on which she had scribbled a cell phone number.

He read the figure, and his heart skipped two beats. "Are you sure you didn't accidentally add an extra zero here?" The business named on the check was Cooper Venture Capital. The check was for fifty thousand dollars.

"I don't make mistakes with money," Zanns said coolly. "That is yours to keep. If you choose to take the position, I will add another one of equal value to it."

"I have questions. First, what is Cooper Venture Capital?"

"That's the firm financing this operation. Steven Cooper is a venture capitalist, a friend and colleague. Technically, you will be working for him until we make the transition to the Colonial brand. They will issue your checks."

"I see," he said flatly. "What's the salary?"

"You currently make about a hundred thousand dollars. Your salary here would be two hundred and fifty thousand dollars, along with an annual bonus of up to half your annual pay if we meet our goals. You'll get a full benefits package, completely paid for. Medical, dental, retirement, stock options. The works."

Jason pursed his lips in thought. "So if I'm this new vice-president, won't you still need a pharmacy manager here at the Colonial?"

"That's correct. And your first job will be to hire that person," said Zanns. "After that you will be meeting with me weekly to get your assignments, and I expect results. Make no mistake. You will be working very long hours. In the beginning, eighty or more a week. That's why you will be paid so well. Failure to produce results will not be tolerated. Do you understand?"

"Completely."

"Good. I have other candidates I am considering," she said. "I need your decision quickly."

Jason wondered if she was telling the truth. How could she have gathered candidates so quickly? "When do I need to let you know?" He expected Zanns would give him a few days.

"I need an answer by nine o'clock in the morning."

"That's not much time."

"I want to move on this."

"I need to think about it," Jason said flatly. "I'll let you know."

CHAPTER 6

"Daddy was forced to sell the business," said Christine. "It's not a well-known fact. Lily came along with a lot of money and bailed him out. He resented her for it."

"Bailed him out? The Colonial is a cash cow," Jason replied. "It's one of the few independents left that makes money."

Jason was nothing if not persistent, Christine told herself. He'd called her again this afternoon, thirty minutes after she arrived home from work, insisting they get together after their aborted rendezvous this morning. She grudgingly admitted to herself that she enjoyed his tenacity. It was a quality she'd admired in him many years ago.

They were sitting in a corner booth of Kevin's Place, a quaint, dark Irish café tucked at the far end of a strip mall on Warwick Boulevard. A half-empty glass of Long Island iced tea sat beside the empty first one in front of her. The long workday and the anticipation of meeting Jason required liquid strength. The waitress arrived with a second tumbler for Jason. Two wedges, one lemon and one lime, floated among the ice.

Jason had slid into the booth only moments ago. She'd spotted him as soon as he walked in, but hadn't waved, preferring to really see him for the first time since his reappearance.

He'd aged, looking thinner but with an athletic mien. *Must be working out,* she thought. His hazel eyes revealed a pensive quality not present thirteen years ago. Faint wrinkle lines had formed at the corners. *How much of those are from our past?* Jason Rodgers's smile was cute and crooked, curling imperceptibly at the right corner. Coupled with his crinkled eyes and thick mane of dark hair, the effect was self-effacing and comfortable, as if a joke was only a few syllables away. His demeanor said, "Talk to me."

"I ordered you a drink," Christine said. "It's been a while. But you always liked gin and tonic with a lemon and lime. Gordon's Extra Dry, if I remember correctly."

"You do." Jason sipped. "Thanks. It's been awhile since I treated myself to one of these."

Christine wasted no time getting to the important question. "So what happened today?"

Jason ignored her question, cocked his head to one side, and studied her. The pupils of her caramel eyes were wide and beginning to glass over. He glanced at the iced teas on the table. "I see you don't share your father's abhorrence of liquor."

"I'm not my father. And apparently, he didn't abhor it. He died driving drunk, remember?" Christine bit her lip and took a healthy gulp of her drink. "So, you met with Lily?"

Jason's expression told her he was bothered by her comment about her father "Lily made me an incredible offer. I told her I wanted to think it over. She has big plans for your father's pharmacy."

"Yes, she does. Ironically, that's what Daddy hated about her."

"Hated? I thought they were fond of each other. Didn't you say she paid for the funeral?"

"She did. But from what I could piece together, he didn't care for her, and they didn't talk often."

"Why?"

"I guess business isn't as good as it once was. I'm not privy to all the details." She hesitated, thinking, then said, "Daddy was in personal financial trouble. He used a lot of capital from the Colonial to fund his own pursuits. He resented having to be bailed out." She uttered the last word as if it were bitter on her tongue.

"I thought he sold the Colonial to cash in. Chrissie, you make him sound like he had an addiction," said Jason, lowering his voice. "Was he drinking the profits?"

"No, I don't think so," said Chrissie, shaking her head. "But he did have an addiction."

"Something chemical? Is that what you're talking about?"

"Another kind. More of an obsession."

"Meaning?"

"Jason, do you ever get paranoid?"

"Sometimes. Doesn't everyone get that way now and then?"

"Exactly. Everybody gets paranoid. But it usually lasts a short time. Then rational, normal people come to their senses. My father wasn't that way."

"What are you saying? Your father was perpetually paranoid?"

"He was a conspiracy nut. He was always looking for the sinister twist, always hunting for bad guys in smoky back rooms. He said the conspiracies were there. You just had to look for them."

"Chrissie, I knew your father. I never saw any of that. And he never mentioned anything like that to me. Ever!"

"It started after you left." Christine absently stirred what was left of her drink with a spoon. She wanted to add that she associated Jason's leaving with her father's new, deviant attitude, but refrained.

"What kind of conspiracies?" he asked.

"Anything and everything. Local, national, international. To him, the world was Machiavellian. Every organization had the seeds of conspiracy in it, he said. Governments, corporations, agencies—everyone was up to underhanded, back-door manipulations. He was always looking for them. He collected lots of documents trying to prove it."

"So when, exactly, did your father become delusional?"

"Just a few months after you left the Colonial."

Jason looked away, studying a waitress serving another table. "No way," he murmured. "I don't believe it." Jason had a faraway look in his eyes. Chrissie sensed he was remembering the past. She was about to ask him what had happened all those years ago, when a fresh round of drinks arrived.

"Shouldn't you slow down?" Jason urged. Chrissie noticed him looking at her empty drinks.

Christine ignored him. "It got worse in the last six or seven years, you know. Conspiracies consumed everything in his life. Money. Relationships. He pushed me out." She locked eyes with him, her voice thicker now. "His whole life became that stupid box of files."

He played with the edge of a napkin and then tried to change the subject. "You look tired. Good, but tired," he whispered.

"Thanks, I think. I *am* tired. It's been a long week. I still have a lot to do to settle Daddy's affairs. I can't believe he's gone. At first, it was almost a relief, but each day it gets harder. I had to identify his body. That's something I never want to do again."

He reached over and squeezed her wrist. "I'm sorry."

The waitress arrived to take their orders. Christine pulled her arm away.

"I'm hungry. We should order," said Jason.

"Yes," she said, tears welling.

After the waitress moved out of earshot, he defended his mentor. "Your father was a good man, incredibly passionate about pharmacy. There wasn't a detail he missed. He was a perfectionist, and he demanded it of his pharmacists and his students."

"That was one of the things that drove me nuts about him," she said wistfully. "He was the most anal man I've ever known. Did you know he folded the end of the toilet-paper roll into a nice little point, like they do in hotels?"

Jason chuckled. "That's what made him a great pharmacist. In our profession, you have to look at the smallest details. Miss a decimal point or misinterpret a doctor's scribble, and it could mean big trouble. That was one of the first lessons he ever taught me. I remember, early on, I filled a prescription for an old man. He was on heart medication, digoxin, and he had liver failure. The doctor made a mistake, prescribed the higher dose. With his advanced age and kidney disease, the larger strength could have been disastrous. Your dad knew the patient and his condition. He let me fill the prescription, then as I was about to dispense it incorrectly, he stopped me and said I was about to kill the man. Of course, he didn't let the patient know what was going on. Later we called the doctor and had it changed.

"The man had a wife, three children, and eight grandchildren. Your father described his hobbies, his concerns about finances and the stock market. How his kids were busy and didn't come by enough. Your father always took the time to know his patients. Not just their medications and medical conditions. He knew their stories. He said if I screwed it up it would affect a lot of people, not just the patient. 'Every prescription should be filled like it was for your own mother,' he always said.

"I looked at your father very differently after that. Before, patients were just a disease, a medication, and a prescription to me. Your father made me see that there were real people behind what we do. That was the first time I realized how important what I do is." Jason stopped, a faraway look clouding his eyes.

"Go on," she said softly.

"We always need to be at our best, perfect. He told me never to forget that. And I haven't."

"Are you okay?"

He nodded. "Fine," he said. "Just remembering too much."

"Is that what happened back then, Jason? Daddy put too much pressure on you?" Christine asked.

"No, that's not why I left. It was something else completely."

"Are you ever going to tell me why you *deserted* me?"

Jason winced as though the word hurt to hear. "Someday soon," he said. "Not tonight. You're drunk."

"No, I'm not."

"You're close."

Through the fog of the vodka, tequila, and gin, she read anguish in his face. "You make him sound like Superman."

"To me he was. He certainly wasn't paranoid. He didn't drink and he certainly didn't drink and drive." Jason opened his mouth to continue, but stopped.

"People change," she said.

The waitress returned with a thick hamburger and steak fries for Jason and an oriental chicken salad for Christine.

"You were going to ask me a question," she said.

Jason nodded, slathering mayo on his burger. "Something's been bothering me about your father's death."

"Yeah?"

"What was your father doing in Smithfield when he died?"

"I have no idea. The police officers asked me that too. Maybe he just went out for a drive."

"After drinking?"

"I told you, we weren't talking much. He could've kept it hidden. What are you trying to say?"

"What I'm trying to say is, in the last thirteen years, did you ever see him take a drink? Beer, wine, whiskey?"

"No, never." Christine had never thought of it that way before. Perhaps she wanted to believe he father had been drinking. It would explain his obsessions.

"Doesn't that tell you something?"

"I don't know what to tell you," Christine replied. "Are you the same person you were thirteen years ago?"

"I guess not." Jason took a large gulp of his gin and tonic.

"So what happened to that, Jason?"

"I was young and didn't know what I wanted."

"What about now? Do you know what you want now?"

"Your Honor," Jason said, chuckling, "counsel is badgering the witness!"

"I think I deserve some answers."

Jason screwed his face up and bit into his burger. A minute passed. They used the food as a distraction. Jason finally broke the silence.

"It's good to see you again," he said.

"Is it?"

"Are you going to keep answering questions with questions?"

Christine could sense the thoughts bounding inside his head like overheated molecules. *He wants to spill out the whole mess*, she thought.

* * *

She's an enigma, Jason thought. He had expected a barrage of questions about their breakup. In a way, he wanted her to be angry. It would be easier to talk about it if she were angry. She would have her guard up, her defenses in place. He could take comfort in the fact that his words would hurt less.

But she was drunk and in no condition to discuss their history. He wanted her at her best, he rationalized. The last thing he wanted was latent, raging emotion combined with alcohol-fueled irrationality.

"Do you remember how we met?" he asked.

Christine looked away, remembering the past. "You were a petrified little extern, waiting for Daddy to come back into the office, trying to figure out the answer to that stupid question he asked all his students. Of course I remember."

* * *

Thomas's tiny office was tucked behind the pharmacy department in a dark corridor. Uneasiness besieged Jason like swarming mosquitoes. At six foot four, Thomas Pettigrew towered over the technicians and pharmacists he worked with and supervised. His hands were so large he could hold a dinner plate by the edges with one meaty mitt. His eyes were older, more intense versions of his daughter's, framed by crow's-feet and mottled skin. His white, flowing hair always seemed to be in desperate need of a trim, which, coupled with his full-length white lab coat, gave him an Einstein-like appearance.

Pettigrew appeared absolutely gigantic inside the closet-sized office. Cramped and miserable, insignificant and puny under Pettigrew's gaze, Jason sat stiffly in the uncomfortable metal chair. His knees rubbed the front panel of the dented metal desk as he fended off the barrage of questions. "Ums" and "ahs" drifted from Jason's lips like chaff in response to Pettigrew's barrage of questions. Jason later learned it was part of Pettigrew's strategy, his game. He didn't care what your answers were. He wanted to see how you handled the stress. The pharmacist's workday was a pressure cooker. It produced diamonds or spit out chunks of dirty, bituminous coal. Jason was failing miserably. Forty minutes after it began, Pettigrew stopped and peered unblinkingly at Jason for a few seconds. An eternity yawned. The old man asked a final, unhurried question. "What philosophy should dictate your practice of pharmacy?"

Jason opened his mouth, unsure what answer might spew forth. Pettigrew raised a long, slender hand, cutting him off. "You and I," Pettigrew said in his powerful baritone, "have undertaken a respected profession. Did you know that pharmacists are more trusted than doctors and clergy?"

"No."

"They are. We are a respected bunch. I've had patients tell me that their doctor instructed them to do such and such. But they wanted to ask me before they did anything."

Jason nodded nervously, already aware he had never considered his professional mantra.

Pettigrew held up a bony finger one more time. "I want you to think about your answer for twenty minutes. I have to check some prescriptions. When I come back, I will hear your response. If I'm pleased, I will consider taking you on as my extern. It should be one short sentence, appropriate and succinct. Then be prepared to defend it." Pettigrew stood and left the small office, brushing past Jason.

A minute later, she poked her head in the door, her lips wide in an impish smile. Dark brown eyes glimmered with a hint of mischief through the curtain of soft brown tresses. Jason smiled weakly, trying to push his dilemma into a cerebral closet.

"Are you the pharmacy student?" she asked.

Jason nodded. His throat was dry, tongue thick.

"Did he ask you the question yet?"

Jason gave her a vacant stare.

"You know, the same one he asks every extern. 'How are you going to be the best pharmacist' or something like that?" The girl-woman added air quotes around the word "pharmacist."

Jason nodded a second time. "He's coming back in a few minutes. Got any advice?"

"I sure do." She smiled. Her eyes sparkled with devilry as she turned and walked away.

Like a largemouth bass taking the bait, Jason followed her into the cramped hall. She was leaning against a wall. She beamed. "That didn't take long."

"Are you having fun?" Jason hissed.

"I sure am. So do you want the answer?"

"I want this externship. If you have information that will help me, I'd like to know what it is."

She looked him up and down. "I like a man that goes after what he wants."

"You're just playing games. You don't have any advice." He turned to reenter the office.

"Oh, I have the exact answer he's looking for," she explained.

Jason stopped, wondering who this woman thought she was. "And how do you know that?"

"Because he told me."

"Who are you? Do you work here?"

"You can call me Chrissie. And I work here, in a manner of speaking."

"So what's it gonna take to get the answer?"

"Dinner."

"Dinner? Do you do this with all the externs, Chrissie?"

"No, as a matter of fact, you're the first," she replied.

"I have two questions. Why am I so privileged? And why don't I believe that?"

"You better decide," she declared. "He's gonna be back soon."

"First, tell me why you want to help me."

"Because you're cute. I saw you come in. You've got a nice ass."

He huffed and looked away, certain he was being played.

"So what's it gonna be?"

"Okay. I'll buy you dinner. But only if I get the externship. Deal?"

"Uh-uh. Maybe you won't use the answer I give you. It's dinner or nothing. What you do with that information is up to you." Christine twirled strands of hair around a finger. "Deal or no deal?"

* * *

Jason smiled again, remembering. "Your father was really impressed by the Latin. *Considera aegrum totum.*"

"I'll let you in on a little secret," said Christine, taking another sip of her iced tea. "He only gave you the spot because of that answer."

"You never told me that before."

"A woman likes to have some secrets. I also never told Daddy I gave you the answer."

"I appreciate that."

"I didn't want it to lessen his image of you. He thought the world of you once he got to know you."

"How *did* you know the answer?"

"I'm a pharmacist's daughter. I heard him say it thousands of times over the years. I liked it. It was catchy. So I translated it to Latin. How did you defend it to him when he came back for the answer?" she asked.

"Well," Jason began. "Your father made me so nervous, I forgot all the tenets I'd learned in school. Your little phrase reminded me what I'd been taught and all the right words came rushing back. *Considera aegrum totum* means 'consider the whole patient.'"

"I know that, silly. I told you, remember? So what did you tell Daddy?"

"I said pharmacists are uniquely qualified to understand every aspect of a patient's condition. Home, work, social. You have to look at the whole person. Look at their overall health, their life. Every organ system. Look at their family and home life, their work situation, and find the therapy that makes the most sense. We see them much more than doctors, and they tell us more than physicians have time for. Sometimes they tell us things they would never tell a doctor. We're more accessible and approachable."

"You got all that from one little statement?"

"It's not a statement, it's a philosophy."

Christine nodded, and another silence descended between them.

"So what have you been doing with yourself?" he asked.

"Working, mostly," she replied. "I'm glad I didn't get into retail like you did. I don't think I could stand the hours and weekends. I prefer dull, drab accounting procedures."

"Are you still with that accounting firm?"

"Collins, White and Casper. Yeah, I am. I've been their lead auditor for almost twelve months now. I finally got the promotion. I work a lot, but I make sure I get weekends off. We're auditing a big auto dealer right now in Williamsburg." Christine took another long sip of her third drink.

"No time for a husband, huh?" Jason asked casually.

Chrissie assumed Jason had kept loose tabs on her through the grapevine. She wondered if he knew about the few boyfriends and her broken engagement. She also wondered why he was so suddenly, pleasingly, curious about her social life. The drinks had peeled back her inhibition and revealed some of her repressed playfulness. "Why, Jason," Christine lilted in her best southern drawl, imitating Scarlett O'Hara, "I do believe that you are fishing for information."

"You didn't answer my question."

"You're right, Ah didn't," she said, batting her eyelashes and pretending to fan her face. She could feel the good ole Chrissie coming out to play. It had been so long since she'd let her out of her cage.

"He must not be very special if you don't want to talk about him," he teased.

"Why the sudden interest?"

"I'm just making conversation."

"No, you're not. Your girlfriend, Ms. Beauty Queen, what's-her-name, probably wouldn't appreciate you asking another woman these kinds of questions."

"Her name's Sheila Boquist, and she's not my girlfriend anymore. Now you're fishing."

"Maybe," Christine replied, smirking.

They held each other's gaze for a long time.

"How's your son, Michael?"

"He's great. He's eleven." Jason pulled out his cell phone and showed her several photographs. "Loves baseball, drums, and asking questions."

"Good lookin' kid. He must get his looks from his mother."

Jason smiled and looked away.

"So why did you ask me to dinner?"

"Can't a friend just take another friend out for a meal?"

"So we're friends now?" The effects of the liquor and his statement ignited her anger.

Jason gave a shrug.

"What happened to you saying what you had to say and then leaving me alone?"

He moved fries around with his fork. "I can't talk about it right now."

"Can't or won't?"

"Chrissie—you're drunk. We should wait."

She knew he was right. And that pissed her off. "You started all this. You asked me to come out so you could say what you had to say—" Christine spread her hands, palms up. "Here I am."

He sighed. "I'm not ready to deal with the—"

"Feelings?"

Jason averted his eyes and studied his food.

Their volcanically painful past was now fully erupting. The words spewed from her like white-hot ash. "You think it was easy dealing with you leaving and not knowing why? All those years, and no answers!" Christine's voice grew louder, her speech slower, more deliberate.

Several diners looked in their direction.

The waitress appeared, looking between them quickly, hoping to broker a truce. Jason asked for the check and handed over his credit card. She rushed away to process it.

"Keep it down," he said.

"You keep it down," she blasted.

"Let's not do this here."

The waitress returned with the credit slip.

"I think we better go," he said. He signed for the meal as Christine glared at him with red, glassy eyes.

"Come on, let's take a walk. We can talk outside."

Christine grabbed her purse and tried to stand. She stumbled. Jason caught her by the elbow, but she wrenched free and marched unsteadily to the door. Other diners cast glances their way.

Jason followed her to the parking lot. "Nice car," he said, admiring the Chrysler 300.

Christine rummaged impatiently through her purse. "I bought it the night Daddy died. It was the last time I spoke to him. You know, he hung up on me." She wiped tears away and in the process dropped her keys. Jason scooped them off the asphalt.

"I need my keys," she demanded.

"I'm not letting you drive, Chrissie."

"I'm fine," she slurred.

He wrapped his arm around her waist and directed her to the passenger side. She resisted, pushing him away. Jason clutched her tighter, pressing her to him. Christine tried three times to free herself, each attempt weaker. She was no match for his strength. She relented, leaning on him as he opened the door. In two minutes, they were in traffic, headed to her house.

"Why did he hang up on you? Were you two arguing?" he asked as they drove.

"No, Daddy was preoccupied with something. Then all of a sudden he stopped talking and hung up. I finally got worried and went over there. Daddy was gone, and the place was a mess. I thought someone had broken in, but nothing was taken. I assumed Daddy was just being sloppy."

"Chrissie, there are too many strange things going on. Your father dies in an accident because he was drunk. His house is a mess and he ends up dead in Smithfield. It doesn't make sense."

"He's dead. What are we supposed to do about it now?"

"Would you mind if I took a look around your father's house? Just to ease my mind."

"I don't see how that'll help," she said, her anger subsiding.

"Humor me."

"Well, okay. I'm meeting the real estate agent at nine. I can show you Daddy's obsession before that."

"The box of files?"

"Yes. A box he's been compiling for nearly thirteen years." Her speech was slowing.

"What's in it?"

"Files that supposedly support his conspiracy theories. There's something else…"

"What?"

"The police questioned me about Daddy's death. They did an autopsy. The coroner said he had a gunshot wound in the shoulder. It was sutured, but didn't contribute to his death. They asked me if I knew anything about it."

"Did you?"

Christine shook her head and laid it back against the passenger-side window. "No."

"I need to see your father's files. The sooner, the better," said Jason. "How about tomorrow morning at seven? I think I'll be pretty busy after that."

"Why?" Christine asked.

Jason negotiated several turns but didn't answer. Christine's head slumped back against the headrest, angled toward the door. Soft snoring soon filled the car.

At her place, he roused Christine, helping her into the house and up the stairs. On the bed, he placed a pillow under her head and removed her shoes. He found a blanket in the closet and covered her with it. Before he went downstairs, he wrote a note about meeting her at her father's house at seven and set the alarm clock for six.

Christine woke and asked him the question again, as if it would keep her from sleep. "Why are you going to be so busy?"

"I'm going to accept Lily's job offer."

CHAPTER 7

Thursday, September 21

"Ever thought of living here?" asked Jason.

Christine shook her head. Her hair was in a ponytail pulled through the back loop of a Virginia Tech baseball cap, and she was dressed in a sweatshirt and jeans. "No way. I have my own place now. I'm going to sell this old house. The last ten years were nothing but painful memories." Christine studied the coffee in her cup.

She looked tired, he thought, remembering her state last night. "Found any booze?"

"I've been through every room at least twice. I never found a drop. Of course, I wasn't looking for it or anything. But you're welcome to take a look."

"We better get started."

"What do you want to see?"

"Let's start with your father's collection of conspiracy information. We'll check for liquor as we go. Where's the box?"

Christine walked toward the study, motioning for him to follow. "He kept it locked in the office closet, and he wouldn't show it to anyone. It was a poorly kept family secret."

"Have you looked at it?"

"I can't find the key to the closet."

They passed through the living room and into the office. The door to the study had been closed when Jason had attended the funeral reception.

"There," she said, pointing.

The room was fifteen foot square with darkly stained wood and retro-seventies paneling. A wooden desk and a swivel chair sat near a window. A credenza struggled under the weight of books and papers. The closet was to the right. Jason tried the knob. It turned easily, and the door swung open.

"You said it was locked," he said, turning to her.

"It was. I checked the day of the funeral. I didn't want anyone opening that door and seeing it." Christine stepped closer, inspecting the closet. "Oh, my God," she said.

Five wooden shelves held office supplies, pharmacy periodicals, and old newspapers. A two-drawer metal filing cabinet was crammed to one side. But an empty space yawned next to the filing cabinet. Jason placed a knee on the carpet and ran a hand over the fibers. A rectangular depression was clearly visible. Except for a few scraps of paper, a filing cabinet, and dust bunnies huddled in the corner, the floor of the closet was empty. The files were gone.

* * *

"Where could he have put it?" Jason asked.

Christine frowned. "I don't know."

"Maybe he moved it to somewhere else in the house."

"I've been through every closet and space in the past week. There's no box."

"And you say this door was locked the last time you were here?"

"Yes. After the funeral. I can't find the key."

"When were you here last?"

"Today's Thursday. The funeral was Tuesday. That's when *you* were here. I checked it then. So, yeah, Tuesday."

"And you locked up when you left?"

Christine nodded. "Someone's been here, Jason!"

"Let's go take a look."

They began in the kitchen, checking doors and windows. The back door and the garage were both locked. Moving to the dining room, every window was intact. The office contained three windows, one behind the credenza and two on a side wall. Sitting on the credenza, he spotted a black console wired to the satellite dish on the side of the house. He'd noticed it at the gathering after the funeral. He read the name of the manufacturer: Digitronics.

"What's the satellite dish for?" he asked.

"I have no clue," Christine replied. "Daddy never watched much television."

Jason tried the window over the credenza. Locked. A window on the side wall was also locked. The third, however, slid up easily. Wet granules of dirt lay on the carpet beneath it. They had been hidden behind the desk.

She grabbed his arm, fingernails digging his flesh. "Look!"

The sole of a boot was outlined in dirt on the carpet. "Someone's been here." Jason knelt beside the print and ran a finger over the granules of dirt and mud. "It looks fresh."

He moved to the window, avoiding the footprint, and yanked it open. The ground beneath the window was damp with morning condensation. Footprints began where the edge of the driveway stopped. He pulled his head back in. "Is anything missing? Has anything else been disturbed?"

"Looks like nothing was moved since I was here last."

"Someone was in the house."

"I don't feel safe," she murmured.

"Have you been in every room of the house today?"

"No, I've been downstairs the whole time."

"I'll check the rest of the house. You stay here."

"I'm not staying here alone."

"Okay, come with me then. You can tell me if anything's been taken."

Squeezing Jason's hand, Christine followed Jason up the staircase slowly. At the top, he pushed open the first door, revealing a bathroom. She stuck her head in and gave him a tentative thumbs-up. Empty.

The next door, on the left, was also closed. Christine whispered, "Bedroom." He cracked the door. It squealed as he slowly pushed it open. The bed was made, covered with a comforter. A dresser, a nightstand, and a lamp were the only other furniture. Christine pulled him into the room with her and opened the closet.

Nothing.

Two more bedrooms and a small sewing room in which Pettigrew had stored an assortment of odds and ends revealed nothing unusual. The last room on the right was the master bedroom. Confident they would find nothing, they entered casually. The room looked as if Thomas Pettigrew would emerge from the bathroom any moment. Nothing had been touched. His effects were still there, on the nightstand, including pictures of his wife, Eleanor, and a conspiracy magazine he'd bought at Dealey Plaza in Dallas. An envelope marked a page. Beneath that was a hardcover book about fake NASA moon landings. Jason felt like he was stepping back in time. He and Christine had made love in this very bed while Thomas was at work many years ago. A chill ran through him.

Jason scanned the room and then looked at Christine. "You haven't packed this room up yet?"

"I didn't have the nerve." She moved to the walk-in closet. "There's no one here," she said, turning toward him.

Her words were cut short. A figure sprang from the shadows of the closet like a cornered panther.

CHAPTER 8

The huge, masculine figure rammed into Christine's back, driving her into the dresser. Two small framed photos of a younger Christine dropped from the dresser top. Even as he was pile-driving her, the hooded man's large, desperate eyes, visible through two wide holes, were focused on Jason.

Christine shook off the blow and watched as the intruder stepped over her and hit Jason from the side, wrapping him in tight bear hug, pinning his arms, and lifting him into the air. Jason, too surprised to react, hit the far wall between two windows, caving in plaster.

Jason's nose and cheek hit first, his arms welded to his side by the bear hug. Hooded Man rammed him into the carpet, pressing his full weight onto Jason. A gloved hand moved to Jason's neck and squeezed, choking him. Jason struggled, his face reddening. His breaths came faster and weaker. As he struggled, spittle flew from his mouth.

The attacker made no sound. The in-and-out pulsation of his mask quickened, but otherwise revealed no stress. Jason tried in vain to pry the hand from around his neck. But against the man's godlike strength, his attempts were anemic. Jason rammed a fist into the mid-section, hoping to release the choke hold. He failed.

A loud shriek filled Christine's ears. She realized it was ema-nating from her own throat as she hurtled through the air. She slammed her shoulder into the side of the cloth-covered head. The man bounced into the wall beside the bed. Christine's baseball cap dropped over her eyes as she gouged skin beneath the mask. She felt Jason scramble free beneath her.

The intruder's arm whipped violently, shedding Christine like a rag doll. She landed in a heap a few feet away. Jason rose up and delivered a trio of punches with alternating fists to the mask Chris-tine had dislodged. The eyeholes were filled with tan skin. The fig-ure, temporarily blinded, was stunned by Jason's blows. Loud cracks penetrated the air. The intruder rolled away. His hands moved to his face, readjusting the mask.

"Chrissie! Police!" Jason shouted, launching a side kick. It was blocked by an unyielding forearm, stopping Jason's foot dead as if it had struck granite.

The man sprinted toward the door, past Christine and toward freedom. She flinched, thinking he might strike again. Jason jumped over Christine, trying to get at the attacker again.

Hooded Man grabbed Jason in midleap and flung him through the bedroom door. Jason's head slammed into the doorframe, bounc-ing on the floor upon landing. The intruder raced to Jason and stood over him ominously, waiting for him to move. He turned toward Christine, who was retrieving the lamp from the nightstand. She took two steps in his direction.

The man sprinted down the hall and disappeared down the stairs. Seconds later, Christine heard the front door open. She ran downstairs and looked out. The figure was racing away through Mrs. Liggieri's yard.

* * *

"I'm fine," Jason persisted.

The paramedics had tried several times to convince him to get in the ambulance and go to the hospital. "You might have a concussion," one said. Jason, steadfast, declined. They packed up their gear and helped him downstairs, planting him on the sofa. They told Christine he should not be alone for the next twenty-four hours, and gave her instructions to get him to a doctor as soon as possible. Jason signed a release refusing treatment, scratching his name without looking at the form.

A police officer waited at the bottom of the stairs, watching silently until the paramedics were gone. He asked Jason a few questions, who answered with his head in his hands.

"He had a tattoo on his arm," said Jason.

"Where on his arm?"

Jason exposed the inside of his right forearm and pointed to the spot on his own arm without looking up.

"What did it look like?"

"Like a squiggly line."

"Can you draw it for me?" The man handed the pad to Jason. He took it without looking up and drew the small tattoo.

The officer left, promising that a detective would follow up in a few days. He said that dusting for fingerprints would not help, since the attacker had worn gloves. "We have several units cruising the neighborhood," he said.

* * *

"Kneel," Lily commanded. Oliver obeyed and knelt on the thick carpet of her expansive bedroom. "Tell me what happened."

He described the events of the altercation with Jason Rodgers, speaking in hushed tones. His Adam's apple bobbed quickly several times during his monologue. Zanns listened patiently until he was finished.

"Did they see your face?"

"I wore a hood," he replied, eyes downcast.

Zanns frowned. "That box must be found, Oliver. Go back to Pettigrew's and search again. Then search the daughter's house. Obviously, if he was looking for it, Jason Rodgers does not have it."

"But the daughter doesn't know where the box is," Oliver offered, hoping this insight might help him win a reprieve.

"Nonetheless, Pettigrew may have hidden it in her house. Search it. You must find that box."

Oliver slumped.

Lily patted Oliver's shoulder. "You have failed me, Oliver. You are a true and loyal servant. If you were not so valuable, your punishment would be much more severe. Consider yourself lucky." Lily could not afford to part with his services. His skill as a pilot and a bodyguard had served her well many times, and would do so again in the near future.

"Yes, Ms. Lily."

Oliver remained, kneeling on the carpet while Lily left the bedroom. She returned with a blanket, bandages, gauze, and a jet lighter. She spread the blanket out and laid the supplies on it. Oliver lay on his back, his right hand and arm across the blanket, wincing in anticipation of the pain.

"Oliver, your incompetence could have crippled our mission had you been caught, stealing from Allah his chance for vengeance. Vengeance we have worked so long and so hard for. He has no patience for such clumsiness. Your deeds cannot go unpunished. It is no different than a thief who is caught stealing a loaf of bread."

Lily recited a verse from the Quran. "As for the man who steals and the woman who steals, cut off their hands as punishment for what they have earned, an exemplary punishment from Allah."

"I will not cut off your hand, Oliver. Only a fraction of it, to remind you that the mission is paramount." The blades of the boning scissors gleamed in the dim light of Zanns's desk lamp. "You will be cleansed of your sin. Do not repeat it!"

She slipped his right pinky between the blades as Oliver sucked in a deep breath. With a forceful, loud snap, the severed finger dropped to the blanket, followed quickly by large droplets of blood.

Oliver's wail shook the walls.

CHAPTER 9

Michael wound up and fired. His fastball zipped at Jason and popped like a rifle shot into Jason's ancient mitt. A plume of dust exploded from the glove. *Not bad*, Jason thought. For the last two months, Michael had worked hard, throwing against the fence and with his father, to strengthen his arm for next year's Little League season. This past summer he'd realized he needed to work on developing a curveball and his arm strength if he was going to compete against the year-round ballplayers.

Jason's head still throbbed and spun like a carnival ride. He steadied himself by placing a hand on the driveway.

"Nice pitch, Son," he said weakly.

Michael had begged him for a round of catch before starting his homework—a report about the code breakers of Bletchley Park during World War Two and their use of the Colossus, the world's first electronic, programmable computing machines.

Michael fired another one straight down the middle.

61

"If you keep throwing them like that next season, they won't be able to touch you."

Jason always loved playing catch with Michael. He'd dreamed about it since before Michael was born. Today, it took his mind off his headache, eased the pain, and made him wonder about roads not taken.

Jason had always placed Chrissie's face in the picture frame of his mind that was saved for his wife. When he'd dreamed about playing ball with his as-yet-unborn son, Chrissie was Michael's mother, even in the years that followed their breakup. Then he met Jenny, married her, and those visions melted away.

Michael threw ten more pitches, mixing in a few change-ups and fastballs.

"That's all for me." Jason sucked in several deep breaths. His temples pounded.

"You okay, Dad?"

"Just fine."

The ibuprofen dulled the pounding, and the nausea had resolved. But balance was still an issue. As a pharmacist, Jason knew he should have gone to the hospital. If one of his patients described the way he'd struck his head, Jason would have strongly suggested visiting an emergency room. X-rays or even a CT scan were called for. But Jason feared if they found something serious, there was no telling how long he would be confined to a hospital bed, and Lily Zanns would find someone else to become her new VP. That was a chance he was not willing to take.

Michael tossed his glove into a plastic bin in the garage. The boy was the spitting image of Jenny. His black, wavy hair spilled over his ears, making putting a ball cap on it an adventure. The gap-toothed smile lit up Jason's world.

"Dad?"

"Yeah, Son."

"Are all criminals in prison guilty?"

"Most of them are. Why do you ask?"

"You know my friend Trevor?"

"Yeah."

"Well, his older brother was arrested last week for breaking into someone's house. Trevor said he did it on a dare."

"That wasn't very smart."

"I guess not. Wouldn't it suck if you were accused of a crime and had to go to prison?"

"Watch your language."

"Sorry. But wouldn't it?"

"Yeah, it would be pretty bad. Why do you ask?"

"If you committed a crime, would you admit it?"

"I hope I wouldn't commit a crime."

"Yeah, but just say you did. Would you?"

Jason smiled. "Yes, I would admit it."

"What if you didn't do it, and no one believed you?"

"With evidence nowadays, it should be easy to prove your innocence."

"If you told me you didn't commit a crime, I'd believe you."

"I'm glad, Son. Now go do your homework while I work on my Hwa-Rang."

CHAPTER 10

Friday, September 22

Oliver slipped in the back door like an apparition. It was his second attempt in the last forty-eight hours to finish the task that had cost him his last remaining pinky finger. He methodically searched each room of Thomas Pettigrew's house using only a three-inch flashlight. Thirty minutes later, empty handed, he exited and moved to the next objective.

He watched from a hundred yards away as the Chrysler 300 backed out of the driveway, the Pettigrew woman at the wheel. She sped away in the opposite direction. The taillights brightened. She paused at the intersection and slowly made the turn. He waited a full minute to be sure she didn't double back.

He rubbed the gauze over the missing finger, grimacing deeply. It hurt incredibly. As usual, he had forgone any painkillers. The agony served as a constant reminder about the consequences of failure. He had successfully completed many missions for Ms. Lily, hundreds in fact. Success was expected and not celebrated. Failures were dealt with harshly. But to her credit, Lily did not dwell on his few failures after punishment had been meted out.

Oliver flexed the remaining eight fingers that were still attached, glad his career was coming to an end. He could ill afford any more mistakes if he expected to be able to feed himself. This mission would be their last and would allow him to live comfortably in self-imposed exile serving Ms. Lily.

Satisfied it was safe, he quietly exited the BMW and walked calmly through the shadows of the sycamores to the back. Ninety seconds later, he was inside. He searched every room with gloved hands. Stymied again, he exited, locking the door behind him. He would not rest until the box of files was in his possession.

CHAPTER 11

Tuesday, September 26

"What's the bet?" asked Jason.

"The usual," Peter Rodgers, Jason's brother, replied. "Loser buys lunch and drives Mom to her doctor's appointments for the next two weeks. I'm particularly hungry today. I see a large steak smothered in sautéed onions and mushrooms in my future while I listen to you tell me about that bitch of an ex-girlfriend of yours, the intruder, and this cushy new job." Peter ripped a few pieces of grass in the air and tossed them. They floated away in the wind. "The wind's strong today. It must be at least eight miles per crossing. Not an easy shot."

They were lying prone on a hill, somewhere in rural Smithfield. They had been coming here weekly for four years. Peter had infected Jason with his enthusiasm for handguns, rifles, and martial arts. Peter, a former Force Recon marine sniper and third-degree black belt in Tae Kwon Do to Jason's fourth-degree brown, had taught Jason how to handle and fire an assortment of weapons, proper breathing techniques, and long-range shooting tactics. Peter had at least ten confirmed kills in the first Gulf War, and probably a dozen more unconfirmed.

66

Jason was a stellar student and had absorbed every fact and detail. He owned a handgun and enjoyed handling it, but was not as fanatical about them as his older sibling. For Jason, it was more about enjoying Peter's company and war stories. Dressed in camouflage fatigues, they looked like two hunters about to drop a twelve point.

Jason eyed the distant target through a large, tactical sighting scope propped on a small tripod. A piece of plywood with the figure of a man outlined in red paint was propped against a stump three-quarters of a mile away. A heart had been painted on the chest. Next to it, a tall stake had been driven into the ground, and an orange rag fluttered in the breeze just above the knee-high, rippling grass.

Peter lay beside him with the sniper rifle nestled in the crook of his shoulder. His intense, cobalt-blue eyes were hidden behind the rear lens of the scope. Their distant, skewed quality and his care-free, I'll-try-anything attitude gave strangers the impression that one too many loose screws were rolling around inside the leatherneck's brain. Jason often joked that the last words his brother would utter would be "Hey, watch this!"

Peter was six foot two, two inches taller than Jason. His strawberry-blond hair was trimmed tightly along the sides, a style held over from his days in the corps. A thick neck and square, dominant chin rounded out the intense, alpha-male persona.

"You ready?" Peter asked.

"Let's do it," Jason countered.

"You remember the rules?"

Jason nodded. "Same as always. One shot, no excuses."

Peter pulled a Kennedy half-dollar from his pants. "Call it in the air." Peter flipped the coin, looking at Jason. A shrapnel scar, left over from the war, ran through his left eyebrow and resumed under the eyelid, imbuing him with a respect mysterious to civilians.

"Heads," said Jason.

The coin dropped into the dirt in a small cloud of dust. Peter smiled. "Tails," he said. "I'll go first."

Peter recited the critical data out loud. "We're exactly thirteen hundred and twenty yards from the target at an elevation of forty feet. The wind is coming from the northeast, behind us, and slanting to the left at eight miles per, pushing the round." The ex-marine twisted the elevation dial a few clicks and adjusted for the wind. He checked the target in the scope and readjusted the dials once more.

Peter peered through the scope, his eye three inches behind the rear lens. "I hope you brought your MasterCard, bro." Under his fatigues, Peter's hard body reflected a daily predawn workout regimen, consisting of a five-mile run, thirty minutes pumping iron, and one hundred marine push-ups, all before opening his gun shop at nine.

Jason smirked. "Blah, blah, blah."

Peter sucked in a deep breath and pulled back slightly on the trigger, removing any slack. He exhaled a half lungful of air and held it. At that exact moment, his trigger finger applied a smooth, gentle pressure. The report echoed through the fall air. The rifle bucked against his shoulder.

A second later, the projectile penetrated the plywood, splintering a quarter-sized hole through the board five inches below the silhouette's heart. The bullet missed the narrow stump, and a plume of dirt erupted in the berm beyond the target.

"You're low and to the left," Jason reported. "Still a devastating shot. I think you ripped out the guy's liver."

"Damn," said Peter.

"My turn," said Jason.

They exchanged places. Jason went through the same ritual his brother had. He had the good fortune of learning from his brother's shot, and made a few minor adjustments to the wind and elevation dials. As Jason let out his breath, he smoothly engaged the trigger. A wisp of smoke floated from the barrel and quickly disappeared in the breeze.

His round had nicked the left side of the fist-sized heart. A kill shot. Jason peered through the scope, smiled, and turned to his brother.

"I think I'm in the mood for seafood," he said.

Peter released a string of curses befitting a marine. "Bested by a sissy-boy, pill-counting pharmacist. I might as well just kill myself now."

"Sorry about your bad luck!" Jason said, echoing one of their favorite childhood taunts. "Don't worry, Pete, I won't tell. Besides, I can't see how I'll ever need this skill. Tell Mom I love her!"

CHAPTER 12

Wednesday, September 27

Jason strode into the Colonial like MacArthur returning to Leyte Island. His retreat years ago should never have happened. His return today was bittersweet. A week ago, the building had been tainted by miserable memories. The phantom ache of the past was still present, but numbed by opportunity. The misgivings he'd had about coming back and replacing his mentor had been bleached away, at least partially.

In the preceding week, he'd lain low. Except for yesterday's shooting competition, each morning had been spent at the Tabb Library researching business tactics and strategies. He was an entrepreneur now. Jason had studied for six grueling years at the Medical College of Virginia to earn his doctorate in pharmacy. For the last eight, he'd been running Keller's Food and Drug, and had done it superbly. Inventory was under control. Waste was minimal. Labor walked a tightrope between efficiency and disaster. His supervisor always complimented Jason on his ability to balance service and financial viability.

A hands-on pharmacist with an excellent rapport with his patients and employees, Jason also understood what he was not—a financial

70

whiz. At Medical College of Virginia, he'd gained only the most basic financial knowledge. Sell prescriptions for more than you pay for the drugs. Keep expenses under control. Minimize waste. But he knew squat about expanding a business, marketing strategies, and financial statements. He didn't quite understand why, but if Zanns said he was the man for the job, who was he to argue? He was determined to prove her a prophet. So he studied tomes on entrepreneurial enterprise, devouring each sentence, chart, and graph.

In the afternoons after Michael finished his homework, they would play catch. Then Jason would listen to him pound out a rhythm on his drum set. The boy was proficient enough now that it wasn't noise, but solid, toe-tapping beats. Dinner would be hamburgers, french fries, Chinese food, or frozen pizza. Jason explained to Jenny that when he started his new job, his ability to see his son would be limited, at least for a while. She told him to take all the time he needed.

On Thursday, Jason helped Michael research his paper about Bletchley Park. They spent several hours on the Internet reading and printing passages. When he wasn't studying in the library or hanging out with his son, Jason took care of personal business. He deposited the fifty-thousand-dollar bonus check, and when it cleared he transferred the funds into his E-Trade account. The second installment would be received today, and would pay off his candy-apple-red Mustang. He also spent an afternoon fixing minor problems around the house: a toilet that continually ran, a broken ice maker, and a squirrelly garage door.

Though he called several times, he hadn't been able to reach Christine. She was either busy or avoiding him. Jason drove by her house twice to check on her. Both times the driveway was empty. Though he was still curious about Pettigrew's death and wanted to locate the box of files, he decided not to stop.

Lily was standing in the pharmacy department as he approached.

"Welcome back, Mr. Jason," Lily said, wearing another flawless, salmon business suit. "I hope you are well rested. You're going to need it."

The headaches had lasted two days, growing weaker with each hour. This morning, a faint patch of swollen, tender tissue still puffed his cheek. Other than the minor aches, he was recharged and ready. "I can't wait to get started," he replied.

"Come. You have paperwork to fill out."

While Sam Fairing was preparing to open up the store, Zanns showed Jason to her small office, the same space that had once been Thomas Pettigrew's. He filled out his W-4 forms and insurance selections. Lily placed a three-page contract in front of him, outlining their agreement, and an envelope with another check from Cooper Venture Capital.

"Take your time and read it," she instructed. Without skipping a beat, she added, "How did you injure your face?"

Jason wrinkled an eyebrow. "Playing baseball with my son," he lied.

"Ah!" Zanns responded with a wide grin that made Jason uncomfortable.

Jason read through the entire document. "Everything appears to be in order," he said finally.

"Then please sign on the line." Lily handed him an expensive fountain pen.

He signed and handed the Giuliano Mazzuoli back to her. "Keep that. It's yours now," she said. Zanns removed a book from her desk and handed it to Jason. "Are you familiar with Peter Drucker?" she asked.

"He was a business management guru, wasn't he?"

"Correct. This is a collection of his writings. Drucker died in 2005, but I feel his thoughts and insights are still valid today. Read through this in your spare time."

Jason took the paperback book from her. It was entitled *The Essential Drucker: The Best of Sixty Years of Peter Drucker's Essential Writings on Management.*

"I will," Jason replied.

She handed him a single piece of paper. "This is what I want you to work on beginning immediately."

He read the three bulleted items on the page.

"Questions?" Zanns asked.

"The first one is fairly straightforward," Jason commented. "Hiring the pharmacy manager. I don't understand the last two. Clean out the back room?"

"Take a look," Zanns instructed.

Jason turned and leaned out the door. Towers of boxes with thirty-odd years of documents and prescriptions choked the hall.

She said, "By cleaning out the hallway and the boxes in the storage room, you will be making room for your office."

"Fair enough," he replied evenly. He was put off. He'd just accepted a promotion to the position of vice-president, and she wanted him to move boxes? He thought about protesting, but held his tongue.

"And how about this other task, finding a new store location in the east end?" he challenged. Over the decades, Jason marveled at Newport News's expansion westward into a vibrant, gleaming city. The east end, however, lagged behind as an economically depressed area. Like most inhabitants of the region, he considered it a black tooth in an otherwise cavity-free smile of civic pride, not a place to seek new business opportunities.

"As I explained to you during your interview, one of your duties will be to find suitable locations for new sites. I would like three locations chosen in the first thirty days. I also expect you to find locations with high traffic volume, high visibility. I want a thorough analysis of the PTA for each site—"

"PTA?"

Zanns sighed audibly. "Primary target audience." She pulled on her cigarette and let the smoke drift from her nostrils. She continued her explanations like a runaway freight train. Jason wanted to step out of the way before he was bowled over. "I want population figures within a five-mile radius with demographic information broken down by age groups, income ranges, and third-party payers."

Her words zipped past him. He was still stuck on the location issue. "Yes, I understand that," said Jason. "But Huntington Avenue? A new pharmacy wouldn't work out in that part of town. I don't need to run numbers to figure that out."

Zanns rose and leaned on the desk, using her knuckles for support. "Mr. Jason, let me be very clear. I am not paying you to evaluate my wishes. I know what I want and I expect you to carry out my plans. Is that clear?" The tone in her voice left no doubt about her annoyance.

"Yes," he replied. "But you're paying me to make this operation a success. To use my pharmacy expertise."

"I'm sure I will be tapping into your expertise throughout the coming months. But you will carry out my wishes and not question them. Are we clear?" She smiled patronizingly and sat back down. "You can begin the interviews tomorrow. Today, you can begin cleaning out the back room. Shred any outdated prescriptions and documents. Those boxes are taking up too much room. We need the space for you to work. I had asked Mr. Thomas to do it months ago, but he refused."

"I can do that. But I'll need time to find some candidates to interview."

"I have taken the liberty of lining up three interviews tomorrow at ninety-minute intervals beginning at nine. You can start with them. They are people who have expressed an interest in working here. They are listed on the document in your hand, and their applications are in the files. I expect you to have a body under contract within the week."

"Why did he refuse?"

"Excuse me?"

"You said Pettigrew refused to clean out the back room. That doesn't seem like the man. Why?"

Zanns removed her half-moon spectacles and placed one of the stems in her mouth. "Mr. Jason, I do not wish to speak ill of the dead."

"There were issues with Thomas?"

"Nothing you need to concern yourself with." Zanns lifted a finger as a thought seemed to strike her. "I just remembered. We are having a gathering tomorrow night. The PRPA is honoring Thomas with a lifetime achievement award. I want you to be there."

"Not a problem," Jason replied.

Zanns smiled. "I thought you might invite Ms. Christine as your guest. She has until now declined."

"Uh, I suppose I could ask her."

"Wonderful. Attire is semiformal."

"Anything else?"

"Yes, we are having lunch today with Steven Cooper. I mentioned him last week. I promised him a face-to-face with you. He wants to meet the man who will be responsible for making him even richer than he already is."

* * *

Half the cartons had been sorted into two growing stacks. Jason called in a part-time pharmacy technician named Brandon, a local high school football player, to help him. One stack was for reports and prescriptions older than five years, and would be destroyed. The second, for more recent documents, would be retained in case of an audit by the DEA, the state board of pharmacy, or an insurance company. Jason's progress was tedious but steady.

The massive collection was completely unorganized. Despite keeping everything, Pettigrew had spent little time collating any of it. Old and new documents were intermingled, and some boxes weren't even labeled. Jason had to sift through the contents to see what they contained. The hallway was more clogged than before, nearly impassable. He scoffed at how much money Lily Zanns was paying him to perform such a mundane task. Today, he was nothing more than an expensive file clerk. Had he anticipated this kind of work, Jason would have dressed differently. His tie was filthy, and circles of sweat under his arms darkened his dress shirt. *Stop complaining*, he told himself. With the money Zanns was paying, he could afford a closet full of shirts and ties.

Drawing a sleeve across his sweaty forehead, Jason left the dark back room and walked into the brightly lit pharmacy. Sam Fairing was on the phone taking a prescription, and Kevin Mitchell, the young black technician, was counting pills. Jason headed for the drink refrigerator in the front left corner. He took three steps and froze.

The man standing at the front of the store looked familiar, but Jason couldn't place him.

CHAPTER 13

Visible only in profile, the stranger appeared to be perusing greeting cards. Where had Jason seen him before? As a pharmacist, he came into contact with hundreds of people daily, mostly patients. In the pharmacy, he could recall a name with amazing speed. But outside work, Jason had to rack his brain to remember who people were or where he'd met them. He studied the man. A sickly and skinny figure with rough-hewn, leathery features. A long, graying ponytail hung down his back. Jason retrieved a Coke from the refrigerator, paid for it, and moved toward him.

As Jason approached, it came to him. Pettigrew's house after the funeral, standing in the corner, watching the mourners. The stranger glanced sideways and saw Jason approach. Their eyes met. A flash of recognition lit the man's face. He turned, heading quickly for the exit.

"Excuse me."

Ponytail picked up speed.

Jason quickened his pace, catching him at the door. "Sir?"

Unable to ignore him any longer, Ponytail faced the pharmacist. His eyes were a dull blue, and held a touch of melancholy. Pock-marked skin hung from his cheeks. He wore a plaid button-up shirt and faded blue jeans. The stench of tobacco and cheap women's perfume seeped from him, stopping Jason like a force field. He held a plastic Colonial bag in one hand. Through the thin plastic, Jason could see a box of condoms.

"My name's Jason Rodgers," he said, extending his hand. It hung there. Realizing no handshake would be forthcoming, he withdrew it. "I saw you the other day after the funeral, at Thomas Pettigrew's house. How did you know him?"

The stranger looked Jason up and down. Then he spoke in hushed tones. "I don't know you." His voice was deep and gravelly, like a country singer's. He glanced around the store to see who might be watching.

"What's your name?"

Ponytail glared, considering the question. Another quick glance around the store. Without another word, he pushed through the door and into the parking lot, where he climbed into his red Chevy Blazer and drove off without looking back.

CHAPTER 14

Thursday, September 28

"Any particular reason you didn't return my calls?" Jason asked into the mouthpiece of the phone. He was sitting at Zanns's desk in the back room of the pharmacy.

"I've been swamped at work," Christine replied. "We had to do an unexpected audit for a local restaurant. What are you doing?" Her voice was tentative.

"I'm getting ready to interview some pharmacists this morning for, uh, your…"

"You can say it—Daddy's job."

"I'm sorry," said Jason. He changed subjects quickly. "I tried to leave you a message. Your mailbox was full."

"I have a bad habit of not erasing my messages. How's your head?"

"Better. I'm only seeing double now. What's up?"

"Not a whole lot. I just wanted to see how you were doing."

"Did you hear anything from the police about the intruder?"

"Not really. A detective called me a couple of days later. Asked a lot of the same questions. I don't think they're going to find him."

"Any other break-ins?"

"I don't know. I haven't been back to Daddy's."

"I can't say I blame you." Jason sucked in a breath. "I'm glad you called. I wanted to ask you something."

"What's that?"

"So, it's like this," he began hesitantly. "Lily's having a little soiree tonight. I know it's short notice and all, but I thought you might like to go. That is, if you're not seeing any of your boyfriends tonight."

Silence.

"Are you there, Chrissie?"

"Yeah, I'm here."

"Can I get an answer before Christmas?"

"Oh, am I supposed to answer you now?"

"Since the party is tonight, that would be a good idea."

"Why are you asking me?"

Jason had no clue what the correct response should be. "You didn't tell me they were honoring your father."

"Oh, it's *that* party. I told Lily I wasn't interested."

"Why not?"

"It's inappropriate for me to be there, considering how he and I had been getting along—or not getting along, if you know what I mean."

"He was your father, Chrissie. The community is honoring him. Don't let the past few years taint everything he did over his career and lifetime. And he was a good father early on, wasn't he?"

More silence.

"I'm not taking no for an answer, you know."

"Oh, really?"

"Hasn't my irresistible charm convinced you to change your mind yet? Usually I have a yes in half this time."

Christine snorted. "So I'm just a check mark in your little black book?"

"I didn't mean it that way. You were never just any woman, Chrissie." Jason paused. "Christine, I'll have your back."

"Oh, no! This coming from the man that disappeared faster than a case of Twinkies at a fat farm. Tell me you just didn't say that!"

"Yeah, I did. That took some balls, didn't it?" Jason could smile at his mistake.

"Big, overinflated ones."

Rachel, the gum-snapping cashier, appeared at his door. "Your first interview is here."

Jason turned back to the phone. "I've got to go. I'll pick you up around five-thirty?" He hung up before she could refuse.

* * *

Lily Zanns leaned over the oversized map laid out on her desk. It showed Newport News and the surrounding area.

"Here, here, and here," she said, tapping the grid, then circling each spot with a grease pen. "These are the locations I want you to evaluate."

Jason shook his head, still incredulous she would even consider such a combat zone. He remained silent, unwilling to create another stir. His counsel had been given. She was the boss and could do what she pleased.

He changed the subject. "I've conducted the interviews. The first two candidates weren't qualified. I want to hire Parks. He's got lots of supervising experience and can handle the prescription volume. If we make him a good offer, I think he'll accept."

"Excellent," Zanns replied. "Offer him twenty thousand dollars over what he's making now, along with a sizable sign-on bonus, say twenty thousand dollars. But he needs to start in three days."

"Consider it done," said Jason. He admired the way Lily did not hesitate to pull the trigger on decisions, even if her stubbornness clouded her good judgment.

"This is for you to use when you view your locations. I want pictures from every angle of each location and also of the surrounding area." She removed a digital camera with a 100 mm lens from her desk and handed it to him. Lily pulled out a second, longer lens from under the desk. "And this is a 300 mm F2 telephoto."

"I'm not sure I can use that to photograph the locations. I'd have to stand too far away," said Jason.

"This is not for the locations. While you are in the area, I want you to get some shots of the shipyard, specifically the ship in dry dock. I want pictorial documentation of the entire area for negotiating purposes. The more evidence I have to show the current owners, the more I can lowball the price. And besides, I'm a fan of the military. When you come over tonight, I will show you my collection of aerial shots of ships. Today, I want you to get some pictures of the dry dock and the aircraft carrier."

* * *

The gleam of midtown gave way to older edifices as Jason drove south along Warwick past Mercury. It was an urban purgatory, where well-dressed white men were eyed with suspicion and targets for a quick, knife-brandishing roll. The only seedling of optimism was a rescue mission, feeding and housing the homeless in exchange for exposure to the word of the Lord.

The first site was an abandoned, dilapidated store on a corner lot, which leaned precariously. Intersections of joints and miters formed parallelograms and trapezoids instead of right angles—a geometry teacher's delight. New graffiti was being painted over the old. A drunk crumpled near one corner was sipping an unknown spirit from an equally crumpled brown bag. Jason walked the site, snapping photographs.

The final two spots weren't much better.

When he'd finished at the sites, Jason parked the Mustang on Riverdale Road on an escarpment overlooking the dry dock.

It would be his final stop of the day. As he climbed out of the Mustang, he'd come to a decision. He would call a commercial real estate agent to search for some realistic sites, and he would push Lily to abandon this part of town. His job was to tell her when she was on the wrong road and get her back on course.

Jason scanned the sight before him. Penrose Gatling Shipbuilders was the only shipbuilder in the nation capable of building aircraft carriers. It had grown steadily over more than a century on the James River, gorging itself on fat government contracts. Locals simply called it the Yard. It had begun as the Jamestown Dry Dock Company in 1902. The first warship had slid into the James River six years later. And in the hundred-plus years since, the Yard had constructed thirty-eight aircraft carriers (including the one Jason looked at now), eighteen battleships, seventy-five submarines, and a host of destroyers, cruisers, and landing ships.

Visible for miles, the words *Penrose Gatling* were scrawled across the beam of the crimson gantry crane, towering two hundred feet over the dry dock. Beneath the crane, in the flooded space, sat the aircraft carrier *Jacob R. Hope*, surrounded by smaller, but still enormous, boom cranes. Workers scurried like ants about on her decks. The number painted on the island superstructure, eighty-one, stretched ten stories. Painted and spiffy, the massive vessel dwarfed surrounding homes and shipyard workshops. Local newspapers and news programs were carrying reports in preparation for its christening, Saturday, October 7. Ten days away.

Jason twisted the two-foot-long, 300 mm telephoto lens and clicked it onto the body. He lifted the camera, rotated the focusing ring, and the fuzzy view came into sharp focus. He clicked off several frames from different angles. Ten minutes later, he put on the smaller 80 mm. As he finished up, a blue pickup truck with a swirling, yellow light pulled to a stop a few feet away.

"Hey, what are you doing, bud?" A rotund, squirrel-cheeked man sat behind the wheel. A lump of chewing tobacco was rammed into one cheek. His face was red and mottled, no doubt from nightly visits to local pubs. He spit a long, brown trail of tobacco juice on the ground near Jason's feet.

"Just taking a few photographs," he declared weakly. The word *Security* was stenciled above the Penrose Gatling logo on the door of the cab.

"You wouldn't be taking pictures of the Yard, now, would ya, pal?"

"Maybe."

"Stay right there," he commanded, lifting a radio handset. He barked instructions. The radio crackled in response. In less than a minute, two unmarked, official-looking sedans skidded to a stop near them. Four grim-looking men in dark suits jumped out, and encircled Jason.

CHAPTER 15

Plastic visitor badges hung from breast pockets and signaled that these men were not shipyard regulars. Jason spotted a gold, star-shaped badge clipped to one man's belt, portending official—and more ominous—trouble. The leader approached Jason. He was tall and wide-shouldered with a blond crew cut. Dark sunglasses obscured his undoubtedly penetrating eyes.

"What's your name?"

"Jason."

"Jason what?"

"Jason Rodgers."

"What were you taking pictures of?"

Deciding it was time to come clean, he said, "Just getting some shots of the crane and the ship."

"I see," he said. "Put him in the car." With a nod, the man motioned to his colleagues to move in. Two men grabbed Jason's arm, while the third confiscated the camera. Within minutes, he was escorted into a nameless, faceless building among the maze of

Penrose Gatling buildings. Three floors up, Jason sat at a table in a small interrogation room.

The leader and two new men entered. Acid began to churn in Jason's stomach. The blond leader now deferred to a new, equally fish-faced man. His demeanor did not instill Jason with new confidence. The agent removed his dark blazer and hung it on the back of a chair. Next the dark glasses were laid on the table, revealing crystal-green eyes. One of those coiled cords dripped from his left ear and disappeared down his shirt collar. Jason swallowed a mouthful of bile.

"Jason Rodgers?" the man said.

He nodded. "Yes. I guess I'm in some kind of trouble?"

The man snorted and glanced at his colleagues. "You could say that. Why are you taking pictures of the shipyard and the aircraft carrier?"

Not wanting to throw Lily under the bus, he lied, "For...for the hell of it." A child caught with his hand in his mother's change purse would have sounded more convincing.

"For the hell of it?" He rubbed his chin. "You sure stepped in it just for shits and giggles, Mr. Rodgers. I need to see ID." Jason fished out his driver's license. The new leader left. Several minutes later, he returned holding two sheets of paper. "Jason," the man said, pulling out a chair and sitting. "Do you know it's illegal to photograph the shipyard?"

"I do now."

"Where do you work? And what do you do there?"

"I work for the Colonial Pharmacy. I'm a pharmacist." Jason squirreled up some courage and asked, "Who are you?"

The man locked eyes with Jason. He pulled out a leather badge case and flipped it open. "I'm Special Agent Clay Broadhurst of the United States Secret Service."

The camera was brought into the room like an incriminating weapon, the 80 mm lens still attached. "It's clean, except for the photos," the agent announced.

Broadhurst examined the camera and switched it on. He scrolled the through the photos. "Why are you taking pictures of empty lots and old buildings, Jason?"

Before he could answer, another agent returned with several cans of soda and placed them on the table. "Where are my manners, Jason? Would you like something to drink?" said Broadhurst.

Jason declined, barely able to shake his head.

"So were you about to tell us why you're taking pictures of empty lots?"

Jason's mouth and throat felt like the Mojave. "Maybe I would like something to drink," he whispered.

Broadhurst slid him a can of Coke, and Jason popped it. The acidy drink hurt going down.

Jason cleared his throat. "I'm looking for sites for a new pharmacy."

"A new pharmacy?" Broadhurst smirked.

He nodded

"In this part of town? You're a long way from home, chief."

Jason nodded again, weakly.

"That's lame," another agent said. "Why don't you save us a lot of time and tell us what you really doing down here?"

"That's the truth," Jason declared.

Broadhurst sighed, shaking his head. "Here's the situation. You were on shipyard property taking these photographs. That's trespassing. You were photographing a Navy aircraft carrier. That could be considered espionage. Spies did the very same thing just before they bombed Pearl Harbor!" Broadhurst let that statement settle for a moment. "I could just confiscate your photographs and the camera and let it go at that. But considering what's going to happen here next week, you're in some pretty deep shit."

Jason remembered that the ship was scheduled for a milestone ceremony. "You mean the christening?" asked Jason.

"You must be a pretty good pharmacist, Jason. You catch on quick. I bet you graduated magna cum laude," Broadhurst said sarcastically.

"What's going to happen now? Don't I get a phone call?"

"You're not under arrest—yet."

The men exchanged glances, left the room, and returned a few minutes later.

"We're confiscating the pictures, Jason. Stay away from the shipyard. If you're caught down here again, you will be arrested and charged." Broadhurst picked up the camera, removed the memory chip, and held it up. "Do I make myself clear?"

"Yes."

"Don't come back here again. Your name and face have been logged into the Secret Service and FBI databases." Jason remembered an agent taking his head shot with a small point-and-shoot camera. "If you do, we'll do more than take your camera away. Understood?"

Jason nodded. His bladder suddenly needed to be emptied.

"I'll have someone drive you back to your car." Broadhurst nodded to one of the men standing along the wall. "Make sure he leaves the area immediately."

In twenty minutes, Jason was driving back to the Colonial. In his rearview mirror, Jason watched the government sedan follow him for several miles before making a U-turn.

Nice job, hot shot!

CHAPTER 16

"Mr. Jason! Ms. Christine! How wonderful to see you again," Lily Zanns called from across the sprawling patio in the backyard of her enormous riverside estate. Jason marveled at its enormity and elegance.

Zanns spread her arms wide in an exaggerated display Jason hadn't expected from the normally reserved woman. "I'm so glad you could join our little gathering."

"Thanks for having us," said Jason.

Zanns wore a silk, royal-blue sari-type dress, shimmering in the flickering tiki lamps. Slanting across the perfect skin of her chest and exposing a bare shoulder, the gown was the antithesis of her business attire. On her, it was almost pornographic. A choker dotted with large diamonds circled her neck, under which dangled the ancient amulet. The ever-present cigarette, perched in a long holder, pointed to the night sky. She placed a hand on each of Jason's shoulders and planted an air-kiss on both cheeks with a familiarity that made Jason uncomfortable.

"Ms. Christine," she said. "I'm so glad you changed your mind about attending." Lily looked her up and down quickly. "Spending time with Jason, I see. Are you two an item again?" Lily smiled slightly.

Christine blushed. "Just old friends. It's good to see you again, Ms. Lily. Thank you again for everything you've done."

"It was my pleasure, child. Come, tonight, we celebrate *un bon homme* who dedicated his life to easing patients suffering, the profession of pharmacy and the Peninsula. Let me introduce you to some of my guests."

Lily escorted them to each gaggle of guests, introducing them to pharmacists, board members of the Peninsula Retail Pharmacists Association, civic leaders, and physicians. They met the mayor of Newport News, several prominent attorneys, and city councilmen. Each offered Christine their condolences. Finally, Zanns stopped at Jasmine Kader and Sam Fairing.

"Ms. Christine, nice to see you again. Your father was a good man. And I see that you have good taste in men as well," Kader said, eyeing Jason.

Christine nodded, narrowing her eyes.

"Jasmine, Jason Rodgers has accepted the position as my new vice-president of pharmacy operations."

Jason took the extended hand. "I remember you from the funeral," he said, glimpsing her skimpy outfit.

Kader responded with a single nod and a lascivious smile. Her black dress clung to her body like a second skin, stopping well north of midthigh, revealing long, dark-skinned legs. A long necklace on a silver chain dangled in her cleavage, holding an onyx stone surrounded by a ring of pearls. Long sleeves, an interesting but not an unpleasant fashion twist, covered her arms to the wrist.

A tall, blond man motioned to Lily. Jason recognized him. He was Lily's business partner, Steven Cooper. He and Lily had lunched with the man. It was a formality Zanns had seemed anxious to end as soon as it had begun. Even now, Jason caught Lily's brief, frustrated moue at the sight of him. Jason had been impressed by both his knowledge of pharmacy business and the size of his investment portfolio. But the tension between Cooper and Zanns was palpable.

Cooper was about Jason's height. His thin frame was unimpressive, with a slight forward roll to his shoulders. His penetrating blue eyes seemed to glow against his pasty skin, which looked even sicklier against his blond surfer haircut. Jason sensed the man never worked out. He was probably more comfortable in front of a computer screen than a piece of gym equipment.

Lily said, "I must tend to our meal and some other matters. Please excuse me."

* * *

Cooper waited inside the french doors. The party and the guests were framed through the large expanse of glass. He and Zanns strolled to her office, followed soon by Jasmine Kader. Zanns sucked a long breath through her nose as Cooper came straight to the point. "He used to work for the Colonial."

"Steven, please tell me something I don't know." Zanns could feel her frustration mount as soon as she stepped within five feet of Cooper. But keeping him happy was a necessary annoyance; without his boss, Hammon, their mission had no chance of success.

"I *knew* I recognized his name. He was removed long before you and the Simoon came on the scene. He was a threat," Cooper insisted.

"What kind of threat?" asked Kader.

"My employer had designs on the Colonial many years ago. It was to be used as a front for a black op. Every employee was profiled and assessed. Jason Rodgers is a dangerously curious man with a penchant for sticking his nose where it doesn't belong. His presence would have caused problems. So he was neutralized. Which is to say we made it impossible for him to stay. I fear, Lily, he will cause you—and therefore us—problems as well."

"Your little cabal had designs on the Colonial in years past?"

"Yes. But before the operation became hot, it was reassigned a lower priority. It was tabled and eventually dropped. But Jason Rodgers had already been disposed of."

"This is a fine time to let us know, Steven," Kader spat.

"Jasmine is right, Steven. This information could have proved useful before I invited Jason Rodgers to work for me."

"Lily, there was no need for you to bring him on board. Our mission will be executed in less than two weeks. And, I might add, you didn't consult me before hiring him. I had to rack my brain and research some old files just to pull up the information. Hammon is not pleased with this development! You told him that there would be no more complications."

Jasmine shot Zanns a glance. Zanns read the concern in her eyes. Cooper had been kept out of the loop for very valid reasons. First and foremost, she did not trust him or his secret splinter group. After their deed was done, she was sure Hammon's people were going to vanish like rats scurrying from the light, leaving the Simoon to take full blame for their actions. Zanns had no intention of letting that happen. Jason Rodgers was her insurance policy.

Zanns turned back to Cooper. "Thank you, Steven. The information is disheartening. But it will be handled. Please allow Jasmine and me to discuss it."

"Make this go away!" Cooper spun and departed.

Lily tapped her chin with a finger, thinking. Jason Rodgers needed to be scrutinized very closely, starting this very moment.

"Come," she said finally to her daughter. They walked out of the office toward the kitchen. The headwaiter walked past at that moment.

Zanns addressed him. "I want you to change the seating arrangement." She turned to Jasmine. "It appears Rodgers may be more virulent than we anticipated." She fingered the amulet around her neck. "But we need him around. I have begun laying the trap for Mr. Rodgers. The Secret Service detained him this afternoon. Stay close to him tonight, find out what he knows. Then we'll decide how to deal with him."

CHAPTER 17

"Impressive," Jason said, looking around the grounds. The bartender had just handed him a gin and tonic.

Zanns's mansion consisted of an enormous redbrick main house surrounded by a smaller outbuilding and a massive three-car garage. The main house was bathed in the glow of huge floodlights. The eight-foot palladium windows yawned like miniature buildings plastered to the side of the structure. The party was under an octagonal gazebo large enough to swallow a small house, on the rear brick patio. The grounds were perfectly landscaped, with accent lighting and expertly trimmed shrubbery. The perfectly manicured lawn sloped regally to the James.

Christine sipped an apple martini. "I could get used to this kind of living."

Jasmine passed them, giving Jason a long, seductive glance. Jason smiled, avoiding her eyes. But they lingered a fraction too long on the long, tawny legs.

"Like what you see, sailor?" said Christine. She poked him with a finger. "Just remember to dance with the one that brung ya."

Lily emerged from the house and clapped her hands crisply three times. The music stopped and everyone turned toward her.

"Ladies and gentlemen, dinner is ready," she announced. "If you would kindly make your way to the gazebo and find your seats."

The throngs eagerly converged on their place cards, anticipating one of Zanns's sumptuous feasts. Jason and Christine were placed halfway down the middle table, ten seats from Lily's position at the head. A moment later, Jasmine pulled out the chair immediately to Jason's right. Her breast brushed his shoulder lightly as she sat. Jason smiled nervously. The scent of her perfume was strong and inviting. "Hello again," she said, placing her hand on Jason's arm. "I was hoping we'd have a chance to chat again."

He glanced at Christine, who was engaged in small talk with a matronly woman, whose diamonds appeared to have been smeared on.

Christine noticed Jasmine and frowned. "Aren't you the lucky man," she whispered to him.

Jason shrugged.

The polished silverware gleamed in the soft lighting. The delicate china was rimmed in gold, the lead-crystal stemware sparkled. Virginal white linens, starched to a wooden stiffness, were draped over the long tables. An army of wait staff bore platters laden with breads and cheeses, working with the speed of an Indy 500 pit crew and the grace of a ballet troupe.

"Before we begin," Lily said to the gathering. "Let's have a toast."

They raised their glasses. "Let us remember what it means to be successful. There is a line which I have always tried to remember from my favorite business philosopher, Peter Drucker. 'The best way to predict the future is to create it.'"

* * *

Jason felt his elbow being gently squeezed. He looked to his right and saw Jasmine staring at him. She smiled seductively. "I have some ideas about programs I would like to see implemented in our office and the Colonial," Jasmine offered. "Perhaps we could meet to discuss them."

"What kind of programs?" Jason asked.

"Perhaps a lipid clinic or a diabetes management program. Patients need more education and reinforcement than we can provide at the office. I'm sure Lily would be very much in favor of such a program, and it would win you points with her."

"I didn't realize I needed to score points," Jason replied.

Jasmine smiled. "Lily wants results, Jason. Score as many points as early as you can."

"I suppose it wouldn't hurt to discuss some ideas."

"Excellent. I'll call you to arrange lunch or a drink." The words glided from her lips. Jason gulped his wine and sensed the invitation was more than just a business proposal.

"How's the fish?" asked Christine. The roasted salmon and asparagus with lemon oil were served beside potatoes, shallots, and chervil, complimented by a citrusy chardonnay.

"Excellent. It's the best I've ever had," said Jason.

"Isn't that right, Mr. Jason?"

Jason nearly choked on a bite of salmon. He glanced up and saw every pair of eyes on him. Zanns had spoken to him, and he'd missed it. He felt like a student caught napping during a lecture.

Zanns said, "I was just saying that you are our new vice-president. How was your first foray into finding new locations for us?"

"Very interesting," Jason said, knitting an eyebrow. "I'll have the information to you tomorrow." *Didn't she want to keep this quiet?* he thought.

"Did anything look promising?"

He hedged. "No, not really. We need to talk about that."

"No, no, please," she said, motioning for him to proceed. "Please, tell me your thoughts."

Heads turned, hanging on his response. He hesitated.

"So," she said, sensing his trepidation. "What did you think?"

Jason gently rotated his wine glass. "Well, since you asked, Ms. Lily, I think all three of the sites—quite frankly—are completely and utterly inappropriate."

A barely audible but collective gasp escaped from the guests. The air seemed to be sucked out from under the gazebo.

"Why?"

"You already know my thoughts on the matter."

She nodded. "Please share them with the rest of group."

"Because it's the east end. It's a bad place to begin." Blood rushed to his face.

Christine's hand squeezed his under the table. "Easy," she whispered.

At the same time, Jasmine Kader slipped her palm onto his thigh, a smile lining her face. Jason glanced her way, gently removed it, and sat rock still. Zanns, Christine, and Jasmine had him surrounded.

"And I suppose you have other locations you think would be more suitable." The other guests had turned to watch their exchange.

"I can come up with some. I believe they will be better choices. Yes."

"Very well," Lily relented. "Bring me your suggestions by the end of the day tomorrow."

"You shall have them," he replied.

"I am curious to see what you come up with," said Zanns. Then, as if nothing had happened, Lily looked to the headwaiter and clapped her hands again. On cue, a peach-and-raspberry crisp was laid before the diners with a flourish. With the showdown over, attention turned to the elegant, calorie-packed creation. Pockets of conversation resumed, and the tension slowly passed.

"That bitch," Jason whispered under his breath. He glanced at her. Lily had turned to the person sitting beside her, oblivious to the stir their interaction had caused. Or, perhaps, reveling in it? Jason sensed her words were some sort of warning.

"Easy, cowboy," said Christine. "You handled her fine."

"I've known Lily Zanns for a long time," Jasmine interjected. "Get used to it. She doesn't care for timid people." Jasmine squeezed

Jason's elbow so Christine couldn't see it. "And I bet you're not timid, are you?" she whispered.

* * *

Later in the study, Zanns said, "Please close the door." Her lips curved into a smile. "Would you like a cigar? I have some Rey Del Mundos in the humidor on the table."

Jason gazed at her with contempt. He was still reeling from their public confrontation. Reluctantly, he closed the door and faced his boss.

With dessert finished, Lily had invited the revelers to dance. At the first opportunity, she'd located Jason and instructed him to follow her into the mansion. The trio of musicians played a spirited number and a smattering of guests had filled the temporary dance floor. The scene, visible through the floor-to-ceiling windows, served as a backdrop for their conversation.

"No, thank you," Jason said stiffly.

"You did not like being questioned in front of my guests?"

"You're damn right, I didn't!"

"I tested you. Unwavering resolve in my employees is a canon for success. I expect it in all my employees. The question of the day is, are you up to the challenge of running my organization. You passed, quite successfully."

"I have resolve, Ms. Zanns. But this was supposed to be a pleasant, relaxing evening."

The phone on her desk buzzed. She picked it up and listened. "Fine, I'll be right there." She replaced the handset. "The mayor wishes to discuss my plans for the expansion. He might be of assistance in securing property. Please wait here."

When he was alone, he scanned the room. Dark mahogany, fine leather upholstery. The chair and desk alone probably cost more than his yearly salary. He opened the large, oak humidor on a wall table, removed a thick, black Cuban cigar, and slid it in his breast pocket. *I've earned it*, he thought.

Framed aerial photographs of the shipyard were mounted on the wall above the humidor. One was of a partially constructed aircraft carrier in the dry dock. It was a bright, sunny day. The large numerals on the island were identical to those on the ship he'd photographed today. Eighty-one. It was the *Hope*. By the state of construction, the photo had to have been taken months, if not years, earlier. Among the framed photos, a large, wide panel with assorted lights and switches was embedded in the wall, blinking at him like a console from a nuclear submarine.

"Sorry for the interruption," Lily said, returning. She noticed him inspecting the panel. "It's my security system," she said.

Jason turned without speaking.

"It's state of the art. Motion and contact sensors in the house, as well as ground and laser sensors ring the property. We have every inch covered."

"Overkill, don't you think?"

"When you become as successful as I am, enemies are inevitable."

"I see," he said.

"Where were we?"

"Discussing my resolve."

"Yes, of course. You handled yourself quite admirably," she explained.

"I'm touched."

"I'll grant you that little bit of sarcasm."

"I have two questions for you, Ms. Lily."

"*Bien sûr.*"

"First, why did you have me take photographs of the shipyard if you already have some? Pictures, I might add, that are much better than I could have ever taken."

Lily ignored the question. "By the way, how did that go?"

"Not well," he replied. "Why didn't you tell me photographing the shipyard is illegal? They thought I was a spy!"

"My new vice-president, a spy? I had no idea," Zanns chortled. "Were you mistreated?"

"No, I believe the matter's closed."

"I'm sorry you were hassled. I have a great admiration for this country, more than the majority of those born on this soil. A person can make himself into anything he desires, if he works. The aircraft carrier is the symbol and the protector of that doctrine."

"The memory chip of the camera was confiscated," Jason said, refusing to be sidetracked. "All the photos are in the possession of the Secret Service now. I was lucky to keep the camera equipment."

She said, "Keep the camera. You'll need it. I have reconsidered my position. Bring me other location options within the next week. What is your second question?"

"I thought the expansion of the Colonial was a secret," Jason said. "Why were you discussing it out there? I'm just curious."

Zanns's mood flipped like a manic-depressive who'd forgotten to take her lithium. "I will discuss my plans when and where I choose. Is that clear? You work for me. Do not question my motives again. My patience and good graces only go so far!"

Then she softened, and picked a piece of lint from Jason's sport coat. "You mentioned being curious. Curiosity. I don't find myself using that word often. In life it can be a valuable asset. But it can also get one in a lot of trouble, *n'est-ce pas*? You are a curious person, aren't you, Monsieur Jason?"

"No more than the next person," he replied.

Zanns pushed out her lower lip. "That's not what I hear. Too much curiosity can be dangerous."

"How so?" asked Jason.

"Sometimes you have to accept things at face value. Too much digging leads to unwanted consequences."

Jason felt as if a veiled threat was being leveled at him. He wanted to say something, but was too shocked to respond. Then Zanns put her arm around his shoulder and led him back to the party. Her tone had changed from a lecturing executive's to that of a doting matriarch. "But to indulge you just this once, it was time that the mayor and his people were made aware of our plans. Before I spoke to you at dinner, I was bringing the mayor up to speed. Now, enough talk about business. Let us enjoy the rest of the evening."

He let the secrecy issue drop, though the inconsistency baffled him. It was her show. She could talk or not talk about it whenever she chose. *Forget about it*, he thought. She had caved, after all, on the east end locations. He smiled inwardly and felt the cigar in his pocket.

"Did you make the offer to Mr. Parks?" asked Zanns.

Jason nodded. "Yes. He was very pleased with the twenty-thousand-dollar raise. I'll get him to start in a day or two. Lily, how do you expect to make a profit, throwing your money around? Besides the cost of medications, pharmacist salaries are one of the costliest items on the balance sheet."

"You let me worry about that," she replied.

* * *

"I want to dance," Christine announced, grabbing Jason's hand and leading him onto the dance floor.

"Are you having a good time?" he asked as they swayed to a slow beat.

Christine shrugged. "I wouldn't write home about it."

"Well, I'll have to try harder."

After a few measures, Christine couldn't resist asking a question that nagged at her. "Do you like her?"

"Who?"

"Dr. I'm-Not-Wearing-Any-Underwear. She's been eyeing you all night."

"Really? I haven't noticed anyone but you tonight, Chrissie."

Christine smacked him on the shoulder. "Nice try, Romeo. That vixen is all over you."

His smile widened. "You're jealous!"

"Don't flatter yourself," Christine intoned. "You mean to tell me you can't see through her advances? She's been on you like flies on a pile of dung."

"That's an appetizing thought. Are you comparing me to a pile of dung?"

"Just dance."

"We *are* dancing. Besides, she's just trying to be friendly."

"With friends like her…"

"Just remember, she's coming on to me, not the other way around. I didn't plan it."

"Oh, so you admit that she's coming on to you."

"Okay, okay. I admit it."

Christine smiled. "Good. Now enjoy the dance."

When the song was over, he grabbed two glasses of champagne from the tray of a passing waiter and led her down the sloped lawn toward the pier and boathouse, passing Jasmine along the way.

"Make sure you save me a dance," the doctor said. Christine shot her a withering glance.

The dim light of the single lamp on the pier glistened off the water. In the distance, Zanns's boat and plane bobbed gently on the water. They climbed into the small launch. *Retribution* was scrawled across the transom.

* * *

Lily joined Jasmine where the patio met the thick lawn, observing Jason and Christine. "Have you made any progress with him?" asked Zanns.

Jasmine shook her head. "The woman is getting in the way. There's history there."

Zanns nodded. "They were lovers many years ago." Lily looked at her illegitimate daughter. "Allow them their time tonight. Get him alone tomorrow. Use whatever you have at your disposal, but be quick about it. In a week, we will have accomplished our mission and your father will be avenged. Nothing will get in the way."

"Perhaps Sam is right. Maybe you shouldn't have hired him."

Zanns sighed. "Everything is under control. Fear not, daughter. I know how to break up this little romance."

CHAPTER 18

"You're still not over her, are you?" Christine asked. She wasn't referring to Jasmine Kader.

"Who?" he replied, feigning ignorance.

"You know who. Sheila. How long ago did it end?"

Sheila Boquist was another failed relationship in a short, painful string following Jason's divorce from Jenny four years ago. Jason had admitted to himself years ago that, compared with his relationship with the woman sitting beside him now, every other woman he'd ever been involved with did not measure up, including Michael's mother.

"It ended two weeks ago. What gave it away?"

"We've both lived here our whole lives, Jason. The area is not *that* big. Word gets around. Did you love her?"

"No."

The water glowed silver with moonlight. A breeze gently moved Christine's hair and a shiver spread over her. Jason placed his arm around her, expecting to be rebuffed. Christine tensed but didn't try to move away.

Christine waited for Jason to offer more. There was only silence. She gazed at the huge yacht, floating a hundred and fifty yards away. "What is it with you guys?"

"What?"

"Why is it so hard for you to talk about your feelings?"

"You're not going to start analyzing me, are you?"

"I'll analyze if I want to," she said.

"What about you?"

"What about me?" she retorted.

"Was there someone in your life?"

"Why do you say 'was'?"

"Because if it was an 'is,' you wouldn't have come tonight. At least, not with me."

Christine shrugged, conceding the point. "It ended about three months ago."

"How serious was it?"

"We were engaged."

"I'd say that qualifies as serious."

"We dated for two years. And he's a good guy, but we just weren't right for each other. If I'd married him, I would've regretted it in five or six years. So I ended it."

"That must have been hard."

"Incredibly. But it was the right thing." Christine faced him, locking eyes.

"Sometimes doing the right thing hurts," he replied.

"Tell me about Sheila."

"She wasn't what she seemed to be. I didn't like her very much after the veil was pulled away."

"How long?"

"We dated for about ten months. The part that really gets to me is the way she treated Michael, my son. It was almost as if she was jealous of him. I never met anyone so selfish."

"Did she physically abuse him?"

"No, she just made his life—and mine—very uncomfortable."

"Kids are resilient. He'll forget about her soon enough. So what are you looking for now?"

He smirked. "Some cheap, meaningless sex."

"You can get that from Dr. Hussy up there."

Jason smiled. "I was just joking. I'm not interested in Jasmine. I don't need the complication right now. That's the word that sums up what I need—uncomplicated."

"Uncomplicated sounds good." She slipped her hand into his. "It's easier to talk when things aren't complicated by emotion. And we still have some talking to do."

"Really?"

"Really. Like why your marriage ended, what you've been doing for the last thirteen years. And that other thing."

* * *

Jasmine's eyes darted between the couple she'd been pretending to be interested in and the pier. The pair ascended the sloped lawn. She heard the Christine woman say, "I have to find the little girls' room." Jasmine did not hesitate, intercepting Jason on his way to the bar. She slipped her hand in his and pulled him toward the dance floor. "You've ignored me long enough!"

She placed a hand on his lower back, toying with the thin line of appropriateness. The other slipped under his jacket between his shoulder blades, pulling him to her. Her floral fragrance and the pressure of her firm body started a chain of involuntary male responses. Restraint and desire became embroiled in a vicious tug of war.

Jasmine moved her lips to his ear and whispered, "Are you afraid of assertive women, Jason?"

"What makes you think that?"

"You *are*, aren't you?" The whispered words were full of implied pleasure.

"No, Jasmine. I'm not intimidated. I'm here with someone. It's proper that I respect that."

"So if you were here alone, you would be more receptive to my flirting."

"I didn't say that either." Jasmine spun them across the dance floor. Jason noticed Christine standing nearby, pretending not to notice.

"Your girlfriend is watching us," said Jasmine.

He tried in vain to appear casual. "She's not my girlfriend. Do you take pleasure in acting this way?"

"I'm enjoying it immensely." Her black eyes tugged at his memory in a way Jason could not put a finger on. It was a quality he'd seen in Sam Fairing's eyes as well, as if he were looking into a familiar but unfriendly face.

"Do you enjoy wreaking havoc with relationships?"

"I thought you said she wasn't your girlfriend."

"You're trying to cause trouble."

"I know what I want and I go after it," said Jasmine as the song ended. She slipped her hand down his backside and squeezed a handful.

Jason pushed her away. "That's enough!"

Jasmine was undaunted. "I'll call you at work and ask you to lunch tomorrow. And you won't refuse me." She spun and wiggled away. Jason turned away from her retreating image in a tangle of bewilderment and arousal.

His cell phone chirped. "Hello?" Static filled the line. "Hello?"

More static. He flipped it closed and walked to Christine.

"Did you enjoy your full-body examination?" She forced a weak smile. "I want to go home."

"It was just a dance," Jason muttered.

"If there was a piece of coal between the two of you, a diamond would have dropped to the floor from all the pressure. That woman wants something from you, Jason," said Christine.

There was a stirring in the crowd, and it parted. Zanns appeared, waving her arms, gathering everyone around her. A wheeled cart draped by a white tablecloth appeared from inside the house, pushed by one of the liveried wait staff. On it rested a large bronze mortar and pestle. The guests circled close.

"And I think we both know what that is," Jason rejoined.

"Think again, horn dog. Some women only use sex or the promise of sex to get what they want."

"Do you speak from personal experience?"

"I speak as a card-carrying member of the female species. Some women use their bodies to get what they want."

"So you're admitting that you possess that power."

"Of course I possess that power. Every woman has it. We have it because you guys are so driven by urges below the belt, you give it to us. All we have to do is turn it on."

"And you've never turned that power?"

"I used it on my fiancé when I wanted him to cut the grass or take out the trash. But I never used it to advance myself in business or get information. See, Jason, honey, I only use my power for good, not evil. That's the difference between me and Dr. Jump-My-Bones over there."

"Where did you get your degree in social anthropology?"

Three quick, loud claps interrupted Christine. Lily Zanns called the gathering to order. "We have gathered tonight to honor a man who was a vital force to the profession of pharmacy over the last thirty years. I had the privilege of knowing Thomas Pettigrew for the last four. Many people have told me what a dedicated pharmacist and wonderful human being Thomas Pettigrew was. I saw those qualities every day as we worked together. We were to bestow upon him the Lifetime Achievement Award from the Peninsula Pharmacists Association for his contribution to the health and well-being of our community.

"Unfortunately, he was tragically taken from us a few weeks ago. Tonight, we honor him posthumously. Tonight is a celebration of not only his professional career but also his life. I would like to invite his daughter, Christine, to join us in accepting this award this evening."

Christine fought the urge to turn and run. Jason gently grabbed her elbow and guided her through the crowd. The levies opened and tears flooded her eyes as Zanns hugged her. Christine stood with her arms hanging limp by her sides, too devastated to return the embrace.

Zanns continued, "I would like to now introduce to you the president of the Peninsula Retail Pharmacists Association."

Chrissie didn't catch her name. The middle-aged woman spoke about Thomas Pettigrew's accomplishments over his long, distinguished service career. His participation in local organizations was well chronicled. The words did not register with Christine as she stood with eyes lowered. Then she was handed the large mortar and pestle engraved with her father's name. Polite applause followed. In the moment of awkward silence that followed, Christine felt all eyes on her. She choked back tears and spoke softly, barely audible. "Daddy would be very proud of this honor," she said. "He was a decent man. Someone who always wanted to do the right thing. It's a blessing to have people in your life who do the right thing." Christine looked at Jason, her eyes delivering an uncomfortable message.

She wiped her eyes, as the sound of her sobs was drowned by more applause.

* * *

Jason, relieved the soiree was ending, guided Christine to the front entrance, where most of the partygoers were headed. Christine clutched the heavy mortar and pestle in both arms.

At the door, Jasmine offered her hand to Jason and said, loudly enough for Christine to hear, "I'll talk to you tomorrow, Jason." The doctor also offered a hand to Christine, who responded only with a frozen stare. Outside, they waited for the valet and chatted with other departing guests.

Then Jason recognized the familiar outline of the approaching figure. "Oh, no," he said.

"What's wrong?" Christine asked, following his gaze.

A woman was marching up the circular driveway, weaving through a line of cars. Her eyes were locked on her ex-boyfriend and the woman standing with him. Her auburn curls bobbed with each determined stride.

"This is gonna be ugly," Jason croaked.

"Who's that?" Christine asked.

"It's Sheila, my ex."

"What the hell is she doing here?"

"I was just asking myself that same question."

Sheila Boquist stomped to a halt. The veins in her neck looked like taut computer cables beneath her pale, flushed skin. Her cobalt eyes burned with anger. "I thought you said you weren't seeing anyone," she snapped.

"Sheila, this isn't the time or the place."

"Bullshit! You've been cheating on me since day one, haven't you? You lying piece of shit!"

Dozens of eyes were fixed on the confrontation.

"Sheila, I'm not going to do this now." Jason's eyes searched the faces of other departing guests. Shocked, tense smiles greeted him.

Sheila looked Christine up and down. "Is this the tart you've been screwing?"

"Sheila! That's enough!" he whispered harshly. He moved between the two women before Christine could react. He put his hands on Sheila's shoulders to turn her away. "Let's just go—"

Distracted by embarrassment and Sheila's audacity, Jason had let his defenses down. Sheila raised her knee quickly and mashed it into his testicles. Bolts of lightning paralyzed him. Air escaped his lungs in a loud whoosh. He sank to both knees and grabbed his groin, retching in a violent, silent scream.

CHAPTER 19

In her living room, Jason looked up at Christine as she assessed his pitiful state. The bag of frozen peas rested gingerly between his legs, darkening Jason's trousers with moisture. He'd been trying to get comfortable for the last ten minutes. After she'd delivered her blow, Sheila had stormed off. He barely recalled being lifted by strong hands into the car. He spent the ride to Christine's house curled into a fetal position in the passenger seat. Christine drove, suppressing a smile the whole way.

"I'd offer to rub it, but I'm not that kind of girl," said Christine.

Jason winced and readjusted. "You think this is funny, don't you?"

"The comedic value is priceless. You're welcome to sleep in the spare bedroom. I wouldn't want you getting in an accident because all your blood rushed to your balls and you couldn't concentrate on your driving," she said. "Now, I'm going to take a shower. I'll check on you before I go to bed." As she turned to go upstairs, Christine stopped, another thought occurring to her. "You can throw the peas away. I don't think I'll be eating them anytime soon."

110

Jason limped to the spare bedroom and dropped onto the bed. It took thirty minutes before sleep arrived. The repose was anything but restful.

The chirping of his cell phone woke him from one of his brief naps. He glanced at the red numerals of the clock on the nightstand. It was 1:28 a.m.

"Hello?" His voice was gritty, his testicles felt like grapefruits. Jason's eyes focused on the shadowy outline of the bronze mortar Christine had left on the dresser.

"I've been trying to contact you all night."

"Who is this?"

"A new friend," the voice said. "Meet me tomorrow morning at the fountains in City Center at eleven."

"Who is this?"

"Be at the fountains at eleven," the baritone voice repeated.

He bolted upright. "I'm not going anywhere unless I know who I'm talking to."

"If you want help finding out what happened to T. P., you'll be there."

The initials brought Jason to full alertness. "How will I know you?"

CHAPTER 20

Friday, September 29

Jason's neck muscles felt like thick, waterlogged ropes twisted into tight knots; his head pounded and his testicles, sore and swollen, tugged at his groin with each step.

Two more stacks to go. White, corrugated-cardboard boxes leaned precariously in varying directions, creating a miniature, cellulose skyline. The "keeper" pile had been lugged to the distant end of the hall near a small bathroom, the "throwaways" to the entrance for pickup by a shredding company. Dressed in jeans and a T-shirt, he and Brandon, the football player, had been shuffling cartons since seven. The high school senior was gone now, having rushed off to his first class.

Jason was taking a break, leaning on the doorframe, when he noticed the black console mounted on the opposite wall. It had been hidden behind the mountain of boxes. Wires, spaced at five-foot intervals, descended from the ceiling, disappearing into the top of the unit. Another, thicker cable meandered from the underside, circling into the ceiling again near the outer wall.

112

He climbed up on a box, pushing a ceiling tile out of the way. He peered over the upper side of the darkened tiles. Slivers of light seeped up through the joints. Sam and Kevin Mitchell could be heard conversing below. The thin wires snaked over the ceiling squares and terminated at small, cigarette-pack-sized boxes. He climbed down and examined the thicker cable. Held in place by U-clamps, it poked through a hole in the roof.

He walked into the pharmacy and spent a few minutes in each bay, pretending to be examining stock bottles for expiration dates. Jason shot furtive glances up at the ceiling. It took a few tries, but he finally spotted the tiny holes. In each bay, a miniscule lens poked through the foam of the ceiling tile, flush with its surface, nearly imperceptible. Pinhole security cameras.

The Colonial had been equipped with a closed-circuit video system.

Jason was familiar with every inch of the Colonial. There was no supporting hardware anywhere in the building. Questions bombarded him. Where were the monitor and recording equipment that must be capturing the images? Who was accessing the images, and where were they being stored? Had there been a problem with theft? Who had installed the system? Lily? Pettigrew?

Jason returned to the hallway, perplexed. He gripped a box on the last stack, holding it by the cutouts. Expecting a packed, heavy load of papers, he jerked it into the air. It was nearly empty, causing him to lose his balance. He tumbled backward, hit the bathroom doorframe, and kicked a wheeled janitor's bucket. The mop it was holding fell away. Dirty brown water sloshed up over the sides, crashing in waves. A flash of metal in the trough of a wave caught his eye, the shine and texture incongruous with the brown muck. He nudged the bucket with his foot as if it harbored a disease, and again saw the flash of metal. Pulling up his sleeve, he plunged his hand in and fished out the object.

A flip phone.

He placed the phone in a plastic baggie, then dropped it into his briefcase. Wondering who might have lost the phone, he checked his watch. Nine thirty. Time to do some real pharmacy work. He abandoned the boxes, promising himself to finish sorting them this weekend. Retrieving his dress clothes from the car, Jason gently rolled the dirty bucket from the bathroom and changed.

* * *

"We'd like you to start right away," said Jason.

"I think it's appropriate to give them some notice," Billy Parks said over the phone.

"I understand that. But if you come on board right away, Lily Zanns has authorized me to pay you quite well and provide a bonus." Jason recited the figures to an astonished Parks.

"Are you shittin' me?" Parks responded.

"No sir, Billy. When can you start?" *Business is business*, he thought.

"I'll be there tomorrow."

"See you then."

He leaned back in Lily's chair and glanced at his watch. He was supposed to meet the anonymous caller in less than two hours. He had slept little. He rubbed his eyes, fighting the headache that was rapidly approaching. "T. P." could only refer to one person. Thomas Pettigrew.

His mentor's death still bothered him. It all stunk to high heaven. He had no proof of anything, mind you. The call last night—or this morning, rather—had rubbed the raw flesh of his curiosity. *Don't let your imagination run wild*, he told himself. *Could be a crackpot. Be very skeptical.*

Rachel, the cashier, appeared in the doorway, announcing a phone call from Dr. Kader. Jason thought for a moment. "Tell her I'm in a meeting, and I'll call her back."

CHAPTER 21

Jason checked his watch and reflected on the lunacy of waiting on a park bench for a covert meeting with a total stranger because he doubted the published facts about Thomas's demise. Jason had always challenged inconsistencies, regardless of their apparent insignificance. It was who he was. That trait had irritated his brother, Peter, from the time Jason was old enough to beginning analyzing his surroundings and the people in them. He'd abandoned it when he was forced to resign from the Colonial. The facts surrounding his departure were troubling. It was the only time in his life when he'd not followed his conscience and he still regretted it. Determined peskiness was a quality that made Jason a very good pharmacist. The most miniscule drug interaction or inconsistency in a patient's drug therapy spurred him to call physicians constantly, to the consternation of the office nursing staff.

In fact, that same quality had saved his father from serious injury when Jason was fifteen years old. Edward Rodgers, a robust, barrel-chested man, had been cutting down the massive, dying oak in the backyard with his aging chain saw. Jason knew the hum and whine of the blades, having heard them often as his father cleared their densely wooded lot. But that day, the sound of the spinning chain was different, strained and warbling. Edward, who was deaf in one ear, failed to hear the change. Jason raced to his father's side, begging him to shut off the machine. When they inspected it, they found the damaged links were ready to fly off in all directions. Jason had saved his father from serious injury.

Bustling foot traffic circled the City Center's enormous reflecting pond. He was lost deep in thought when the gravelly voice came over his left shoulder, interrupting his reverie. "Don't look over."

Jason turned.

"I said don't look over here!"

Ponytail, the tobacco-reeking, cheap-perfume-smelling Willie Nelson look-alike, sat on the opposite end of the bench, looking straight ahead.

"You're late," said Jason.

"No, I'm not. I've been here since you arrived."

"I've been here for fifteen minutes. You weren't here."

"I was checking to see if you were followed."

"Are you kidding me? Do you have a message that will self-destruct in five seconds, too?"

"Just pretend you don't know me."

"What's with the spy routine? First the phone call. Now this."

Ponytail coughed and wiped his nose with the sleeve of his shirt.

"Who are you?" asked Jason.

More silence. Jason did not smell cigarettes or perfume today; either Ponytail was sitting downwind, or he'd showered recently. "My name is Walter, Walter Waterhouse. I was a friend of Thomas Pettigrew's."

"How do you know me?"

"I earn my living knowing things about people," said Waterhouse.

"You guess people's names for a living?"

"Are you going to be a wise-ass the whole fucking time? I'm a private investigator." He had a faint, nasal, New England twang.

Jason shifted, allowing some blood flow in his backside. "What do you want with me? And how did you know Thomas?"

"Thomas was an acquaintance of mine. He thought he was being pursued. His death may not have been an accident."

"Thomas was murdered?"

"I'm saying that Thomas was onto something. He told me as much. The part about murder is a guess."

"Do you have proof?"

"Yes and no."

"Is it 'yes' or 'no'?"

"Do you want to hear what I have to say, or should I just kick that scrawny pill-pushing ass of yours right now?"

Jason arched an eyebrow. One side of his mouth curled into a snarl. He thought, *I'd like to see you try.* But he bit his tongue. "This better be worth my time," he said, as he calculated how much Zanns was paying him per minute.

"Thomas passed the message on to me before he died."

Waterhouse pulled a crumpled pack of Marlboros from his shirt pocket. He shook one loose and produced a lighter. Three puffs later, he said, "How did you so conveniently come to be employed by the Colonial?" The exhaled fumes evaporated in the breeze.

"Not that it's any of your damned business, but I interviewed. It's called free market capitalism."

"Pretty convenient, that job opening up for you, wouldn't you say? I was at Thomas's house after the funeral, remember. We made eye contact. I saw you with Christine, his daughter. There's a history there."

"What are you trying to say?"

"Just making an observation." Waterhouse took a drag. "I did some checking. You worked for Thomas a few years back, and left under less-than-ideal circumstances. You haven't kept in touch with Thomas—or his daughter. Then all of a sudden Thomas dies, and you get his job. Pretty damned convenient."

Jason glanced over and saw Waterhouse's crooked, yellowing teeth appearing and disappearing behind his thin, quick-moving lips. *How much does this guy know?* Jason wondered. Thomas wouldn't have revealed the incident to anyone, would he? The last thing the old man would have wanted was for the details of Jason's departure to become public. Pettigrew's career and reputation would have suffered as much as Jason's. Jason sat stone-faced, giving nothing away.

"See, as I said, I was an acquaintance of Thomas's. I met him six years back. He never mentioned you. Thomas left reason for me to believe things aren't what they seem over at the Colonial. Since you benefited from his death, I'm thinking you might know something about what's going on. Or maybe you're involved somehow?"

"Screw you! You want my help, don't give me the third friggin' degree! Why the hell did you ignore me at the Colonial, anyway?"

"Timing wasn't right. By the way, do you know where the term 'the third degree' comes from?"

"What?" Jason's irritation spilled over into his voice.

Waterhouse ignored Jason's tone. "It's a Freemason thing."

"What?"

"Thomas told me about it," said the investigator, like a teacher explaining a lesson. "The term 'third degree' comes from the Masons. There are thirty-three degrees. The first three are actual degrees, the next twenty-nine are administered at the Scottish Rite level—"

The words were like a foreign language to Jason. "Now I have to sit through this?"

Waterhouse huffed and stared straight ahead. Jason could feel the man's frustration. Waterhouse continued. "The third degree is that of a master Mason. The candidate is subjected to intense questioning and physical challenges. Hence the meaning of the term."

Jason narrowed his eyes, his cheeks bulging with air. "You say you knew Thomas, but how do I even know if that's true?"

"You want proof? I thought you might." Waterhouse reached into his leather jacket and handed him a photo. In the photograph, younger versions of Thomas Pettigrew and Waterhouse stood with their arms around each other's shoulders, smiling in a yard somewhere. Waterhouse held a Michelob in his hand, Pettigrew a Diet

Coke. People were in the background, talking in groups at some kind of backyard gathering.

"I knew him," Waterhouse continued, "and I owe him. And I pretended not to know you, because there are problems at the Colonial. There's a fly in the ointment, to use a pharmacy metaphor." The edge in his voice had melted.

"What kind of problems?"

"Before I tell you anything, I need to know I can trust you. The information must be handled prudently."

"So why call me? Talk to Lily Zanns."

"Everyone at the Colonial is suspect. You're the only person that's new. So I figure you're probably not involved. But I checked you out anyway. You've been a pharmacist at Keller's for eight years. Before that you worked at Rite-Aid, and before that, the Colonial. You own a house, have a kid, and no criminal record. I have a pretty good idea you're okay, but you can't be too sure. I needed to look you in the eye."

"Is this Let's-Dig-Up-Shit-on-Jason-Rodgers Month, or what?"

"What's that supposed to mean?"

"Never mind."

Waterhouse leaned closer, his voice conspiratorial. "How did you come to get the job at the Colonial? The second time, I mean?"

"Getting the job wasn't planned. It just kind of happened. I saw the article in the paper about Pettigrew's death. I went to the funeral—"

"And you met up with your old flame?"

Jason shrugged. "I met Christine at the Colonial so we could catch up. She was picking up her father's things from the store. The next thing I knew, I had an interview. I had no plans to take the job, but the offer blew my socks off."

Waterhouse nodded. "Thomas said Lily Zanns was a piece of work. Don't trust her. Things aren't right."

"I know what you mean, Walter," Jason agreed. "And I, too, think something's rotten in Denmark. But it has nothing to do with the Colonial. What bothers me is the way Thomas died."

"The alcohol?"

"Exactly."

Waterhouse turned toward Jason. "Thomas always tried to get me to stop drinking when we got together. Even as a late as a week before he died."

"I knew it. He couldn't have died the way he did," said Jason.

"Thomas wanted me to tell you something," said Waterhouse.

"You said he never mentioned me to you."

"He didn't."

Jason turned his palms skyward in a what-the-hell-are-you-talking about motion. "You doing the psychic thing?"

Waterhouse smiled. "You're a wise-ass, kid. You remind me of me a lifetime ago." He interlaced his fingers and pushed them away from his body, cracking his knuckles. "Thomas wanted me to tell you he was sorry. He also wanted me to tell Christine that he loved her. I haven't had a chance to pass on that message to her yet, though."

Walter—Ponytail—whoever this man was, reached into his shirt pocket again and pulled out a folded piece of paper. Jason took the crinkled paper, unfolding it slowly. It was a computer-generated report, listing patient names and prescriptions. It contained seven items. "This is some kind of drug audit," said Jason. "Pharmacists use this type of report often."

"Turn it over."

Jason flipped the paper and saw a messy scrawl that would have made a doctor proud. His gut clenched and he swallowed hard. Thomas was reaching out to him—and Chrissie—from the grave. His mouth became dry; his throat clogged.

Walter:

Keep these files safe and tell no one at the Colonial about them.

Bring this evidence to the authorities. They are after me.

Thomas

P.S. Tell Christine that I love her.

P.P.S. Tell Jason I'm sorry.

CHAPTER 22

"Thomas left a box of files with me," said Waterhouse, "stuffed with information. He was afraid it would fall into the wrong hands—"

Jason's stomach somersaulted as he read the handwritten missive. He remembered the indentation in the carpet of Pettigrew's office closet. "Is the box about twelve by thirty-six inches?"

"I didn't measure the darned thing. But that sounds about right. I figured you were the Jason he meant, seeing as you're the only Jason that's ever worked at the Colonial. That, and the way you and his daughter were talking after the funeral. You two an item?"

"We were," he replied. "We dated for a year."

"Why did he want to apologize?"

Jason dodged again. "Didn't you speak to him when he dropped the box off?"

"I wasn't home at the time. Thomas had a key to my house."

"I thought you said you were acquaintances. I don't give acquaintances keys to my place."

"Okay, we were friends."

"If you two were friends, why didn't Thomas tell you what was going on over there?"

It was Waterhouse's turn to shrug. "Thomas got burned because of these conspiracies. I guess he wanted to make sure he had all the facts before he told anyone."

"What do you know about the past? My past?"

"Not much, really. Thomas and I were friends in the present. We never talked about the past. What was so important he was apologizing after thirteen years?"

"I don't know," Jason lied.

"I was a cop for twenty years. My bullshit detector is dead-on-balls accurate," said Waterhouse. "Something happened. Something so big and so awful you left the Colonial. And you never kept in touch with Thomas or Christine. Thomas never spoke about it directly. Now suddenly you're back. What was it?"

Jason pushed a hand through his hair. "Leave it alone. How did you come to know Thomas?"

"We don't have time for that right now. I have to be in divorce court in an hour. I have some juicy video on a philandering husband who's dipping his pen in company ink."

"What is—was—Thomas hiding with you?"

"Look straight ahead," Waterhouse commanded. "That's why I wanted to meet you. To find out what these papers mean. Can you be trusted, Jason Rodgers? Thomas seemed to think you were important enough to mention in a note to me thirteen years after the fact."

"I'm the second-most trustworthy person I know."

"Who's more trustworthy than you?"

Jason was tiring of the questions, so he changed the subject again. "I was also a friend of Thomas's. He was my instructor a few years back."

"What ended the friendship?" Waterhouse snapped.

"We just never stayed in touch."

"So why is he apologizing?"

"It's complicated."

"And why did you go to work at the Colonial for a second time?"

"I told you! I was offered the job." Jason whipped his head around, looking directly into the skinny man's eyes.

Waterhouse nodded, apparently satisfied with Jason's indignation. "I have more documents like that one. There, in his files. I need a pharmacist to interpret them, tell me what they mean."

"What's going on at the Colonial?"

"That, Jason," Waterhouse said heavily, "is the Final Jeopardy question."

Waterhouse removed the crumpled pack of cigarettes from his shirt pocket a second time. He lipped one out and snapped open the lighter. He took a long drag, exhaling smoke through his nostrils. "I'm going to trust you, Jason Rodgers. Not because your past is on the up-and-up, but because it seems Thomas did. I don't have the answers to your questions. But they're the same questions I've asked myself for weeks. Meet me tonight at six thirty, and we'll try to figure it all out. Come alone, and tell no one about this meeting. And I mean no one, especially the people at the Colonial. Thomas had a reason to think something was amiss. That's good enough for me." Waterhouse twisted his upper body toward Jason. "If you fuck with me, I'll make you sorry we ever met."

Jason studied the rustling leaves of the birch tree above them. "I want to bring someone with me tonight."

"Who?"

"My brother, Peter."

"Why?"

"Because I trust him more than I trust myself. I'm a little too close to the situation. I need someone who's objective."

"I don't think that's a good idea."

"He comes, or I don't."

* * *

The man codenamed Boreas sat behind the wheel of the car, watching as the tall, thin man with the ponytail walked to his Blazer. *Fucking amateurs*, he thought. Their attempts to conceal their conversation were painfully inadequate. They had been engaged in an animated discussion. About what, he had no clue. He picked up his secure cell phone and dialed. "The pharmacist just met with someone." Boreas listened for a moment, then spoke again. "About six feet, skinny…long gray ponytail. We're getting photos now."

His partner, Jack McCall, another codename, snapped several shots of the man through his digital camera from the passenger side. He connected the camera to a small laptop sitting between them.

Boreas listened. "Okay, we'll stay with the pharmacist. McCall is uploading the images to you now."

"We'll identify him and gather whatever information we can," the voice on the other end replied, "and pass it on to Cooper."

Boreas disconnected, and the two men waited to see what Jason Rodgers would do next.

CHAPTER 23

"You didn't call me back!"

Jason spun to see Jasmine Kader, a few feet away, smiling at him. A large shopping bag dangled from her left hand. How long had she been there? Had she seen him with Waterhouse?

Jason had been window-shopping along the open-air market, pondering the conversation he'd had minutes ago. Waterhouse had not been gone more than fifteen minutes. "I was busy."

"Well, it appears you're no longer busy. You're wandering around City Center shopping. Your workload must have lightened."

"Don't you have patients you should be seeing?" he asked.

"The office is closed for lunch until one thirty. Why don't we grab a bite to eat, since we're both here? The Southern Belle is right around the corner."

Jason glanced at his watch again, hoping it would give a reason for him to decline.

Kader read his thoughts. "You're the vice-president now. You mean to tell me you can't take a few minutes to have lunch?"

126

Jason hesitated. The come-hither smile was hard to ignore.

"I won't bite," she said. "At least, not on the first date."

Unlike last night at the gala, her clothing today was clinical and professional: white lab jacket, pink silk blouse, and black knee-length skirt. Yet sensuality still managed to ooze from the woman. Jason had never been uncomfortable around women. In fact, in his college days, he'd considered himself something of a ladies' man, witty and smooth. But for some reason, he was nervous and self-conscious around Jasmine Kader.

"Sure," he said, unable to come up with a good excuse to refuse. "Lunch would be fine. Just keep your teeth to yourself."

* * *

Crowded with city bureaucrats, bank tellers, mothers and their adult daughters, and solitary businessmen with loosened ties, the Southern Belle was a favorite lunchtime spot. Jason and Jasmine were seated at a window table overlooking the fountains by a green-aproned, matronly waitress.

Jason returned to the table after stepping outside to call his brother. Peter told him he'd meet him tonight for their rendezvous with the private investigator.

"If I didn't know any better, Jasmine," he said upon returning, "I would say you had this little meeting planned. How did you just happen to come equipped with wine and a corkscrew?"

Jasmine smiled and said, "Guilty as charged. Do you want to handcuff me now or later?"

"Were you following me?"

"I just seized an opportunity, that's all. By the way, who was that man you were talking to?"

"An old friend of mine. Why do you want to know?"

"No reason. So, did you have a good time last night?"

"Yes," Jason lied, taking a long pull on the pink liquid. The public confrontation with Lily, Jasmine's overt attempt to fondle him, and the final coup de grace by Sheila to Jason's groin made the night quite memorable for all the wrong reasons. He wondered who regretted going more, him or Christine. "You mentioned last night you wanted to talk about some programs for our pharmacy and your clinic."

"I did say that. But that's not the only reason I wanted to meet with you." Jasmine flipped her long black hair over a shoulder. "I want something from you. No, I need something from you. And—Jason—I'm a woman who gets what she wants."

Christine's words flashed through his mind. *That woman wants something from you!* "And what is it that?"

His hand rested on the table. She placed hers over his, but exerted no pressure. The touch and her gaze were electric, stimulating nerve endings that ran deep inside him. The exquisite, tan skin on her hand was a perfect contrast to the pink silk of her sleeve. Jason avoided her eyes as if to ward off her spell. He wanted to slide his hand away, but it felt welded to the table.

Jason registered a strange fact. For a woman who flaunted her skin and body, Jasmine always wore long sleeves. At Pettigrew's house after the funeral, last night at the party, and today, despite temperatures close to eighty degrees, her arms were covered.

"What do you think I want?" she asked, playing with him.

"Dr. Kader—"

"Call me, Jasmine, please."

"Dr. Kader, I don't think I'm the type of man you're looking for."

"You have no idea what kind of man interests me."

"True. And you have no idea what kind of man I am."

"That's why I want to get to know you."

"I don't have time for a relationship. Lily plans on keeping me very busy." He managed to drag his hand out from under hers.

"There's always time for fun. Work hard, play even harder, I say."

He'd downed two glasses of wine. "Do you always mix business with pleasure?"

"If you're successful, they're one and the same." Jasmine glanced at her silverware. She picked up her fork and inspected it. "This is filthy. Look! This knife is as well. Jason, would you be a dear and go ask for some new ones at the waiters' station?"

* * *

Kader watched Jason walk to the small cubby used by the wait staff as she slipped her hand into her sleeve.

This man was not like her usual targets, who became weak-kneed at the sight of her body. Usually, the alcohol, perfume, and promise of sweaty bodies pressed together was enough to have them hollering for the check. Kader enjoyed the hunt, the banter and the coy double entrendres. Normally, she would pursue her prey more patiently, more subtly. Two factors did not allow that tact. Jason Rodgers was resisting her, and time was limited. His temptation was strong, but so were his defenses. The woman, Pettigrew's daughter, was in play. She thought getting him alone, away from her, would make him pliable; most men were. But Christine had some sort of hold over him, even when she was not around. Drastic measures were warranted.

Kader slipped her hand into the sleeve of her blouse and removed a small vial. She unscrewed it and poured its contents into Jason's glass, keeping an eye on Jason. The clear fluid trickled into the empty wine glass, settling on the bottom. She filled both glasses again. With a long, slender index finger, she swirled. In seconds, the thicker liquid mixed with the wine. He returned to the table as she moved her hands back to her lap.

"I took the liberty of pouring you another glass," she said.

"Thank you. This'll be my last. I do have return to work."

Don't worry. It will definitely be your last, she thought. She lifted her untainted wine in the air. They clinked and drank.

"Do you always drink with such gusto?" she asked.

"As a matter of fact, I don't. Must be the company," he said.

"I don't know if I should take that as a compliment or not."

"Neither do I."

"Do you always play this hard to get?"

Jason emptied his third glass of wine. The final drops were bitter tasting. He studied the bottom of the glass as if he had been bitten. "If I'd played harder to get, my life would be a lot simpler. I told you, I'm not interested in a relationship."

"Who says I want a relationship?"

"What do you want?"

Kader raised an eyebrow and quirked a corner of her mouth. "You know," she said. "That, and information," she said.

Jason cleared his throat. "What kind of information?"

"Business information."

"About the Colonial?"

She nodded and caressed his forearm.

Christine was right, Jason thought. "Subtlety isn't one of your strengths, is it? Why not just ask me?"

"This is much more fun. You're a very attractive man. Life is too short to be a shrinking violet. Most people miss out because they are afraid to go after what they want." She touched his arm again. The effects were felt much lower.

"You're not making me feel all warm and fuzzy. I don't intend to be just another notch on your stethoscope." A flushing sensation came over him. *Too much wine, too fast*, he thought.

"I don't give up easily, Jason. I intend to pursue you." She paused for effect, the consummate actress, and then she whispered the next word. Jason leaned in to hear it. "Vigorously."

The waitress arrived, and Kader straightened her blouse. "Lily has asked me to invest in her pharmacy venture. I want to know if it's a sound investment."

"Why don't you ask her yourself?"

"Lily and I are friends. She's very persuasive, but she isn't objective. I need someone who will be honest with me."

"I work for Lily now. How do you know I can be objective?" He pushed the empty glass to the center of the table.

She saw this and emptied the remaining liquid into it. "You haven't been with Lily long enough to be corrupted by her passion."

"Corrupted? That's a strange word."

"I meant it in a good way. She has a way of making you see only her way. Like drinking the Kool-Aid."

"What would you like to know?"

"Do you think the Colonial concept will succeed? Does Lily's plan make sense?"

"If we make wise investments, yes, it will. Lily's a go-getter and can make it work. But there'll be a few bumps on the way—she likes to throw her money around. Or, should I say, Steven Cooper's money."

"Last night you disagreed with her strategy."

"Just with her east end idea."

"But you changed her mind?"

"It seems so."

Kader tossed back her head, arching her spine, stretching the silk of her blouse against perfect, round breasts. She dawdled there for an agonizingly long moment. "If you were me, would you give a large sum of money to Lily?"

"I'm not in the habit of telling other people what to do with their money, Dr. Kader—Jasmine."

"Fair enough. But I dare say you wouldn't have taken this job if you thought it would fail."

"I wouldn't say that. If it doesn't work out, I can always find work. It's a no-lose situation for me." The words were coming slower, hesitantly, not quite slurred, but close. His tongue felt like it had doubled in size.

"I understand you worked at the Colonial quite a few years ago."

Jason squinted at the question. "That's right. I was an extern there. Then I worked as a staff pharmacist."

"So you were familiar with Pettigrew, the former owner?"

"He was my mentor."

"His death must have been a shock."

"It was."

"I've heard rumors that he was into some strange stuff."

"Like what?"

"That he was a member of some secret organization. And that he was slightly touched or into drugs. And, of course, that he was a drinker."

He began shaking his head before the sentence was complete, the temperature under his collar growing. "That's totally wrong. Thomas had his peculiarities, but he was one of the most grounded men I knew."

"So what was he into? Where there's smoke, there's fire. Even rumors have some basis in truth."

"I can tell you that he wasn't part of some secret club. And I don't believe he was into drugs or alcohol."

"Then how did he manage to wrap his car around a tree?"

"Why are you so interested?" His voice had a clumsy edge to it now.

She waved it away. "His death was so sudden and so tragic. People speculate, fill in the gaps. I'd just like to know what to believe."

"Thomas's death was a...shock and...very...tragic. And I don't know what to believe about his accident. It was...incon—sistent with the person I knew."

"Didn't the papers say he was drunk?"

"Yes, they...did."

"Are you saying you don't believe he'd drink and drive?"

"It wasn't in him." Jason saw Kader inch his glass closer to him with a fingernail. He snatched it up and downed it without thinking. "Unlike us," he said, lifting the now-empty glass. "He didn't touch alcohol. Why are you so interested...in this?"

"So then how did it happen?"

"I can't explain that." His skin was tingling. The room suddenly felt like an oven. He loosened his tie. His eyelids seemed to be attached to anchors, pulling them closed.

"I'm sorry," she said, sensing his frustration. "So tell me about your girlfriend, Christine."

"She's not...my girlfriend." His speech was thicker now, out of his control.

The waitress appeared and placed their orders on the table. "Will there be anything else?" she asked. They both shook their heads.

Kader persisted like a prosecutor cross-examining a witness. "She may not be your girlfriend, but there's an attraction there."

"Just...history," he replied, cutting into his steak sloppily. He misjudged and spilled some green beans onto the tablecloth. He didn't dare afford himself the luxury of assuming he and Christine could be together again.

He was agitated now. After three glasses of wine—or was it four?—the uncomfortable topics, combined with Jasmine's overbearing presence, became a roiling brew. He jabbed at the food as if the steak needed to be killed all over again.

"Have I upset you?"

"I'm...fine," he replied, ramming a square of meat toward his mouth, almost missing. "Just need...to eat something."

"You don't seem fine."

Enough, he thought. He rose unsteadily, removed his wallet, pulled out a hundred-dollar bill, and tossed it on the table. "Time for me to go! This should...cover it," he said. He zigzagged toward the door, which he shoved open clumsily, banging his head on the glass. As Jason staggered to his car he knew he shouldn't drive. He tried to decide what to do. The answer came moments later.

* * *

Jasmine smiled, sipped her wine, grabbed Jason's wine glass with her napkin, and slipped it in the pocket of her lab coat before walking briskly after him.

CHAPTER 24

Jason and Peter trailed Waterhouse single file toward the rear of his small Poquoson one-story bungalow. A large-breasted woman, wrapped in a frayed towel, emerged from the bathroom. Her hair, still dry, looked as if it repelled water better than Kevlar, and appeared to have been dipped in undiluted Clorox. Waterhouse filed past, foregoing introductions. The same strong scent of cheap perfume Jason had smelled on Waterhouse during their first encounter permeated the house. Jason averted his eyes and ran a hand over his throbbing head, but the woman showed not a scintilla of embarrassment at her state of undress.

Jason's brain felt like an overinflated balloon pressing against his cranium. He'd woken this afternoon to Peter pounding on his front door. He had no recollection of leaving the Southern Belle, or of how he'd even managed to get home. But his car was in the driveway, and the keys were on the counter. What bothered him even more than the headache was that he didn't remember anything that happened between leaving the restaurant and waking up. Had he done something with Jasmine he was going to regret?

"Have a seat," Waterhouse instructed.

The cramped dining room had been converted into a command center, stuffed with a myriad of electronic assets. On a long table in front of a drawn curtain sat a large-screen computer surrounded by a digital video recorder and several cameras. Three telephoto lenses stood inverted, like oversized chess pieces. On the opposite wall, a desk with another computer was flanked by two large filing cabinets.

Three chairs huddled in the center of the room, surrounding a tattered, bulging, white banker's box. The sides were dotted with gouges and lengths of duct tape.

"Here it is. Thomas's pride and joy." Waterhouse pulled a chunk of files from the box. He squinted against the smoke rising from his cigarette.

"You mind if I light up?" Peter asked, rubbing the scar over his eye. It was an unconscious habit, Jason noticed, his brother fell into when he was about to stress that gung-ho, "ooh-rah" brain of his.

"Be my guest," the private investigator replied. Peter shook a cigarette loose, and with the two of them puffing away, a velvety cloud soon hung below the ceiling.

Waterhouse continued, "It's his collection of material on any kind of conspiracy he could get his hands on. The moon landings, the Kennedy assassination, crop circles, September 11, UFO sightings of all kinds, Freemasons, the Illuminati, Operation Valkyrie, the Trilateral Commission, Bilderberg and anything else he could think of." He paused. "Did you know he actually spent four days, on two separate trips, at Dealey Plaza investigating Kennedy's murder? He stood behind the picket fence on the grassy knoll with his camera and tape measure. He also visited Ground Zero a year ago. Claims there's evidence that the Twin Towers and the smaller buildings were intentionally brought down by preset explosives, not the planes crashing into them. He also went to Shanksville to see the crash site of Flight 93. Said no bodies were ever recovered from the site."

"He was a conspiracy theorist?" asked Peter, giving Jason a look. "Is that what this is all about?"

The next twenty minutes were spent leafing through the dog-eared collection of papers. "I have to admit, Walter. This doesn't look good," said Jason. "The man *was* paranoid." He tossed a stack of papers about a UFO crashing somewhere in Pennsylvania in the fifties on the floor beside the box. A sliver of doubt entered Jason's mind about Thomas's activities.

"I show you this so you know what kind of man Pettigrew was."

Peter fanned through paper, pamphlets, and brochures. "It looks like he was a quack. How did you know him, anyway?"

Waterhouse leaned back and clasped his hands behind his graying head. "Thomas and I became friends about six years ago. He hired me to investigate the death of his wife—"

"His wife died of cancer. She wasn't killed," Jason declared.

"I know that," Waterhouse replied. "But Thomas was convinced her chemotherapy was diluted. Asked me to investigate her outpatient intravenous pharmacy."

Peter leaned forward. "And what did you find?"

The naked woman had emerged from the bathroom, clothed now, and was rummaging around the kitchen. "You're leaving, Becky Sue," Waterhouse called to her.

She grunted in the negative.

"He paid me to become a certified pharmacy technician and infiltrate the pharmacy. It took me three months to get my qualification, then I applied. They denied me at first, but eventually I got the job. Meanwhile, he was paying me eighty dollars an hour to do this undercover work."

"Again, Walter, what did you find?" Jason was growing irritated.

Walter rubbed his beard stubble. "I couldn't find anything wrong."

"What made Pettigrew think that the pharmacy medications weren't correct?"

"He'd read about some pharmacist in the Midwest who was mixing IV bags with subpotent medications to save money. Thomas thought this pharmacy was doing the same thing. In fact, he started accusing the doctors who owned the pharmacy before we had any hard evidence. It turned out to be very embarrassing. Luckily, I—and his attorney—convinced him to apologize and zip his mouth."

"This is ridiculous," Peter mumbled. "This guy was a fruitcake."

Jason held up a hand, quieting Peter. "So you took his money to investigate this pharmacy, and it turned out to be nothing?"

"Mind you, I didn't know it was nothing until I got in there. Once I realized they were legit, I stopped taking payment. By that point, I felt sorry for him. I began to stop by the pharmacy once a week to talk to him. We became friends, started meeting for chess and dinner."

"How much did he pay you before you stopped accepting his money?"

"About thirty-eight thousand dollars."

"Sweet Mother of God," Jason whispered. The guy's stock dropped several points in his eyes; was he trustworthy?

He looked hard at Waterhouse. "I thought you wanted to keep this quiet," he whispered, jerking his head toward the kitchen, and the girlfriend.

Waterhouse waved the comment off. "She doesn't care about this stuff. She'll be outta here in a few minutes."

Jason squinted then said, "You were saying?"

"His money paid for a lot of the equipment you see here. I'm a retired police officer, moved down here from Massachusetts after my divorce. Worked homicide in Boston. I was just starting out in the racket when I met Thomas. At the time, I needed a break. Thomas gave it to me."

"And once you found out the scam was bogus?" Jason's tone left no doubt about how he felt about Waterhouse's actions.

"I told you, I stopped taking his money! I didn't call Thomas. He called me!" Waterhouse, now agitated, sat up. "Listen to me, you good-for-nothing pill pusher. Who the hell do you think you are?"

Waterhouse and Jason locked eyes. The tense, testosterone-laced moment passed. Waterhouse blinked, and Jason continued. "How do you know his daughter, Christine?"

"I don't know her very well," the private investigator replied, relaxing a bit. "I went to the house because I overheard her inviting other people. I told her the truth. I was a friend of her father's. Since I was curious about his death, I wanted to check out folks at the Colonial, see if anyone might be a person of interest." Waterhouse handed Peter the drug report with the handwriting on the back he'd already shown Jason.

Peter read the report and looked quizzically at the two men.

"There's more," Waterhouse said. "Turn the page over."

Peter turned the page over and saw the note. He handed it back to Jason. "What is it?" Peter asked.

"That's what I was hoping your brother could tell me," Waterhouse replied, looking at Jason. "Here's the rest of what was in that particular file." He handed over a thin sheaf of documents and six paper prescriptions. "Then there's this." He handed Jason a DVD in a thin, clear plastic case. "It's a video of a day at the Colonial taken from a security camera. I've looked at the thing four times. I didn't see any unusual activity on it. But I'm not a pharmacist."

"What day was it recorded?" Jason flipped the case over, remembering the video equipment in the pharmacy.

"September 15."

"That was the night Pettigrew died."

"Exactly."

"What's this?" Peter asked, holding a palm-sized device.

"It's a GPS. Evidently, Thomas tracked one of the pharmacists the night he died. Sam Fairing. I believe you've met him. There's only one file on the hard drive. The trail ends at the Lions Bridge."

"Pettigrew left this box and these reports the night he died?"

Waterhouse nodded once more.

"What time did he leave them?"

"I was on an assignment that night. I left the house about eighty thirty. I didn't return home until about half past midnight. That's when I found the box inside the door. He had a key to this place." Waterhouse snapped his fingers. "Oh, yeah, there's one more thing. He left a message that night on the landline at a quarter to twelve. He called my cell, but I leave it off when I'm on assignment. I saved it." Waterhouse moved to his equipment and pulled a CD from a stack on the table. Placing it in a tray, he pressed a button, and the message played.

"I found one, Walt. I found one. I know I've been wrong in the past. But this time it's real. It's urgent, very urgent!"

CHAPTER 25

Pettigrew's deep, scratchy voice competed with the harsh background noise. It sounded as if he was in a hurricane. He might have been driving fast with the windows down. The recording stopped and left the three men in smoky silence. These were some of the man's final words, now spoken from the grave.

"What did he find?" asked Jason.

"That's what I was hoping you could help me with. It's in these papers somewhere and on the DVD."

"You haven't gone to the authorities?"

"With what? There's no evidence of foul play. All we have are some reports and a message left by a man notorious for jumping to conclusions about wild conspiracies. They'd boot me out on my ass."

"If he was killed, what would be the motive?" Peter leaned back and stroked his eyebrow.

"I don't know. But these reports and invoices are the only documents in his file box that aren't of national or international scope.

They involve the Colonial. The last entry on that report was for the day before he died. It's the only connection I have right now."

Jason shuffled the reports again. "I'm going to need a few minutes to review these. Don't you two have some death sticks you need to smoke?"

"That's our cue," said Peter, slapping his hands on his thighs. "Walter, my man, let's go take a few minutes off our lives thanks to the United States tobacco industry."

Jason sat at Waterhouse's desk and inspected each document, placing it neatly in a pile before moving on to the next. After he had reviewed each, he rummaged in the desk and found a writing pad and a pencil. He began again at the beginning of the stack and hastily scribbled notes.

An hour after he'd begun, Jason walked outside. Waterhouse was on the tail end of telling Peter about a firefight outside of Khe Sanh.

"What did you find?" asked Peter.

"There's a pattern to the paperwork. But I'm not sure I've found anything yet. I'll walk you all through it."

Back in the makeshift command center, Jason explained. "These are six prescriptions for the same medication written over the course of more than a year. They are all for the same patient, some guy named Douglas Winstead. And they're all for the same medication, a chemo drug called Prucept. It's used for liver cancer. And they were all written by the same doctor, Dr. Jasmine Kader."

CHAPTER 26

Jason held the report in his hand uneasily. If Jasmine Kader was somehow involved in Thomas' death, the implications were enormous. But Jason needed more. If Thomas was following a trail of prescriptions written by Jasmine, the old pharmacist must have suspected something was amiss. And, according to this sleazy private eye, he had literally followed Sam Fairing the night he died. The anxiety Jason felt was growing as he dealt the prescriptions, laying them out as if he were playing solitaire.

"What's it mean?" Waterhouse asked.

"I don't know. Nothing yet. Then there are these invoices." Jason referred back to the hastily scribbled notes on the yellow pad. "Each prescription corresponds with one of the listings on the report except one." Jason showed them his notes. The dates of the prescriptions and invoices were laid out in two columns. "There are seven invoices, but only six prescriptions."

"There's a prescription missing from the collection?" asked Waterhouse.

"Definitely, the one dated June 18," Jason replied. "This other report is a drug audit. A pharmacist can run one to find all the prescriptions written for a certain medication during a specific time frame. We use them all the time. This one"—Jason shook the report—"is a printout for all the Prucept prescriptions. Pettigrew must have run it. Each hard copy of a prescription is listed on this report, including the one dated June 18. But the actual hardcopy from that date is missing. Is it still in the box?"

"Let's take a look," said Waterhouse. The front door clicked closed. Waterhouse's lady friend had left.

The men paused briefly before taking sections of the documents and papers and leafing through them, looking for the missing prescription. They sat on the floor beside the battered box, legs crossed Indian-style, perusing the papers and files. Thirty-five minutes later, Jason looked up. "There's nothing in my pile."

"Nothing here," Peter agreed.

"Same," said Waterhouse. "So, where's the seventh prescription?"

"Wait a minute," Peter interjected, rubbing his eye. "What do the invoices have to do with the prescriptions?"

Jason turned to his brother. "The Colonial, being an independent pharmacy, doesn't have a warehouse. They buy their drugs directly from a wholesaler. We did the same thing at Keller's."

"So?" Waterhouse asked.

"These prescriptions were put into the computers at the Colonial and ordered from the wholesaler. But the shipment wouldn't have arrived until the next day. The invoice would be dated for the day the shipment arrived."

It was Peter's turn. "Wait one minute. Some of the dates you have for these invoices aren't for the next day. Two of the invoices are dated two days after the drug was put into the computer. Explain that one, boss man."

Jason puckered his lips, thinking. "Walter, you have a calendar on your computer, don't you?"

They spent the next twenty minutes reviewing dates on the calendar and matching them with the prescriptions and invoices. They had an explanation for each instance. If an invoice was dated two days after the prescription was entered into the computer, it was because a holiday or a weekend intervened.

Peter put a hand on Jason's shoulder. "Why would these prescriptions have to be ordered? How come they weren't on the shelf?"

"Good question. But I have an answer, O Dimwitted One. Prucept's very expensive. I believe it costs upward of a thousand dollars for one bottle of a hundred pills. Thomas was very cost conscious. He would never allow such an expensive drug to sit on the shelf tying up his money."

"But didn't he sell the Colonial? So it wasn't his money anymore."

"Old habits die hard," Jason replied.

"Why is any of this important?" Waterhouse swiveled in his chair to look at Jason and Peter, who were standing. "So they have a patient on a chemo drug. They filled his prescriptions. Big deal."

Jason touched his forehead. "You know what? I didn't realize what it meant until just this second." He picked up the invoices, then another sheet of paper from the stack. "I should have looked at this before! Look here, this report is a printout of the signature log for these prescriptions. When a patient picks up a prescription, he signs the electronic record to indicate he received the medication. The log is kept so that when an insurance company audits, a pharmacy can prove that the medication was picked up by the patient." His confidence in Thomas's sanity was returning.

"What if the patient forgets to sign it?" Peter asked, playing devil's advocate now, his second-favorite sport after guns and shooting.

"It happens. But look at this second report. Douglas Winstead never signed for any of his Prucept prescriptions."

"So you're saying he never received the medication?"

"That's exactly what I'm saying," Jason intoned. He snapped his fingers and rifled through the invoices. Then he said, "On each of these invoices, there's no listing for Prucept. The drug was entered into the computer, the insurance company was billed, but the drug was never delivered to the pharmacy. So how could they dispense it to the patient?"

Peter asked, "Why wouldn't they just have this patient Winstead sign for the drug or fake his signature to cover up the fact he never received the medication?"

"Good question, Pete," Jason replied. "It's one I can't answer at the moment."

"You know what you're saying, don't you?" Waterhouse furrowed his brow.

"You're damn right I do. The Colonial is guilty of insurance fraud."

"Son of a bitch," Peter swore under his breath. Then he said more loudly, "The old man *was* on to something. But how do you know those prescriptions were billed to the insurance company."

Jason thought for a minute. "That's easy. I can check the activity on each prescription. Anytime anyone does something to a prescription file, there's an electronic tag of everything that happened. I'll check each prescription and see if they were billed to Winstead's insurance. If they were, I'll also check to make sure no one reversed those claims. If the claims were reversed, there's no fraud. They billed the drug and ordered it. When it didn't come in from the wholesaler, they should have reversed it. If that's the case, everything's peachy. If they didn't, we're talking fraud."

"I wonder why Pettigrew didn't check the claims and reversals himself. You'd think they'd be in this box," said Peter.

"Did the insurance carrier pay the Colonial for the prescriptions?" asked Waterhouse.

"Another good question," Jason replied. "I'll find the remittance statements from Winstead's insurance company. They're probably in a file somewhere in the pharmacy. They send a statement along with a check to reimburse the pharmacy for payment of the prescriptions for all filed claims each month. I'll dig up each statement corresponding to each one of these prescriptions."

"Again, why didn't Pettigrew do that?" asked Peter.

"Maybe he didn't have access to those documents. Lily Zanns wouldn't let him have free run of the place once she bought the pharmacy. Or maybe he died before he could get to it." He pulled out two more items from the pile of paper. "There's more," said Jason. One was a wax-paper prescription bag with a Colonial receipt fastened to it. The bag and receipt were crumpled, and specks of claylike dirt granules were inside. The second was a white piece of paper with a drawing and a word scribbled on it. "This"—he held up the crumpled bag—"is the prescription bag from the last prescription fill. Why would Thomas keep it?"

Waterhouse and Peter shot each other confused looks.

"Then there's this drawing. There's a word under it. It says, 'Simoon.'"

Peter grabbed the sketch from his brother. Blood drained from the ex-marine's face.

"What's wrong?" asked Jason. "Have you seen this before?"

"Nothing. Never mind," Peter muttered tersely. "Let's just take it to the cops."

"No, not yet," Jason answered, eyeing his brother. The drawing had evoked a reaction in his brother, but he knew better than to press the matter.

"Why not?" asked Peter.

"Because if we do that, we may never find out what happened to Thomas."

"What are you saying? That he was murdered?" Peter seemed irritated.

"I'm saying we need to look into that possibility."

"Sheesh, bro. You've been watching too much late night TV. How are we going to look into something like that?"

Waterhouse held up a finger. "If he died in a car accident, it's considered an unattended death. Since there was alcohol involved, they probably did an autopsy. I might be able to get a copy of it."

"Do that," Jason commanded. "There's also this." He pulled the now-dead cell phone from his jacket pocket. It was in a ziplock bag. "I found this in the Colonial. Can we find out who it belonged to?" Small droplets of brown water clung to the inside of the plastic bag.

"Where'd you find it? In the shitter?" asked Peter.

"It was in a bucket of dirty water in the Colonial. Why would someone drop a cell phone in a bucket and leave it there?"

"I can find out who it belongs to. Leave it with me," said Waterhouse. "Thomas had a phone just like that."

"Where do we go from here?" asked Peter.

"I'll follow up on the cell phone and the autopsy," Waterhouse said.

"We know three people who're involved," said Jason. "We can start with them."

"Three?" asked Peter.

"The patient, the doctor, and the pharmacist," Jason replied.

"The patient is Winstead, the doctor is Kader. Who's the pharmacist?" Waterhouse asked.

Jason smiled tightly at the private investigator. "Sam Fairing."

CHAPTER 27

Walter Waterhouse stubbed out the cigarette in the ashtray sitting on his crowded nightstand. It sat in a valley between prescription containers. The large vial of generic Vicodin was as wide and round as a mortar shell and was half filled with the horse pills. A muscle relaxant, cyclobenzaprine, stood next to two containers of high-blood-pressure pills, a vial of antidepressants, and those damned capsules to keep him from having to take a piss every hour during the night.

A box of tissues hung precariously over the edge of the nightstand. Discarded tissues lay piled on the floor beside the bed, crumpled and stained with a brown substance that had come from deep inside the private investigator's respiratory tract.

Waterhouse sensed that the brothers Rodgers did not trust him. He could see it in their exchanged glances when they were asking about his investigation of Thomas's wife's death. He couldn't give two shits. It was his time to cash in. He'd spent the better part of his life taking down scumbags and murderers while in Boston. And all he had to show for it was a painful leg wound that flared up when clouds rolled in.

148

Waterhouse had seen enough violence and death in the last twenty-odd years. It'd begun in the army during his two tours in Vietnam. As a lowly grunt, he'd volunteered for every patrol he could, walking point under the hot sun by day and in the stiflingly humid nights. Remarkably, he received not even a scratch in country over twenty-four months. Two acts of bravery had earned him a Bronze Star with oak leaf clusters and a promotion to lieutenant.

There'd been one close call. In the jungles of Ia Drang valley, a mortar round landed nearby, leaving him unharmed but totally disoriented. Had it not been for Clint Jones dragging his ass to safety, the next round, which hit ten seconds later, would have ripped him apart.

Though physically intact, the experiences had left him emotionally shattered. Withdrawal and panic attacks never affected his police work. They only haunted him after the sun went down as he lay in bed. The recurring nightmare of a black-clad, yellow-skinned warrior about to plunge a bayonet into his chest visited him nightly for the next ten years. Sometimes, he wished he *had* been wounded in battle. He heard that those guys actually had an easier time making the transition back to normalcy.

The war had cost him his marriage and any meaningful relationship with his three daughters. They'd had enough of the long, unpredictable hours followed by the silence and the booze at home. They took a permanent tour of duty to California. His daughters, whom he hadn't seen in almost seven years, had made their own lives. And he was not a part of them.

Vietnam left him with other, invisible scars. He was a first-rate racist when it came to anybody whose eyes weren't round. Having grown up in the lily-white neighborhoods of eastern Massachusetts, he'd have hated blacks also, if it hadn't been for his army buddy, Clint Jones. Jones had saved an entire race from Waterhouse's internal wrath. A massive former defensive lineman who'd flunked out of Purdue, Jones had been as dark as midnight with pearly whites that could light a small city. Waterhouse had often ordered Jones not to smile on patrol at night, so the enemy wouldn't get a make on their position. They'd become good friends in the four weeks after Jones had saved his skinny white ass. When an NVA ambush occurred in broad daylight and Jones was bayoneted by a gook regular, Waterhouse's hatred toward Asians multiplied. The attack on 9/11 had immediately and effectively transferred that hatred to Arabs and Middle Easterners as well.

The physical injuries that he'd avoided in Southeast Asia managed to catch up with him back home. After being discharged and spat upon, Waterhouse became a cop walking a beat in the small town of Medford a few miles north of Boston. Muscle strains and sprains were common. Five years later, he was promoted to detective, investigating small-time break-ins and minor drug trafficking. A buddy got him an interview with the Boston Police Department in narcotics. He took the job, and his life intensified. Two years later, Cathy left him, taking their girls with her. Fifteen years after that, a whacked-out drug dealer accused of murder put a round in his right leg. Three months and two surgeries followed. Waterhouse walked out of Mass General, sold everything he owned, which wasn't much, and moved to southeastern Virginia. He'd given more than his share for his country, and he'd paid dearly for it. No two-bit, legal pill pusher would shame him into a guilt trip.

As he sat on his bed and hawked into a tissue, Waterhouse heard a high-pitched, short squeak from the rear of the house. Waterhouse knew instantly someone had opened the screen door. He was suddenly glad he hadn't gotten around to lubricating it. His senses on high alert, he rolled silently out of bed and crept to the kitchen entryway.

Waterhouse peered around the hallway doorjamb into the kitchen. The doorknob jingled softly as the intruder manipulated it. The kitchen was dark. The figure, dressed in black, was silhouetted against the soft glow of a neighbor's porch light.

His heart kicked into overdrive when he saw the hood covering the face. Waterhouse snuck back to the bedroom, reached under the nightstand, and pressed the panic alarm. Run-down though his house was, he'd spared no expense in outfitting it with a monitored security system. Forty grand in cash hidden in various places known only to him and God made one very careful—and very suspicious. The police would arrive quickly. Poquoson was a small town.

He pulled the Sphinx AT 2000 Police Special from under the bed, released the safety, and headed back to the kitchen. As he left the bedroom, he was slammed in the face. The blow connected with the bridge of his nose. His head snapped, and white bolts of light filled his vision. The fist slammed him again. Waterhouse slumped to the floor, releasing the gun.

When he awoke, he had no idea how much time had passed. It couldn't have been long. He heard no sirens. The enormous hooded man towered over him. A gun pressed against Waterhouse's temple. His hands and feet were bound with some kind of cord. Waterhouse could see the man's tan skin and dark eyes through the wide eyeholes.

"Where are the files?"

The deep, raspy voice confirmed the man was from the deserts of the Middle East. *He's a freakin' oversized camel jockey*, Waterhouse thought. He scowled and spat on the man's boots. "Puta!"

The gun struck him on the right cheek, crashing down like an ironsmith's hammer. *Where the hell are the cops?*

"Where are Pettigrew's files?" the man boomed.

"Fuck you, Ahmed!" He tasted blood on his lower lip.

Another blow snapped his head to the side. His right eye began to swell. Waterhouse glared defiantly at the figure. He only needed to hold out a few minutes longer. *How does this guy know about the files?*

"The files!"

After the third blow landed, Waterhouse's head began to swim. The man wrestled with the fingers of Waterhouse's right hand. He produced a pair of needle-nosed pliers and grasped the fingernail of the index finger between the blades. Waterhouse shook it loose. A firm foot pressed against Waterhouse's belly and the pliers were reapplied to the nail.

"I'm not going to ask again."

The wail of approaching sirens shattered the sleepy night. The eyes under the hood widened.

Waterhouse smiled and told the man what he could do to himself.

The warbling grew louder. The hooded face turned to listen. He cursed in a guttural dialect. Suddenly, he removed the pliers.

"Hey, Mustaffah! Hang around and meet some of my friends!" Waterhouse spat.

He backhanded the private investigator again and departed through the back door.

Waterhouse was trying to wriggle free when the first Poquoson police officer knocked on the front door.

CHAPTER 28

Saturday, September 30

The diminutive pharmacist appeared to Jason in a new, sinister light this morning. He studied Sam Fairing from the shadows of the rear hallway. The dark-skinned man worked the counter with Kevin Bryant, the technician, in a calm, efficient manner, dispatching each prescription carefully and precisely with minimal discussion. It was the weekend, so business was slower than normal. Despite the desire to grab Fairing by the neck and squeeze a confession from him, Jason grudgingly admired his orderly approach to his craft. Regardless of the man's proficiency, Fairing was involved in a nefarious—or at least criminal—plot, and was now tainted. The luster of Jason's new job had begun to fade.

Lily was probably at her mansion, doing whatever multimillionaires do to unwind. Thankfully, he didn't have to deal with her for two full days. Jason relished the opportunity to snoop in relative privacy. And hopefully have the whole picture by Monday.

Seven prescriptions, all run through the Colonial's prescription dispensing software. Three people—two of them professionals—Fairing,

153

Kader, and some guy named Winstead, the supposed "patient." In addition to the lingering headache from his lunch with Jasmine Kader, another question refused to go away.

Was Lily Zanns involved?

If it was fraud, then why? The Colonial was thriving, and had been for years. At two thousand prescriptions a week, the prescription count was robust. They weren't overstaffed. There was enough help; in fact, they could probably use another technician. Inventory was under control at about at six hundred and fifty thousand dollars, a mere six weeks of sales on hand.

Why fill seven phony prescriptions in a fourteen-month period? It translated to a total of just over thirty-two thousand dollars in gross revenue over a fourteen-month period. A pittance for a business that did $6.1 million in sales annually. Why risk defrauding an insurance company for such a small amount of money? What purpose would it serve? Were they billing other medications falsely? Jason made a mental note to check the financial statements. Maybe Christine could help in that area. In any case, it was time to let her know what they'd found.

Billy Parks entered the store and walked toward Jason. "Everything going okay, Billy?" Jason asked with more cheer than he felt. Since Billy was new, he knew this man was untarnished by the Colonial's sins.

"Just fine there, young fella," Parks responded. A rotund man with a protruding belly, Park's gold tie rested on the white fabric of his shirt and was two buttons short of his waist. "Anxious to get started."

* * *

"He suspects something unusual about Pettigrew's death. But he knows nothing of our plan." Jasmine crossed her long legs in the spacious backseat of Zanns's blue stretch Mercedes. "He met with the same man who was at Pettigrew's house after the funeral. The one with the ponytail."

Lily placed the thin Turkish cigarette to her lips. "His name is Walter Waterhouse. Cooper's men photographed him. Oliver tried to search his house last night, but the police showed up."

"Has Oliver found the files?"

"No, I have tasked him to keep searching. Right now, he's out of leads. If Waterhouse had the files, they most certainly have been moved by now."

"What about Rodgers?" asked Jasmine.

"Rodgers knows nothing important. The operation is less than a week away. He will not have time to do us any damage."

"Did you place the evidence in his house?"

"I did. The notes about Torpedo and Thunderbolt were left in the pages of a book. Not easy to find unless you're looking for them. A competent search of his house will uncover it. Once the deed has been done, they will look to him for answers. I have also taken his gun and the wine glass with his fingerprints on it. They will be useful later."

"Excellent. The evidence will confuse the authorities for a little while, at least," said Zanns. "The gun and the wine glasses we will hold in reserve. Continue to engage him. If he learns anything, I want to know it immediately."

"Mother, your plan to frame him is ingenious."

"Thank you, my dear. Find out more about this Waterhouse. I do not trust Cooper or Hammon. We must divert focus away from us until we have time to make our escape. Jason Rodgers will be that diversion."

CHAPTER 29

Jason and Peter exited Peter's Hummer and walked to the entrance of Peter's Gun Shop. Not a creative name, but effective. They were clad in their sparring outfits and drenched in sweat after an hour-long workout and sparring session at Charles Kim's Tae Kwon Do dojang. They each wore the black-striped ha'i pants and T-shirts, and had donned sneakers. Their belts were still cinched around their waists, Peter's black, Jason's brown.

Inside, they sat at a table in a small conference room, and analyzed their gruff new friend.

"What's up with Waterhouse?" asked Peter.

"I don't know if I trust him," Jason replied. "He took almost forty grand of Thomas's hard-earned cash. And he's obsessed with money." Several times in casual conversation, Waterhouse had broached the subject of money in front of Jason. The private investigator had questioned Jason intently about how insurance companies pay their claims and how pharmacies billed them. He'd asked Jason a lot of questions about how insurance companies deter fraud. Jason had explained that they send in

156

auditors periodically to look at high-dollar claims. As Jason watched the man listening, he could see the gears grinding behind the pale blue eyes.

"He gives me the heebie-jeebies," Peter replied. "You think he's on the up-and-up?"

"He's an ex-cop. And Thomas left the files with him, so the old man must have trusted him."

"He may be an ex-cop, but that doesn't mean he's trustworthy."

"True," said Jason. "We just need to keep an eye on him. Let's not give him too much rope. We need to run this thing. Not him."

"You mean you, little brother. I'm following your lead."

There was a knock at the door. Christine and Walter Waterhouse stepped into the conference room.

"Morning, gents," said Waterhouse. The pasty skin on the right side of his face was swollen, pushing his eyelid closed. He cradled Pettigrew's files in his arms.

"What happened to you?" asked Jason.

"It seems we're not the only people interested in these," said Waterhouse, dropping the box onto the conference table. "I was visited last night by someone looking for these. He asked me to part with them, in a not-so-friendly manner."

"I see you refused," said Peter.

"I have a silent alarm in the bedroom. Luckily the police showed before he could do any more damage."

"Were you followed here?" asked Jason.

"No," Waterhouse replied. "I was worried about that, too. I doubled back several times along the way."

"Let me have those." Peter motioned for Waterhouse to slide the box to him. Waterhouse did so. "We can keep them here," said Peter. "I have an empty gun safe. It would take a forklift to move it and a carton of C-4 to blow it open."

Peter left the room with the box in his arms. He returned a few minutes later empty-handed. "They won't be disturbed now," the ex-marine said.

"Let's get down to business," Jason demanded.

Jason relayed details of their conference in Waterhouse's command center to Christine.

"I called the wholesaler this morning," he continued. "They're open Saturday. They confirmed that the Colonial has not purchased any Prucept—*ever*. And yet, these prescriptions have been billed to this patient's, Douglas Winstead's, insurance company. It's fraud, plain and simple."

Jason slid each document toward Christine as he outlined each point. She studied each one. The three men watched her try to assimilate the information. Her eyebrows furrowed then relaxed several times.

Finally, she pushed the papers to the center of the table. "My father is dead and buried. None of it matters anymore. What good can come from pursuing this?" she hissed.

Jason gathered up the papers and gently rapped them into a neat pile. "Your father may have been obsessed with conspiracies, but the evidence we have here is pretty solid. He discovered that the Colonial was into something underhanded. He was trying to bring it to light."

"So?"

"Christine, these documents are proof of a crime."

She was unconvinced and shook her head emphatically. "And when it gets out that this was going on, Daddy will be guilty by association. His reputation will be further damaged. Even though he sold the pharmacy, everyone associates it with him. He *was* the Colonial."

"Your father never would have stood for any of this," said Jason. "And it's serious enough that Walter was attacked last night, and I'm being followed," he added.

"Followed? By whom?" Christine asked.

"I don't know. A car's been following me." He'd first noticed them last night driving home from Waterhouse's. Jason suspected it was the Secret Service, still keeping tabs on him because of his photography at the shipyard. But after hearing of the attack on Waterhouse last night, Jason was having doubts. He hadn't told anyone about the tail until now. Not even his brother. "Maybe it's the same folks that beat up Walter here."

"That mean they're outside now?" Peter was immediately concerned.

"No, I rented a car and parked it in the alley behind the store. I left the Mustang parked out front at the Colonial, and snuck out the back door. They're probably still in the parking lot waiting for me to leave." Jason had spotted them again following him to work. Either they were bad at it, or they wanted him to know he was being tailed. If it was the latter, Jason was sure it would be the Secret Service. He didn't like the idea of anyone following him—including the feds. He'd arranged for Rachel, the cashier, to meet him behind the Colonial with her car. She had driven him to the car rental business two miles up the road. Jason had then driven straight to the gun shop in the rental, a Ford Fusion, and then rendezvoused with Peter for their early-morning workout.

Christine had been half-listening. Jason could see her mind was somewhere else entirely, probably focused on the ramifications of more negative publicity. Suddenly, her face softened as a thought struck her. "Are you suggesting that this insurance fraud had something to do with Daddy's death?"

Jason leafed through the pages in his hand and pulled out the report with Pettigrew's handwriting on the back. He turned it facedown and slid it toward Christine. "Read that. This note was left with Walter by your father."

She slid it over. Christine wrinkled her forehead as she read the words. Her lip quivered. She buried her head in her hands and began to sob.

Tell Christine that I love her.

CHAPTER 30

Christine had run from the building. Jason caught up with her in the parking lot near his rented Fusion. Tears were streaming down her face.

"Get away from me!" Christine shrieked through watery mascara. A man walked past them toting a gun case and headed toward the shop, trying not to stare. Jason stepped toward her, extending some tissues. She snapped them from his hands.

"Your father worked his whole life to build the Colonial into what it is. If someone is breaking the law there, they're tarnishing that image. Isn't that your father's legacy, too? It seems he was trying to find out what was going on. We need to finish his mission." He leaned closer and whispered the next few words. "We need you to tell us what you remember about the night your father died. We need your professional expertise, too."

"I'm an accountant. How's that going to help you?"

"Lily and Fairing keep records. We're dealing with fraud."

He surveyed her, silently imploring her. Her eyes shrank to narrow slits. Emotions pulsed through her in spurts. Hurt, frustration,

160

anger, confusion. She hit him, slamming her closed fist into the side of Jason's head. "You sorry son of a bitch," she seethed.

"Damn it!" he exclaimed, reaching for his face.

"I want to know why you left!"

The sting of a hundred yellow jackets set in. "I promise I'll tell you," he said. "Not here, not now."

"When?"

"Soon."

Christine flaunted her new bargaining chip. "If you want my blessing to continue this little investigation, you better tell me something."

Jason sighed. "I'll tell you. I promise. I've always wanted you to know what happened. But I couldn't—wouldn't—for your father's benefit—and yours. But not here. Not now, not like this."

"You keep finding excuses not to tell me!"

"Today's Saturday. Tomorrow night, after I drop Michael off at his mother's, I'll buy you dinner and I'll tell you the whole damn thing."

Christine eyed him. "You're trying to get out of it. I want assurances."

"Christine, I'm not trying to get out of it."

"Give me your wallet."

"What?"

"Give me your wallet!"

He hesitated, frowning. "Why? The answer's not in my wallet."

"Do you want my help or not?"

Jason shook his head. "Okay, fine," he said, fishing his wallet out and handing it to her. "You realize that my whole life is in there."

Christine removed the cash, three twenties and three ones, along with his driver's license, and handed them to Jason. "You'll get the rest back when I see you tomorrow night."

"You don't trust me?"

"Your track record ain't that good, honey. I live by an old proverb: love all, trust few. Right now, you don't fit into either category."

Jason frowned. "Can we go back inside now?"

* * *

Inside, Christine and Jason returned to the meeting room. Christine had dabbed her eyes dry. But they were still red, and faint streaks of mascara were visible. Without hesitation, she made an announcement. "I want to go on record. I'm against anyone meddling in this matter. But I'll go along for now. If anyone discovers any information which further impugns my father and goes public with it—or allows it to go public—I will personally cut his testicles off."

The men's eyebrows jumped. Peter smiled and saluted. "Yes, ma'am."

Jason waited until her anger subsided, then asked, "What do you remember about the night your father died?"

Christine glanced at the wall, but did not focus on it. She was in another place and time. "I'd bought my new car that afternoon, the 300. I called him to ask if he wanted to have a look. We hadn't talked a lot in the last six months. He seemed distracted and didn't say much. Then suddenly,"—she snapped her fingers—"he hung up. He wasn't mad. It was almost as if he'd thought of something and had to take care of it right away.

"I didn't think much of it at the time. He'd been doing that more and more lately. I tried to call back, but he didn't answer. Later, I drove to his house. He was gone, and the house was a mess. I couldn't find him, so I called the police. Nothing was missing. The next day I found out that he was dead…" Her eyes became moist again.

"Was there anything else?" It was more a demand than an inquiry. "Anything, no matter how insignificant it may seem."

Christine shook her head, then stopped and said, "I didn't think much of it at the time. But that night, I got a voice mail at home from Daddy's cell. There were no words, only static and some sort of scratching noise. I just figured he accidentally called me and didn't know it. You know, like he butt-dialed his cell phone."

Waterhouse asked, "What time was that?"

"A little after midnight," Christine replied. "I don't erase my messages, so we can check the time."

"Is it possible he'd already gotten in the car accident and was trying to phone for help, but couldn't speak?" asked Waterhouse.

"Maybe," Christine replied, stricken by the thought.

Jason interlaced his fingers in front of his face. "I need you to find that message."

CHAPTER 31

Jason scanned the parking lot under a clear night sky. The men following him, whether they were Secret Service or conspirators associated with the fraud, were probably gone by now. But he was taking no chances. Confident it was clear, Jason gently depressed the accelerator, and the two-vehicle convoy slid into the far end of the Colonial Pharmacy's parking lot. The first vehicle was Jason's rented Ford, the second Waterhouse's red Blazer, on which an extension ladder was tied down with bungee cords. Four car doors opened silently. Jason's Mustang was parked where he'd left it, three rows from the front door to the pharmacy.

"Christine and I'll go into the pharmacy through the front door. You two sneak around back and wait by the rear entrance," Jason said to Waterhouse and Peter. "I've already called the security company and explained we're having a plumbing emergency, so they don't call Lily and alert her."

"Why can't we all just go in the front door?" Peter asked irritably.

"Will you stop thinking like a marine for once," Jason shot back. "I don't want to attract attention. The pharmacy closed two hours ago.

164

The last thing we need is for someone to call the police. I know it's hard for you, but subtlety is required."

"Just hurry up, will ya?" Peter shot back.

Waterhouse and Peter circled the building on foot. A minute later, Jason slipped his key in the lock, and they entered. He punched in his access code and deactivated the alarm. Leaving the lights off and using the light provided by the emergency beacon, they made their way to the pharmacy. Jason unlocked the folding steel gate of the pharmacy itself. They ducked under it and into the back room. Jason unlocked the back door, letting Peter and Waterhouse in.

"Here it is, over here," said Jason, leading the private investigator to the wall. They stood single file in the box-filled, cramped hallway. Jason slid containers out of the way, revealing the video equipment and the wires. Jason pointed to the thicker cable. "That goes through the ceiling tile up through the roof. These other cables come from the tiny cameras in the ceiling."

"And you say there're no monitors in the store?" asked Waterhouse.

"None. If it's a closed-circuit television system, where are the monitors? I don't even think Lily knows it's here."

"Daddy probably had it installed or did it himself. That would be just like him," Christine murmured. "He spent his money on crap like this all the time."

"I've seen everything I need," said Waterhouse. He turned to Peter. "Let's get the ladder. We'll bring the truck around back."

"While you're doing that, Christine and I can look for the missing prescription," said Jason. "And I have some reports to run."

The ex-marine and former cop propped the back door with a box of prescription vials, while Jason led Christine into the pharmacy department. He pointed at the drawers holding hundreds of bundles of prescriptions. "We need to find that seventh prescription."

* * *

The Cadillac pulled up perpendicular to the driveway of Jason Rodgers's Yorktown home. Two silhouetted figures circled around back, carrying two black bags as the car slipped off. They checked windows and doors for an alarm system. Finding none, they moved to the back door. The house had been unoccupied all day. The pharmacist had never come home after leaving for work this morning. They had monitored the pharmacy from across Jefferson Avenue from several restaurant parking lots. They changed positions every hour. It wasn't until 9:00 p.m., when Sam Fairing locked up the pharmacy alone, that they knew they'd been duped. After the pharmacy was dark, they'd returned to Rodgers's vehicle and planted a GPS tracking beacon in the wheel well.

While McCall kept watch, Boreas picked the deadbolt. It clicked open. Pausing a second to make sure no sirens sounded, they slipped inside. A light on one of the end tables was lit. Boreas turned it off and produced a small flashlight.

They moved with the speed and precision of veteran spies. In twenty-five minutes, they had placed the tiny cameras and listening devices in strategic locations in every major room. McCall jotted down the location and type in a small notebook for quick retrieval. The phones were already monitored by other means.

With the devices expertly placed, they slipped away into the night.

* * *

"I don't see any prescription," Christine said in frustration.

The missing prescription was another link in the chain of evidence Jason was constructing. He was sure that chain would be significantly longer before they were done. Together, they would pull each and every instance of fraud out of the sea of papers and seal the fates of Jasmine Kader, Sam Fairing, and the patient named Winstead—perhaps even of Lily Zanns.

Little had changed in the Colonial since Zanns had purchased the business. It was a place Christine had literally grown up in.

And though she wasn't a pharmacist or a technician, she knew the pharmacy better than anyone.

She examined the numbered California folders where the prescriptions were filed. The folders were bound with rubber bands in lots of one hundred, and numbered sequentially for easy retrieval. The Colonial had been in business so long that it used a seven-digit number code for each prescription. Millions. Many of the boxes Jason had been collating in the back were filled with these old prescription bundles. The last two digits ranged from double zero through ninety-nine. It was system that had been used by every pharmacy for prescription filing and retrieval for more than thirty years. When done accurately, retrieving a prescription from such a huge haystack could be accomplished in under thirty seconds. Even this method was becoming obsolete; the large chains were now scanning prescription images and storing them electronically.

Christine had been filing prescriptions since she was a schoolgirl. The missing prescription was not in its folder, which simply meant that Pettigrew had probably removed it. She had opened all the drawers as well as the two filing cabinets. The drawers themselves had been pulled out, and the space behind them checked, along with the floor. Christine even checked behind computer screens, under computers, and in every crack and crevice. The task was made more difficult by the darkness. The faint bluish glow of the computer terminal Jason was using provided the only light.

"It's been weeks since Daddy collected this information," she said to Jason. "This prescription could be anywhere. It could have been thrown away. Sam or Lily could have found it. Hell, it could be somewhere in his house."

* * *

Jason didn't hear Christine's words. He was completely engrossed by the data on the glowing screen. The printer hummed, spitting a report of all drugs costing more than five hundred dollars per bottle. Jason spoke out loud, as if he were explaining his rationale to Christine. "If someone were going to defraud an insurance company, they wouldn't waste their time on inexpensive medications. They'd fill phony prescriptions for expensive ones."

"Whatever you say," Christine answered.

Jason pulled the page from the tray and scanned it. The report outlined more than fifty expensive prescriptions filled in the last six months. Tomorrow, he would spend his time rummaging through the files looking for the prescriptions and signatures. He folded the page and placed it in his jacket pocket.

"Did you find it?" he asked absently, still staring at the screen.

"Didn't you just hear what I said?"

"Sorry. What?"

"Never mind. It's not here," she sighed.

"I've got what I need for now," said Jason. "Let's go see what they found." He shut down the terminal and walked to the rear with Christine in tow. Peter and Waterhouse were still on the roof. Jason walked down the crowded hall, peering at Zanns's office door. He tried the knob. It was locked.

He brushed past Christine and exited through the propped back door. Peter was coming down the ladder. Waterhouse was lighting a cigarette in the alleyway.

"What did you find?" asked Jason.

Waterhouse took a long pull on the cigarette. "Close up, and I'll tell you when you get back here."

"No, there's one other thing I want to see. Come inside for a minute."

All four filed into the cramped hallway once more.

"I want to get into Lily's office."

"What are you looking for?" Waterhouse asked.

"I'll know if and when I see it."

Waterhouse tried the knob. "I'll be right back," he said.

He returned with a leather case containing small, awkwardly bent instruments. "Just what every private eye needs," he said.

Waterhouse manipulated his lockpick tools, trying several times to engage it. He thought out loud. "How much do you guys figure she's worth?"

"Who?" Jason whispered.

"This Zanns lady," Waterhouse replied, "you think she's got any cash in here?"

The door opened with a soft click.

Jason rolled his eyes. "Walter, you take anything, and I'll break every one of your fingers."

Jason flipped on the overhead fluorescent lamp to the window-less office. He saw the hurt expression on the ex-cop's face. But he didn't give a shit.

"Where do we start?" asked Christine.

"Try the computer," he commanded. He moved to the desk be-side her and yanked drawers open. Christine took a seat and switched on the computer.

"I'm sure she's changed Daddy's password."

Peter motioned for Waterhouse to follow him outside. "You got any smokes?" Peter smiled. "Look's like they're gonna be awhile."

His brother was right. "You two head on home," said Jason. "No sense all of us losing sleep." Jason motioned for them to come into the hallway.

"You sure?" asked Peter.

"We'll be fine," Christine chimed in. "We'll be outta here in a couple of hours."

Peter and Walter followed Jason through the storage area and into the alley.

"What's up there?" Jason asked, gesturing toward the roof.

"A wireless transmitter and a dish. Whoever installed it can look at the video images from a remote location. I'm familiar with the com-pany. Digitronics. It's top of the line."

"You don't say."

"Yep," said Waterhouse.

"Why? What's going through that mind of yours?" asked Peter.

Jason scratched his cheek with a forefinger. "That's how Thomas made the surveillance video. The receiver is at his house."

"How do you know?" asked Peter.

"I saw the receiver in his office. It's a model made by Digitronics and wired to a satellite dish outside his home office."

CHAPTER 32

Jason went straight for the middle drawer of Lily's desk, and found it secured by a flimsy lock. He could force it, but he didn't want Lily knowing anyone had been in it. Fishing his keys out, he tried each of them. The blades were too wide and long.

He cursed because he'd sent Peter and Waterhouse home, thought about calling them back to the pharmacy, but decided against it. Instead, he returned to the pharmacy and found a thin-bladed spatula and a paper clip. Returning to the desk, Jason inserted the spatula blade and the clip into the keyhole, manipulating them in unison. After several unsuccessful attempts and some whispered curses, the cam turned, and Jason slid the drawer open.

At that moment, Christine sighed. "I can't figure out the password. I could call a friend who works in our IS department at the firm. He could break it, but we'd have to come back."

"No can do. We need to keep this to ourselves for now. What about these filing cabinets? Are there paper copies of the transactions?" Jason asked, as he slid Lily's checkbook from the drawer.

* * *

Two hours later, the floor around them was littered with stacks of bank reports, financial statements, invoices, insurance remittance summaries, and payroll and billing statements. Jason stretched his aching back. They'd located every document pertinent to their investigation going back fourteen months since the first fake prescription had been billed. Christine had sorted them into piles and clipped them together with binder clips from Lily's desk. She'd labeled them with sticky notes to indicate the file and drawer they had been stored in.

Jason had scrutinized Lily's checkbook register. That task alone had taken him an hour. He'd found a yellow legal pad and jotted down every entry for the last two years, including the two checks Zanns had made out to him. Most appeared to be ordinary expenses.

Each insurance remittance statement listed the prescription claims billed by the Colonial to ShieldCare, Winstead's carrier, the previous month. Jason also pulled the same documents for the months following each of the seven phony prescriptions. Jason highlighted each claim. ShieldCare had paid for each bogus prescription. He'd found no evidence that any of the claims had been reversed. Another damning piece of evidence.

He glanced at his watch as Christine returned unneeded documents to the filing cabinets. It was one fifteen in the morning. He was about to suggest they take the documents to an all-night copy place, when a loud rattling came from beyond the pharmacy department.

"What the hell was that?" Christine whispered.

CHAPTER 33

They scampered into the pharmacy, staying out of sight. Jason rose up, peeking above the frosted glass of the pharmacy counter. A uniformed man stood inside the double doors, scanning a flashlight in a wide arc.

Jason cursed and sank down beside Christine. He had not locked the door after entering the pharmacy. He motioned with his hands and mouthed the words "Someone is inside."

Christine's eyes went wide. She mouthed a question. "What do we do now?"

Jason held up a finger. He rose again, slowly elevating his eyes above the glass. The figure had moved deeper inside the store, swiveling the flashlight 360 degrees. The beam sliced through the darkened building as the man moved to their left. The guard had yet to notice the open grate that separated the pharmacy department from the front store.

Jason sank to Chrissie's side again and placed his lips to her ear. "Go back to the office and gather up the papers. Take them to the back door and wait there for me. When I get there, be ready to run. Make sure you close up Lily's office. And be quiet!"

He carefully pulled his car keys from his pocket and slid them into her hand. Jason reached above him, groping along the pharmacy counter. He touched something heavy, grabbed it, and lowered it to his lap. It was a box of staples. Jason turned and crouched, ready.

Chrissie was terrified, her irises completely encircled by the whites of her eyes.

"Go, now!" Jason said.

As she crawled away, Jason turned and launched the staples through the darkness. They landed with a metallic crash in a corner, far from the flashlight-wielding man.

Christine crawled on all fours into the hallway. She stood and found an empty cardboard box in the storage room, tiptoed back to Lily's office, and stuffed the documents into the box. Thirty seconds later after locking Zanns's door, she carried it into the storage room, setting it beside the back door.

* * *

Uniform whipped around, shining the beam of light in the direction of the sound and away from Jason. Jason saw a pistol clutched in his hand, backlit by the light beam.

The figure moved toward the source of the sound. Jason watched for a full minute as he made his way, ducking through aisles. At times, only the faint wash of the flashlight's beam jerking this way and that was visible. Finally, Uniform was as far away from Jason as he could be, in the front corner.

Jason rose and began a slow turn toward the hallway and escape. His elbow brushed something on the pharmacy counter. It was a plastic counting tray that had been hanging over the edge. It teetered briefly over the floor before dropping. Its journey lasted only a second, but it seemed like an eternity. It clattered on the floor, sounding like a thousand rapid-fire gunshots.

Jason ducked. The beam wheeled, filling the pharmacy department with dust-speckled light.

"Who's there?" the voice hollered.

Bent at the waist, Jason raced to the hallway. Christine waited by the back door, her hand on the knob. He motioned frantically for her to open it. They shot into the alleyway just as the light beam and heavy footfalls reached the entrance of the hallway.

Taking her hand in his, he cradled the box in his left like a football. "Go, go, go!" he hollered. "Get the keys ready!"

Thirty seconds later, Christine jumped behind the wheel as Jason slid into the passenger seat. She fired the engine. Tires squealed, and they sped off.

They exchanged relief-filled smiles. They had gone two blocks when Jason turned to her. "I've got to go back, Chrissie. I've got to go back, or Lily's going to know we were in there. Take me back now!"

CHAPTER 34

Sunday, October 1

A cup of coffee cradled in his hands, Jason sat on the edge of the sofa in his living room, watching the television screen, with the kind of anticipation he'd experienced when his Red Sox were one out away from winning their first World Series in eighty-six years. He was exhausted, but with help from his fourth strong cup of Folgers and the residual adrenaline of their early-morning adventure, he pushed himself to focus on the Colonial security camera video Waterhouse had given him.

Jason had realized as they sped away from the Colonial hours earlier that he'd deactivated the alarm system using his alarm code. It was unique to him, and would indicate to Lily or anyone with access that he'd been the one in the pharmacy. A call to the security company would be all it would take. He'd dropped Chrissie at a coffee shop with instructions to wait for him while he returned in the car to the Colonial.

Jason was fairly confident he'd mitigated the chances a report would be filed by the shopping center's rent-a-cop. He had approached the man at a dead run, flashing his pharmacist's license and door keys to

176

the Colonial. "I'm the VP of operations," he explained, out of breath from the run and the near miss of being caught. He'd received a phone call from the security company, Jason said, and had rushed right over. It took fifteen minutes and a tour of the pharmacy under the pretense of looking for signs of theft to convince the rent-a-cop that the situation was under control, and that there was no need to call the police. The man relented, but did not look convinced. The promise of avoiding paperwork, however, appeared attractive to him.

"You must have scared the thieves off before they had a chance to take anything," Jason said. He watched the security guard's chest puff with self-importance. He would file a report in the morning with police and make a call to his supervisor explaining his exemplary action, Jason promised. Reluctantly, the man let the matter drop. Jason locked up and watched as the guard walked away to finish his rounds. Jason had no intention of calling the cops.

The anticipation he'd felt over finding more evidence on this video slowly waned. It had been recorded two weeks ago on the hidden security cameras. He fast-forwarded at four times normal speed. Sam Fairing and Kevin Mitchell, the technician, worked the counter, filling prescriptions and answering the phone, ringing up patients. They scurried around like actors in a choppy, but silent, color movie. After an hour of fast-forwarding, the recording ended. The entire twelve-hour day at the Colonial had been saved. And it seemed to be just as ordinary as a thousand other days Jason had experienced over the course of his career.

What was Thomas trying to document?

Jason lifted copies of Pettigrew's reports, along with his handwritten notes. None of the prescriptions for Prucept were filled on the same day as the video. The last prescription on the list was filled one day before, the fourteenth. What happened on the fifteenth that was so important Pettigrew wanted a record of it? He'd been murdered that night. Was there a clue here that would point Jason in the right direction? He felt the answer was staring him in the face, but he was groping like a blind man in the dark.

With his anticipation turning to frustration, he went upstairs, hoping a hot shower could scrub it away.

He returned to the kitchen twenty minutes later in only a slightly improved mood. He toasted two English muffins and nuked them in the microwave, melting a slice of Swiss cheese on each. He washed them down quickly with orange juice. His impotent angst over the Colonial mess was rising like a storm surge. He opened and closed drawers, slamming them recklessly, hunting for his favorite four-inch knife, part of a set given to him by Keller's on his fifth anniversary. Unable to locate it, he crashed a final drawer closed and grabbed another.

Ten minutes later, he was out the door to pick up Michael from his friend's house after a sleepover and bring him back to his mother.

Two hours beyond that, Jason was knee-deep in computer printouts inside the Colonial.

His cell chirped. Christine didn't wait for Jason to offer a greeting, sounding like an excited little girl. "I found it!"

Chapter 35

"You're sure it's from your father's cell phone the night he died?" asked Jason.

"The message still has the time and date stamp on it."

Jason did not answer, frustrated with his lack of progress in finding more phony prescriptions.

"Are you there?" Christine's voice punctured the trance.

"Sorry. Yeah, I'm here."

"What are you doing?"

"I'm at the Colonial to see if I can find any more fraud."

"Let me know if you have any luck."

"What would you consider luck? Finding some or not?"

"Good point."

"I'm just about done. I've found nothing. I've checked fifty more prescriptions for other high-cost drugs. Every prescription is authentic and original. Plus, the invoices and the software show that the drugs were in stock on the shelf when the prescription was filled. Only the Prucept prescriptions are fakes. Plus I've printed all the electronic signature files for the fifty prescriptions. A signature means the prescription was picked up by the patient. All but three John Hancocks were present. The signatures were all different, written by different hands. Some were perfect cursive, others just scribbles. The ones that had no signatures were the three Prucept prescriptions, which we already know are bogus."

"I'd say that's good news. Maybe the problem's not that big."

He grunted.

"I'll let you finish up. Call me before you come by."

"Will do. I'll be in a better mood by then."

"You better be," said Christine.

"Chrissie? Did you make the copies?"

"Uh-huh. I spent two hours this morning at OfficeMax, copying every side of every document."

"Good girl."

"I'm glad I can help," she said.

"I'll see you in a little while." Jason hung up.

He stretched the tight muscles in his back. The last time Jason had experienced this kind of fatigue, he was back in college cramming for pharmacology exams.

"Damn!" He seethed. He still didn't have an answer to his question. Why would they only fill seven fake prescriptions?

* * *

It wasn't like running a marathon or climbing the steps of a stadium, but the exertion of moving the heavy file boxes worked off some frustration. Jason had not bothered to call Brandon today. He wanted no witnesses to his sleuthing and needed the time alone. The lifting and carrying forced blood to his muscles, which demanded more oxygen. Blood flow was diverted from his brain. That was a good thing. It slowed his mental gymnastics.

Frustration, one of his college professors had once said, was the result of unmet expectations. To quell your frustration, he explained, change your expectations. Presto! No more frustration. Jason had never agreed with that statement. All that changing your expectations did was make you settle for less. Sometimes, you had to bust your ass to get results. Break down walls. See what was on the other side! There would be no settling, he thought. The answers were here somewhere. He was going to find out what the hell was going on.

He had expected to find the answers stuffed away in the prescriptions files of the Colonial. But after pulling a half-dozen real prescriptions, Jason realized it wasn't going to be as simple as waltzing in and plucking the evidence from the computer databases and the stored files.

He leaned against the wall between Lily's locked office and the storage closet, admiring his handiwork. A patina of perspiration coated his skin. He wiped his brow with a sleeve. With just a few boxes left to stack, the task of sorting the files was almost complete. The hallway was still jammed with paper and cardboard in various forms. Jason made sure the "keeper" boxes were arranged so as to hide the surveillance system Pettigrew had installed. If Lily didn't know about it, he didn't want her finding out now.

His stomach growled. Besides his small breakfast this morning, Jason hadn't really eaten in two days. When he finished, he was going over to his favorite steakhouse to gorge himself on their largest steak, the fattest baked potato, and as many buckets of sweet rolls as his belly would hold. He would top it all off with a tall, icy beer, maybe two.

The first of the last three boxes was old and taped together at the corners. Jason grasped the tattered container by the cutouts. It felt like it contained lead. He sucked in a breath and heaved. As he turned, the left cutout gave way, tearing. One end of the box dropped toward the floor. He tried to catch it, but missed. Prescription bundles scattered everywhere.

He cursed and sank to his knees, gathering the bundles. A stray prescription lay on the floor like a lost child. He picked it up and examined the thin strip which had been affixed to the face of the prescription, assigning it a prescription number. He didn't know why he looked at the number rather than just stuffing it back in the box, which would be shredded anyway. Just part of a pharmacist's anal nature, he would later recall. Find the correct bundle and put it back.

He scanned the prescription numbers scribbled on the outside of the California folders, looking for the bundle from which this prescription had spilled. The number did not belong. It was not part of the sequence of this box.

When he turned it over and looked at it more closely, Jason's heart nearly jumped out of his chest.

CHAPTER 36

"What does this say?" asked Jason. His forefinger tapped the copy of Pettigrew's autopsy on the kitchen table.

Peter and Waterhouse had been tasked with scouring every bar and pub in Smithfield and the surrounding localities. Their goal was to find anyone who might recognize Thomas. Someone who'd seen him drinking the night he died. They'd found no one. It was another missing link fueling Jason's suspicion.

The three men took seats at the table as Jason opened the report.

"My buddy in the Newport News PD," Waterhouse said, "was able to get a copy of that from someone he knows at the medical examiner's office. It's inconclusive—"

"What else is new?" Peter chimed in.

Jason scanned the pages. "His neck was broken, so were three ribs, both arms and legs. His face was badly smashed. His blood-alcohol level was equivalent to 0.13 measured by extracting vitreous humor. Well above the legal limit."

Waterhouse said, "What kind of alcohol?"

"What the hell is vitreous humor?" asked Peter.

"Eyeball juice," Jason replied.

Peter cringed and rubbed his eye.

"The stomach contents show no food, only some kind of distilled spirit like whiskey," Jason continued.

"This guy had everybody fooled," said Peter.

"No way," Jason declared. "Maybe he was forced to drink it."

"You know, Jason, I'm tolerating your little investigation here," Peter sighed. He scratched the gap in his eyebrow where the scar cleaved it. "But let's face facts. Pettigrew was drunk. Now you're telling me someone forced him to get drunk. Then they faked his car accident."

"It's possible," Jason replied. "None of the facts point to Thomas being a drunk. Chrissie found no evidence of booze anywhere in his house. No one saw Thomas drinking anywhere in Smithfield. Hell, Walter even said Thomas was trying to get him to stop drinking a week before he died. And anyway, how the hell did he drive thirty miles when he *already* had a BAC high enough to stop an elephant? It doesn't add up."

"I'd believe it more if he was just hit over the head or shot," said Peter. "If they were going to kill him, why go to the trouble of making it look like an accident? Why not just put out his lights and dump his body in the Chesapeake?"

"Maybe whoever did it didn't want an investigation. If he disappeared or turned up murdered, then people would ask questions. If there's an insurance scam, they wouldn't want the scrutiny."

Peter shrugged. "I'm not convinced."

Walter produced the cell phone wrapped in its plastic bag. "I had a friend check the serial number with all major carriers. It was Thomas's. He used AT&T, purchased the phone a year and a half ago. Where did you say you found it?"

"In a bucket of water in the back room of the Colonial."

"Christine said he called and left a message on her phone from his cell. The phone was found in the pharmacy. I pulled his phone records. The last call was to Christine's landline. It must have been made before the phone ended up in the bucket."

"He was in the pharmacy the night he died," Jason explained. "Christine said it was late when he made the call, close to midnight. The autopsy said he died somewhere between two and four in the morning."

Waterhouse shuffled the phone logs. "According to the records, the call was made at 11:27 p.m. What was he doing in the pharmacy at that hour?"

"I'm guessing he wasn't getting drunk. Maybe doing exactly what we've been doing?" Peter said.

Jason withdrew the folded prescription from his pocket, opened it, and laid it on the autopsy report. "Or maybe he was looking for this. It's the missing prescription."

Peter picked it up and examined it. "Big whoop! We knew the prescription existed. That doesn't prove he was murdered."

"Thomas thinks he was." He turned the prescription onto its face.

Peter and Waterhouse leaned over the table as if they were looking at a rare diamond.

It read,

If you find this, I was murdered.

T. P.

CHAPTER 37

"How do we know Pettigrew wrote this?" It was Walter questioning Jason this time.

"I pulled several prescriptions from the files. Prescriptions Thomas had taken from doctors over the phone and written down. They were written months ago. They're the same. Take a look." Jason removed six more prescriptions from a folder.

"The handwriting looks the same, I'll give you that." Peter nodded. "But just because he wrote it doesn't mean he was *actually* killed. Maybe he wrote it in a fit of paranoia."

"C'mon, Peter. Give me a break!" Jason glared at his brother. "Can you use that pea brain of yours for a second?"

"So now you're a conspiracy nut too. I think you're partaking of some your own product, Jason."

"That's enough, you two," Waterhouse interrupted. "The autopsy..." The private investigator flipped the pages of the report. Finding the section he was looking for, he read from it. "Right here, it says he had two sutured wounds, front and back, in his right shoulder. The wounds were relatively recent but definitely inflicted before the death occurred. The ME opened the sutures and reported a pulpified track between the scapula and the left humerus radiating to the surrounding tissues. It's consistent with a gunshot wound. The bullet went clean through."

"Two wounds?"

"One in front of the shoulder, one in the back."

"Entry and exit?"

"Yup." Waterhouse pulled several eight-by-tens from the stack.

Jason winced at the first photo. "It appears our dearly departed Thomas was shot in the back, and the bullet exited through the front."

"He was running away."

"Damn," Jason said. "What do you think?" He passed them to Peter. There were four photographs. One of Pettigrew's torso, one of his upper back, one of both legs, and a close-up of the face.

Waterhouse said, "The coroner is certain it's a bullet wound. But he said it had nothing to do with the cause of death."

"So why wasn't it investigated?" asked Jason.

"I can't answer that. But as a former cop, if I saw the gunshot wound and thought he died in a car wreck, I probably wouldn't pursue it either. Especially if it was sutured. What would be the point?"

"The guy was shot!" A look of incredulous disgust spread across Jason's features. "The last time I checked, that was a crime."

"The police are overwhelmed with cases. He's dead. The result of drinking and driving, supposedly. The two had nothing to do with each other."

"Isn't this enough to take to your buddy the cop?"

"Not really. It's all circumstantial."

"These files and notes are *not* circumstantial," Jason pleaded.

The three men contemplated the photographs in silence.

"If he was seen in an emergency room, wouldn't they file a police report?" Peter rubbed his eyebrow.

"Yes, they would," Waterhouse replied.

Peter shook a cigarette loose from a pack. "I need a smoke. Let's go outside."

They withdrew to the back porch, the same porch where Jason had first seen the article about Pettigrew's death in the *Hampton Roads Gazette*. Peter and Waterhouse lit cigarettes, while Jason sipped from a bottle of water.

"My buddy on the force checked for reports of gunshot wounds treated in emergency rooms in the area for the last month," said Waterhouse. "There were none for Thomas's wound. He wasn't treated in a hospital."

"So who sutured it?" asked Peter.

"I'm no doctor," said Jason, "but whoever did it knew what they were doing. A physician—or someone with that kind of skill—sutured those wounds." Jason did not voice his thought that Jasmine Kader *was* a physician. Had she been involved in Thomas's death? Did she suture the wound, and if so, why?

Waterhouse said, "I know you don't want to tell Christine about the autopsy results. But we need to find out what she knows. Maybe she remembers if he looked or sounded like he was in pain."

Jason drained the water bottle and they moved back inside. "What about you? You were his friend. When was the last time you saw him? Did he appear to be injured?"

Waterhouse shook his head. "Thomas and I had dinner a week before he died. We played chess and talked for a few hours. He was his usual self. If he was hurt, I would have noticed. He was fine."

"What date exactly?"

"Thomas died on the night of the fifteenth, a Friday. His body was found on the sixteenth. We had dinner at Outback on the Saturday before, September ninth."

Peter shook his head. "What if he was shot the same night he died?"

"You coming over to the dark side, Pete?" asked Jason.

"Don't go there, brother," Peter shot back. "As you so eloquently put it, I'm trying to expand this itty-bitty brain of mine."

"What if we ask someone at the Colonial?" Waterhouse said, thinking out loud.

"That's not a good idea. It might raise alarms. Someone might mention that we were asking."

Waterhouse persisted, glaring at Jason. "There's no police report about a shooting. You don't want to ask anyone at the Colonial. You don't want to ask Christine. What the hell *do* you want to do?"

"I don't know," Jason replied.

"Jason, I was a cop for more than twenty years. It's never easy to investigate a murder. You have to scramble some eggs to get answers. If we want to get to the bottom of this shit hole, we need more answers. Christine might have them."

Jason looked between the grungy private investigator and his skeptical brother. "I don't want to hurt her again. But you're right, it needs to be done. I'll talk to her."

* * *

In a dark room surrounded by glowing electronic instruments, a female technician with thick glasses, spiked hair, black nail polish, multiple earrings, and a top-secret clearance watched the graphic display of the audio recording pulse with every word. With the exception of the few minutes the three men had been outside, every word had been captured with remarkable clarity.

She quickly encrypted the vital passages and forwarded them to Hammon.

CHAPTER 38

All three men rode to Christine's house in silence. Christine showed them in, offered sodas and snacks. Jason hesitantly asked her about the days leading up to her father's death, explaining that they were trying to pin down exactly when Thomas had suffered the gunshot wound. Christine nodded once and reminded them that she'd seen the wound when she'd identified the body. But she hadn't known it was a gunshot wound at the time. She hadn't found out until a police detective asked her about it. The second to last time she'd spoken to her father was three days before the accident. It was on the phone, and he sounded like his usual grumpy, distracted self. She didn't know anything more.

Relieved to be done with the questions, Jason brought up the voice message, which was the primary reason for their visit tonight.

"I don't erase my messages until the mailbox is full. It's a bad habit," said Christine.

"Don't apologize," Jason replied. "Your bad habit might help us figure out what happened that night."

190

"I didn't have much trouble finding it. It's just noise. I don't see how it's going to help. It was between eleven thirty and midnight when he left the message. Obviously, I wasn't home when he called. In fact, I was at his house looking for him. He tried my cell earlier and didn't leave a message. I'd left it in the car. The second time he called the house directly."

She punched the speaker button and hit play. The generic female voice recited the date and time of the call, September 15, followed by Pettigrew's cell phone number.

The first sounds were whooshes of air. The breaths were hushed and hurried, overlapped by the rustling of clothing. They paused briefly, as if Thomas had ceased all movement and was remaining perfectly still. The silence was broken by muffled voices. Peter and Waterhouse leaned in, angling to hear.

Jason, instead, studied Christine. She was hearing the final sounds her father had made hours before he died. The noise that had held no meaning for her that first night was now eerie. She looked pained, forlorn.

The aging pharmacist seemed to be tapping—no, scratching—the mouthpiece of the phone. Intermittent bursts of varying duration, some shorter, some longer. In the longer noises, it became apparent he was using a fingernail.

Peter elbowed Waterhouse lightly. Waterhouse nodded. Both former military men recognized the patterns. They asked Christine for a pen and paper.

Christine returned with the items and handed them to Peter. "What's this for?" she asked.

"Can you please replay the message?"

She punched a button and the message began again. Peter marked the paper with dashes and dots. After the third replay, the message was complete.

After the scratching ended, rustling and garbled words followed. The word "you" came through loud and clear in Pettigrew's husky voice. He sounded disgusted, shocked; he'd recognized the person he addressed. Finally, a metallic clank and the sloshing of liquid. Then the line went dead.

"That's when the cell phone ended up in the bucket," said Jason.

The two other men nodded in agreement.

Waterhouse and Peter hunched over the paper. "Mine's a little rusty," said Waterhouse. Peter had jotted a string of letters under the dashes and dots.

threemengunssos

The significance of the letters became apparent as Peter rewrote the string with the correct spacing inserted.

Three men. Guns. SOS.

PART TWO

CHAPTER 39

Monday, October 2

"Mr. Jason," Lily Zanns lectured, "I was counting on your youth and energy to allow you to keep up with the demands of the work. Have I not made my expectations clear? Or was I faulty in my judgment?" She sat behind her desk, a chief executive handling an underachieving underling. "Please tell me why I shouldn't fire you immediately." More than her words, the expression on her normally stoic face told him he was on the brink of being out of a job again, this time involuntarily.

Jason gazed at Zanns, trying with every sinew in his body to hide his contempt. The millionaire entrepreneur had been scolding him for ten minutes, her words uncomfortable and self-righteous. *I'm going to put up with it to get some answers*, he told himself as he half listened.

The current objective overrode all else. At the same time, Jason wanted to retain his position. Not because he desired the salary or the prestige, but because finding the truth and restoring Thomas's reputation were paramount. A small part of him even hoped that Christine might be a term in that equation.

"No, Lily," he replied, leaving out the "Ms." on purpose. "You made yourself quite clear."

Did Lily know about what Fairing was up to? He was her employee. Zanns was cordial but firm with her pharmacist, not like her convivial relationship with Jasmine Kader. Fairing seemed to have a healthy respect for Zanns. Yet Jason sensed a deeper connection between them. He couldn't quite put his finger on it. Would that connection cause her to protect Fairing? Or would she condemn him for the scoundrel he was?

Jasmine Kader's involvement also worried Jason. Zanns and Kader had spent a lot of time together at the gala for Thomas, whispering and smiling. Jason didn't want to jump to conclusions and make Zanns guilty by association. But then again, everyone around her was up to their eyeballs in corruption.

He hadn't seen nor spoken to Jasmine since his drunken episode at the Southern Belle on Friday. He'd drunk too much before, especially in college, and as much as he hated to admit it, he recognized he'd had a blackout. It had never happened before.

But he needed to see her again. There were unanswered questions. Had Jasmine sutured Thomas's wounds? Had Jasmine been a party to Thomas's death? He was going to look her in the eye one more time to see if the truth was there.

"Then where are the pharmacy locations we talked about last week? Have you contacted the commercial real estate agent? Have you even set up a meeting with them?"

"I haven't had time."

Zanns bit her lower lip. "Excusez-moi? You haven't had time?"

* * *

Zanns bored into Jason Rodgers with her unrelenting gaze. She'd been keeping him on the defensive, but he was a cool cucumber and did not easily give up. Cooper's assessment of his tenacity was spot on. Rodgers was driven by the need to know what had happened to his mentor. It was obvious he would not give up until he had answers. He'd been digging around in the pharmacy files. That much she knew. The night security guard had called and informed her that he had found the pharmacy unlocked the other night. He said that a man named Rodgers had shown up because the alarm had been triggered. But the guard was suspicious that the man hadn't wanted to report it to the police.

A call to the monitoring service told her that Rodgers had used his access code to disarm the alarm system. They'd notated that Jason Rodgers had deactivated the alarm, saying there was a plumbing emergency. She'd had Sam do a quick search, but he found nothing out of the ordinary. Zanns had checked her files and found insurance remittance statements missing. Statements corresponding to the months in which the bogus prescriptions had been delivered to the pharmacy. Rodgers had been searching her office. He probably suspected her of complicity in the crime. It was time to flush Rodgers out and trick him into letting on what he knew. If she played it correctly, she could keep him as an ally for just a little longer and stall his probing. She needed him around. Her bluff would be risky, but she suspected Rodgers would take the bait.

"You haven't had time?" she repeated. She shook her head slowly, like a disapproving parent. "Jason, I made a gross error in judgment by hiring you. I want you to turn in your keys. It is time for you to end your employment with us."

* * *

Shit!

Jason couldn't believe what he was hearing. In all his years of work, in high school, college, and as a pharmacist, he'd always prided himself on his work ethic and quality. Not once in his professional life had he ever been close to being fired. And if she canned him, he would never figure out what happened to Thomas; he needed to stick around if he was to continue his investigations.

Jason leaned forward and sat on the edge of the metal chair. He had been wrestling with confronting her with what he knew. Though he had no direct knowledge of her involvement in the fraud, it was a strong possibility. It was also possible she was unaware of any fraud. She didn't actually fill prescriptions or get her hands dirty with the day-to-day operations. There was still a chance she might be above it all.

He made a snap decision sitting in her office to reveal to her some of what he knew about the fraud. Lily had in effect just fired him. If she was innocent, he'd save his job—and if not, then maybe her reaction would reveal her involvement.

"Ms. Lily," he began. Despite wishing he could tell her to pound sand up her petite backside, Jason kept his voice calm and serious, as if the world's existence rested on what he was about to say. "Listen to me very carefully. There's something I need to talk to you about. Some...activity at the Colonial I've been tracking. It's taking more time than anticipated. That's why I haven't completed my assigned tasks." His hands gripped the armrests of the chair, causing his knuckles to blanch.

Zanns's left eyebrow jumped. "What kind of activity?"

Jason paused, placed a closed fist in front of his mouth, and cleared his throat. "Over the last fourteen months, there have been...prescriptions fraudulently billed to a patient's insurance company."

"Did you say fraudulently?"

He nodded.

"Go on," she said, mashing a cigarette in the ashtray.

He fired the facts in fast, confidential whispers. "Seven prescriptions to be exact. For Prucept, a cancer medication. All for the same patient, written by the same doctor. The medication was never ordered. None of the prescriptions have been signed for. Only one conclusion can be drawn."

She pursed her lips. "Show me!"

Jason picked up the folder sitting at his feet and dropped it on the desk. "It's all here. The last one was billed September fourteenth."

He'd prepared copies of the prescriptions, invoices, drug reports, and the blank electronic signature logs. The originals were in the front seat of his rental, destined for a detective's eyes. A third copy was stashed safely in his home office.

As she turned pages, Jason observed her carefully, looking for an indignant or surprised reaction. Thomas Pettigrew's involvement and death would be omitted from the discussion for now. Neither the dead pharmacist's notes nor the crumpled, dirt-encrusted prescription bag were in the file.

Reviewing the papers, she made periodic guttural noises. Jason glanced around the small office, checking to ensure everything was where it was supposed to be.

"How did you come across this information?"

He'd anticipated this question and was ready with a lie. "I ran a check on signature capture efficiency and saw several prescriptions that weren't signed for. They were all Prucept prescriptions. I did a little probing and came up with what you have in front of you. I think it's important for you to know what's going on."

"Mon Dieu!" she said slowly. "It is important. Thank you for bringing this to my attention. You have shown me why I was correct in choosing you for this job." Closing the folder, she leaned forward. "We, you and I, will need to come up with a strategy on how to tackle this problem."

"So I get to keep my job?" he said with just a hint of sarcasm.

Zanns smiled. "You get to keep your job, monsieur. For now!"

Jason sat back in the chair again and exhaled. "We should call the police."

Zanns recoiled and held up her hands. "Let's slow down for just a moment."

"We need to do something before it happens again."

"Rest assured this matter will be looked into. Does anyone else know about this?"

"No," he lied. "Did you happen to notice which pharmacist entered all these prescriptions?"

Zanns made a half-hearted motion to look at the documents again. "Yes, I did see. It was Sam. And I see that Dr. Kader is the one writing the prescriptions," she said a little too quickly.

"This could land the Colonial in a lot of trouble."

"You are quite right. First, tell no one about this. I do not want to tip off Sam or Dr. Kader. I appreciate your diligence in investigating this matter. I will consult my attorney."

* * *

Jason ignored Zanns's directive to avoid telling anyone about the problems at the Colonial.

The four men sat around the large conference table inside a flag-draped meeting room in the Newport News police administration building. One wall was floor-to-ceiling glass with a view of a highly polished corridor. Detective John Palmer sat on one side of the table in front of three large flags: the Newport News city banner, the state flag of Virginia, and the Stars and Stripes. He was faced by the Jason, Peter, and the private investigator, Waterhouse.

"He was murdered," Jason declared. "Thomas Pettigrew was murdered. There's no other conclusion to be made."

Palmer tucked his chin to his chest and looked down his nose at the pharmacist. "Murdered?"

Palmer was six two with a long face and black hair streaked with white, a testament to his twenty-three years of police work. Fine wrinkles fanned out from the corner of his hazel-green eyes. A toothpick protruded from the corner of his mouth.

"He *was* murdered," Jason repeated.

"Just a minute!" Palmer held a finger up, halting the pharmacist. He turned to Waterhouse. "Walt, I read that report before I gave it to you. It didn't say anything about murder. The injuries were consistent with a car accident. The cause of death was blunt-force trauma. The guy was drunk. More than two times the legal limit."

"Can we start from the beginning, John? We're putting the cart before the horse. We want you to see everything we have," said Waterhouse.

"Fine." Palmer leaned back and steepled his hands in front of his face. "Go ahead."

Waterhouse turned to Jason. "Start from the beginning and tell Detective Palmer what we've found. Don't leave anything out."

It had been decided that Jason would do the talking. Jason had thought Waterhouse was deferring to him, but after seeing Palmer's reaction, he suspected Waterhouse didn't want to sound like a fool in front of his police comrade. Nevertheless, over the next forty minutes, Jason recounted everything in excruciating detail, laying before the cop every piece of evidence. Jason had perfected his presentation with each telling. Palmer listened and did not interrupt. But he was having great difficulty masking his skepticism.

When he was finished, the detective asked one question. "What would you like me to do?" Palmer scanned the documents on the table and readjusted the black pistol in its leather holster.

"We'd like you to investigate," Jason replied. "That's why we're here. What about the gunshot wound in his shoulder?"

Palmer met each pair of eyes as if he were about to scold his children. "It says the wound was sutured and in no way contributed to his death. The wound is certainly strange, but there were no reports from any of the local hospitals or doctor's offices. The coroner said it didn't contribute to his death." Palmer turned to his friend. "Seems to me like you've got a case for insurance fraud, but I gotta tell you, there's no murder here. Leave me these documents, and I'll forward them to our economic crimes unit. Don't hold your breath; they're totally backlogged. And, Walt, you should have told these guys the evidence is slim for murder."

"I did," Waterhouse said.

CHAPTER 40

The black-and-white images were frozen on the television screen. Sam Fairing was in midstride from one of the pharmacy bays to a computer terminal. Kevin Mitchell, the technician, hunched over the pharmacy counter, head down, spatula in midswipe over a green counting tray.

Examining the DVD for the second time, Jason wondered again what—if anything—was so important that Pettigrew would include it in his collection of evidence. Every other item was a piece in the puzzle creating a picture of fraud. The video did not fit, and seemed to serve no purpose. But Jason, understanding the anal nature of his former teacher, knew it was in there for a reason. He just had to find it. *What was he missing?* Thirty minutes into fast-forwarding through the twelve hours of recording, he stopped the playback and moved to the kitchen table.

Jason's thoughts drifted back to the meeting with the detective. Waterhouse had thrown them under the bus, as far as Jason was concerned. Sure, their case was weak, but Waterhouse could have sided with

202

Jason. Jason had blasted Waterhouse as they walked to their cars. Peter had moved between the two men, afraid that it would come to blows.

He was jarred out of his reverie when the telephone rang. Jason answered. He didn't recognize the voice. The caller spoke again and he realized it was Jasmine.

"Let's have lunch today. Do you like Italian?" she asked.

"I won't have time," he responded. Jasmine persisted, but Jason held firm.

"Well then, perhaps I'll stop by the pharmacy," she said. "Or better yet—your place."

"We'll talk *very* soon, Jasmine. I promise you. But the time's not right."

"Someone's grumpy," she teased.

"I've got to go," he snapped.

After he ended the call, he walked to the small black box sitting on the kitchen table. He stood there for a moment shaking his head. *She's still after something*, he thought. Whatever it was, Jason was determined not to give it to her. He desperately wanted to confront her about the phony prescriptions. But Lily had cautioned him to keep Jasmine in the dark about their knowledge of the phony prescriptions. Jason would bide his time. When the moment was right she, would have her comeuppance.

Jason picked up the handheld device Waterhouse had found in Pettigrew's collection and turned it over in his hand. A GPS. The private eye said Thomas had followed Fairing to the Lions Bridge. Flipping on the power, he saw this was not one of those everyday GPS devices sold for use in the family car. This was designed to track vehicles remotely. Businesses used them, police forces, anyone who wanted to know where a vehicle was or had been.

A menu listed the different vehicles tracked. There was only one entry: "Fairing Lexus." Jason clicked on it, and the menu showed trips tracked for that car. There was only a single entry. He had only used the device once, on September 15.

The same night Pettigrew died. The same night he recorded the video Jason was now watching. The tracking on the GPS was time-stamped. It began around nine fifteen and ended just before ten that same evening.

He didn't know why, but it suddenly occurred to Jason that Thomas had probably watched the action in the Colonial's pharmacy department live while he was recording it. Maybe he saw something that disturbed him and raced from his home office to follow Sam Fairing the night he died. Sometime before that night, he'd planted a tracking beacon on Fairing's Lexus.

Jason pressed enter, and the small computer thought for a minute, then switched to a map of Newport News. Jason zoomed in several magnifications, bringing the street names into view. A thin red line snaked southward along Jefferson Avenue, turned right at J. Clyde Morris Boulevard, and hit Warwick. The line turned left and headed south. Before reaching the Hilton Village area, it turned right again on Cedar Lane. A half-mile later, the path indicator bore right where Cedar Lane ended and merged with Museum Drive. The line followed Museum Drive and crossed over Lake Maury at the Lions Bridge, where Fairing had evidently stopped for several minutes, as indicated by the timer on the screen. The line circled back across the bridge, returned up Museum Drive, and backtracked down Cedar to a point farther south.

An urge struck him. Jason grabbed his rental car keys and the crumpled prescription bag, and headed out the door.

CHAPTER 41

As soon as he opened the front door, Doug Winstead knew his house had been violated again. They'd been inside. As usual, there was no damage. Nothing had been disturbed. No doors had been kicked in, no windows broken. Whoever they were, they were real professionals. They'd snuck in, left their calling card, and left as quickly and silently as they had entered.

The old, worn bills were bound with a thick rubber band. Five stacks, lined neatly in a row, sat on the kitchen table under the glare of the overhead lamp. A photograph and a handwritten note lay next to them.

He always left the house dark. Never waste anything, including electricity. The first time he'd come home and seen the lamp burning, he'd freaked. Now, the infrequent, but lucrative, visits were a disturbing reminder of what was at stake.

Winstead put the photo under his nose, smelling it. He didn't know why he did it. Somehow it made him feel closer to his daughter. The memory of the first night he was abducted and given instructions

205

unfolded in his mind, as it did every time he saw the cluster of green-backs. He put the photo down and picked up the note.

Last one, Douglas. Another installment upon completion.

Winstead breathed a nervous sigh of relief. Was it almost over? Like a disease finally cured, would this ordeal finally be coming to an end? Would it ever really end? Would he ever stop looking over his shoulder?

He cradled the five stacks of bills with both hands and carried them to the living room. He shoved a chair aside, knelt, and peeled back one corner of the area rug. He pushed down on two slats of the hardwood flooring, revealing a hole. Most of the cash was stashed here. To date, he'd earned seventy thousand. He spent some on a few luxuries, including the new Harley in the garage, leaving him with fifty-five thousand. Tonight's payment made it sixty-five, with another ten after he delivered the last prescription. He would end up with seventy-five grand. *Not bad*, he thought. *Not bad at all.*

He'd give it all back in a flash, though, to know Charlie was safe. As soon as it was over, he told himself, he was getting the hell out of here. He would find Charlie and keep her close. Very close.

* * *

Why had Pettigrew followed Fairing here?

Jason watched the activity in and around the area from his position on the hill just above the Lions Bridge. Joggers and walkers completed their treks around the Noland Trail, and automobiles moved up and down the shoreline of the James River along Museum Drive. The bridge sat atop a berm, a short roadway over an earthen dam, bottling up waters flowing into the James River and creating Lake Maury. Its signature feature was four eight-foot stone lions perched regally on each parapet, globes resting between their paws.

He stood on the knoll beside a mammoth sculpture, *Conquering the Wild*. A man grasped the rope bridle of a rearing steed, straining to contain the beast on a fifteen-foot pedestal guarded by four naked men sitting in the style of Rodin's *Thinker*. He and Jenny had taken Michael for walks in his three-wheeled stroller around the Noland Trail, years before the divorce. Jason came here often to relax, and was intimately familiar with the area.

The northern entrance of the trail disappeared around a bend, past a granite marker engraved with the trail's name. He walked the thirty yards to it. Beyond the marker, a small clearing opened to the right. A break in the thickly wooded forest led to the edge of Lake Maury. He descended the path. A large, fallen tree lay to one side. He rotated 360 degrees, looking for a clue, a sign of what had happened here the night Pettigrew died.

He noticed a small depression had been dug out in the claylike earth under the dead tree. Jason remembered the dirty, crumpled prescription bag among Thomas's files. He pulled it from his pocket and unfolded it. Some dirt had managed to trickle inside the bag. Kneeling, Jason dumped the specks of red earth from the bag into his hand. He compared it to the dirt under the rotting log. The two samples consisted of identical red clay. The earth here always clung to the bottom of his shoes. It wasn't a scientific analysis, but it was good enough for Jason. This bag had been here, or somewhere close by, the night Pettigrew was murdered.

Thomas had followed Fairing here. Had Fairing been meeting with someone, the "patient" Winstead? Or was he delivering something, a payment perhaps?

Searching the entire trail for clues would be a gross exercise in futility. It was five miles long and cut through dense forest; a team of a hundred men combing the area for days stood little chance of finding anything. Worse yet, he didn't even know what he was looking for.

Jason dialed the number to the Colonial. Kevin Mitchell, the technician, answered. "Kevin, this is Jason. Can I speak with Sam, please?"

"Sam left about two hours ago. Billy's here."

Perfect, he thought. He didn't want to speak with him anyway. "Really? I'll speak with Billy, then. Is he keeping up?" asked Jason.

"He's a real pro," Kevin replied. "We don't have to worry about him. Hold on, he's on the line with a patient."

"Okay. While I'm waiting, would you please get me Sam's home phone number."

Bryant placed him on hold, then recited the number. Jason memorized it.

"Billy's done now. Here he is."

Parks came on the line a moment later. "How's your day going?" Jason asked his new pharmacist.

"Smoother than a baby's ass," Parks responded.

"Very good. Well, I hope the rest of the night goes well for you. Call me if you have any questions." Jason was comforted by Park's proficiency. Jason could chase his demons and not worry about the pharmacy's state of affairs.

"Thanks. Oh, Jason, by the way, Sam said he really needed to be off Saturday. Said he's going to Canada for the weekend. I'm gonna cover for him, if that's okay."

Jason had completely forgotten about Fairing's request. Sam had demanded the day off when Jason started as vice president. But for the first time in his professional career, he didn't give a crap about his responsibilities as supervisor. "Sure, that's fine, Billy. Thanks for being so flexible."

He hung up and called Peter's cell phone. "I need you to do me a quick favor. Can you do a reverse look-up on this phone number and get me an address?" He recited the number Bryant had given him.

Jason heard the muted clicks on the keyboard. "8888 Riverdale Road with an apartment number, Newport News," said Peter. "It's Sam Fairing."

He walked back to the Ford and climbed in. The dark blue sedan was parked a quarter mile up the road, watching him. Jason saw it but pretended not to notice. They, whoever they were, were still following every move he made. He reminded himself to change out the Ford rental for a newer one. He didn't know if he could keep them off his ass, but he'd certainly try.

CHAPTER 42

The sandstone guardhouse had a flimsy, swing-up gate painted with red-and-white barber-pole striping. A uniformed black man, looking bored, then irritated, pushed open a sliding glass window.

"Can I help you?"

"I was hoping you could help me find an address," said Jason.

"Yeah, what it is?"

"8888 Riverdale Road."

"Well you found it," the guard said dryly, looking at him as if he were a moron.

"This is it?"

"Which number you looking for?"

"17-A. Sam Fairing."

The guard punched a few keys on his keyboard. "He's in the south tower. I have to announce you first. Give me a minute."

"That's okay. I was just trying to make sure I knew how to get here. It's late. I'll catch up with him tomorrow."

"You sure, man? Ain't no problem."

"I'm sure. Thanks anyway." He backed out of the small driveway and headed home.

Another piece of the puzzle had fallen into place, unlocking another trunkful of questions. The night of September 15, Sam Fairing had left work at the Colonial and driven to the north end of Lions Bridge. With Thomas Pettigrew following, he'd parked and done God knew what with the crumpled prescription bag there. Then Fairing drove home to his condo in the Windsor Towers on Riverdale Road.

And somewhere in the course of the night's events, Thomas Pettigrew was murdered.

* * *

The guard watched until the Ford Fusion disappeared from view. Fairing had given each guard on all three shifts five hundred dollars and a promise of a thousand more to the man who reported anyone asking for him. A jealous ex-wife might send people looking for him, he'd said. He lifted the handset from the phone and dialed Fairing's number. No answer. The guard left a message as he thought about where the new big-screen television would fit best.

CHAPTER 43

Jasmine Kader fired a fifth round at the ten-ring target painted in the torso of the silhouetted figure a mile away. Oliver lay next her, calling out the results of her efforts. The cloth target was lit up by a small but powerful infrared laser registered only through the rifle's scope. The success of their mission depended entirely on the infrared aspects of their weapons.

"Six ring at about five o'clock," he said, his eyes not leaving the large spotting scope. Jasmine rotated the elevation turret two clicks.

She was having a hard time keeping tabs on Jason. Her trips to the Camp had become more frequent making it practically impossible to monitor the pharmacist. Lily was unaware of the predicament and Jasmine, thinking the matter of minor importance, was content to keep it that way.

Situated deep in the thick woods of northern North Carolina on a fifty-acre tract of land purchased three years ago, the Camp, as it was known, was miles from the nearest town or road. Constructed by a small army of now-deported immigrants, the camouflaged range consisted of an elevated, wooden firing platform and numerous human-form targets positioned a mile downrange under an equally dense canopy of foliage obscuring the view of passing aircraft and satellites. A short, dirt landing strip carved from the forest flanked them. The wheeled float plane sat pointed for a quick takeoff under netting stretched between thick, rough-hewn logs on the runway.

Oliver spent his afternoons shuttling Kader and Fairing to the site. Sam had traveled down the previous day. Tomorrow, both would be flying down with him.

Kader pulled off five more shots. Oliver announced the results after each volley. Kader made her adjustments. Her final three rounds were placed in a nearly perfect cluster dead center from a mile away.

"That's all for tonight, Oliver," she said. "I'm dialed in."

"It's a pity that the world cannot appreciate your talents, Ms. Jasmine. The infidels will pay dearly."

* * *

"He made a trip to the Windsor Towers this afternoon," the young Secret Service agent explained. "Our guys followed him to some bridge near Lake Maury a couple miles up the road. He made a phone call from his cell phone, then proceeded to the towers."

Special agent in charge Clay Broadhurst was reviewing the security procedures for the christening, reading from a list he'd prepared on his laptop. Everything was progressing as planned, except for one disturbing fact. Jason Rodgers was ignoring Broadhurst's warnings to stay away from the shipyard. He was becoming a pain in the ass of enormous magnitude. "What did he do there?" Broadhurst demanded.

"We don't know. He stopped at the gate, spoke to the attendant, then left. The agents followed him home. He's there now."

Broadhurst glanced at his watch. It was eight forty-five. Night had descended over Newport News. He looked out over the dark waters of the James from his borrowed work space, which served as one of two command centers on shipyard property. The small, windswept waves were colored orange by the lights of the marine terminal.

"What's the status on Rodgers's background check?"

"I sent it to IB," the junior agent replied. IB was the investigative branch of the service. "We're still waiting for it."

Broadhurst shook his head in displeasure. "Call them and tell them to get their asses moving! And I want that search warrant to examine his finances. I want to know what he eats for breakfast and what time he takes a shit every day."

"I'll get right on it. What do you want me to tell the guys on surveillance?"

Broadhurst stretched and clasped his hands behind his head. He removed a plastic container of Tums from his suit coat, shook two from the bottle, and popped them into his mouth. The heartburn felt like it was eating a hole in his stomach. It always got worse as the big day approached.

"Tell IB I want that report first thing in the morning. Then tell our guys to watch his house tonight and pay Jason Rodgers a visit before he leaves for work in the morning." He held up a thumb and forefinger. "Make sure Rodgers knows he's this close to finding his ass in jail."

CHAPTER 44

Tuesday, October 3

Her naked form hovered over him. She bobbed up and down in slow motion, as if floating on gentle, unfelt waves on an invisible ocean.

Jason's head shifted fitfully as the image played out with his bedroom ceiling as its backdrop. Jasmine Kader's stern demeanor in his dream was markedly different from her come-hither persona in real life. Her voice filled his ears with radio static, never rising to the level of coherence, but filling Jason with unease. Yet, in the time and space of this nightmare meaning penetrated, dredging the grooves of his subconscious, excavating memories of his noontime meal with her and the events that had followed, which until now had been locked away.

Jasmine Kader had interrogated him, probing, threatening, groping for information. His mind tried to grasp the purpose, but came up empty.

The sightlines of the dream blurred, wavering like a pane of glass coated with cascading water on a rainy day. He looked up from his bed at her naked form. At the caramel skin, delicate breasts, and soft curves. She was a perfect female specimen. Though he had never seen her undressed, his imagination filled in details. His loins

214

stirred. He reached for her with a tentative hand. Kader, the apparition, smiled and drifted out of reach.

Her right arm, covered by a sheath from shoulder to wrist, extended toward him gracefully. Her left hand slowly pulled back the sleeve. Jason shrank from the sight even before his eyes fully focused on the image.

The arm was not abnormal or grotesque. In fact, it was perfect and unblemished in every way, except for the tattoo. Through the wavy, undulating curtain, he discerned the marking. Jasmine moved her arm closer to him. It broke through the wavy drape as if coming from another dimension. The body art on the flawless skin repulsed him, convulsing him with dread.

Jason awoke with a jerk, eyelids fluttering. Temporarily paralyzed, stuck on the cusp between dream and reality, his chest heaved rapidly. Eventually, his muscles regained feeling. Movement returned, first to his fingers, hands, arms. He flexed his feet up and down, back and forth. He managed to find the floor, walked slowly to the bathroom, and splashed water over his face. Downstairs, he made coffee, turning the dream over, centrifuging two important realities into focus.

First, the tattoo was real.

Jason had seen it in the flesh through his drunken mist. His mind replayed snippets of their conversation at lunch. Staggering to his car. Jasmine grasping his arm. Heavy, pleasing perfume filling his nostrils. Then everything went black. He must have passed out. The next recollection was that of Jasmine and a man, helping him up the stairs. A liquid was squirted up his nose. His nostrils burned and his eyes watered. A minute later, the room began to roll and wave. He felt as he had after waking from an appendectomy many years ago.

He realized that he'd been drugged. Words had flowed from him in response to her pointed questions. Lies had been impossible. He couldn't remember exactly what he'd said. But he told her what he knew. Why his mind was revealing it to him now, he would never know.

At some point, Jasmine had leaned in close to make sure he heard her words, her nose nearly touching his. Jason had reached out and grabbed a fistful of blouse in an attempt to pull her close. Jasmine had been caught by surprise. He was a man under the influence of a narcotic and she, after all, was an extremely attractive woman.

Kader had tried to pull away, but Jason had held tight. She'd broken his grip, but not before her right sleeve rode up, exposing the forearm—and the tattoo. He'd seen the image before. It was identical to the one etched on the attacker's arm at Pettigrew's house. Jason hadn't realized it until this very moment, but the hand-drawn sketch that Thomas had left in his files was a cruder version of the same design.

Jasmine Kader was tall and athletic, but she could never be confused with the brawny man who'd broken into Pettigrew's home. They were two different people. Two identical tattoos in the same location on the forearm. Were Jasmine and the intruder part of the same organization or group?

Jason had assumed his attacker that day had been a robber, looking for loot. Now, Jasmine—adorned with the same tattoo—had drugged him and was asking difficult questions about his knowledge of the Colonial. He grabbed a pad of paper and a pencil and sketched the image across the entire page. Ten minutes and three drafts later, he was satisfied. He folded it twice and put it in his wallet. He would compare it to the sketch Pettigrew had left in his files. But Jason was confident they were identical.

He gulped down the last of the coffee. The doorbell rang twice impatiently. Padding to the door, he threw it open. Two serious-faced men in dark suits and sporting sharp crew cuts glowered at him. The closest man held up an identification wallet. A bright gold badge with the star of the Secret Service was rammed into Jason's face.

CHAPTER 45

Lily Zanns's policy forbidding electronic communications or over-the-air transmissions had been successful in keeping their operation undetected. Eavesdropping devices were everywhere. Hammon, she knew, nonetheless communicated by very advanced, high-tech methods. She was quite certain he was an American, with access to vast resources. The secret group he headed had access to a plethora of sophisticated devices. The Simoon did not. That was fine. There would be no e-mails, cell phone calls, or text messages about their mission. The only compromise she allowed was the rare coded phone call to the pizzeria in Hampton to set up the meetings with Cooper. So far, the strategy had worked.

Having to meet with Cooper face-to-face was becoming a chore. He had called an hour ago requesting another meeting. She despised the man sitting in her Mercedes more every time she laid eyes on him. "What is so important that you had to get me out here at this early hour?" she demanded.

The circular parking lot on the banks of the York River was deserted. They stood at redoubts nine and ten in the Yorktown National Battlefield. These two fortifications, held by the British, were vital to the defense of the hamlet more than two hundred years ago. If they'd fallen into the insurgent American hands, the small village would have been within range of the Continental Army's cannons. An assaulting party led by Lieutenant Alexander Hamilton and supported by French troops stormed the earthworks in October 1781, capturing them, thus signaling the beginning of the end for the British.

Zanns had picked this location to have her clandestine meetings with Steven Cooper for its ironic historical significance. Zanns's own assaulting party would be launching their attack on the imperialist nation that had become exactly what they'd despised so long ago in the British.

Zanns had driven herself to the meeting, a rare occurrence. Oliver had arrived late last night from taxiing Jasmine Kader to North Carolina and would be making a return trip in a matter of hours. The trips to the Camp in the deep woods were now daily. Preparation for their task on Saturday took precedence. So Zanns was relegated to the menial task of actually getting behind the wheel of her Maserati.

"Rodgers," Cooper began, "was spotted at the Windsor Towers last night. We intercepted him calling the Colonial asking for Fairing's phone number. He then called his brother and had him do a reverse look-up to get the address. Rodgers knows that Fairing lives in the towers. Hammon is extremely concerned!"

Zanns was already aware of this fact. Fairing had retrieved the message from the towers guard and had called her last night warning about Rodgers's visit. Cooper's men had followed the pharmacist as well. Cooper's call this morning asking for a meeting was annoying but not unexpected.

"We've had a team following him since we learned of his return. He and two other men were seen coming out of the Newport News Police building," Cooper continued.

She knew this also, but feigned ignorance. "You've been following him? There was no need! I have someone handling that. My person says Rodgers knows nothing about the real plan. He thinks it's insurance fraud."

"Who, your tramp, Jasmine? We saw her meet with him for lunch."

Zanns leveled a disgusted look at the spy. Cooper was unaware Fairing and Kader were Zanns's offspring. She hid her anger, resisting the urge to reach out and slap the tight smirk from his face. "I wouldn't want to be on Jasmine's bad side. She's skilled with many weapons."

Cooper ignored the threat and replied coolly, "When was the last time she spoke with him? My men haven't seen her with Rodgers in days. What he knows may have changed. They've visited the police, and we have no idea what they said. He needs to be disposed of."

"Rodgers is not to be killed. Two pharmacists dead at the Colonial in a matter of weeks would raise suspicion. He has no obvious vices that we can use to stage an accident, no drug use or alcohol. Anyway, there's not enough time for him to put everything together."

"Pettigrew was not a drunk. That didn't stop you with the old man!"

Zanns glared. She was clutching at straws. There were many ways to eliminate Jason Rodgers without arousing suspicion. He would remain alive until such time she deemed it necessary to eliminate him.

"We'll find out what he knows," Cooper continued. "His house and car have been bugged. Cameras are in place. His cell phone is being monitored. He'll be meeting with the brother, Peter, and two others. We suspect one of them is Christine, the daughter. The fourth person is the private investigator."

"Where will the meeting take place?"

"At Rodgers's house. We should know more then. He may have to be dealt with."

"If suspicions are raised, they will look to me, Fairing, or Kader. We cannot have the police investigating before the plan is executed."

"Lily, you're a fool!" Cooper's statement was calm and analytical.

Zanns aimed a string of French expletives at Cooper. She paused and gathered herself. "I will be confirming receipt of the funds by tomorrow night. Every penny needs to be in the ten different accounts, or the plan will not be carried out. Are you ready to move it?"

Cooper bristled. "Of course. Twenty-four million dollars, to be wired into an escrow account in the bank in the Caymans. The flow of money cannot be reversed, our account will be closed, and the records deleted immediately after the transfer. Once the plan is executed, you can activate the password. The bank has specific instructions that the money is not to be moved until Sunday, when the password is presented. You will be given the password after the event, in a secure e-mail. The letters of the password will be embedded in a seemingly inane message, and can be retrieved using the predetermined numbering sequence. It will be routed through untraceable servers in Europe and Indonesia. We've paid a bank employee to monitor the news channels. Once news of the deed is public, he will know to release the funds to the password holder. If there's no news, the password will be voided, and the funds will be rerouted to other accounts. Naturally, the bank employee will be eliminated shortly thereafter.

"If the funds aren't moved before 9:00 a.m. Atlantic time—whether or not the deed is accomplished—they will be recirculated back to my agency through another string of accounts." Cooper hesitated. "Suffice it to say, Lily, failure to produce results will not be looked upon favorably. You and your protégés will be marked and hunted. You've already been given earnest money." Three years earlier, Zanns and her team had been given a nonrefundable deposit of twelve million dollars.

Zanns wanted to spit in the face of the American weasel sitting beside her. She suspected Cooper, an alias no doubt, would fold when the pressure intensified. She'd seen it before in so many other weak-kneed Americans. He was nothing more than a pontificating sycophant who dissected others' decisions in hindsight, but didn't have the mettle to step forward and think for himself.

Cooper switched back to the pharmacist. "If we deem that Rodgers knows too much, Hammon has authorized me to have him neutralized. Tonight will tell us more," he said.

Zanns turned, acid in her tone. "*Cul!*" Ass. "If Rodgers dies before Saturday, we will not carry out the killings. Is that clear?"

"Rodgers had better remain contained."

"What about the courier?" asked Zanns.

"Mr. Winstead will be making his last delivery to the Colonial today. And I do mean *last*."

"Have you taken delivery of Cyclops?"

Cooper nodded. "Tomorrow. It's been tested four times in the last two months with excellent results."

"Very well," said Zanns.

"There's one small matter that has yet to be resolved, Lily."

"And *what* is that?"

"Delivery of the device will only be completed upon receipt of payment."

"Payment? What payment? That was not part of the original agreement."

"Most true. However, I have decided that *I* need some insurance."

So, Zanns thought, *the man has some balls after all.* The snake was going to hold Zanns and their plan hostage in order to cash in. Bile rose in her throat. There was no one to whom she could appeal this blackmail. Steven Cooper was her only contact to Hammon and the rebel faction financing her operation. If given enough time, Zanns could unearth it. But there were only a few days left until D-day.

"I see you waited until we were beyond the point of no return before blackmailing us, Steven. For once, I'm impressed. How much?"

"Five million is fair," Cooper said flatly. He handed her a slip of paper with an account number scribbled on it. "Transfer the funds by midnight tonight, or I'll develop car trouble on my trip to take delivery of Cyclops."

"But the deposit has already been spent. I do not have that kind of money, and—"

Cooper raised a hand, stopping her. "I know who your benefactor was, and his history. He raped and pillaged his homeland. You have access to much more. Consider yourself lucky that I'm only asking for five. Without Cyclops, the mission is guaranteed to fail!"

Lily wrung her gloved hands as she glared at Cooper. Her Amo had been dead for almost three years, hung like a common criminal. Now, his memory was being thrown back in her face. "Bastard! Are *you* prepared to incur Hammon's wrath?"

"You let me worry about that. Make sure the money is in the account tonight. If the attacks fail because Cyclops is not in place, Hammon will think you reneged. In fact, I'll make sure he knows you did. You'll become hunted, forever on the run. No corner of the planet will be safe."

* * *

Every nerve in Douglas Winstead's body was frayed. His eyes darted about. He despised this place more with every visit. When this whole thing was over, he promised himself, he'd never set foot within three miles of the pharmacy. He shifted his weight from one foot to another as he waited in the four-person queue. A damned blue hair was talking up the fat pharmacist about her godforsaken bowel movements. In between questions, she had to tell him about her family and grandchildren and how they never visited anymore. The woman was in her own little time warp, the pharmacist her own personal consultant.

Hurry up!

Winstead had never seen the pudgy pharmacist before. A grandfatherly type, his bald pate was ringed by a furry, horseshoe-shaped patch of hair, like monks Winstead had seen in history books. The name plate on the high counter read "William T. Parks, RPh."

The short, dark-skinned raghead had always been on duty when he delivered the prescription. Was he supposed to turn it in only to him? The last thing he wanted to do was screw this thing up now. Winstead drummed his palm faster against his thigh. A trickle of sweat made its way down his back.

Get the prescription to the pharmacy. That was his only task. Did it really matter who took it from him? Like all the other times, the unmarked envelope holding the prescription had been left in the front seat of his truck during the night. He'd given up long ago trying to learn who was delivering it. They knew every move he made.

The line inched forward as Blue Hair shuffled off to wait for her medication. Ten agonizing minutes later, Winstead bellied up to the counter. The young cashier snapped her gum as she took the prescription and asked if he wanted to wait for it.

"No," he replied. His throat was dry and felt like it might close up. *Who gives a shit? Take three weeks to fill the goddamned thing!*

Winstead turned to leave. Entering one of the aisles, he almost bumped into the short Arabic-looking pharmacist. The pharmacist's eyes widened, recognizing him. Winstead nodded and kept walking. Fairing stepped behind the counter and up the steps, looking for the slip of paper Winstead had just dropped off.

Winstead could hear him say, "Billy, I'll take care of this prescription." Winstead breathed easier and felt a few ounces lighter as he stepped into the morning sun.

* * *

"Where's Lily?" asked Jason of anyone who would answer. He waited with hands on hips for a response. He had no desire to be dressed down again for neglecting his duties.

"She called earlier and said she was going out of town on a meeting. She said she'd be back in the afternoon," Parks replied. "Something about meeting with the lawyers."

She's meeting with her lawyers, Jason thought. *Good!* At least he wouldn't have to listen to her rant about why he hadn't found any locations. He had no intention of completing that task until the Pettigrew matter was resolved, one way or another. He would not, could not, focus on anything else. In fact, he decided that when he'd gotten to the bottom of this whole mess, he was going to resign. The fact that the Colonial was engaged in fraud would lead to years of investigation and litigation.

"Fine," he said in response to no one in particular.

The visit from the Secret Service agents had shaken him. Jason had refused to let them into his house, stepping out and confronting them. They demanded to know why he'd been on Riverdale Road yesterday. Jason told them the truth. He was looking for an address, a fact he guessed they already knew. Jason tried to look unfazed by their aggression, but wasn't sure he succeeded. Their warnings this morning were more virulent than at the shipyard. They leaned into him, invading his personal space. Jason stood firm, refusing to back away. The leader jabbed his finger at Jason's chest and said, "We better not see you near the shipyard again, or your ass will be cooling it in a federal lock up!"

After they'd gone, Jason did an Internet search and found Jasmine's address. He didn't want to wait any longer to confront her about the fake prescriptions she was writing. She'd drugged him, pumped him for information. It was all too clear now: she wanted to know what he knew.

Jason felt violated. He'd decided he could wait no longer. To hell with Lily and keeping quiet, he thought. He needed answers. Before coming to work, he drove to her house and rang the bell several times over five minutes. But there was no answer. He drove to her office. The receptionist said she was not in, and was taking the rest of the week off. Something about vacationing in Hilton Head. Frustrated and confused about her sudden vacation, Jason drove to the Colonial.

He approached a computer terminal away from the main filling area. He accessed the drug audit function and queried the databases for the drug Prucept. The last time a prescription for the medication had been put into the system was September 14. He entered the search parameters to include September 15 through today. Jason had run the same report yesterday and it showed no data. No prescriptions for Prucept had been entered since the last one on the fourteenth.

He hit enter. The hourglass popped onto the screen. Then he heard the hum of the printer as a single sheet flowed into the output tray. His heart fell into his stomach. Repressing the urge to run, he walked over to the printer and casually removed the page. Folding it in two, he walked back to Lily's office, leaned against her door, and read the document.

One prescription was listed, dated today. Prucept. It had been put into the computer at 10:53 a.m. *It's happening right now.* Winstead had dropped off the prescription forty minutes ago. He opened his cell phone and dialed Waterhouse. Then he closed it. He walked into the pharmacy department and went to the will-call bin. Prescriptions were held in the plastic trays until patients picked them up. Pretending to be looking for something, he looked in the W tray. There it was. A flat pharmacy bag with the bag receipt stapled to it. The name in big, bold, black letters. Winstead, Douglas. It contained no prescription vial and no medication. A quick scan of the sales floor revealed no one waiting. As expected, the man named Winstead was long gone. Sam was standing at another terminal, engrossed in entering prescriptions. Jason repressed the growing urge to confront him then and there, to wrap his fingers around Fairing's throat and squeeze the truth from him. But he needed to act. Now!

He walked back into the office area and, this time, completed his call to Waterhouse. "Winstead dropped off another prescription for Prucept."

"Stop him and hold him there until I can get over there!"

"He's gone. It happened forty-five minutes ago. It's time we talked to him. Can you find out where he is?"

"Get me his cell phone number. It'll take about an hour."

"I don't want to wait that long." Jason scanned the drug audit. The phone number listed on the form looked like a landline. "Hold on a second."

He returned to the terminal, pulled up Winstead's address, and found what looked like a cell phone number. Returning to the hallway, he recited the number to Waterhouse.

Jason issued an order like a battlefield general. "Trace Winstead's whereabouts immediately. Then meet me in the alley behind the Colonial. We're taking your car. Fifteen minutes."

CHAPTER 46

Having spent the last hour hunkered down in the front seat of Waterhouse's Blazer, nervously watching the greasy spoon on the southern stretch of Warwick Boulevard for signs of the fraudster Winstead, Jason spied the scruffy-looking man as he exited the eatery and climbed into his black Ram 1500. They'd found the pickup using information given to Waterhouse from a buddy at the DMV. Three hang-up phone calls later, they'd triangulated his location to within three square blocks and eyeballed the vehicle in the parking lot.

"Here we go," said Jason.

Winstead wore faded, holey jeans and a denim jacket over a black Harley T-shirt. His dirty-blond goatee and curly hair completed the grunge look. Waterhouse handed the field glasses to Jason and started the Blazer.

Jason peered through the glasses, trying to catch a better glimpse of the man. "He's not what I expected."

They followed the pickup to Winstead's house. Like most in this part of town, it was past its prime, built just after World War Two.

227

Long and narrow, it was crammed onto a skinny lot. The paint peeled like a bad case of psoriasis. Holes left by missing shingles dotted the roof. The house fit its occupant—or vice versa.

"Mr. Winstead is home," Waterhouse announced. "Let's go ask him a few questions."

* * *

Jason ran up the painted concrete steps, leading the older, out-of-shape Waterhouse. The floorboards creaked under their combined weight. He tried the doorbell and rapped three times, but heard no sound inside. They stared at the dark, stained curtain behind the window in the door.

The drape in the picture window to their left shifted. A few seconds later, the curtain on the door was pulled back. The blonde goatee, the scruffy hair, and a pair of sky-blue eyes appeared behind the dirt-encrusted glass.

"What do y'all want?" The voice was high-pitched and muffled from behind the door. It sounded like a teenage boy's in the throes of a voice change.

"Douglas Winstead?" Waterhouse asked.

"Who wants to know?"

Waterhouse, standing beside Jason, reached behind his back and produced a leather case, letting it fall open. The gold badge glinted. "I'm Waterhouse. This is Rodgers, my partner. We have a few questions for you."

The curtain fell back. Another minute passed. Finally, the dead bolt slid and the lock clicked. Winstead opened the door partially, leaving his right side concealed.

"Can we come in?" asked Waterhouse.

"You're fine right there."

"Whatever." Waterhouse hesitated, pulling out a notebook. "You're Douglas Winstead, correct?"

Winstead nodded.

"You brought a prescription to the Colonial pharmacy two hours ago," said Jason. It was not a question.

"Yeah, so?"

Jason saw anxiety flash in the man's eyes.

Waterhouse coughed, bending over as he did. When he stood, he extended his right arm. The sideways-tilted Glock was trained at Winstead's forehead. "Don't move there, Douggie." Jason twitched at the sight of the gun.

Waterhouse spoke calmly. "I know you have a piece behind that door. So you're going to slowly take two steps to your left so we can see that hog leg you're holding." Waterhouse flicked the Glock twice.

Winstead hesitated, then slid from behind the door. In his right hand, he held a four-inch 357 magnum revolver.

"Thank you very much," said Waterhouse, as if he were talking to a waitress who'd just poured him coffee. "Now, bend slowly at the knee. Keep your eyes on me and place that gun on the floor... Good...Now back away."

The private investigator picked up the gun and handed it to Jason. "Take the rounds out." He turned back to Winstead. "Now we can have a nice, polite sit-down," he said, motioning to a beat-up sofa.

Waterhouse reholstered the Glock while Jason emptied rounds, scattering them and the gun on the coffee table. Waterhouse sat on a threadbare, cushioned chair across from Winstead. Jason took the only other chair in the room, a spindly wooden contraption.

"You guys aren't cops," Winstead hissed.

"You're right about that, Douggie."

"I ain't telling you guys nothing."

"You know the penalty for insurance fraud?" asked Jason.

Winstead hiked an eyebrow.

"How about murder?" Jason added.

The man flinched and his jaw sagged. "I ain't killed nobody."

"A man was killed because of what's going on at the Colonial," said Waterhouse, "because of the prescriptions you're bringing over there. We know you're doing it. You drop off the prescriptions and never pick them up. Isn't that right?"

Winstead's eyes seesawed back and forth. "Who got wasted? That pharmacist?"

Waterhouse leaned back again. "Yeah, *that* pharmacist. *That* pharmacist was a friend of mine, asshole."

"I didn't off him. Never even met the man."

"You going to tell us who's running the show," Jason ordered. "Or do we have to get the police involved?"

Winstead sucked in a deep breath and dropped his gaze to the floor. His cheeks began to quiver. Jason sensed the man was about to lose it.

"The first admission is always the hardest, Mr. Winstead," Jason persisted. "Start from the beginning."

Winstead leaned forward, burying his face in his hands. He rocked slowly back and forth. Jason saw Waterhouse open his mouth to speak, but held up a hand to stop him.

"Go on, Doug," Jason said calmly.

"I can't. They'll kill her if I talk."

"Who?"

"Charlie, my daughter." His voice was soft, almost a whisper.

"Doug, we don't really care about you. We need to know who's behind this," Jason replied. He still had his hand in the air, keeping Waterhouse from involving himself in the conversation. "Who are they?"

Winstead looked up at Jason. "Did you hear me? They'll kill her."

Waterhouse jumped in, his voice hard. "You leave us no choice. We'll have to go to the police. Then they'll know you talked."

Winstead's face flashed red with anger. He grunted, leapt across the table, and was on Waterhouse before he could react, toppling over the chair. Winstead was on top of Waterhouse, reaching and clutching at the Glock. Waterhouse was moving his arm back and forth, trying to keep the man from getting hold of it.

Jason pounced on the two men. Winstead had wrestled the gun from Waterhouse's hand. Jason, in turn, ripped it from Winstead's a split second before he could turn it on either of them. It slipped from Jason's fingers and dropped to the floor.

Winstead was not deterred. He forgot the firearm and slammed a fist into Waterhouse's jaw, ramming his head into the dark, hardwood floor. Winstead cocked for a second blow. Jason placed both hands under Winstead's arms and flung him off the private investigator.

Winstead rolled to the wall under a window and staggered to his knees.

Jason collected the pistol and leveled it at the kneeling Winstead. "That's enough!" Winstead looked like a feral animal, trapped and contemplating his next attack. He flexed his right hand repeatedly, balling it into a fist for a beat, then relaxing it. His cheeks puffed with every breath.

Waterhouse wiped a streak of crimson from his mouth with the back of his hand. His tongue moved inside his mouth, massaging another swollen area on his face. "I'm getting too old for this shit," he muttered.

Winstead stood up to his full height. "I need you both to leave. Now!"

A dull thump sounded from beyond the window. The glass shattered, exploding tiny shards into the room. The front of Winstead's head came off as if an explosive had detonated inside it. Red chunks of matter rained tissue, bone, and blood over Jason and Waterhouse.

CHAPTER 47

Several seconds elapsed as they processed what they'd just witnessed. In the moments that followed the disintegration of Winstead's skull, Jason, covered in splattered blood and chunks of gray matter, dropped to the floor. He collected himself, then slid along the floor, raised himself up beside the shattered window, and checked the narrow space between the houses. It was clear. Whoever had killed Winstead was gone.

Sucking in a deep breath, he summoned a grit he'd never known he possessed, going into damage control like a seasoned pro. "Don't touch anything," Jason commanded, as the pool of blood from the mangled head expanded in every direction.

"Hey, dipshit, I've been handling murder scenes since your mama was wiping snot from your nose," retorted Waterhouse.

"We need to search the house," Jason urged.

"We need to call the police!" said Waterhouse.

"Not yet," Jason countered. "Let's see if there's anything here that might give us any clues."

Waterhouse picked up Winstead's weapon and wiped Jason's fingerprints from it. "Let the police investigate it."

"Walter! We don't have time to discuss this. I'll go upstairs and search the bedrooms. You stay down here and look around. Don't leave any fingerprints. Remember, this is for Thomas."

Waterhouse mumbled something Jason couldn't here. Jason knew it was not complimentary. "Before we look around, follow me," said Waterhouse, stuffing his pistol into his waistband.

They jogged back to the Blazer. Walter replaced the gun in the glove box and found a box of latex gloves in the bed. They returned to the house, donning the gloves as they re-entered.

* * *

Jason raced upstairs, searching as if for a ticking bomb, finding nothing. He checked the final room and returned back downstairs.

Jason saw Waterhouse kneeling over a hole in the floor holding a crumpled, paper grocery bag.

"It's the freakin' mother lode," said Waterhouse with some excitement.

"How did you find this?" asked Jason, frowning.

"When the chair toppled over, one of the legs must have knocked some of the floorboards out of place. The carpet was sticking up, so I looked under it."

Jason peered into the bag. "Holy shit." Bundles of twenty-dollar bills bound with thick rubber bands filled the bag.

"We can't let the police see this," said Waterhouse. "I have an idea." He grabbed the bag from Jason and ran out the door.

They jogged to the Blazer one more time. Jason didn't want to let the private investigator out of his sight while he was holding the cash. Waterhouse removed the spare tire from the rack under the rear end. He rolled it quickly to the back door and into the house, while Jason carried the bag. Waterhouse punctured the black sidewall with a folding knife, and forced the bag of cash into the tire. He then replaced the tire under the chassis, ensuring the slice was against the underside of the truck. He returned to the house and dialed 911. He hung up and made another call.

"Jack, it's Walter Waterhouse. I'm at a crime scene. I need your help." Waterhouse gave the address.

"Who'd you call?"

"John Palmer."

"The detective?"

Waterhouse nodded. "Believe me, we're going to need a friend inside the department."

As they waited, they went over their stories three times.

CHAPTER 48

Two hours after Winstead's murder, Jason stood close by as a reluctant Waterhouse retrieved the money from the spare tire. "You mind backing up a little," Waterhouse chirped.

Jason complied with a very small retreat, staying within arm's length. Two minutes later, Waterhouse pulled the bag from the mangled tire. When the bag was free, Jason ripped it from the private investigator's hand. "I'll hold this," he said as he marched inside.

"What the fuck?" Waterhouse spat. Muttering virulent curses under his breath, he followed Jason inside. Christine and Peter were waiting for them.

"Did you two have fun today playing cops and robbers?" Peter kidded them upon seeing their clothing. Jason and Waterhouse had both surrendered their clothing as evidence and were wearing blue police jumpsuits.

Jason filled them in on the details.

It hadn't taken long for the police to figure out Jason and Waterhouse were innocent, as the splatter pattern indicated they'd been standing in front of Winstead when the shot tore his head open. Their statements had been taken by different detectives and must have sufficiently jived because they were allowed to go with warnings that more questioning would follow. Jason spotted Detective John Palmer at the scene and confronted him, saying Winstead's murder was a direct result of the activities at the Colonial. Palmer admitted something very strange was afoot, but the evidence in Winstead's death still didn't support murder.

Jason held up the bag and told Christine and Peter how they'd discovered the money.

"*How* much did you say it was?" asked Christine.

"Sixty-five thousand. And that's just what's left. We have no idea how much he may have spent," Waterhouse replied.

"They were paying Winstead to deliver the prescriptions," Jason said.

"You two do realize that you've stolen evidence in a criminal investigation, right? If the police find out, I'm sure it's a felony," Peter added. "Why didn't you just leave it?"

"Winstead ain't gonna be needing it," said Waterhouse. "This hunt we're on ain't paying none of my bills."

Peter stared at the skinny man.

"The money stays with me until we figure out what's going on," said Jason. He turned to the private eye. "You're welcome to walk away anytime."

"Screw you, jack wagon."

Jason stepped toward the scrawny man. "You want to mix it up, peckerhead? We can step outside anytime. 'Cause I'd hate to get your blood all over my carpet."

Peter stepped in, blocking his brother. Waterhouse moved away and sank into a chair like a scolded child. Jason glared a moment longer at Waterhouse, then managed to focus on Christine who was asking herself a question.

"How big is this thing Daddy stumbled onto?" She leaned with both hands on the table and appeared as if she might vomit.

Jason placed a hand on her shoulder. "Whatever it is, it's something much bigger than insurance fraud," he said.

"What makes you so sure?" Peter opened the fridge. "You got any beer?"

"There's sixty-five grand here. Hardly seems worth the thirty-two thousand the insurance company paid the Colonial."

"You all should have let the police handle it," added Peter.

"Well, we didn't and it's a little late for that now, isn't it?" Jason barked. Waterhouse wanted to keep the cash for obvious reasons. Jason had another. Because it was connected to Pettigrew's murder, he didn't want it out of his sight until all the dots were connected.

"How do we know Winstead wasn't just saving the money?" asked Christine.

"No way," said Jason. "There's a note about another payment coming after the final delivery. And…there's something else." Jason pulled the folded piece of artwork from his pocket and showed them all. Peter had seen it before at Waterhouse's place. His reaction was the same as it had been before: Jason saw his brother's eyes harden.

"What is it?" asked Christine.

"It's a drawing of a tattoo. Your father had the same design among his files. It was on the attacker's arm that day at your father's house. And I saw it on Jasmine's forearm. In the exact same spot. I think it's some sort of cult or group."

Christine rose up and scowled at the mention of Jasmine's name. Jason glanced away quickly. He handed the paper to Peter. "Don't you have a friend in DC who can find out about this?" Jason asked.

"Yeah, I do," said Peter. "He's an analyst in the counterfeit division of the Secret Service. His name's Tom Johnson. He was in my squad. Smartest man I know, got a PhD from MIT. He was recruited by the CIA, FBI, and every other alphabet in Washington. The guy's definitely wired in, but asking him to track down some obscure symbol from a dream seems like a helluva stretch."

"It wasn't just from a dream. I've seen this before. And by your reaction, so have you," Jason shot back.

"I'll see what I can do," Peter replied.

* * *

Zanns watched Cooper smile and pull a cigarette from his jacket. He took his sweet time lighting up and blowing the smoke in her direction. "The shit pile you find yourself in is getting deeper and smellier than you could ever imagine, Ms. Lily," he drawled.

The desire to reach out and grab the weasel by the throat welled inside her. She smiled, trying to hide her murderous ire. "Your men eliminated Winstead before he could say anything. It seems to me the problem is resolved."

"You're wrong. Rodgers is at his meeting with the three others. You remember, we spoke about it this morning." Cooper's tone was patronizing and sarcastic. He continued, "As I mentioned, the house is under electronic surveillance. We've been monitoring his phone calls and conversations for several days now." Cooper smiled.

"Have they mentioned a box of files?" Oliver had yet to find the files. With his flights to North Carolina, he'd been unable to continue his search.

"What kind of files?"

"Never mind, Steven. It's nothing."

"Rodgers and his gang are discussing Pettigrew's death and the fake prescriptions at this very moment. They've found Winstead's cash. They suspect something larger. Hammon is worried."

I don't care what Hammon thinks. "That's completely unjustified!"

"There's more," said Cooper.

Zanns shook her head, marveling at the man's audacity.

"They have a drawing of the tattoo."

Cooper had Zanns's full attention now. Her eyebrows arched. "Go on!"

"Rodgers saw the tattoo on Kader's arm. He saw it on the intruder's arm as well, during their struggle. They know the two are connected. Jason Rodgers is slowly connecting the dots, Lily."

Her goal had been to retrieve the files (and the drawing of the tattoo) before anyone could connect it to their organization. Now the tattoo had been uncovered, all her plans were endangered.

The same tattoo, stenciled on all of their arms, was the Arabic symbol for *Simoon*, "the Poison Wind." It was the only link to her ultrasecret group—and to the group's architect. Zanns had made them get the body art many years ago. The select few remaining in her homeland carried the same design on their arms. If the Americans figured out who was behind the Simoon before the event, they'd cancel it, and all their work would be wasted. As much as she wanted Rodgers alive to serve as their red herring, Lily Zanns understood the deeper, more pressing implications of his discovery.

How Pettigrew came to be in possession of it, she didn't know. At this point, it really didn't matter. What did matter was that Jason Rodgers and his three cohorts had seen it twice and knew there was a connection to her, to Jasmine, Sam, and Oliver. Rodgers had shown it to the three other members of his team. And because of that, all four had become liabilities. Rodgers's cronies would be rewarded with painful deaths. Jason Rodgers himself would be neutralized only after he'd served her purposes. It was time for the evidence Jasmine had planted in Rodgers's house to be put to use.

Cooper continued speaking, his words barely registering as Lily pondered the situation. His final statement jerked her back to reality. "If this blows up because of your incompetence, the deal's off—and you're out twenty-four million dollars."

Zanns studied him briefly. "Tell Hammon it will all be taken care of in twenty-four hours—including that pain in the ass, Rodgers."

CHAPTER 49

Wednesday, October 4

Peter Rodgers traced his finger over his brother's drawing. To the un-initiated, it resembled a fragment of an electrocardiogram, a squiggly line, nothing more. But it stirred in him distant yet painful memories. Memories he'd spent years conquering.

If there was anyone who could figure this out, it was Johnson. The last time either of them had seen it had been about thirty seconds before Lance Corporal Rodriguez had been blown into three large chunks and Tom Johnson lost both legs. Afterward, Peter had passed the intel up the chain, then went back to his other duties. In weeks, the symbol—but not the carnage—had been forgotten.

Peter dialed the number. Three rings later, Tom Johnson picked up.

"You legless good-for-nothing computer hack. You couldn't find your ass with a GPS, a compass, and a blood hound," said Peter.

It took a moment, but Johnson recognized his friend's voice. "Peter-fucking-Rodgers, how they hell are you, Sarge?"

"Earning an honest living, giving Americans a choice when it comes to buying firearms. Tom, you're not going to believe what I'm looking at."

240

* * *

Both her children were soldiers of the cause and knew nothing else. They'd been indoctrinated from a young age. Zanns knew that someday they would give their lives for her purpose. But in very different ways.

Lily Zanns possessed no maternal emotions. She did not think of Jasmine as her own flesh and blood. Though she'd given birth to her in a difficult twenty-hour labor and nurtured her into a beautiful, intelligent woman, Lily viewed her daughter as a soldier to be sacrificed. Of course, she would be martyred, hailed as a heroine. But ultimately—though she did not know it—Jasmine was expendable. She was, after all, female, and therefore had no claim to her father's birthright.

Sam was a different story. He, too, was a soldier and had been groomed for a historic fate. He was as skilled as his younger sister in weapons, hand-to-hand combat, explosives, and military tactics. His future, however, held no bounds. Because he was male and her firstborn, Sam was destined to fill his father's shoes in a spectacular fashion. Zanns had revealed that destiny to him almost a year ago, while she mourned the death of Sam's father. It was then that she'd told him of their real plan. Like a true patriot, he hadn't shrunk from it, but instead relished the idea.

At that time, Zanns had been two years into planning the jihad. First they would strike the infidels a crippling blow. Then, using the momentum from the devastating attack, they would set in motion the tumbling political dominoes that would cast out the imperialistic bastards, returning their country to its rightful place atop the Muslim and Arab world.

Zanns had already begun to lay the groundwork for Sam's ascent. Through other, trusted members of the Simoon back on the Arabian Peninsula, their coalition had been taking shape. Inside her homeland, they had reached out to potent Shi'a and Sunni power brokers and select religious leaders who were unhappy with the American occupation. Members of the Islamic Dawa Party and Supreme Islamic

Council who had been wooed with the money and the promise of power were already on board. Outside her country, factions sympathetic to their cause would provide soldiers, intelligence, and funds. Hammas, Hezbollah, al-Qaeda, the Palestinian Liberation Front, the Islamic Jihad Union, Al-Shabaab. Each in turn would be promised a seat at the table when the new order took shape. They would cast the American pigs out of their homeland and the Middle East altogether, and then they would turn their attention to annihilating the dirty Jews from the face of the planet.

At the head of that table would sit her son, Sam. By then he would be known by his given name, Sharif. When Sam's bravery in striking down the infidels became worldwide news, he would be positioned to fulfill their glorious mission. His father and Allah would look down from heaven and smile upon them.

Her bastard children had been her ticket to a life of privilege because of their father's prominence, status, and wealth. Her countrymen had starved and cowered under an oppressive thumb, but Zanns ignored those inconsistencies. After all, she loved the dictator, *her* dictator, Amo. Amo was his favorite, pet name. A name he let only those close to him use.

His real name was well known to the entire world—infamous, in fact. It was a name synonymous with death and suffering.

Zanns reflected as she took in the furniture, artifacts, and photos around her spacious study. She felt a brief twinge of sentiment. She recalled the turbulent twists and turns that had led her into his arms, and ultimately to this moment. Allah truly had tapped her for immortality.

Her biological parents were kind, loving souls who'd named her Delilah. Henri was a large black man with massive, gentle hands, who would lift her high above his head to squeals of delight. Imane was a dark-skinned Catholic missionary of Middle Eastern descent. They lived a quiet life in Iraq in a small village near Babil. Zanns smiled to herself. She was the only person still alive on the planet who knew that she'd been born to Christian parents.

At the age of ten, she'd returned home from school and called for her mother. When there was no response, Delilah began to look for her. Her search ended quickly and tragically.

Upon entering the bedroom of the small house, Delilah was assailed by the sight of blood everywhere. Her mother's throat had been slashed. Her dress was pulled up around her waist. Delilah knew unspeakable acts had been perpetrated on her before she died. Her father, on the other hand, had been shot twice. His testicles had been cut off and stuffed into both cheeks.

The hard-packed, earthen floor had turned black as it mixed with her parents' blood. The walls were smeared with cursed writings, using the crimson ink from her parent's veins.

Delilah screamed and fled the house, fearing the attackers would come for her. The next ten days were a blur. She roamed the desert, stopping to steal food and sleeping in the cold night air under the stars. On the tenth day, she snuck into a house whose occupants appeared to be away. Delilah found several pieces of bread and some goat's milk, devouring them quickly. She roamed the house. Finding a shawl, she swung it around her shoulders. When she turned, she saw the man standing in the doorway. She could see in his eyes that her-now tragic life would take another step downward into the pit of fire.

The man looked over his shoulder out the door to be certain they were alone. He blocked Delilah's only avenue of escape. The rape lasted hours. The man relented only because he grew tired. Delilah was tied and left exposed and bleeding until nightfall.

His name was Muhsin, which means beneficent and charitable. He was far from it. The wife's was named Fadwa. They kept her tied her up for two straight weeks. She was not allowed to bathe and was only untied so she could relieve herself while Muhsin watched. Her captivity lasted nearly a year. Muhsin beat her mercilessly, making her an example to his three daughters. During her slavery, Fadwa gave Delilah the most unpleasant of chores. The daughters ridiculed her. Once, she tried to run, but Muhsin ran her down a few hundred meters from the house. He unleashed on her a savage beating. Delilah knew then she would only be free when Muhsin and Fadwa no longer drew breath. That day, she began devising a plan.

Muhsin enjoyed his opium. As she performed her chores, Delilah stumbled upon his stash one morning. She scraped some of the powder from the small container into her palm. Over the course of a few months, Delilah managed to squirrel away enough to kill a horse. Her opportunity came one night when Fadwa had taken the girls to visit her mother in a village up the road. Delilah knew what would happen that night. Muhsin came to her. Delilah endured it. When Muhsin demanded tea, Delilah mixed a large amount of opium into it. Thirty minutes later, Muhsin was in a drug-induced coma. She found a large boulder and caved in his skull. For good measure, she cut off his manhood and stuffed it into his mouth as revenge for her father's mutilation.

Delilah ran for hours through the night, stopping to rest for a few minutes every so often. Fearing Muhsin would awaken from death and drag her back, she refused to stop. She stumbled upon a road in the dark night. As luck would have it, a large, dark sedan was passing and nearly hit her. The car screeched to a halt. A stout, robed man emerged from the backseat along with the driver and helped her into the car.

Seeing her state of malnutrition and uncleanliness, the man questioned the young girl. Delilah sat rocking in the soft leather, crying, unable to put into words what had happened or what she had done.

"My name is Ahmed," he told her. "Whatever you are afraid of cannot hurt you here. You are safe, my child."

She slept on the soft leather during the ride. When she awoke, it was daylight. Ahmed coaxed her from the vehicle. They had stopped outside a beautiful religious building. "Come, child," he said. "You are safe now. This is my mosque. No one can hurt you."

"Where are we?" asked Delilah.

"Far away from your tormentors. Near Tikrit."

He took her inside, where he knelt in prayer. Delilah watched, fascinated. When he was finished, he led her outside and down a path to his house a hundred meters away. The imam's wife made her a sumptuous lunch. Delilah showered, was given fresh clothes, and slept restfully for the first time in over twelve months. Never again would she experience poverty or fear.

The cleric and his spouse guided her to adulthood, educating her and revealing to her that Allah was the one true God and Islam the one true faith.

During that time, the cleric introduced her to a very good friend of his. A young man, tall and dark, with a thick, bushy moustache. He had been exiled, had returned, and was soon to be jailed. Over the course of the next ten years, she would meet him several times more. Though he was married to three other wives over the years, that young man gave her two children and changed Delilah's life forever. Delilah, a.k.a. Lily Zanns, had even taken his name.

Now her every action had been in preparation to avenge him, to perpetrate the ultimate jihad. Three years of tedious preparation would come down to an event that would last less than five seconds. Her children, her soldiers, were prepared, ready for battle—ready to die. After tonight, she would never see Jasmine again. She would only look upon her son many years from now. They would avenge their father, a man they had never known.

The whole world knew the public person. Zanns knew the private man—intimately. She had caressed his warm, olive skin and looked into his soulless eyes as he ravaged her in animalistic love. Though they would never be together again, she ached for those long-ago days. This mission was her final tribute to him.

Zanns removed a folded piece of paper from inside her blouse. She always kept it close to her heart, stuffed inside her brassiere. Unfolding it, she scanned Amo's final letter to his people, penned days before his death. She read the final paragraph, her favorite passage:

Dear faithful people, I say good-bye to you, but I will be with the merciful God who helps those who take revenge in him and who will never disappoint any faithful, honest believer...Allahu Akbar...Allahu Akbar...Long live our nation...Long live our great struggling people...Long live Iraq, long live Iraq...Long live Palestine...Long live jihad and the mujahedeen.

Saddam Hussein Abd-al-Majid al-Tikriti, President and Commander in Chief of the Iraqi Mujahed Armed Forces

With two fingers, she stroked the amulet hanging around her neck. Opening it, she gazed down at his smiling face. Amo, her beloved Amo, had been taken into custody years ago, captured in a spider hole by the Americans. She'd tracked his case through the media and secret messages embedded in the web site, which were relayed through his incompetent lawyers. Then she had watched the horrific cell phone video as he was ridiculed while the noose was placed around his neck.

She missed him deeply, but she knew Saddam would be pleased by her work.

* * *

It had happened again. She'd made a fool of herself over a man.

Jason had been the latest in a string of failed relationships. Initially, he'd seemed different than the others. He was so kind and attentive. But then that brat of a son demanded too much attention, getting in the way of her quality time with Jason. And that bitch of an ex-wife was always calling to talk about the Little Prince. She, Sheila Boquist, deserved some consideration, some attention, too. What was so difficult about that?

Thinking back, the signs of the impending breakup had been painfully obvious. She'd ignored them, as always. Longer intervals between phone calls followed by less-frequent dates. Jason delivered the blow, quick and hard. His words reached inside her like hot, searing tongs, ripping out her heart and with it the painful memory of every failed relationship she'd ever had. A tear inched down her face. She shook her head, trying to shake the pain and memories.

Bastards, she thought. *All men are bastards.*

She inserted the key into the lock of the community mailbox and opened the tiny door. Three envelopes. Two were bills. The third was a card of some sort with her name typed on it. She opened it, read the typewritten words, and her heart soared.

Sheila,

I would like to meet you tonight to talk about our relationship. Please meet me at Maggie's Tavern at seven.

Jason

CHAPTER 50

Christine scrutinized Jason coldly. Jason's wallet in her pocket pressed against her thigh. It was her small, leather hostage. He was not getting it back until she knew the truth. They had agreed to meet on Sunday. But her father's coded voice message had disintegrated those plans.

"It's a cover for something larger. It has to be," said Jason. "It's more than insurance fraud."

"We already talked about this," Christine said impatiently. Jason had agreed to meet her to discuss their past, not his obsession. "We're here to talk about what happened between us. Stop trying to avoid it. I want answers. It ends here and now!"

They were at a table in the rear of Maggie's Tavern, an upscale but generic eatery in the Port Warwick section of Newport News. Jason sat with a view of the entrance. After following the now-dead Winstead, Jason had left the rented Fusion in the parking lot at the Colonial. That left him without a ride. He now had two cars parked at the pharmacy. Peter had given him a ride to rent another vehicle. This one was a Saturn

248

SL1. Jason hadn't seen anyone following them, but he just didn't know anymore. Sometimes it felt as if he had a fleet of cars on his tail.

"Cut me some slack, will you? We'll get to that."

"Make it quick."

He leaned over the table, closer. "I watched the DVD your father left in his files again. I'd looked at it for hours, but didn't see anything that looked important. Then I saw it."

Christine looked to the ceiling in disgust. When she looked at him again, she saw reflected in Jason's eyes her own expanding frustration. *Get to the point!*

"What?" she asked with a roll of her eyes.

"It happened just as Sam Fairing was leaving the Colonial. He'd finished closing up and shutting down. Then, as he was walking out the door, he grabbed an empty prescription bag from the will-call bin."

"So?"

"It was the same dirty, crumpled bag your father left for us in his files. The one with Winstead's name on it. You see, after Sam left the pharmacy, he drove immediately to the Lions Bridge with the empty prescription bag. Don't you see what this means?"

"I don't feel like playing twenty questions. Why don't you tell me?"

"The bag was stained with red clay. The kind of clay you find over there near the bridge and the Noland Trail. Sam left the bag there. I think I know the spot, it was a depression under a dead tree. Sam was sending a signal. It's an old spy trick—a dead drop. Sam was signaling someone about something, or he retrieved some information and left the bag as a signal that the package was received. My guess is he retrieved a package of information or money. Then he left the bag to confirm the pickup. Except your father got there and found the empty prescription bag. That's when he got caught."

Christine stared at him with utter contempt.

"Don't you see? There's a conspiracy. The last time it happened, Winstead dropped a prescription at the Colonial on September 14. On the fifteenth, Thomas died. Your father was following Fairing the night he was killed. They found out he was on to them, and they killed him. Maybe he saw what was happening at the bridge, retrieved the bag, and whoever was supposed to find it caught him. Your father ran. He ran to the Colonial, where they caught up to him. Somewhere in all that, he was shot through the shoulder. They sutured him up, got him drunk, and made it look like he died in a car accident—"

"Enough!" Christine's hand made a wide arc toward Jason's face.

Jason was prepared for it. With the reflexes honed by years of training in Tae Kwon Doe, he reached up and grabbed her arm in midair, stopping it cold with a dull smack of skin on skin. Christine tried to yank her arm away. Jason held tight.

"I don't want to talk about it anymore. Do you understand me?" Christine seethed.

Jason held her gaze, clamping her arm in a viselike grip. He lowered it and pressed it to the tabletop. "No, it's not enough. There's more," he said. "When I was looking at the DVD, I got frustrated because I couldn't figure out what was going on. I threw a book at the mantel. A vase fell and broke. I found something inside it. It was a tiny camera and microphone. Chrissie, they bugged my house! People are following me, watching me. They're concerned about what I know. That's why Jasmine is so interested in me. Someone wants to know what I know. They probably heard everything we were talking about last night!"

Hearing Jasmine's name only fueled her ire. "I don't care! Do you hear me? You owe me answers. And I want them *right now!*"

"But you also want to get some things off your chest as well, don't you?"

"You're damn right I do."

He raised his hands into the air, releasing her arm. "I need a drink." Jason waved at the waitress and ordered a gin and tonic. When the waitress was gone, he said, "Okay. Go ahead. Tell me what you've waited all these years to say."

Christine bit her lip, collecting her thoughts. Old passions and new jealousies swirled inside her. This was the conversation she'd dreamt about. A longing that began the day Jason had dumped her. She swallowed and began. "You really crushed me, Jason. I was screwed up for a long time. No, you know what? There's no word close to describing what you did to me. You effed me over and effed up my head for years, in ways I could never imagine one person doing to another!"

Jason looked directly into her eyes. He nodded slightly, acknowledging his guilt. He opened his mouth, but Christine cut him off. "I spent a lot of nights wondering what I did wrong," she continued. "What did I do to deserve to be treated that way? You freakin' disappeared! You never returned my calls. Why? Why now, after all these years, did you come back? You owe me an explanation." As the words flowed from her, Christine could feel the pulse in her head pumping like a jackhammer.

The waitress returned with their meals and a round of drinks. A burger, coleslaw, and steak fries for him, and for Christine, a chicken caesar salad. They ate sparingly, looking everywhere but at each other. Christine focused on a couple with two small children eating and laughing together. The kids jabbered incessantly, laughing at silly faces made by their father. Mom rolled her eyes. That family was the antithesis of her life.

Jason paid no attention to his food. "Chrissie, I'm ashamed of what I did. But not for the reasons you might think. I ran away from a problem that I should've hit straight on. In the years since we stopped seeing—I mean since I left—I've been married and had a wonderful son. Now I'm divorced. Michael's a great kid, and I can't imagine my life without him. But not a week goes by that I don't think about what might have been if I stayed around. In some ways, I regret it immensely."

"Then why *did* you leave?"

"Because your father's business depended on it."

"*What?* So it's Daddy's fault?" Her voice regained its steely timbre. "You're blaming him now that he's gone and can't defend himself!"

"No. I became a liability to your father. I made a mistake."

"You're damn right you made a mistake!"

"That's not what I'm talking about. I made a medication error." Jason toyed with a fork on the table. "This is hard. It's hard to find the right words, so please don't interrupt me until I'm done."

Christine sensed the forced determination in his words and read it in his tense neck muscles.

"I'd been with the Colonial for about nine months. One day in May, I refilled a prescription for a nice, elderly woman named Ada Mae Renforth. She was seventy years old and taking several heart medications.

"Two days later, your father called me into his office. He said that he'd got a call from the patient's daughter saying Ada Mae was dead, and we'd filled the prescription with the wrong medication. She said we—I mean, I—killed her mother. After that everything happened very quickly. The family hired a lawyer who sat down with your father and his lawyers. According to them, the evidence against me was overwhelming."

His voice cracked. He cleared his throat for what seemed like the tenth time. "The whole matter went on for a month. Your father's lawyers said that he was underinsured and when the family sued he would lose the business—"

"I remember Ada Mae. But I never heard about any of this," said Christine.

"Your father didn't want you to know about it. It looked like your father and I were going to be taken to court. They would sue and win a multimillion-dollar settlement. Needless to say, I was paralyzed with fear. I thought my career as a pharmacist was over before it ever really began.

"But the thing is, I remembered filling those prescriptions, and I *know* I filled them correctly, because the technician at the time had dropped Ada Mae's pills all over the floor. We spent fifteen minutes picking them up. We tossed the dropped pills and refilled the prescription with new ones. I spent an hour making sure those pills were right. I checked and double-checked them. I remember comparing the spilled pills to the fresh ones. They were the same—round and white.

"You know, I fill hundreds of prescriptions a day. Some you don't ever remember. Some you do, because you can associate certain events with them, like a customer yelling at you. That's what this was like." Jason covered his mouth with his hand. "I filled the prescription correctly.

"Your father and I met with the lawyers, and they showed us the bottle. It was the highest strength available. Blue, oblong tablets. Four times Ada Mae's regular dose. She had renal failure. The excessive dose built up in her blood and killed her, so they said. It was the correct medication, just too much of it. I *didn't* make that mistake. But they said I did."

"So why didn't you fight it?" Christine demanded.

"I was young and inexperienced. I was still trying to figure out how to be a pharmacist. I guess I questioned myself enough at the time. But the more I thought about it and recalled it over the years, the more certain I was that I'd filled it correctly." He paused and took a large gulp of gin. His quaking hand rattled the ice in the glass.

"After I found out about the mistake, I could barely concentrate. I couldn't sleep. I was depressed." Jason's eyes were beginning to glisten.

Christine had listened to his tale with a volcanic anger only barely contained. Now, her indignation found its voice. "You never confided in me, Jason. For Christ's sake, you could've said something!"

"It wasn't because of you. Your father said I couldn't tell anyone, not even you."

"Damn you!" Christine slapped the table with the palm of her hand. "Who cares what Dad said? Why! Why did you have to keep quiet about it? I wouldn't have told anyone. We were in love!" *We could have worked it out!*

"Calm down!" Jason demanded. "Lower your voice! I'm trying to explain!" Jason ran a hand through his hair and pushed a lungful of air at the ceiling. A few seconds later, he reached over and touched her arm. Christine leaned back and yanked it under the table. Jason shook his head in frustration. "I *did* have to keep quiet! Your father's lawyers told him to keep the whole thing under wraps. It was a condition set by the people advising him. I continued to work my regular shifts, petrified with every prescription I filled. He could've fired me. But they said that would be as good as an admission of guilt. So I worked.

"Then something unexpected happened. Suddenly, the family said they would drop the charges and promise not to sue. But there were some conditions."

"What conditions?" she demanded.

"The woman's family received a large payment. I don't know how much it was. Your father would never tell me. But whatever it was, it was enough to satisfy the family and their lawyers. Your father hinted that the suits who were defending him, the lawyers and the insurance company, contributed the money. These guys were well connected and had *very* deep pockets.

"As long as I left the Colonial and never worked there again or had any contact with him or you, they'd let me and the Colonial off the hook. If I stayed or resisted in any way, they'd pursue the matter in court. Your father came to my apartment with tears in his eyes and told me about the offer. I'd explained to him that I'd filled the prescription correctly. And he truly believed me. He said he'd stand behind me and fight it in court if necessary. That's the kind of man your father was. He was ready to put his career and his business on the line for me. I think that's because he knew how we felt about each other. But in the end, the choice was mine."

Christine placed her fingers near her temple. "Jason, I believe that you *think* you filled the prescription correctly—"

"*Think?* I filled it correctly!" Jason shook his head. "You think I'm imagining all this?"

"I'm just saying, if you filled it correctly, then how did the wrong pills end up in the bottle?"

"Chrissie, I don't have all the answers. I'm telling you what I remember."

Christine sighed. "I'm sorry."

Jason sipped his iced tea. "Your father gave me a day to think it over. If I stayed, your father would've lost the business. I decided to leave. In a weird sort of way, I kind of did it for you. Better your father kept the pharmacy and provide for you. I owed your father. He was ready to fight for me. Everything I'm doing now is my repayment to him. That's why I need find out who killed him."

Christine lowered her face into hands. "This is not what I wanted to hear!"

"I know it's not. But it's the truth."

Thoroughly confused, her emotions listed from side to side like a ship's mast in a hurricane. Her hatred for Jason was being battered by the realization that he'd tried to do the right thing, the best thing, considering the circumstances. "Damn you!" was all she could say again.

Jason continued. "The whole matter was never made public. I guess it was part of whatever settlement was reached. The State Board of Pharmacy was never notified. If they'd found out, I would've lost my license to practice." Christine felt Jason's hand touch her elbow. The contact seared her skin. She hesitated, then moved it away again.

Jason didn't let up. "I loved you very much. I'll always wonder what would have been if we'd stayed together. I think about you a lot, even more now that I've been able to see you again." His voice cracked on the word "think."

Christine felt the room begin to spin. She summoned the courage to meet his eyes, which revealed the roiling emotions he was trying to keep at bay. The last time she'd seen him this tormented was the day on the bench down by the river, when he told they were through.

She sat paralyzed. Part of her wanted to revive her dead father and tell him off, to give him the type of tongue-lashing the Pettigrews were known for. Another part wanted to slap Jason. Still other parts, those being trampled on by her selfish, unfulfilled wants, were trying to understand what kind of choice Jason had been asked to make.

He said softly, "I'm sorry, Chrissie."

A third time, his hand glided toward her. She pulled away again. As she did, she saw Jason's eyes register something over her shoulder.

"Oh, no. Not again," he said.

Christine turned and saw Sheila Boquist, eyes narrowed and fists clenched, storming toward their booth. Her rage was palpable.

Sheila arrived at the booth and—without uttering a word—pummeled Jason with her fists in a clumsy, spastic attack. She landed several futile blows. Unhappy with her mosquito-like punches, Sheila swung her purse in wide arcs, landing it about his head. She paused and screamed for the whole restaurant to hear, "You lying piece of shit! You invite me to dinner, just to humiliate me in front of this tramp!" Sheila jabbed at him four more times as Jason covered his head with his arms. "It's not bad enough you dump me, you have to rub my face in it. You fuckin' weasel! You want to see how it feels—"

"That's enough!" Christine shrieked. "Stop it!"

Sheila paused at the sound of Christine's voice. It was as if Sheila realized she was expending her energy bashing the wrong person. Sheila wound up, arcing her heavy cloth purse at Christine's head.

"Shut up, you stupid bitch!" Sheila screamed.

CHAPTER 51

Sheila stormed about her bedroom. She ripped her pump from her right foot and fired it against the far wall, screaming obscenities. She tromped back and forth lopsidedly, shedding clothes, imagining the wonderful, dreadful deeds she'd like to inflict on Jason. Ten minutes later, she was in the shower, letting the steaming water pummel her skin. She thought about the chilled Chardonnay sitting on her nightstand. Her heart had begun to slow, along with her heavy breaths. The wine would glide down her throat easily, calm her nerves. With the wine at her side, she'd phone Amy and tell her what the horse's ass had done.

She stepped out of the shower, still muttering to herself. After toweling off, she walked naked into her bedroom. Then she halted, as if hitting an invisible wall. She instinctively covered her breasts.

Two hooded figures clad in black stood among the discarded clothes. One was tall and lean, with breasts protruding from under her dark sweater. The other was shorter, more masculine.

Her self-consciousness did not last long. "Who the hell—" Sheila stammered. She spun and raced back into the bathroom, trying desperately to slam the door. The short one threw his body into it before it closed, knocking the door and Sheila backward. Wood splintered. Screws ripped from hinges. Sheila stumbled to the cold tile and scooted away, attempting to put precious inches between her and the intruder. He was too fast. Grabbing a fistful of her ruby hair, he wrenched her up by their roots.

His fist pounded her face, knocking her down again and into the wet shower stall. The plastic curtain popped from its hangers, cascading over her. Blinded by the curtain, she kicked wildly. Her foot connected with flesh, but the short man cast the blow aside with ease. He clamped two hands around an ankle, kicked the fallen door out of the way, and dragged her back into the bedroom. Sheila yelped in fear and pain as he nearly tore the hair from her head, yanking her to her feet.

"Restrain her," the masked woman commanded her companion.

Behind Sheila now, the man wrapped an arm around her neck while pulling back on her hair, thrusting her chin into the air. The man leaned against the wall, wrapped his left leg around Sheila's left knee, and repeated the procedure with the other side. He released her hair and slid both his arms around her, pinning her arms to her side. Her right arm was slung behind her back, exposing her right side. Sheila's panicked gasps filled the room. The masked woman moved in, her left arm hiding something behind her.

Sheila struggled with every ounce of strength she possessed. Her spasms were puny and weak against the man's restraint.

"It's too bad such a beautiful body has to go to waste," said the woman, bringing the knife into view. The glint of the short, steel blade flashed.

Sheila tensed, redoubling her efforts to break loose. Panic boiled into sheer terror. She whimpered, cried, and groaned all at once. The woman removed her hood. Sheila stared into two black eyes contemplating her naked body.

"The least I can do is let you look into the eyes of the person who'll send you to hell."

The woman sank the four-inch knife to its hilt, piercing the perfect skin. Sheila shuddered. Her green eyes widened, whites on all sides, as she realized death was at hand. Every muscle contracted. Sheila seized, clenching as her killer sliced toward the midline, stopping when the blade connected with the sternum. In her last, terrifying moments, Sheila saw the murderess's eyes sparkle.

As the life ebbed from her, Sheila heard the woman whisper, "Simoon."

Then everything went black.

* * *

Jasmine Kader released the knife, leaving it protruding from the wound as blood pulsed over the handle. The woman's muscles relaxed, and Sam released her, letting her fall to the floor. The woman landed on her side, literally dead weight, and half rolled onto her chest. The knife, taken from Jason Rodgers's kitchen and imbedded in her ribcage, stopped a complete roll onto the stomach. Blood oozed onto the carpet, creating a dark crimson puddle. Urine dribbled from the bladder.

Fairing stepped over the body. Kader produced Rodgers's stolen gun from her waistband, a Smith and Wesson 645 semiautomatic. She removed it from the clear plastic bag and dropped it onto the carpet. The crumpled typewritten invitation followed. Kader strolled out of the bedroom to the top of the stairs, retrieving the small plastic bag she'd left there. From it, she removed the wine glass taken from the Southern Belle coated with Rodgers's fingerprints. She placed it beside Boquist's glass. Kader smiled at her good fortune. Allah had truly blessed them. The woman had decided to have a glass of wine. Perfect.

The brother and sister assassins departed through the back door, sneaking through backyards to Kader's waiting Lexus. She removed a cell phone. It had been purchased this afternoon under an assumed name by Oliver.

"Nine-one-one operator. What's your emergency?"

"There was yelling and screaming coming from next door. It was a woman. Then a man ran out of the house. He was driving a red Mustang. I think she's been hurt." Jasmine was aware that Jason had not been driving his Mustang in the last few days. By mentioning Jason's vehicle, she would cement his fictitious presence at the woman's house.

"What address are you calling from?"

"I'm calling from a cell phone. But I can give you the address." Kader gave the dispatcher the house number and street.

"And what is your name, ma'am?"

Kader gave a phony name.

"I'll send a unit out there right away. Can I have your phone number, please?"

Kader recited it, then added, "Please hurry. It sounds bad."

CHAPTER 52

The small, beach parking area sat across the street from the Windsor Towers. A tall hedgerow at the edge of the lot, combined with the landscaping and shrubbery of the towers, obscured the view. Pettigrew's GPS locator beacon was active and still transmitting a signal from somewhere on Fairing's Lexus, which was parked across the street in the Windsor Towers lot, and had been for some time. Apparently, Sam wasn't aware of the beacon's existence.

Jason had reconnoitered the parking lot, spied Fairing's vehicle, and returned to the SUV. Peter in the backseat, Waterhouse behind the wheel, and Jason in the passenger seat were perched in a Dodge Durango waiting for the Lexus to move. Waterhouse had decided it would be best henceforth not to use their own vehicles, in order to avoid Jason's tail and any tracking devices they might have used. Waterhouse had borrowed the SUV from an associate he contracted with occasionally. Neither the parking lot nor the lower fourth of the Windsor Towers were visible from their vantage point. The only other car in the beach parking area was a sedan parked four rows away, and as far as Jason could see, it was empty.

When Sheila had begun hitting Christine with her purse in the restaurant, Jason had stood up, wrapped his arms around her, and literally carried her out of the restaurant. Jason returned, paid their bill, and sneaked out a back door with Christine, while the manager of the restaurant argued with an apoplectic Sheila out front.

Christine distanced herself from Jason and sped off angrily as he climbed into his new car, the Saturn SL1. He caught a glimpse of her face before she turned away. Tears glistened on her cheek.

Numbness overwhelmed him as he drove straight to Waterhouse's to meet up with the private eye and Peter. Jason pushed aside his emotions, and explained his hunch to Peter and Waterhouse.

"Are you sure about this?" Peter asked, expelling a lungful of smoke out the window.

"I wouldn't bet the house on it. But pretty sure," Jason answered. "I told you, Winstead dropped off the prescription on the fourteenth. The next night Pettigrew died. Thomas followed Fairing to the Lions Bridge. Fairing stopped for ten minutes, then went home. Pettigrew saw something he wasn't supposed to, and that's why he was killed."

"And you think the same thing is going to happen tonight?" Peter persisted.

Jason explained again, "The prescription dropped off at the Colonial is a signal for a meeting or a pickup. If my guess is correct, Fairing will be leaving shortly to go to the Lions Bridge."

As if on cue, the device in his hands beeped. The beacon began to move. "Fairing's car is leaving the parking lot," Jason bragged.

"Well, I'll be damned," Waterhouse said as he turned the ignition.

"He's at the intersection, just up ahead," said Jason.

"We'll let him make the turn and then we'll catch up. We can't lose him with that thing," the private investigator advised.

Two minutes later, Fairing turned right onto Mercury Boulevard from Riverdale Road. "If he takes the most direct route," Jason said, "he'll go north on Warwick."

Waterhouse drove to the intersection. When the light turned green, Jason announced Fairing had taken the off ramp to Warwick Boulevard. "He's waiting at the light there. Make sure you stay out of sight. We don't want to get too close."

Fairing's Lexus followed the exact route to the bridge Jason had predicted. Waterhouse, a half mile behind, stayed out of sight. Three minutes after Fairing parked on the north end of the bridge, the Durango rolled over the span.

"Keep going," Jason instructed. All three craned their necks. The Lexus was there, but unoccupied. Waterhouse turned left onto Museum Parkway, out of sight.

Just past the bend, they parked and exited, jogging back to the corner. They kneeled near a tall, wide pine tree, watching and waiting. Minutes later, Fairing descended the knoll, walking down the slope past the statue of the man and the rearing steed.

"He's carrying something," Peter whispered, pointing.

Fairing carried a flat, dark package under his arm. He looked around, climbed in the Lexus, and backed out. "Let's go see what he did," Peter commanded.

"No, wait," Jason ordered, stopping Peter and the investigator. "If I'm right, there will be another car shortly. Someone's going to retrieve the prescription bag. Let's give it thirty minutes."

Fifteen minutes after Fairing had backed out of the parking spot, a pair of headlights rounded the bend on the far side of the bridge.

"That's not Fairing coming back, is it?" Peter asked.

"No, it's someone else," Jason answered, examining the GPS monitor.

The vehicle was a dark blue or black sedan. It was hard to be sure in the dim moonlight. The driver exited the car and jogged up the incline to the entrance of the Noland Trail. He returned two minutes later carrying the slender, waxy-white prescription bag.

CHAPTER 53

"We need to find out what's going on in there," Jason whispered. "And what's in that package."

Fairing had driven directly from the Lions Bridge to Zanns's mansion. The three men were watching the mansion from a quarter mile away.

Waterhouse walked to the rear of the borrowed SUV and opened the hatch. He climbed back in holding a large black bag filled with electronic gear. He withdrew a small, satellite-dish-like contraption and a camcorder. "We can use these," he announced.

"What is it?" Jason asked, taking the gadget.

"Parabolic microphone with a high-intensity laser. It works off of the vibrations in the window. We can record what we see with this small camcorder. Hopefully, they'll discuss what's in the package, and we can nail 'em."

* * *

The package sat on Zanns's elegant desk. Another cardboard shipper wrapped in black plastic. Sam and Lily sipped coffee in silence from demitasses.

"Where is Jasmine?" she asked her son.

"She dropped me off about an hour ago," Fairing replied. "If she is late, she must have a good reason."

As with all the other deliveries, the packaged contained highly classified information. With each shipment, Zanns and her Simoon had been able to plan their attack with amazing precision. The pearls contained within tonight's package would finalize their attack. Would it be the final go-ahead? Or would all of their work be cancelled? Zanns silently recited a verse from the Quran, praying to Allah that everything was in place. The package would not be opened it until everyone was present and they were well up the York River. The hyper-sensitive nerves in her gut danced to a rapid tempo.

* * *

Jason explained Zanns's security system to Peter and Water-house. He remembered her bragging about the ground sensors and infrared lasers.

Waterhouse found a gap in a hedgerow, a quarter mile downriver from Zanns's estate. They followed the slope to the James and made their way north along the shore to the edge of Zanns's property. They moved only when the clouds sporadically hid the moon.

Waterhouse carried bags with the parabolic microphone and its camcorder in a case slung over his shoulder, along with another bag of electronic equipment. Jason lugged a video camera and tripod. Peter had jammed his pistol into the waistband of his back and was on point.

Along the water's edge, they hunched low, heading north toward the mansion. They passed through three properties, staying as far from the houses as possible, skirting the water, and staying out of view of the houses' occupants. Piers berthed large powerboats suspended from covered lifts. The third dock sported a small, metal johnboat outfitted with a small outboard motor and three fishing rods.

Peter held up a clenched fist, stopping the trio. They knelt near a hedge, looking out over the water. Zanns's yacht, moored a hundred yards offshore, was backlit by the moon. The low rumble of its idling engines caught their attention. Twenty-five yards beyond, the float plane bobbed, unattended.

The motorized dingy *Retribution* was tied to the larger vessel, and though a service boat, it was larger than any vessel Jason could afford. The clanging of hatches interrupted the humming engines. They watched as a tall man walked along the port side and climbed a ladder to the bridge.

"That's Oliver, Zanns's assistant. What the hell is he doing out there at this hour?" Jason asked.

"I don't know, but if they're going for a ride, we've got a problem," Waterhouse replied.

"We've got to know what they're discussing, or we may never find out what this is all about," Jason whispered sternly.

"If anyone's got any bright ideas, now's the time to speak up," Peter said.

* * *

Zanns answered the bell herself.

"Daughter, what kept you?" she asked when she opened the door and saw Jasmine climbing the steps. The sensors out front chimed that a car had entered the drive.

"I drove by Ms. Boquist's house to make sure that the police are making the appropriate progress. I apologize for my tardiness."

"Nonsense. What did you find out?"

"They are on scene now. My contact in York County says they're tracing the gun. They should know that it is Rodgers's in about thirty minutes."

"Excellent," Zanns said, smiling. "Let us have a drink before we sail. Cooper's men have placed tracking devices on the cars of Rodgers and his accomplices. Those cars are sitting idle. Do you know where Rodgers is right now?"

"Unfortunately, I don't," Kader replied. "After the incident at the restaurant, he did not go home."

* * *

Peter and Jason humped back to the dock. Waterhouse stayed behind, keeping an eye on the house and yacht. Finally, Oliver climbed into *Retribution*, leaving *Vengeance's* diesel engines purring. The engine of the powered launch whined to life. With a turn of the wheel and a push on the throttle, the launch zipped into a tight turn, heading for shore.

Using the cover of the high-pitched engine noise, Waterhouse whistled two short blasts. A minute later, Jason returned to Waterhouse's side. "The big guy just headed for shore," the private investigator said.

"Pete's got the boat ready," Jason replied. "He won't start it until everyone's on board and they're under way. They're definitely going for a ride."

"We need a different plan. We can't get close enough to use the parabolic mike without being spotted. We'll have to get this contact mike on board." Waterhouse held a tiny listening device. "It's small enough to be put anywhere. In a lamp, under a desk, in a bookcase. Then I can tune a radio and a recorder to the frequency, and we'll be able to hear what they're saying. Someone's going to have to swim out there and place it on the boat."

"We don't have time. They could come out any minute."

"We have to make time."

"How?"

"You said she has sensors around the property?"

Jason nodded. "Every ten feet around the perimeter."

Waterhouse scratched his three-day beard. "Trip 'em. Should be enough of a diversion to give us time. But we have to move fast."

* * *

Zanns, Fairing, Kader, and Oliver marched to the French doors. Just before Oliver reached for the handle, a red light in the corner of the living room began flashing. A muted klaxon sounded in sync with the pulsing beam.

"A ground sensor's been tripped," said Oliver.

"Sam, Oliver, check on it," said Zanns.

Oliver walked quickly to the office, checked the console, and returned quickly. "Southwest corner near the water! I'll go."

"Take Sam with you. Call the monitoring company and tell them it's a false alarm. No police tonight!" Zanns barked at Jasmine, who complied.

Fairing and Oliver jogged out the door carrying pistols. Jasmine, waiting inside the house, pulled a weapon from her boot. Zanns joined her, toting her own handgun.

* * *

Peter eased the johnboat away from the dock, heading south. The neighbor's house was dark, and luckily no one came running as Peter yanked on the pull cord several times before it caught.

Waterhouse crouched low in the bow. Peter wheeled right and headed toward the anchored yacht only after reaching midriver. In the distance, the heavy night air carried the intermittent, muted tones of an alarm. He maneuvered upstream until the small craft created a straight three-point line with the mansion and the ship. The huge ship obscured the house. Peter jerked the wheel right again and headed straight for the massive vessel, the throttle set as low as it would go. The drone of the engine could be heard, but, God willing, in the darkness they would be invisible. Twenty feet from the yacht, he cut the engine and drifted in. Waterhouse kneeled on the bow, ready to stop their forward progress. The puny johnboat looked like a barnacle on the belly of gigantic whale.

* * *

Jason was in the water under the same dock from which Peter had stolen the boat. He'd crept straight toward the house after Waterhouse left. Eighty feet away, a dim red glow began to flash inside the downstairs living room. He had tripped one of the sensors. Dropping to his belly, he crept back on all fours quickly and quietly, not waiting to see who emerged. He lay on the dock and slipped into the shallow, cold water under the wooden pier as two figures emerged from the house.

Floating on his back, his face inches from the weathered wood, Jason pushed his hands against the rocky bottom to keep his head above water.

* * *

After being hoisted up in Peter's cupped hands and hidden by the yacht's enormous superstructure, Waterhouse rose to full height on the starboard side. The bow aimed toward the James River Bridge. The massive vessel's engines vibrated beneath him. He slipped aft, toward the door to the main salon. Seconds later, he dropped onto the deck.

* * *

Oliver and Fairing circled three times, finding no sign of intruders. The neighboring house was dark. The hum of a small outboard motor wafted to them. It was not an uncommon sound on the river at night. Even that had stopped. Satisfied, Fairing motioned for them to return to the house.

"It must have been an animal, a deer perhaps," Fairing said.

"Perhaps," Oliver replied before placing a hand on Fairing's arm.

"What's wrong?" Fairing asked.

Oliver pointed to the neighbor's dock. "The boat is gone from its berth on the dock. I haven't seen it used in weeks."

* * *

Jason moved out from under the dock. He grabbed the splintering planks and began to pull himself up. Two shadowy figures emerged from the tree line heading straight for the pier. The sight of the weapons in their hands caused his heart to skip a beat. Jason froze.

Had they seen him? Had they spotted the missing boat?

If he ran, he was sure to be spotted. Praying he hadn't been seen, he dropped beneath the water's surface once more. Footfalls grew louder, swooshing in the ankle-length grass. He closed his eyes, and Michael appeared in his mind. Jason mouthed the words to the Lord's Prayer, hoping he would live to see his son again.

They strode onto the pier. The soles of their shoes were inches above his head. He squeezed his eyes shut, sucked in a quiet breath, and ducked under the frigid water.

* * *

Waterhouse looked high and low for several minutes, choosing where to plant the microphone. The hands of his internal clock seemed to accelerate the longer he was inside. The cabin was lit by bursts of moonlight streaking through the tinted glass of the salon. He moved to a lamp situated on the table in the center of the room and stuck the tiny microphone in place.

Time to leave. He crawled aft and hopped onto the starboard walkway. As he was about to stand up, Peter waved him down. "Two of them are on the dock. Stay right there!" he whispered from the bow of the johnboat.

Waterhouse dropped to his stomach. He couldn't see what was going on, so he watched Peter, whose eyes never left the men on the pier. Peter walked the boat aft to stay out of sight, gripping the yacht's metal rail with his powerful hands.

* * *

"They're leaving," Peter whispered.

He reversed course and pushed the boat toward the bow. Using the yacht's railing, he walked it hand over hand, matching the pace of the two men on shore. They were a hundred yards from the water. Waterhouse crawled along on the starboard side, staying with Peter. Waterhouse ducked under the metal rail onto the launch. Both men crouched low, hugging the hull.

"Let's get out of here," Waterhouse said.

Peter knelt at the engine and pulled the starter rope. He tried six times in rapid succession, but it would not turn over.

* * *

Jason slipped out from under the pier, gasping for air. Peter and Waterhouse were nowhere to be seen. When Oliver and Fairing disappeared through the trees, Jason heaved himself onto the dock, soaked and dripping. He hadn't taken two steps on shore when he saw two men and two women emerge from the house. He dropped to his stomach. Zanns led the quartet across the patio, past the gazebo, and onto the lawn. Fairing's flat package was under her arm.

In the dim light, he could make out the form of a long-legged woman with straight black hair. Jasmine Kader walked quickly beside Lily Zanns, along with Oliver and Sam. *So much for a vacation in Hilton Head,* he thought. His disgust quickly turned to concern.

Where are you, Peter?

* * *

Peter swore as he continued to pull the cord.

The boat had drifted, allowing Waterhouse a view of the yard and the mansion's pier.

"Shit, they're heading this way," he gasped.

The group of four walked with a determined purpose toward the pier.

Peter pulled furiously, cursing and praying simultaneously, telling the Mercury engine what he was going to do to it if it failed to cooperate.

"They're on the dock, getting into the dingy!"

Retribution's engine turned over. A moment later, the bow lifted as the launch rocketed directly toward the yacht.

* * *

"Please, please, please!" Peter pleaded. Suddenly, the engine sputtered and caught. "Thank you, Jesus! Let's go!"

Waterhouse shoved the tiny boat away from the yacht. Peter thrust the rudder hard to starboard, gunning the throttle, twisting it to the stop, keeping the yacht between them and the launch. Peter smiled a relieved, shit-eating grin at Waterhouse as they raced away. "How far away was the yacht from the dock?" he yelled.

"About a hundred yards!"

Peter estimated where a hundred yards from the yacht was, then subtracted twenty. When he reached that point, he cut the engine and turned the wheel, throwing the boat into reverse to stop any drift.

"Quick, over the side," he commanded.

"But my equipment!" Waterhouse said.

"It's got to go!" Peter grabbed Waterhouse and the black bag. They jumped over the side. Waterhouse swore as he fell into the river. They surfaced and clung to the gunwale, using the boat as cover.

They peered around the outboard engine, watching and waiting. The conspirators climbed aboard *Vengeance*. The two women made their way into the main salon. The men were visible on the bridge. After a few minutes, the yacht's screws engaged, and the vessel made a slow turn in their direction.

Peter released another virulent string of curses.

* * *

"We are behind schedule," Zanns said. "Let's go."

Fairing and Oliver climbed the ladder to the bridge. Zanns set the package on the table in the center of the cabin. The women relaxed as the engines revved. The yacht began to inch its way downriver.

On the bridge, Fairing pointed to something in the water. "There! What's that?"

Oliver craned his neck. A small boat drifted in the dark, rippling water.

"It's the Quigley's boat. It must have come loose from the pier," Oliver said. He called down to Zanns to explain what they'd seen.

"Check it out," she commanded.

Oliver spun the large, stainless-steel helm and headed toward the small craft bobbing in the water.

CHAPTER 54

Jason waited until the yacht was fifty yards away before climbing out from under the dock for a third time. Where were his brother and Waterhouse? What was happening in the middle of the river?

The yacht headed for the small johnboat. Then *Vengeance* appeared to swallow the tiny vessel whole. Minutes later, the yacht towed the boat as close to shore as it could. Fairing hopped onto the craft and heaved the anchor overboard. After climbing back aboard, the yacht sailed away.

A shudder, not caused by the October chill, ran through him. Did Zanns have his brother and Waterhouse?

He slipped quietly into the water and swam. Two minutes later, he pulled himself over the gunwale of the small craft.

The johnboat was empty.

He scanned the vessel. No blood. No equipment. No clothing. Jason struggled to his knees and looked toward the James River Bridge. The *Vengeance* had passed under the drawbridge, and was dwindling in size with each second.

Jason sat on the middle bench, his clothing and shoes heavy with water. A slight breeze blew across the water as guilt clutched him by the throat. He—and he alone—had dragged his brother into this affair. And now his brother and another man were either dead or soon to be.

Get moving! he told himself. They must have been taken aboard the yacht. He would follow and figure out how to help Peter and Waterhouse.

Jason moved to the engine, renewed by conviction and desperation.

He knelt and tugged at the cord. Nothing. For three minutes, he tried unsuccessfully to start it.

Finally, he slammed the plastic cowling covering the engine. "No!"

Jason paused to rest, hoping he hadn't flooded the carburetor. Then, in the distance, he heard water splashing. Quiet ruled for thirty seconds as Jason listened. Splashes mingled with another noise. Gasping breaths.

"Jason!" a voice whispered between splashes. "Jason!"

"Pete, is that you?"

"Get your ass out here and help me! This mother's heavy."

Jason nearly shredded the cord when he pulled it. The engine sputtered, caught, and puffed oily smoke. He turned the throttle wide open and pressed the choke closed. He whirled the boat in the direction of his brother's voice.

Jason found Peter thirty yards away, side-kicking an unconscious Waterhouse to shore.

"He's breathing, I think," Peter gasped, as they pulled him into the launch.

Back at the pier, they laid Waterhouse on the creaking planks.

Jason thrust two palms down on Waterhouse's belly, forcing water to dribble from his mouth. Peter turned his head to the side as Jason leaned on his stomach again. Waterhouse sprayed a plume of water and lurched into a coughing spasm, sucking in short, gurgling breaths.

"He'll be all right," Jason said. "Man, am I glad to see your ugly mug. I thought they took you—or worse. What happened?"

"We had to dive off the boat when the yacht approached. We were underwater for a long time. He wanted to surface," Peter pointed to Waterhouse, "but I had to hold him under or they would've seen us. He sucked in some water. And passed out on the swim back." Peter's chest heaved with each sentence. "Damn, I've got to quit smoking," he said.

"Is the device in place?"

Peter nodded, still trying to catch his breath.

"We need to get out of here. You got enough left to carry him to the truck?"

"No, I don't." Peter smiled at Jason, then at the unconscious Waterhouse. "He's going to walk."

CHAPTER 55

The sound quality was passable. Ambient noise, combined with the creaking of chairs and the shuffle of papers and clothing, obscured patches of conversation at times. The three men sat in the SUV, dripping wet, listening to the real-time conversation on the *Vengeance*. Waterhouse had tuned the car radio to the listening device's frequency. The signal on the miniature microphone had a range of miles. The private investigator was holding a palm-sized recorder he'd pulled from his glove box up to the car speaker to capture the conversation.

The first hour held nothing but stray noises interrupted by snippets of inconsequential conversation. The hum of the engines could be heard. Words or phrases came and went as people walked in and out of range. An hour later, the engines died. The yacht had stopped.

Zanns voiced came over the speaker. *My children…is the final package…our source inside the Beltway…*

There was a rustling, closer to the microphone. A creak. Someone sitting in a chair, perhaps. Lily Zanns's voice came through loud and crystal clear at the moment. *If the package contains the requi…*

•

formation…have a green light for our operation. The plan…so carefully and patiently waited for…

The next words seemed to be spoken by Zanns, though it was hard to determine. She was speaking in a guttural dialect, and it wasn't French. Jason and Walter understood none of it.

One phrase jumped out at Peter.

Allahu Akbar!

The other voices joined what sounded like prayer recital. More rustling. Plastic crinkled.

Zanns in English this time. *Torpedo and Thunderbolt will fall in the poison wind of the Simoon! Allahu Akbar!*

A pause in the chanting caused the speakers in the car to fall silent. Waterhouse glanced at Jason in the front seat and Peter in the back.

"Who are Torpedo and Thunderbolt?" Jason asked.

"What's Simoon?" Peter said.

Waterhouse shrugged.

"They all must belong to this Simoon," Peter said more to himself than to his two car mates.

Torpedo and Thunderbolt will fall…

"They're planning to kill again," said Jason.

"Not again," Waterhouse corrected him. "I think the murders of Torpedo and Thunderbolt seems to have been their objective all along…"

Conversation began again.

The seating chart and itinerary are set. Everything is a go. Cooper has taken possession of Cyclops and will set it up in the condo…target the white screen. Sam…in the north tower. Jasmine will be in her location on the other north tower… The last words were drowned out by a noise inside the cabin of the yacht.

"Cooper's involved!" Jason said out loud. Peter and Waterhouse did not know who Steven Cooper was. "But what the hell's a Cyclops?"

Peter shrugged. "Not a clue."

A man's voice began, concerned, rigid.

"It's Fairing again," Jason explained. He was the only one who knew the sounds of their voices.

Will Jason Rodgers…eliminated…his team?…obstacles to our success.…too risky leaving…the police…We should have killed him like we did Pettigrew!

The final burst of conversation came through so clearly, it was as if Fairing were sitting in the vehicle. A thousand knife stabs of fear pricked Jason's body.

Enough! Rodgers may already…no longer a threat…the decision has been made. As for the rest of his team, Hammon's assassins…care of them. They will commence their assaults…focus on the task…"

Jason started to speak. Waterhouse shushed him.

"What about the escape r—"

The woman's voice, Kader's, was cut off midsentence. The sound just stopped. Nothing was coming from the speakers, no static, no hissing, nothing.

"Well piss on me and tell me it's raining," Waterhouse swore. "The microphone failed."

CHAPTER 56

Tentacles of fear and guilt engulfed Jason. The air around him seemed to collapse with the pressure of a thousand atmospheres. Breathing was no longer automatic. The three of them, and Christine, were marked for death. Jason was responsible for the mortal danger each of them found themselves in.

Zanns, Kader, Fairing, and Oliver had planned all along to murder two people. It was going to happen soon. But when? They called them Torpedo and Thunderbolt. Codenames, no doubt. Who were they? The names meant nothing to him, Peter, or Waterhouse. But for some reason, Jason sensed he'd seen them before.

Jason had once heard you never really forgot; your mind just wasn't able to access the information. The names "Torpedo" and "Thunderbolt" had passed before his eyes at one time, fragments of data on the hard drive of his mind. But he couldn't remember from where.

"We're marked men," said Peter.

Hammon, another codename probably, was sending killers after them. They thought they were too close, knew too much. If Zanns only knew how little he actually understood.

"I'm sorry I've dragged you two and Chrissie into this," Jason said. "A lot of people are in danger now."

"These people have killed before and they plan on killing again," Peter said. "Our families could be targets. I have to get Lisa and the girls to a safe location. Jason, you need to call Jenny and tell her what's going on. Michael isn't safe." Peter ran a hand through his spiked hair. "You need to warn Christine too."

"You think they'd be after her?" asked Waterhouse.

"She knows what we know," Jason said. "She was in your house when we were talking about what we found. Your house was bugged."

Peter looked to Waterhouse. "What about you, Walt? Is there anyone you need to call?"

"My daughters live out west and my ex-wife is living in New England. That's it."

"Sorry about your bad luck," Peter said. "We better get moving. We're going to see a lot of shit go down—if we live that long."

CHAPTER 57

Jason mashed the bell four times in rapid succession. He waited five seconds and pushed six more times. After a third round of bell-pushing, shuffling could be heard coming from behind the door.

"Hold on!" Christine hollered.

"It's Jason. Open up now!"

The door opened a crack, revealing a sleepy set of brown eyes.

"We need to talk."

"Now?"

Jason pushed through the door past Christine. "It's a matter of life and death."

"You do realize what time it is, don't you?"

"Where's your computer?" he asked, ignoring her comment.

"How's Sheila?" she asked, her tone petulant and mocking.

"We've got more important issues right now."

"By the way, why did you invite her to Maggie's Tavern when you were having dinner with me? If I'd known, I would've worn some body armor."

"I didn't invite her. I don't know how she knew. Where's your computer?"

"You woke me up at four in the morning to use my computer?"

"Where is it?"

"It's upstairs in its case, next to my bed, where I should be."

He held up a plastic CD case. "You're going to find this very interesting."

"Is this going to take long?"

Jason leaned closer. "Get…your…computer."

Christine went upstairs and returned with her laptop.

Jason's eyes never left the screen as the CD loaded. "We made this recording of Zanns, Fairing, and Kader on her yacht tonight."

"How did you get on the yacht?"

"That's not important right now. Listen!" Jason skipped ahead to the incriminating parts. Christine listened in silence then asked, "Who are Torpedo and Thunderbolt?"

"Keep listening. We're still trying to figure it out."

We should have killed him like we did Pettigrew!

He stopped the playback.

"They did it! Chrissie, Zanns and her people murdered your father!"

Her mouth hung open. "No," she said. "No, it can't be." She lowered her head, then jerked it up to look at Jason. "Lily did this?"

"Yes." Jason grasped her hand.

"He found one? A conspiracy?" Tears welled in her eyes.

"Yes, he did."

Christine stood fully erect. She paced the full length of the kitchen, then turned around. "I never believed him. I ridiculed him!" Christine gently banged the table with a closed fist. "Never in a million years…"

"There's more," he said. Christine listened as Zanns and her cohorts discussed the elimination of Jason, Christine, Peter, and Waterhouse.

"She's going to kill us?"

He nodded. "Not without a fight. But she's going to try. We're all taking precautions. You need to get to safety!"

Christine asked, "How did it all come to this? Why are they trying to kill these two people?"

"I don't know. Something massive is going down, and we've got to stop it. You need to go into hiding until we can get a handle on this."

"Hiding? Where am I supposed to go?"

"I don't know, don't you have a girlfriend out of the area you can stay with?"

"I'm sure I do." Christine thought for a moment. "But I'm *not* going into hiding."

"What? Why? Chrissie, that's insane. These people already killed your father and Douglas Winstead. Whatever they're planning, they not going to stop until whoever is in their way has been eliminated. You could be next! You have to leave, *now!*"

"I can take care of myself." Chrissie's eyes held a determination which dwarfed her stubbornness.

"These people are professional killers. They may already be on their way over here—"

"I have a life here! I can't just leave my job. This is where I live."

"It could also be where you die."

She leaned in, her lips no more than two inches from his nose. She emphasized each word, as Jason had a few minutes earlier. "I'm...not...going!"

CHAPTER 58

Jason slammed the steering wheel. F-bombs flew about the Saturn in unison with the thumping of his fist against the hard vinyl. He railed against her stubbornness and stupidity. The harder he'd pushed Christine to leave, the more forcefully she'd pushed back. How could she be so naïve? How could she not see the danger? Thomas Pettigrew had been just as stubborn throughout his career. It had made him successful. Chrissie came by it honestly. Reluctantly, Jason left. He didn't know how he would do it, but he'd figure out a way to get her to safety.

From Victory Boulevard, Jason turned south onto Big Bethel Road at the fire station. Commuters and housewives were still in their beds. But early risers were beginning their days. Morning was a time of renewal. The worst evils were dampened, tempered by the sun's rays. This morning, though, foreboding filled the air. While everyone around him went about their daily routines, Jason's life was disintegrating. Sheila, even after their breakup, was still harassing him, and she seemed to know where he was going to be almost as quickly as he did. Every part of his life was splayed open like exposed organs after a Y-incision. His new career was a disaster—a deadly venture not bargained for. Two men were dead, and two more were in danger. He feared for his own life and that of his son, his brother, and the woman he'd loved many years ago.

What the hell was happening? Everything was spinning out of control.

Before going to Christine's, he'd woken Jenny with a phone call. He tried to keep his voice steady. But the urgency seeped into his words. Perhaps that was best. Jenny, Michael's mother, reluctantly met him on the front steps of the home she shared with her new husband.

He knew he sounded like a crazy man as he explained to her that she needed to get Michael to safety. He couldn't explain, he told her. "Just trust me, Jenny!" he pleaded. They argued until Jenny's husband, the architect, appeared. Jason made her promise to get Michael out of town before he departed. He would check to make sure they were gone. Jenny knew how much Jason loved his son and that he wasn't prone to melodrama. It took less than thirty minutes to convince her to take Michael on a short vacation. After a shower and a change of clothes, he would go back and talk some sense into Christine.

Jason pulled into the driveway, parked the Saturn, and alighted from it. He stepped to the keypad mounted on the garage's doorframe and punched in the code. The door ascended slowly. Behind him, headlights arced into the driveway. Two men in suits emerged from either side of the car, advancing cautiously toward him.

Confused, Jason walked toward the rear of the car. "Can I help you?"

"Are you Jason Rodgers?" asked the driver.

"Yes."

The driver flipped open a leather wallet, revealing a badge. "I'm Investigator Calvin Baxter. This is Investigator Clyde Stevens. We're with the York County Sheriff's Office."

"What's going on?"

Stevens had wide shoulders and a thick torso, none of it soft. "We'd like to ask you some questions."

"Now? It's two in the morning."

Baxter was black and six four, wider, more menacing than his tough-looking partner. "We're investigating a crime. Do you own a gun, Mr. Rodgers?"

"Yes, I do. Why do you want to know?"

"Where is the gun now?" asked Stevens.

"It's upstairs in its case. Why?"

"Can you please go get it, sir? We'd like to see it."

"Why?"

"There's been a homicide tonight, sir."

"And you think my gun was involved?"

"Please get the weapon, sir."

Jason's eyes seesawed back and forth between the two cops. His gut began a slow twist into pretzel-like knots. "I'll be right back," he said weakly.

He climbed the stairs two at a time. Jogging into the bedroom, he pushed open the closet door. It crashed into the wall. Falling to his knees, Jason pushed several shoe boxes and a carton of photographs to the side. The gun case slid out. Immediately, he realized something was wrong. It was too light. He fumbled at the combination lock, which was not engaged. He opened the case and stared down at the empty gun-shaped depression. Bile welled in his throat. "Son of a bitch!"

Jason returned with the empty case. The officers had their hands on their holstered weapons.

Jason stammered, holding the case up for inspection. "It—it must have been stolen."

"I see," said Baxter. "We have your weapon, Mr. Rodgers. It was found at a crime scene this evening."

"How long has your gun been missing?" Stevens added.

"I have no idea. I haven't used it in a couple of weeks."

Baxter nodded knowingly. Stevens moved behind Jason toward the garage, taking great interest in its contents. Baxter said, "You haven't been home all night. We've tried to ring the bell several times. There was no answer. What have you been doing tonight, sir?"

I was trying to figure out why my boss is trying to kill two men. "I had dinner with a friend."

"What time was that?"

"About seven."

"What time did dinner end?"

"Maybe eight o'clock."

Stevens moved back into Jason's field of vision.

"As you said, it's after two in the morning. What did you do between eight and two?"

"Why are you asking me these questions?"

"Do you know a Sheila Boquist, Mr. Rodgers?"

"We dated for a while. Why?"

"Because she was murdered tonight."

Jason's knees buckled. He staggered but caught himself on the trunk of the Saturn. "What?" The white cop grabbed Jason by the arm.

"Your weapon was found at the scene. Where were you this evening after dinner?"

Jason looked at the two deputies as if he was trying to convince himself they were real and he wasn't having a nightmare. "Are you suggesting I killed her?"

"Did you?" Baxter asked.

Jason roughly rubbed his head with both hands. "No!"

"Then please tell us where you were," Baxter persisted.

Not sure how much he should reveal, Jason said, "I had dinner with a friend. Her name's Christine. Then I was with my brother and another friend, Walter Waterhouse. I met up with Christine again and then I drove home." Jason prayed it would be enough to satisfy them.

"What were you, your brother, and Waterhouse doing?"

"It's complicated."

Stevens chimed in, "Mr. Rodgers, we'd like you to come to the sheriff's office and answer some questions so we can verify your story."

"I didn't do anything."

"Then we should be able to clear this up fairly quickly," said Stevens.

"Can't it wait until morning?"

"No, we'd like you to come with us now."

CHAPTER 59

Thursday, October 5

Jason clasped the chair arms in a white-knuckle grip.

The six-by-fifteen-foot interview room in the sheriff's office was smaller than a jail cell. The furniture consisted of three chairs and a rectangular table topped with a fake-wood veneer. Jason's wooden chair had a green back and two long, flat, wooden armrests. Add a few leather straps and some current, and it would pass for a homemade electric chair.

The walls were white and naked. The inch-thick glass of the lone window did not invite escape. A framed certificate hung from the skinny wall beside the window. It proclaimed the expertise of some guy named Richardson in the art of polygraph examination. A camera encased in a white cylinder sat mounted high in the corner, pointing down in judgment. The space was designed for extracting confessions from lowlife scumbags. Jason didn't belong here anymore than did a pimple on Mona Lisa's nose.

He had no idea how much time had passed. Ten, fifteen minutes. What was taking so long? The door was open an inch. A deputy, looking stern and militant, stood outside, making sure Jason Rodgers, the dangerous pharmacist, didn't try stabbing anyone with his counting spatula.

Though he knew he'd done nothing wrong, frightening thoughts materialized and accelerated in his imagination.

Confident of his innocence, he'd allowed fingerprints to be taken. The investigator asked if they could swab his cheek to obtain a sample of his DNA. One of them had even asked if he would provide a key to allow a search of his house. Even the most incompetent of lawyers would have been apoplectic at the thought. Jason knew he should protest just on principle. But he had done nothing wrong. He still couldn't believe Sheila was dead. The woman was a mercurial, selfish bitch. And though at times, in fits of irrational rage, he'd prayed for her demise, he'd never want anyone, even her, to suffer such a horrific fate.

Should he ask for an attorney? He'd watched enough television to know that if he did, the police were required to cease all questioning. Would they arrest him if he invoked this right? *What the hell are you thinking? You haven't done anything. Tell them the truth and get the hell out of here!*

But he couldn't tell them the whole truth. His activities *had* been illegal. Skulking around spying on people wouldn't make the cops think he was the innocent type. He'd implicate himself in other crimes. If these cops got wind of his brush with the Secret Service, they'd look at him even closer.

Hopefully, Waterhouse had made copies of the conversation they'd risked their lives to record and e-mailed a copy to Detective Palmer in Newport News. The compact disc Waterhouse had given Jason was still in Christine's laptop.

Shouldn't he just tell these investigators that he was collecting evidence against Lily Zanns? That was, of course, his alibi. Peter and Waterhouse would back up his story. The recording would tell them everything they needed to know.

Five more minutes passed. Twenty altogether.

Before he could organize his thoughts, the tall, black man returned followed by another investigator. The second man wasn't Stevens, the man from the driveway. This one was bookish in appearance, with glasses and a legal pad.

Jason got a better look at the lead investigator in the stark light of the interview room. His shoulders, wide and rigid, spawned two arms that looked like the trunks of small trees. Baxter had played some sort of contact sport, probably football, in his past. The rolled-up sleeves of his shirt were stretched tight by muscles rippling like steel cords. The man's eyes pierced Jason. Despite his innocence, Baxter's countenance alone made Jason want to drop to his knees and beg for forgiveness.

Cal Baxter dropped a manila folder on the table with a loud crack. The second man seated himself and placed the yellow legal pad on the table, pen at the ready. Baxter unloaded his two hundred and fifty pounds into the puny, standard-issue chair.

"I didn't kill anyone," Jason said quickly, before Baxter even opened his mouth.

"May I call you Jason?" Baxter's voice was deep and friendly, as if he were Jason's only friend on the earth. Nonetheless, a latent desire to inflict pain seemed to surround him.

Jason nodded stiffly.

"How about something to drink? Coke, coffee?"

Jason declined. The back of his throat was a sun-baked, gritty desert, but accepting any kind of graciousness would be letting his guard down. He needed to stay as sharp as possible. The fatigue and fear, though propped up by adrenaline, were growing heavier.

Baxter began matter-of-factly. "Your weapon was found at the murder scene. We traced the serial number through our databases with NCIC and ATF. It's yours, Jason. There's no doubt about it."

"I just found out it was stolen. I don't know how it got over there."

"You said that before."

"Did you see Sheila Boquist tonight?"

"No," he lied. No sense giving them any more reason to suspect him.

"She was your girlfriend, correct?"

"Ex-girlfriend," Jason corrected.

"Ex-girlfriend, right."

The notetaker, a small, wiry man with rimless glasses, scribbled some notes.

"When did you stop dating?"

"A couple of weeks ago." Jason glanced up at the video camera mounted at ceiling level in the corner of the room. He wondered how his words would sound when played back in court.

"Did you two get along?"

"For the most part," he lied again.

"Did you see her tonight?"

"No," he persisted.

"You sure?"

"I just said I didn't."

A knock came at the door, and a deputy stuck his head in. "Cal, you got a minute?"

"Jason, we'll be right back."

Both men walked out. The uniformed deputy took up his place outside the room once more.

When Baxter returned, he asked, "What time did you see Sheila tonight?"

"I told you I didn't see her—"

"Did you have dinner tonight at Maggie's Tavern?"

Jason felt his eyes widen. How did Baxter know that? "Yeah…I did."

"Did you invite Sheila to meet you there?"

He looked at Baxter like the cop had sprouted a third arm. "No! What the hell makes you think that?"

Baxter removed a plastic bag from his folder. In it was the small, typewritten note card. Jason grabbed the corner between a thumb and forefinger as he read.

"I didn't write this."

"So you didn't invite Sheila to meet you?"

"No, I didn't."

"But you said you did have dinner at Maggie's Tavern?"

"Uh…yeah."

"So who did you meet there?"

"Christine Pettigrew."

"How do you spell that?"

Jason spelled her name. Baxter asked for her address, home, and cell phone numbers. Jason recited them.

"How long did dinner last?"

"An hour, maybe."

"Where did you go after your dinner date?"

Jason looked at him like the words were spoken in Mandarin.

"Jason, where did you go after dinner with your friend—" Baxter checked his notepad in front of him. "Christine?"

"I—was with my brother, Peter, and Walter Waterhouse."

More scribbling. "What were you doing?"

We were hunting down a group of assassins! "We were…investigating."

"Investigating what?"

"There's been some unusual activity at the pharmacy I work at. First, it was an insurance scam…but it turned into something else, something worse. We know two people are going to be killed," Jason said. "We have evidence, a recording."

"So you and your brother and this guy, Walter, are trying to stop two murders?"

Jason nodded intently.

"Who's going to be killed?"

"We don't know their names."

"Who's going to do the killing, Jason?"

Jason lowered his head. His words sounded ridiculous, like those of a man trying to save his own skin. But they had proof now. It was time to let the experts handle it. "Her name is Lily Zanns. She owns the Colonial Pharmacy in Newport News. She and two other people are planning it. Walter should be e-mailing a copy of the recording to Detective John Palmer in Newport News."

Baxter looked at Jason as if he were a ten-year-old boy, trying to explain how the water from the bathtub had managed to flood the bathroom floor.

"We'll check out your story. I need the phone numbers for your brother and this Walter character."

Jason recited the numbers. Notetaker scribbled them on his legal pad.

Notetaker asked Baxter a question. "Do you want me to start having the boys make the phone calls?"

Baxter shook his head and leaned over, invading Jason's personal space. "Not yet."

The notetaker stopped writing and looked up.

"Why don't we cut the bullshit, Jason," Baxter continued. "Tell me where you were last night after seven o'clock. We already know where you were, at least for part of the night. So just come clean."

Jason squirmed in the chair. "Well, if you know, you tell me."

He expected Baxter to recite the litany of events. The yacht, the package, following Sam Fairing. Deep down, Jason knew that wasn't going to happen. He also knew Baxter wasn't buying his story. "Jason, we also know you had an altercation with Ms. Boquist on the twenty-eighth of September. Witnesses saw you and the victim argue after some party. She then kneed you in the cojones. We also have some witnesses that confirm Sheila was at Maggie's tonight."

Jason sat perfectly still, afraid to move.

"Being a guy, I can understand how embarrassing that would be. I bet it really pissed you off. So you invited her to the restaurant tonight to get a little payback. You know, rub her face in it. That's what happened, isn't it?" Baxter smiled at Jason. His expression said he thought he was right on.

Jason shook his head. "No," he whispered.

Baxter removed three photographs from the folder and laid the first one on the table. Jason's eyes widened and his jaw dropped as the images registered. He had spent a rotation in pharmacy school in surgery at Medical College of Virginia. He'd peered over the surgeon's shoulder, watching various procedures over the course of two weeks. A triple bypass. An aortic valve replacement. A splenectomy. The inside of the human body, blood, entrails were not something that caused him shock or revulsion.

But when he saw the blood, the open, unseeing eyes of his gutted ex, he leaned forward and opened his mouth and began to dry heave. The photographs were in full, living color, every nuance, every detail captured expertly by the crime-scene photographer.

Sheila's naked body lay sprawled almost facedown in the blood-soaked carpet. The hilt of an everyday kitchen knife protruded from her abdomen, glistening, slick with blood. Her glassy, green eyes stared like those of a discarded doll.

Baxter laid the next picture on top of the first. This one had a better view of the fatal slice. The wound yawned across her belly. From inside the gash peeked out severed layers of skin and yellowish subcutaneous fat, a bluish-purple haze of some internal organ, probably the liver. The third photograph was much like the first two.

An electric charge zipped through him. He shuddered. "Holy shit!" he muttered, burying his head in his hands.

Baxter did not speak for thirty seconds. Finally, he said, "A neighbor phoned the police and said she heard fighting and arguing from Sheila's address. The woman also said that a red Mustang was seen leaving the scene shortly after the fight. You own a red Mustang, Jason. You weren't driving it when you came home. Where is it?" It was not a question.

Jason knew he'd been set up. He hadn't driven his Mustang since he'd rented his first car, the Ford Fusion. He opened his mouth to explain, when Baxter interrupted him.

"Jason, here's what I know…" Baxter paused and leaned back in his chair, leaving the photographs in plain view. "Sheila Boquist was killed with a knife stabbed in the abdomen. There was a five-inch gash from here to here." Baxter motioned with his hand over his own chest. "She bled to death. She was stabbed with a four-inch blade. That knife had fingerprints all over it. Your fingerprints. And only your fingerprints. The knife is one that came from your kitchen set."

Jason felt as if a knife had been stuck in *him*. "I didn't kill her!"

"Your gun was also found at the scene."

"I told you, it was stolen. I didn't kill her!"

"Two wine glasses were found. One of them had your fingerprints on it. We'll be checking it for your DNA as well. I'm sure that it'll come back positive. Stop wasting everyone's time. Just tell me what happened."

"I didn't do it!"

"You invited her to the restaurant to teach her a lesson. It got heated. You followed her back to her apartment. You argued some more and then it turned really violent. The body had some bruises on the arms and legs. So you grabbed her. She fought back and you stabbed her. It got out of hand and then you—"

"No!" Jason screamed. *This can't be happening!* "No!"

"The question I have," Baxter continued, "is when did you decide to take the knife from the house? Did you take it to the restaurant, or did you stop home after you left dinner? Why not just shoot her?"

Jason sat with his head in his hands, trying to catch his breath.

Baxter waited for Jason to calm. "I want to take an impression of your shoes, Jason. Will you allow us to do that?"

He was doubled over now, like he was in pain. "I didn't kill her!"

"Jason, the hardest part is taking the first step. After that, everything is easier. Just tell me why you killed her."

In his whole life, Jason never thought he'd ever utter the next words, which came out in a tense whisper. "I want to talk to a lawyer."

CHAPTER 60

Notus stepped off the Air Tran flight 707 at Newport News–Williamsburg International Airport and strolled up the Jetway. He had killed in far more sophisticated places. London, Paris, Prague, and Zurich, to name a few. Newport News, Virginia, was a working class town by comparison. But a job was a job. And this one would pay well.

Notus was not his real name, of course. It was the pseudonym given to him specifically for this assignment. Notus, a god of Greek myth, carried the wet, storm-laden southern winds of late summer.

The call had come three hours ago. He'd been banging the cute waitress with the nice ass and small tits. The ringing cell phone had interrupted him before he had a chance to finish the job. He'd pushed her out the door wearing nothing but her panties and an armful of clothes. The mission was a priority delta.

There'd be plenty of time for Carol or Cheryl or whatever the hell her name was later. Maybe he'd make it up to her with a weekend in the Bahamas. Hell, after this job, he could afford to take a whole year off. The money was that good and—from the sound of it—this assignment was going to be a walk in the park. Notus was unrivaled at what he did. His business was death. In ten years, he had compiled an impressive resume.

They would be paired in two-man teams. Notus noticed his soon-to-be partner, Deacon Jim Miller—also an alias—sitting at the small bar watching CNN. Notus had had no idea what Miller looked like until that very moment, and didn't know his real name. If things went to shit, the less they knew about each other, the better.

Their target, a certified public accountant, was a woman. She was an average citizen who'd managed to get mixed up in something she shouldn't have. Notus didn't know what that was, and he didn't give a shit. Nor did he know why Hammon wanted her dead. Her photo and data had been securely e-mailed to his Blackberry. She was the cute next-door-neighbor type every guy wanted to bang. The job should be easy.

Each man wore a dark blue baseball cap totally absent of insignias, emblems, or logos. Just plain blue caps. On the right side, pinned just above the ear, was a small gold ankh, the Egyptian symbol of life that had been all the rage many years ago. Now, ironically, it symbolized not life but death.

Miller sipped a Heineken and watched Notus file slowly past. They nodded imperceptibly to each other. Notus strolled down the long glass corridor to the baggage claim. He didn't know who'd come up with these names. "Deacon" Jim Miller, gun for hire in the late eighteen hundreds, had been a teetotaler, a devout Methodist. He'd been hanged in 1909 for a contract killing of an Oklahoman cattle rancher. These names were a piece of work, he thought.

Never looking in the other's direction, they waited at the baggage carousel. Twenty minutes later, Notus exited the terminal, pulling his bag behind him. He found the car. The keys were hanging in the ignition. He paid the fee and circled back to the terminal to pick up Miller, who climbed in without a word. They drove to a motel on Jefferson, staying cautiously under the speed limit.

* * *

To the north in Richmond, Zephyr, the west wind of Greek mythology, walked out of another airport terminal. Tom Horn, another gunman and killer for hire whose namesake had dispatched seventeen men in a span of four years in the late nineteenth century, climbed into their rented car. They would drive to Newport News in an hour's time. Their target was a man named Peter Rodgers, an ex-marine sniper.

* * *

Eurus, the east wind in Greek myth, slipped the sedan under the awning at a hotel just north of the Coleman Bridge in Gloucester, Virginia. He'd driven three hours since the call. The man known as Robert Ford, the cowardly assassin of Jesse James, opened the passenger door and plopped onto the seat, slinging his bag into the backseat. In another hour, they, too, would arrive in Newport News. Ford placed the dossier on the seat between them. He leafed through it. "His name is Walter Waterhouse," he told Eurus.

CHAPTER 61

"This is Baxter," the deep, gravelly voice said.

Peter spoke quickly. "Detective Baxter—"

"That's Investigator Baxter," the man interrupted.

"My name is Peter Rodgers. I'm Jason Rodgers's brother. You're holding him right now."

"That's correct. He's under arrest for murder."

"Jason just called me. I'm calling to tell you Jason was with me most of the evening. I'm his alibi."

"Okay," Baxter replied. "What were you two doing tonight?"

"Are you going to—check out—what Jason told you?"

There was a pause on the line. Baxter's heavy sigh communicated his displeasure. "Peter!" he began. "To be quite honest, your brother didn't tell us a whole lot about where he was. Another investigator is looking into his alibi. He's probably tracking you and your friend down—" Baxter paused. Peter heard a page moving and guessed he was checking his notes. "Walter Waterhouse, right now."

Peter had called Waterhouse after hanging up with Jason. The call rolled to his voice mail. That was right before Peter put in a call to the lawyer who'd handled the incorporation of his gun shop. The man said he knew a good criminal attorney. He'd call him first thing in the morning.

"We have strong evidence that two men are in danger. We have a recording." Peter then outlined what had happened.

"Mr. Rodgers, can you provide me with proof as to where Jason was and for how long this evening?"

"You think I'm lying?"

"You're his brother. It wouldn't be the first time someone covered for a family member. We have some very hard evidence against your brother. In fact, I have just been handed some evidence which puts this crime into a whole new light."

"What's that?"

"We have strong evidence your brother killed his ex-girlfriend. And was planning much more. Let us conduct our investigation. Someone will be in touch."

* * *

Who were Torpedo and Thunderbolt?

The question had haunted Jason in the hours since he'd asked for legal counsel. As soon as the words were uttered, Calvin Baxter had calmly stood up and ended the interrogation. He'd motioned with his head, and he and the notetaker left. Baxter returned and, with the calm of a librarian, said, "Jason, we're placing you under arrest for the murder of Sheila Boquist. Please stand up and put your hands behind your back." Baxter read Jason his Miranda rights as the metals cuffs cut into his wrists.

The next thirty minutes were a collage of images interspersed with bouts of panic. Phone calls were made. He was driven to the regional jail in Williamsburg, where he was fingerprinted again, photographed, and his belongings confiscated and catalogued. His cell phone, car keys, clothes, driver's license, and sixty-three dollars were placed in a large manila envelope. He donned the orange jumpsuit and flip-flops and was escorted to a cell. Thirty minutes later, he phoned his brother.

He asked him to find a lawyer and make sure Jenny had taken Michael to safety. He'd learned no one had questioned Peter about Jason's alibi. Jason explained what he had told Calvin Baxter. When he'd hung up, a sinking feeling consumed him. Baxter did not believe his story. Jason had given him Peter's, Waterhouse's, Christine's and Lily Zanns's names. Baxter would probably make the calls or have someone do it for him—eventually. But there didn't seem to be any sense of urgency. Peter had promised to call Baxter personally. Jason wondered if he had.

Since then, Jason had lain on the uncomfortable steel-framed bed, which was bolted to the floor, brooding over the identities of Torpedo and Thunderbolt and the sight of his ex-girlfriend gutted like a trout.

Torpedo and Thunderbolt. Where had he seen those names before?

Of course, he'd been expertly and convincingly framed. It had to be part of Zanns's plan. Jasmine must have stolen his gun the day he passed out and taken his knife from the kitchen.

Jason finally realized what he'd managed to stumble into. The doomed men attached to those names were the reason he was in jail; the reason Thomas Pettigrew was dead; the reason Douglas Winstead's head had exploded. Zanns been setting him up from the beginning to take the blame for Sheila's death. But why? Something else was going on.

His fate rested with the identities of those two people—Torpedo and Thunderbolt. Figure out who they were, and maybe he could keep them from being murdered. In the process, he might be able to convince someone who carried a badge that he wasn't a killer. But all of that was impossible while sitting in a jail cell.

It was all about context. If he could remember the circumstances in which he'd seen these names, he could open the right mental file and snatch the information. He examined every avenue of his life. Work, pharmacy school, friends, anyone who may have mentioned the words. Nothing jogged his memory.

Stretched out on the bed, he thought of Michael, just as he did whenever work at the pharmacy threatened to overwhelm him. Michael represented pure innocence, pure peace. He closed his eyes and flipped through a cerebral slide show. Michael on the pitcher's mound; Michael banging out a beat loud enough to wake long-dead revolutionary war heroes buried in Yorktown; Michael on his bike trying to catch up to his buddies in the neighborhood; the innocent smile spreading across his face as he told one of his inane jokes; the incessant questions; Michael sitting in front of the computer surfing the web for baseball statistics and YouTube videos…

Torpedo and Thunderbolt.

He shook his head. The names kept jumping into his mind, crashing the calming party like an uninvited guest. Several more deep, cleansing breaths, and he started the show again—

Again the words, the sounds and syllables filled his mind, shutting out his son.

"Damn," he said loudly. A passing guard shot him a curious look.

Michael reappeared. Jason prayed he was out of danger. Jason wanted desperately to talk to his son. Knowing that it was impossible at the moment made the desire even greater.

Michael's angelic face smiled at his father. The boy was sitting in front of the computer, as Jason looked at what Michael had pulled up.

As with his dream about Jasmine, he would never know why the image flashed to him at that moment. The mind had its own agenda. It was a memory that held no special significance. Until now.

A book of codes, encryption codes. The kind used during warfare to keep the enemy from stealing them. The same kind of Nazi codes the Allies had broken during World War Two to help win the war. Michael was writing a report on these codes and the code breakers of Bletchley Park in England.

He'd asked if he could use the computer to Google the subject.

Michael had searched on several variations of the word "code." Jason had happened by as he typed the word "codename" into the search engine. A list of web sites loaded. Michael clicked on the first link. Being a ten-year-old, he'd quickly forgot his homework and began reading. There, on the screen, was the list.

Deacon

Lancer

Volunteer

Rawhide

Timberwolf

Torpedo

Tumbler

Thunderbolt

Pass Key

Searchlight

Beside each codename was a name corresponding to the person to whom it referred. Jason sat bolt upright as if a spring had released.

"Son of a bitch!" Beads of sweat sprouted on his forehead and upper lip. He brushed away the moisture with a trembling hand.

Deacon—Jimmy Carter

Lancer—JFK

Volunteer—LBJ

Rawhide—Ronald Reagan

Timberwolf—George H. W. Bush

Torpedo—Jacob R. Hope

Tumbler—George W. Bush

Thunderbolt—Gary Hope

Pass Key—Gerald Ford

Searchlight—Richard Nixon

The White House Signal Corps assigned codenames to the presidents. Codenames used by the Secret Service. Torpedo and Thunderbolt were the monikers for presidents Hope, father and son—42 and 44. The news shows, the aircraft carrier. Penrose Gatling Shipbuilders was hosting the christening of the *Hope* on Saturday.

What day is it?

Thursday. Today was Thursday. No. It was Friday morning.

The christening was tomorrow! Twenty-four hours!

Sam Fairing's request to take off Saturday, October 7. It was the first request he'd made of Jason after he'd taken the new job. The seventh was Saturday, the day of the christening. Peter and he had talked about taking the kids to the ceremony. Both presidents were going to be in attendance.

Jason swung his feet onto the floor. "Holy shit!" he said out loud. "It's the presidents! It's the damn presidents!"

PART THREE

CHAPTER 62

Friday, October 6

Christine drove past the mansion twice, scanning the grounds. She saw nothing unusual; if she'd been out for a leisurely drive, she would have taken no special notice of the place except for its architectural beauty. But Christine had an agenda this morning. She was measuring her plan of attack. It was a simple, straightforward strategy.

Parking her Chrysler 300 down the street, she walked back, her gait determined but unhurried. Her heart pounded inside her chest like a blacksmith's hammer. Sweat trickled down her back toward the revolver nestled inside the waistband of her jeans. Her hands flexed and relaxed with each step.

Standing across the divided roadway of Riverside Drive, she studied the redbrick mansion. Two cars were parked in the circular drive. She recognized Zanns's blue Mercedes, but the green, expensive sports car was a make unknown to her. Beyond the vehicles, the granite, circular steps led to the high-columned portico.

She reached under her leather jacket and checked the Colt one last time. *Fitting*, she thought. Her father's gun would be the weapon used to end the bitch's life. Lily Zanns probably hadn't committed the deed. The woman lived atop the food chain. She wouldn't have soiled her precious, manicured hands. But Lily Zanns's fingerprints were all over her father's murder. The recording proved it.

Christine had looked upon the elegant matriarch as her father's savior. Zanns had ripped Daddy from the drooling jaws of his self-made financial ruin. Her cunning business sense and uncompromising deftness had seemed magical, inimitable. Though reviled by Thomas Pettigrew, she always carried herself—in Christine's eyes, anyway—with grace and tact. That supposedly generous person had orchestrated her father's demise and then paid for the funeral, feigning love and empathy. The deep respect Christine once felt had transformed into a raw, festering hatred in the time it took for her to hear Zanns's words on the recording. During that brief span, she had determined she would kill Lily Zanns. That was why she'd refused Jason's request to flee.

Christine took two steps into the street…

The blaring wail of a car horn interrupted her trance, stopping her cold. She jumped at the screech of locked rubber. The sedan's front bumper stopped inches short of her left knee. The driver screamed profanities from behind the safety glass.

Christine looked at him, disoriented and unfocused. She composed herself and staggered across the street. As the car drove off, she tugged down on her jacket with both hands, took a deep breath, and marched up the drive. On the portico, she peered inside the tall, shuttered windows, but saw little past the thick drapes. She removed the revolver and checked the load again. She wasn't an expert marksman, but her father had shown her the basics. Shielding the gun from view, she advanced to the eleven-foot, ornately carved door.

She drew in two long, deep breaths, expelling them slowly.

It wasn't enough to simply kill her. She wanted to see the look in Zanns's eyes when she realized Christine was avenging her father.

Gun pressed against her thigh, she closed her eyes and whispered a short prayer asking for God and her father's forgiveness. The irony was not lost on her. She was praying for strength to kill another human being. She whispered, "I love you, Daddy."

She pressed the door chime and moved the gun into position.

* * *

Jason heard the keys sliding into the lock of his cell door. The guard stood beside a tattooed man in handcuffs. Every inch of exposed skin was covered in body art. His bald head and forehead were covered by a flowing, black-and-green dragon with three drops of blood dripping from its jaws. The lowest droplet was situated between the man's eyes.

Jason sat up on his elbows and watched the guard remove the cuffs. Then he saw something that left a twinge in his gut. Tattoo Man smiled discreetly at the guard, who winked back at him. Then the guard locked them in the cell designed for only one human being.

* * *

The door swung open.

The tall, swarthy manservant peered into Christine's eyes and then the barrel of the Colt. Even though she was the one holding the weapon, Christine swallowed hard. The revolver trembled in her petite hands. Oliver's demeanor showed no more alarm than if she'd been a door-to-door salesman.

"Can I help you, miss?" His eyes darted about, assessing the situation.

Christine cocked the hammer and deepened her voice. "I want to see Lily. Now!"

Oliver contemplated the quaking barrel. "As you wish."

Christine flicked the weapon twice. Oliver backed in, his eyes never leaving her.

"Move away from the door! Stay where I can see you!"

Oliver retreated farther into the mansion.

Christine stepped inside, backing into the door until it latched. She never once averted her gaze from the enormous man.

Zanns appeared from the study in a silk green sari, holding a cup and saucer. She noticed Christine and froze. The dark tea spilled, staining the white carpet. Zanns glanced at Oliver, then back to Christine. "Well, well, my child. What brings you to my humble abode—with a gun no less? Have we done something to offend you?"

Christine twitched the gun with more bravado. "Get over there, next to him!"

Zanns placed the cup on an ornate end table and moved beside her employee.

"You killed my father!"

"I don't know what you—"

"Shut up!" Christine raised the gun higher, aiming between Zanns's perfectly trimmed eyebrows. "Don't—don't you dare—lie to me. I know the truth!"

"Ms. Christine, you must put the gun down. Then we can talk."

A single tear streaked down Christine's cheek. She dared not wipe it away. The Colt was too heavy for her to hold with only one hand.

"Stop! Stop with the lies. Everything that comes out of your mouth is a lie. We know about the murders!"

"I did not kill your father, Ms. Christine—"

When the gun went off, it sounded like a clap of thunder. Chunks of plaster rained down. Oliver and Zanns ducked reflexively. The recoil jolted Christine backward.

Zanns and Oliver stood erect again. Christine releveled the weapon as a coil of smoke escaped the barrel. "I know about his so-called accident. I don't know how you did it, but *you...you* had him killed."

"What makes you think that I would do something so vile? Your father was a good man. He had a drinking problem—"

Another shot rang out. A tall vase behind Zanns disintegrated.

"Shut up!"

Oliver took another step in her direction.

"I want to hear you say it!"

"Say what, my child?"

"That you murdered my father and Douglas Winstead. You're responsible for their deaths—their murders!"

It lasted only an instant. Zanns's eyes displayed a nanosecond of alarm at the mention of Winstead's name. Her stoicism returned instantly.

"It's all on tape. The phony prescriptions. I've seen the files and heard the recording. And we know you're planning on killing again. Two more men are scheduled to die. You won't succeed—"

Oliver was a step and a dive away. As if she were reading his mind, Christine pointed the gun at him. Oliver held up his hands in surrender. Two facts registered in her frantically working mind. First, she noticed the missing pinky fingers on each hand. Her eyes moved lower. He wore a pullover with short sleeves. His arms were exposed. Christine recognized the small tattoo etched into the skin of his forearm. "You! It was you in my father's house that day!"

Everything made sense now. Oliver was the same height as the attacker. The skin filling the eyeholes of the mask was bronzed. Then there was the tattoo.

Waves of rage pummeled her, washing away any remnant of self-control. Tears welled and spilled down her face. Christine jerked the gun back and forth between Zanns and Oliver. "It stops right here, right now!"

As she waved the weapon between her two captives, frantic pounding rattled the front door. Voices shouted, demanding entry. It was the police.

CHAPTER 63

Tattoo Man had been eyeing him for thirty minutes—him, and the camera mounted in the corner just under the ceiling. His body was like an NFL linebacker's. Hard sinew rippled the decorated skin. Chemically enhanced workouts, Jason thought. The man would never pass a piss test.

Jason focused on the ceiling again. How had he ended up here? He felt like he was strapped in an out-of-control carnival ride that was rapidly gaining speed and on the verge of flying apart.

The audio recording made in the small hours of this morning confirmed an assassination was being planned in twenty-four hours. Jacob R. Hope, number 42, and Gary Hope, number 44, were targets. A multitude of scenarios real and imagined played out on an endless loop in his head.

He toyed again with the idea of calling Detective Baxter and laying everything out for him. But he rejected it, again. Baxter believed he was a killer. Lily Zanns and her cabal had framed Jason and tidily shrink-wrapped it for the police. Baxter thought Jason was concocting stories to save his own skin. Even as Jason spoke the words, they sounded incredible.

Peter would know what to do. His brother would arrive this morning with the lawyer, and they'd explain about the assassination. There was still time to prevent the attack. Waterhouse should have contacted the police by now. They would take the information to someone at the Secret Service, and Zanns's plans would be squelched.

What was the name of the Secret Service agent at the shipyard?

Jason checked Tattoo Man, meeting and holding his gaze. The man glanced at the camera again, then back at Jason. The corner of his mouth lifted in a sardonic smile. He shifted, shuffling his boots on the cold, concrete floor.

Two things about the man bothered Jason. First, his skin. Second, his presence. The jail was not crowded, and he was sure they had room for this human art collection elsewhere. Jason could handle himself well. His skill and training in Tae Kwon Doe had prepared him for any conceivable threat. Nonetheless, he'd give this massive wall of brawn and bone a wide berth.

As that thought crossed Jason's mine, Tattoo pushed himself off the wall and moved toward the pharmacist, his steroid-engorged right arm holding something behind his back.

Shit!

"Time to die, motherfucker!" Tattoo Man hissed.

* * *

Everything happened in a split second that elapsed in agonizingly slow motion. The pounding on the door and the shouts jolted her. Christine jumped and turned her head toward the sound.

Oliver sprang.

Christine noticed the darting movement out of the corner of her eye and barely sidestepped his tackle. He grazed her, knocking her into a wall table and spilling expensive knickknacks. The wall broke her fall. Oliver grabbed her arm and pushed the gun into the air. She wrestled with the behemoth. Oliver was on his knees when Christine slammed her own knee into his gut.

He shoved her backward. This time she landed on her backside and squeezed the trigger. The muzzle flash lit the room, and another deafening report pounded their eardrums.

Instantly, the commotion on the other side of the door intensified. The police were trying to kick in the massive oak portal.

* * *

Jason was halfway to standing when Tattoo Man landed on him. He extended his arms to stop the man's forward movement, but was forced back onto the steel bed. Jason's spine felt like it was going to snap. Jason used the momentum to roll Tattoo Man to the side. They landed on the floor, Jason on top. A large hand found Jason's throat. Jason wrapped both hands around the massive wrist, trying to peel it away.

The metal shank arced through the air. Jason tried to block the blow, but only managed to slow it. The shank pierced his orange jumpsuit and the skin beneath. Jason let out an agonized grunt and rolled onto his back.

White-hot pain seared his left side. Tattoo Man buried the shank deeper, forcing a more rigid spasm from Jason. He fought the pain, reached down, and grabbed a handful of testicle, squeezing with all his strength. The gargantuan screamed, releasing the shank, leaving it protruding from Jason's flesh.

Jason cocked his head and slammed it into the tattooed face, crunching the nose, all the while continuing to crush testicles. The pressure around Jason's throat relaxed. Jason rolled off the man and began reaching for the object in his side. Before he could, the large assailant was over him. Jason hoisted a foot to the man's sternum and kicked, propelling him backward. Tattoo

Man flew several feet through the dank air. Upon landing, his bloodied head bounced off the unyielding floor.

Jason instinctively withdrew the shank, tearing away a chunk of flesh, sending another swirling impulse through him. A quarter-size morsel dangled from the tip like bait on a hook.

Riding an adrenaline surge, Jason maneuvered the bloody weapon in his hand for a downwards thrust into Tattoo's chest. But Tattoo Man recovered in time to counter the attack. His fist connected with Jason's head, knocking him toward the stainless steel toilet. The shank clattered to the floor, the chunk of human tissue rolling with it. Tattoo Man staggered to vertical, lunging at the pharmacist like a drunken bull.

Jason snapped off a close-quarter front kick to the chin, snapping the lower jaw with a loud bone-on-bone crack. Tattoo barely slowed. Droplets of blood and sweat showered Jason.

Jason rolled under him, cutting the man's legs as he did. Jason scrambled under the falling body and spun, preparing for the next attack

Tattoo pushed himself up as Jason unleashed a right cross that would have made a heavyweight champion proud, connecting with the shattered jaw. His fist met with a mushy tangle of skin and bone. Tattoo howled and dropped. The back of his head connected with the stainless steel commode, ringing it like a bell. He rolled over, blood, teeth, and mucous dripping from the hole that would not chew solid food again for months.

Chest heaving, Jason, winced at the carnage he'd inflicted. Barely conscious, Tattoo rolled onto his back, unintelligible noises emanating from his gurgling throat. The eyes were filled with pain, fear, and the knowledge that he'd been bested by a man he should have eaten for lunch. The eyes darted about, looking for a way out. Jason winced as he reached down with his right hand and pressed a finger into the left cheek and jaw. Chunks of bone grated under skin. Air escaped from Tattoo's lungs, spewing Jason with a fine mist of red spittle. His high-pitched scream cut through the jail. "Do you even know why you were sent to kill me?"

He managed a feeble shake of the head. Jason didn't care; he could already guess who'd sent him. Two deputies arrived at the cell door and charged in. One was the same deputy who had allowed Tattoo Man access. The shock and disbelief on his face told Jason he was part of the conspiracy.

Jason slumped, his eyes never leaving the shocked deputy. Reaching across his body, he touched his left side. His jumpsuit was soaked in red. His fingers found the gaping wound. The room began to waver, shimmering like a mirage on a summer day. Jason was unconscious before he hit the floor.

Chapter 64

Panic overtaking her, Christine fled, bolting through the house. Oliver was still on his knees, clutching his abdomen. Christine crashed through the french doors into the backyard. The front door continued to rattle as she made her escape. She dashed down the sloped lawn to the water's edge, afraid to look back. Her arms pumped like a sprinter's. Her eyes alternated between the ground and the yardage beyond. The heavy Colt was still clutched in her right hand. At the pier, Christine turned, veering north across the neighboring yard.

* * *

With the tenth kick, the dead bolt splintered the frame. The door swung wide. Zanns watched as a tall, thin, plainclothes police officer charged in, gun leveled. Two more men followed. The tall man, the leader, pointed and shouted commands. One man went left, disappearing into the kitchen, while the leader and another man turned right into an enormous living area. They moved cautiously, crouched, weapons ready.

"Freeze! Hold it right there!" Palmer yelled, aiming at the woman. "Let me see your hands!"

Zanns tried to look shaken and nervous, which wasn't hard. "She tried to kill us. She went that way. Hurry!"

The tall police officer motioned with a flick of his head for his partner to give chase. The younger detective jogged off toward the river and the dock. The tall man lifted a radio, calling for backup. K-9 units would arrive within minutes, he was told.

* * *

Christine's lungs burned. She stopped and rested with hands on knees, wheezing as if sucking air through a coffee straw. She had put four spacious properties between her and the mansion, each separated by tall hedgerows. She could hear a body crashing through bushes in the distance behind her.

The gun felt as if it were growing heavier with each second. She waded into the shallow, murky waters of the James and released the weapon, letting it sink out of sight. The sound of rustling bushes grew louder. Christine sucked in three deep breaths, climbed out of the river, and jogged through the next yard, staying low.

Lily Zanns, she knew, was spinning this incident, accusing Christine of attempted murder. Christine hopped over a row of low shrubs and, ignoring the pain in her limbs and burning in her chest, turned her jog into a dead sprint.

* * *

Zanns informed Palmer that the intruder was named Christine Pettigrew.

"Why was she trying to kill you?" the detective asked. He flashed a badge and introduced himself as Detective John Palmer.

Zanns placed the flat of her palm on her cheek, thinking. "It seems she blames me for her father's death. She wants vengeance."

"By her father, you mean Thomas Pettigrew?"

"That's correct. How did you know that?"

He ignored the question. "Why does she blame you?"

"I purchased her father's pharmacy several years ago. Had I not, the business would have failed. But she does not see it that way. To her, I am the person that destroyed her father, drove him to drink, and ultimately into a tree in Smithfield."

"I see," Palmer replied. "She won't get far on foot. We'll have more units and canine patrols here in a matter of minutes."

He moved to a virginal white sofa on the opposite side of the sunken living area. Oliver returned with a gleaming, sterling-silver tea service. He placed it on the coffee table and offered a cup to Palmer, who declined, and then served his boss.

She sipped the pungent liquid. "It's quite good. I have it imported from Egypt."

"Can you continue?" Palmer asked, seemingly annoyed.

"Of course. The tea helps to relax me," she said, reading his mood. "That whole episode was quite frightening. How on earth did you show up at the moment she was about to shoot us?"

"Ms. Zanns, that was pure luck. We were coming to ask you about certain…irregularities with the billing of some of your prescriptions. Does this incident have anything to do with these irregularities?"

"And how did you come across this information?"

"I would rather not say for the moment. So, what do you know about it?"

"You are well informed, Detective. I have recently been made aware of some problems in that regard. I found out earlier this week. I have been consulting with my attorneys."

"What are you doing about it?"

"We are going to investigate it thoroughly. And the perpetrators will be fired and prosecuted to the fullest extent of the law. Perhaps you may be of assistance?"

"I am referring the case to the state police's white-collar crime unit. I'm sure you'll be able to talk to the trooper in question, Trooper Levinson. At the moment, he is chasing down Ms. Pettigrew."

"That would be perfect. I wish to cooperate with the authorities in any way I can. I hope it can be handled quietly."

"I can't guarantee anything." Palmer hesitated. "Jason Rodgers is one of your pharmacists, correct?"

"Yes, he is. I hired him a short time ago."

"What kind of an employee is he?"

"He has been a disappointment. It seems he is not focused on his job, but on other issues."

"What kind of issues?" Palmer scribbled in a handheld notepad he'd pulled from his suit.

"Christine Pettigrew has convinced Rodgers—they are former lovers—that her father's death was a murder and not an accident."

"And she thinks you murdered him? Is that right?"

"That's correct."

"Did you?"

"I am a business woman, not a killer."

"Who is Douglas Winstead?" asked Palmer.

Zanns looked surprised, then confused. "I believe he is one of the persons involved in this insurance fraud."

"You mean 'was.'"

"Was?"

"Winstead is dead. He was murdered yesterday."

Zanns brought a hand to her mouth. "Mon Dieu!"

"Where were you last night between five and nine in the evening?"

"I was here all night."

"Can anyone vouch for your whereabouts?"

"Oliver, my servant, can."

"Anyone else?"

"I was here with Dr. Jasmine Kader and my other pharmacist, Samuel Fairing. I'm sure they can vouch for me as well."

Palmer flipped the notebook closed and stood. "Thank you, Ms. Zanns. There will be some activity up and down the street while we track down this woman. If you think of anything else which could be helpful regarding this incident or the killing of Douglas Winstead, please call me." He handed her a business card.

Zanns made a show of trying to get out of the chair. Palmer assisted her. She shook his hand weakly and led him to the front door. "Trust me, Detective. We will be securing the house immediately. I do not want that crazy woman coming back."

Five more cruisers and two canine units, lights flashing, rumbled to a stop out front.

* * *

Christine knelt in the water before the concrete pipe. Two feet in diameter, it was barely wide enough to squeeze her shoulders through. At its mouth, a stream of water trickled into the river. Beyond that, thick blackness quickly overtook the gray concrete of the pipe's interior.

Her clothing was soaked to midchest. Her muscles trembled. Outrunning the cops would not happen. Their voices were getting closer. Police cars sped past on Riverside Drive, no doubt en route to Zanns's.

So much for being brave and not worrying about consequences, she told herself. The police had showed up at the precise moment she was about to kill Lily Zanns.

How had they known? Who had tipped them off?

Stretching her arms in front of her, she squeezed into the pipe to the waist. Her delicate hands found the rough concrete, and she dragged herself inside until her soaked tennis shoes were blanketed in shadow. The pipe seemed to constrict around her.

"Oh God," she whispered, fighting the urge to back out. "Please help me!"

Inchworming her way, Christine pulled her body through the rivulet of water. She scraped her head looking back to check her progress.

Keep moving!

The circle of light shrank slowly. Her heavy breathing echoed inside the pipe. Soon her hands, elbows, and knees became raw. In time, the circle of light grew to a tiny, glowing speck. Christine could only guess how far she'd crawled. Unable to pull herself farther, she stopped. Her body would not produce another ounce of energy. This would have to do.

She lay on her stomach. The water, coming from God only knew where, cascaded around her. Her thoughts turned to Jason, the man who'd abandoned her so many years ago. The same man who, hours ago, had run to warn her. Christine wished she'd heeded that warning. Now she wanted him beside her. Jason would know what to do. He always did.

CHAPTER 65

"You have a lacerated kidney. You're going to need surgery," the young female doctor informed Jason.

He writhed in pain on the gurney. She lifted her bloodied, gloved hand to avoid his restrained thrashing.

The trauma room at the Tidewater Regional Medical Center in Newport News was crammed with medical equipment mounted from floor to ceiling, from an X-ray console and crash cart to cabinets stuffed with intravenous solutions. The two guards that had appeared after the attack stood outside the door. Jason lay naked except for his blood-stained underwear and flip-flops. His legs were covered by a hospital blanket. The orange, blood-soaked jumpsuit lay in a heap in the corner. Jason could hear shouts and orders being barked from the hallway. A patient was making some sort of commotion.

The doctor continued to urge Jason to lie still. "I need to finish my examination, Mr. Rodgers!" Jason pushed her hands away. "Call the OR and get a room," the doctor barked to a nurse. "I want an IV of D5W and one-half normal saline, wide open. Type and cross match four units of blood. I want a Chem-12. Give him 50 mg of meperidine IV. Let's pack that wound until we can get him to the OR. Also, I want to start intravenous antibiotics. Start with Zosyn 3.375 mg every six hours. Who's the surgeon on call?"

The nurse replied with a name. The doctor turned back to Jason. "You've got a pretty severe wound here, Mr. Rodgers. You're bleeding pretty heavily. We're going to start you on a medicine to prevent any infection and give you something for the pain."

"Marvelous," he groaned.

The trauma room was flanked by other treatment rooms filled with patients. Nurses, doctors, attendants, and paramedics—all wearing different-colored surgical scrubs—hurried in every direction. Their numbers did not instill Jason with confidence. If Zanns had the ability to buy off a deputy, who else might be on her payroll? He might go to surgery and wake up dead.

The portly nurse entered, pulled down Jason's drawers, and stabbed a needle into his buttock.

He had to leave! Now! As he told himself this, a sliver of opportunity presented itself.

Outside the trauma room, shouting and screaming erupted. Apparently, another patient was causing some trouble. Nurses and doctors ran past. Probably a drunk or a druggie flipped out on meth.

The deputies at the door glanced at Jason. Jason peeked out through a forest of lashes, pretending to be unconscious—and waited.

"Haldol 5mg IM now," someone shouted.

"More restraints!"

One deputy moved toward the noise, out of sight, motioning for the other—the one that had betrayed Jason—to stay put.

Seconds later, a scrum of three people crashed to the floor. Another explosion of noise erupted outside the door.

"Get hold of his hands!"

Struggling, grunting, swearing.

"Grab his arm! I need some help here!"

Two bodies flew onto the floor in full view of Jason's room. The patient landed on top of the first deputy. The second deputy glanced at Jason, who lay perfectly still.

The scuffle moved farther down the hall. Another look.

"He's trying to get my gun!"

The second deputy shook his head, sighed, and moved off.

Now!

Jason leapt from the bed, his side screaming in protest. He darted from the room toward the emergency entrance, clad only in his blood-stained skivvies and flip-flops. He raced past the nurse's station and the med room. The portly nurse looked up and saw the half-naked blur. Her eyes popped. "You! Stop!"

Two paths were open to him. Straight ahead, a hallway led deep inside the hospital. To the right were the sliding doors of the emergency entrance, the same doors through which he had been wheeled less than an hour ago. An ambulance had pulled in. Two paramedics were unloading an elderly patient on a gurney. The glass doors were sliding open.

Jason arrived before they were fully open, hitting them hard with a shoulder. The doors crashed outward, off their tracks. The paramedics' heads whipped toward the sound.

Jason rammed the closest paramedic and the gurney simultaneously. He bolted around the stretcher and the stunned paramedics on his way to the truck cab. He climbed in, found the gearshift, and punched the accelerator. The rig lurched forward, its two rear doors, still open, swinging violently.

CHAPTER 66

The sparse traffic on Interstate 64 yielded to the flashing lights of the ambulance. Jason had driven through every traffic light between the hospital and the on ramp, attracting attention but no concern. He was doing eighty, heading out of the city without a destination. A fleet of police cruisers would soon be hot on his bumper like rabid hounds.

Air rushed through the open windows of the cab. Blood continued to trickle out of the gash in his side, adding a fresh layer to the crusted bandage. His eyelids felt heavy, and the pain and his consciousness lessened with each minute. The meperidine, a potent narcotic, was slowly exerting its grip on his senses.

Jason mashed the accelerator to the floorboard. The eight cylinders kicked in. The vehicle lurched, notching the speedometer toward ninety...ninety-five. It zipped under the Jefferson Avenue overpass toward the northern stretches of Newport News and Williamsburg beyond.

Have to...get...word to Peter.

He shook his head, trying to clear the accumulating cobwebs. All that did was make him dizzy. The ambulance drifted onto the solid,

328

white line of the service lane. Jason overcorrected, swinging back over the dotted center line. Fortunately, traffic was very light. Ten minutes later, the exit ramp sign for Route 199 in Williamsburg zipped past.

Have to find...another car! Through the fog, he remembered the hotel across from Water Country. *Ditch the ambulance...*

He hit the exit too fast. He jerked the wheel to the right to keep from soaring into the wooded ravine. The front left tire flirted with the edge of the asphalt, spewing dirt and debris. He jerked the wheel even farther right. Equipment crashed about in the cabin behind him.

Speeding onto 199, he sideswiped two sedans, crunching fenders and spinning them into the median. To his left, brief glimpses of white caught his eye. Large alabaster busts towered behind the thin green foliage.

Presidents Park! Through the drug-induced fog, Jason concocted a plan.

His forearms sagged on the top of the steering wheel. His eyelids struggled to stay open, and his head bobbed. The vehicle slowed to sixty-five, teetering on the edge of control, drifting into the grassy median, jostling Jason to semialertness.

He hit the intersection just beyond the hotel, driving though the oncoming traffic. Blaring horns and screeching, smoking rubber filled the air. A row of hedges were flattened under the wheels of the rescue vehicle. It wasn't pretty, but he managed to find the roadway curving behind the hotel toward the tourist attractions.

Jason stopped dead center in the deserted parking area, lights still flashing. He fell out of the door, landing on his chest and face. Stumbling to his feet, Jason attempted a run, managing only an unsteady, weaving gait. He pressed on. The adrenaline coursing through him was fighting a losing battle with blood loss, pain, and the narcotic. He staggered through a thicket of trees onto the adjacent hotel campus. What little food there was in his stomach wanted out, and began crawling to the back of his throat. In the distance, he heard the thump-thump of rotors. A helicopter.

Have to find...someplace to lie...down!

Guests were few and far between. After Labor Day, the tourists dried up, closing Water Country and Busch Gardens. The hotel was operating on a skeleton crew. A few cars dotted the asphalt of the hotel parking lot.

Heading away from Jason, a hotel employee pushed a cart to a trash enclosure. He had propped open the back door with a plastic dustpan. Jason raced unsteadily to the doorway and stepped inside.

A stairway sat to the left. He opened the stairwell door and slipped in. Falling to his knees, he crawled under the angle of the stairs behind a collection of toilet paper cartons and cleaning supplies. The outer door swung shut on its hydraulic closer as the Newport News police helicopter appeared over the trees two miles downrange, its rotors thumping as fast as Jason's heart.

It was the last sound an exhausted and medicated Jason heard before he passed out.

CHAPTER 67

The mere mention of Jason Rodgers's name was enough to get Special Agent Broadhurst to drop everything and rush over to the York County Sheriff's Office. He sat impatiently in a conference room. With the christening only twenty-four hours away, he had a thousand things to do. The only reason he was here was because Investigator Baxter had phoned, mentioning Jason Rodgers's name and claiming he had information Broadhurst would want to see. He'd refused to discuss it over the phone. That rare but familiar feeling had sprouted in his gut. It was more than the acid eating away at the lining of his stomach. He'd only had it twice before in his career. Both occasions had required firing his weapon.

Hundreds of threats were investigated every month by the service. Each and every lead had to be checked out. Most were crackpots blowing off steam. Some were real and had to be squelched before they amounted to anything. A rare few made the news. If they had to act to protect the "Man" from an assassin the day of an event, the service had failed. Broadhurst hoped the Rodgers case was not going to be one of those failures.

331

On the way over, Broadhurst discussed the latest intelligence with Simon Vanover in the Norfolk field office. The tension in Vanover's voice was palpable. The news would not be good.

The agents tailing Rodgers had lost the suspect outside a local restaurant after their car had been struck by another vehicle, Vanover explained. By the time a backup vehicle could be obtained, Rodgers had slipped away. His residence was dark and vacant. Rodgers had been smart enough to stay away. There had been no hits on his credit or debit cards. A trace on his cell phone revealed it was locked away in a drawer at the jail in Williamsburg.

Jason Rodgers had vanished.

Until an hour ago, Broadhurst hadn't considered the pharmacist a legitimate threat. He didn't fit the profile. His past was devoid of controversial political activities. He hadn't had a traffic ticket in the last three years. There was no history of mental illness. Rodgers just seemed incredibly stupid or naïve.

Vanover's next tidbit sent Broadhurst's gut into a fiery eruption. The forensic accountants in the investigative branch had completed a background check and hastily obtained a search warrant to examine Rodgers's finances. Fifty thousand dollars had been deposited from an enterprise named Cooper Venture Capital in two separate transactions within the last two weeks, by far the largest deposit the man had ever made. It was the first hard evidence corroborating what Broadhurst's gut was telling him. Photos of the carrier at the dry dock, the pharmacist's visit to the Windsor Towers yesterday, and now the revelation that he'd pocketed a large amount of cash...

It was time to bring in the pharmacist for more intense questioning. It was Friday afternoon. The christening was tomorrow morning. Broadhurst would make sure, at the very least, that Rodgers remained out of commission until after the christening.

Broadhurst shook two Tums from the plastic container and popped them in his mouth, crunching them. He'd devoured half the bottle since this morning.

What the hell's taking so long?

A large black man walked in. "Agent Broadhurst, I'm Lieutenant Cal Baxter. Sorry to keep you waiting." Baxter eased into one of the chairs.

"What's all this about?" Broadhurst demanded. "I've got a lot to do."

"You'll be very interested in what we found," Baxter replied. He removed a plastic bag containing several papers from a file folder. "We executed a search warrant today on Jason Rodgers's residence. We found these documents. He's a prime suspect, the only suspect actually, in the murder of his ex-girlfriend, Sheila Boquist."

"Is that the one I read about in the papers this morning?" The article had been a two-column job above the fold of the *Hampton Roads Gazette* and hadn't mentioned suspects.

"One and the same. These documents were found among his things. I thought you'd be interested in them." Baxter slid the plastic bag across the table.

Broadhurst studied the documents for two minutes. "Jesus, Mary, and Joseph," he whispered.

One was an itinerary of the events for Saturday's christening. The second was a seating chart with the names and locations of each of the dignitaries attending, including both presidents. Two large red *X*s marked the current president's seat and the podium, where dignitaries would be delivering remarks. The final piece of paper was a list of speakers and times.

All of it was classified.

The fact that Rodgers had this kind of information sent a cold shiver down Broadhurst's spine. There were only a handful of people on the planet privy to these details. A few were in the administration; the rest were employed by the Secret Service. Someone had leaked information about the presidential trip to Newport News. It made finding Jason Rodgers job number one.

Broadhurst was hoping the good Lord was looking over his shoulder as he asked his next question. If Rodgers had been arrested, it would explain why Vanover's men couldn't find him. And it would make the Secret Service agent's job much easier. "I want to talk to him immediately," he said. "Do you have him in custody?"

Baxter cleared his throat. "Unfortunately, Rodgers was stabbed by another prisoner while in custody and was taken to Tidewater. He escaped. That's why I kept you waiting. I was getting the rundown from the Newport News PD."

"How the hell did you guys manage to let this guy escape? He's a potential assassin!"

"Why is Rodgers a threat to the president?"

"He was detained for questioning a few days ago after photographing the aircraft carrier. Claimed not to know it was verboten. Based on *this* evidence"—Broadhurst shook the papers—"it seems he's been scouting out the location. We had agents tailing him. They lost him last night, probably because you guys had arrested him."

"You have been tailing him, and you didn't bother to let us know?"

CHAPTER 68

The cool cement smelled like a mildewed men's locker room. Jason's eyelids fluttered. The cinder block wall and brown cardboard boxes gradually came into sharp focus. He sat up and bumped his head on the underside of the stairs, jogging his memory of recent events.

Jason crawled around the supplies to the stairwell door and peeked down the hall. The corridor ran the length of the building and emptied into the small foyer at the front. The voice of a woman making small talk drifted from the foyer.

Through the outer door, voices and the drone of engines drifted to him. The clipped conversations were sharp and tense.

Jason fought his sluggishness and moved to the emergency exit. The outside of the door had no handle. If you exited through it, there was no way back in. Hence the dustpan doorstop the attendant had used earlier when emptying the trash. He cracked the door and peered out.

A blue uniform walked past, followed by another, then a third. The squawk of a radio. Swirling lights pulsed against the building. Police swarmed like moths to a floodlight.

Jason heard one of them say, "He's not in the hotel; we searched every room."

A few seconds later, the voice emanating from the foyer, which had been jovial and relaxed, became filled with concern. "Hold on, let me go check out this alarm. Patrick probably propped the door open again. The police are everywhere looking for some escaped prisoner."

Jason inspected the doorframe. A contact sensor was mounted on the crossbeam. He had activated an alarm.

The metal dustpan leaned against the wall. Quickly, he grabbed it, sticking it between the frame and the door. He retreated into the stairwell and climbed the stairs three at a time. A minute later, sweaty and panting, he cracked the stairwell door on the third floor. A maid's cart sat near an open room five feet away. The metal catch lock was stuck between the door and the frame, keeping it from fully closing. The cleaning woman was not in sight.

He pushed out of the stairwell, stepped to the room, and peered in. He found it empty. The beds were made and towels were neatly folded in their metal racks. Jason ducked inside the closet and quietly slid the door closed.

A few minutes later—it seemed like an eternity—the cart rattled and footfalls shuffled just outside the closet. Jason tensed. Just as quickly, the footfalls retreated, and the door swung closed. Jason breathed again. He waited thirty seconds and stepped out into his new sanctuary. The police had already searched every room in the hotel, so he relaxed a little. He was trapped at the moment, but relatively safe.

* * *

I'm too old for this shit, Waterhouse thought.

The forecast called for heavy rain and thundershowers tonight and tomorrow. The dreary day added to Waterhouse's monumental fatigue. He hadn't slept in thirty-six hours. Some expensive surveillance equipment was at the bottom of the James. He was pissed—and tired. The adventure on the *Vengeance* and his near drowning had caught up with him. Becky Sue had called an hour ago, ready for some adult fun. Waterhouse had begged off, promising to call her soon.

Waterhouse had attached the handheld recorder to his laptop and burned a CD for Jason to share with Christine. The "Conversation," as Waterhouse now referred to it, had been sent as an e-mail attachment to Detective John Palmer. Waterhouse was sure Palmer would run it over to the Secret Service within minutes of receiving it. For good measure, a copy had been sent to Jason's account and also to his own. Finally, he'd wrapped the recorder in plastic and duct taped it to the underside of the fireplace near the flue.

Fifteen hours had passed since Rodgers had departed for the Pettigrew woman's house. In that time, he'd even gone to Rodgers's house and scanned it for electronic surveillance, spending nearly two hours checking the place. It was clean. That meant that the small camera Jason had come across was the only device planted, or that the bad guys had come back and removed the rest. Waterhouse guessed it was the latter. In any event, the space was now righteous again.

His cell phone was in the Blazer, and had been since he'd arrived home. He'd returned the borrowed Dodge to his buddy and driven home in the Blazer. Waterhouse thought about retrieving it. If the Rodgers brothers tried to contact him, he wouldn't know it. His landline was unlisted. He'd learned long ago not to give it out. There were angry spouses out there who didn't like being spied on. *No matter*, he thought. The Conversation had been sent. For now, his job was done. He didn't want to hear any urgent messages which might nag at his conscience and interfere with his ability to catch some shut-eye. He would get the phone when he woke. He laid his head on the sofa and was fast asleep in seconds.

* * *

Robert Ford peered through the binoculars at the small, square house in Poquoson from the passenger seat of the Lincoln. His driver and leader, Eurus, had pulled to a stop a hundred yards up the street, in the shadow of a large elm.

"He's in there," Ford said, his lips moving beneath the field glasses. "I saw him going past the window. In the living room."

"He's got to be alone," Eurus said. He was pointing a device at the window. Its laser beam picked up the vibrations of the glass. His headphones captured sounds inside. "He hasn't said a word since the woman called. It's been over an hour."

"Are we going in?" Ford asked.

Eurus paused and said, "No, this guy's probably armed. I've got a better idea. Hand me the rifle."

Eurus picked up his phone, looked up the phone in the dossier, and dialed. Ford pulled the long, silenced sniper rifle from under the blanket on the backseat.

* * *

Waterhouse's landline chirped beside his head, stirring him instantly. Years of stakeouts and surveillance had honed his ability to wake to alert status quickly. He didn't recognize the number.

"This is Mike with Glencoe Home Exteriors. We have a man in your area and we'd like to give you a free estimate on covering your home with premier vinyl siding—"

"I'm sorry, I'm not interested. How did you get this number?"

"If you'll just give him a minute, I'm sure we can make you a great offer—"

"I said I'm not interested!"

"The man is in your driveway right now. It will only take a minute—"

Waterhouse ended the call and marched to the door, yanking it open. Damned telemarketers! He stopped on the stoop when he realized the driveway was empty except for the Blazer.

What the hell?

The round struck Waterhouse above the left eyebrow, snapping his head back like a doll's. He tumbled back into the house, crashing back through the open front door.

CHAPTER 69

The circle of light had vanished. Christine had no idea how long she'd been inside the pipe. The darkness was absolute, a three-dimensional shroud that seemed to possess mass and weight. It pressed down on her. She flexed her neck, looking back to the now-invisible opening. Two sensations told her she was still alive: the coarse feel of the cold pipe, and the sound of frigid water dribbling around her.

The voices of cops mingled with the barking dogs lingered for what seemed an eternity. The commotion was barely audible from inside the pipe, but nerve-racking nonetheless. Twice, water sloshed near the entrance. A beam of light lurked near the opening but was swallowed by the darkness. Both times, it disappeared. Eventually, all sounds of her pursuers died away.

Keeping her eyes closed, Christine crept backward, aided by the downward incline. Minutes later, she dropped silently into the water of the James.

340

Trying to take vengeance on Lily Zanns had been stupid and juvenile, that was obvious now. She'd barely managed to evade capture— or worse. By now, the police knew who she was and where she lived.

She had to find the one person, the only man she trusted. Jason had always looked out for her, even when he'd left all those years ago. His decision had been steeped in concern for her and her father's well-being. He'd sacrificed his professional and personal life for her. It was a totally selfless act. After he'd found out that Zanns's people were sending people to kill them, he'd run to warn her. Selfishly, she'd ignored him and sent him away. Then, foolishly, she'd tried to take matters into her own hands.

She knew now what she wanted. She wanted Jason Rodgers at her side, now and forever. She needed his help to get out of this mess. And she wanted to make up for the years they'd missed together. She wanted to erase the past and create a new future. She had to get back to Jason.

Christine prayed she hadn't jeopardized her relationship with him. More importantly, she appealed to the Almighty that her miscalculation hadn't put his life in greater danger.

Dripping wet, she crawled out of the river onto the grass. Staying in the shadows, she moved south to where she'd left the car. It was gone. Scanning potential escape routes, she decided on one and slipped into the trees, the night swallowing her.

* * *

Jason peeked through the thick drapes. From the hotel room window, he spotted a car fitting his needs, and an escape plan quickly materialized.

The police had departed an hour ago. In that time, Jason had paced the hotel room. Every creak and sound echoed like a hammer coming through the wall, causing him to freeze and take cover.

Lily Zanns and her team of killers were going to shock the world, and he was stuck in a third-floor hotel room. Waiting for the cops to leave made him want to jump out of his skin. But he saw no other options. If he were apprehended, he would be powerless to stop her.

The cops were gone. It was time to move.

Keeping the lights off, he moved the curtain back an inch and studied the grounds one last time for lingering signs of police activity. Satisfied it was safe, he retraced his steps down the stairs and sneaked out the same service entrance door he'd entered hours ago. He made his way over to the dumpster and knelt behind it. On cue, a head poked out the alarmed door, looked around briefly, and, apparently satisfied, retreated inside. He waited another minute to make sure no one would make a delayed search of the lot. When nothing happened, Jason moved.

The car was a faded green Ford Taurus coated with dirt and sporting Michigan tags. Jason crept to it, kneeling beside the trunk. Along the way he found a large rock, twice the size of his fist. Still almost naked, he moved to the passenger-side rear window. Through the filthy glass, he saw three large suitcases in the backseat. Maybe his luck was changing: a car he could steal, loaded with clothes.

The meperidine had worn off hours ago. An intense, stabbing pain throbbed up and down his left side. A headache was forming at the base of his skull. And the chill of the night air raised goose bumps on his skin.

He tried the handle. Locked. The car was an older model and probably didn't have an alarm. He could break the window, pop the trunk, and pray there was a toolbox with a screwdriver he could use to strip the ignition and start the car. He raised the rock above his head to smash the glass when voices stopped him.

"Why are we leaving now, at this hour? Let's wait until tomorrow," a girl said.

"I told you. We'll beat the traffic this way. We'll be halfway home before noon," the young man replied.

The young couple chatted and split as they approached the car. The man headed for the driver's side, jostling keys. The woman, a brunette with large green eyes, turned the front corner of the Taurus.

Jason lunged at her. He clamped a hand over her mouth and spun her around before she could react. Boyfriend jerked at the noise, stunned. His eyes widened at the naked, blood-covered man who had his girlfriend by the neck.

"I want the keys. Now!"

"Don't do this, man."

Jason moved both hands to the woman's head. "I'll snap her neck!"

Slowly, the man reached out, the keys dangling from his fingers. "Here!"

"Get in and start it up!"

He moved to the door and climbed in. The car rumbled to life.

"Now get back out and come over here!"

Boyfriend hesitated.

"Move! Leave the door open!"

Boyfriend rounded the car. Jason backed toward the rear of the car, out of the panicked man's reach, dragging the woman with him.

"Stop there! Now, go over to the end of the lot, near those woods, and lie facedown!"

Boyfriend backed off, inching away, his concerned eyes never leaving his woman, who shook and struggled with a renewed intensity. Whimpers and stifled breaths escaped her lips. The woman pivoted, dropped her right shoulder, and rammed her elbow into Jason's abdomen between his wound and groin. He released her. Wriggling free, she ran toward her boyfriend, who was thirty feet away.

Jason pushed her as she fled. She stumbled and fell. As she clambered to her feet, she screamed at the top of her lungs. Jason hopped in the car and jammed it in gear. He hesitated, because the coed was in his path. She staggered to the side as the engine revved, never ceasing her ear-splitting wail. When she cleared, Jason slammed the pedal to the floorboard.

Minutes later, he was on Interstate 64 headed south toward Newport News, shaking his head in disbelief. Grand theft auto and kidnapping were in keeping with the severity of his other felonies.

A desperate man with dwindling options, he decided to take matters into his own hands. The christening was twelve hours away. One sunrise lay between the presidents and a disaster that would dwarf the events in Dealey Plaza. Jason sped past lagging cars, weaving with abandon, headed for the last place anyone would expect him to go and the last place he wanted to be.

CHAPTER 70

Five miles up the James River, Oliver pressed the button on the console, and *Vengeance's* anchor descended into the dark water for the final time. He maneuvered the massive ship alongside the float plane. Using the stern-mounted crane, the powered launch *Retribution* was lowered into the water. He stepped over two black body bags as he assisted Zanns, holding a small suitcase, into the craft. Three minutes later, Oliver helped her into the aircraft. Then he left Zanns and returned to *Vengeance*.

Thirty minutes later, he was done with his preparations. Three clusters of six five-gallon plastic fuel cans duct taped together, filled with diesel, had been scattered on the bow, amidships, and aft. To each six-pack two sticks of dynamite had been fastened, taped securely to one of the spouts, with the distal end protruding into the fuel and rigged with a remote detonator. Plastique had been placed at strategic points on the hull, ensuring the vessel would sink quickly. The fuel tanks had been topped off. The vessel had been transformed into a floating bomb. It was overkill, but Oliver was taking no chances.

When he'd finished placing the charges, he unzipped the body bags on the aft deck. One contained a woman in her midsixties, whose height and skin tone were identical to Zanns's. The other was a male, Oliver's height, also with tawny skin. For good measure, Oliver had snipped off the pinky fingers of both hands. Both victims had been chosen months ago, murdered in their sleep, and kept in cold storage in a locked freezer in a subbasement under the mansion's garage.

A corrupt dentist in Kansas had taken X-rays and made plaster impressions of Zanns's and Oliver's mouth after they had flown out in the float plane. A month later, the dentist had been blindfolded, flown in, and promised a handsome payday. From the X-rays and impressions, it took him three long days to prepare both corpses' teeth to be dead-on matches to both Oliver and Zanns's dental profiles.

When his work was complete, Oliver had snapped his neck as if it were a matchstick with his powerful hands. The body was stuffed in a large drum, filled with cement, and dumped from the plane ten miles off the Virginia coast in the early morning hours.

Every contingency had been covered. Even in the unlikely event the authorities figured it all out, Zanns and Oliver would be half a world away by then.

Since the male was bigger and heavier, he was dragged a few feet back to the transom and placed directly beside the six containers there. Oliver doused the body with diesel from a separate fuel canister. The female's final repose was belowdecks, in the bow, beside another cluster of combustibles.

The female was dressed in one of Zanns's leisure outfits, while the male wore one of Oliver's white shirts and a pair of his black trousers. He didn't bother wiping any fingerprints. The fire would destroy them anyway. If they didn't, this was Zanns's yacht. Their prints were supposed to be all over it.

With everything set, Oliver motored back to the plane with the small fuel can and the empty body bags. He set the dingy adrift after opening the sea cocks, allowing it to fill with brackish water.

He taxied the plane to the middle of the river and gunned the twin engines. In the air, he banked the craft and circled twice. On the second lap, Oliver depressed a button on a remote activator. Charges fired, igniting the fuel. The fuel tanks exploded five seconds later. A mushroom cloud rose forty feet into the night air, sounding as if the gods had slammed a large steel door shut, and lighting up the sky for miles. The plane teetered from the concussion.

* * *

Three years of planning had come down to these final moments. Her beloved Iraq and her beloved Amo would have their vengeance in twelve hours.

But Hammon and his small, ultrasecret organization had their own lethal agenda. As much as the Simoon wanted the elder Hope dead, Hammon wanted the son, the current president, eliminated. Theirs was a fragile alliance born out of common hatred. Though she did not know why Hammon wished the younger Hope killed, she would lose no sleep over it.

The last four American presidents, two pairs of fathers and sons, had overseen the rape and destruction of her homeland. The first president Bush had begun the downward spiral by ousting them from Kuwait. Hope Sr. followed, energizing the cataclysm with devastating economic sanctions and US-led UN resolutions. The second Bush invaded again, conquering and occupying. Finally, Hope Jr. was left to water the vile seed of democracy, coaxing it to sprout like a weed.

Hell, all four men deserved to die. In fact, the Simoon had made attempts on the lives of the Bushes. The attempt on the Bush, the father, had failed in Kuwait. Attempts on Bush the son were planned but unable to be carried out. The Bushes were out of office now and therefore nonfactors. So they had turned their focus on the second pair of father and son presidents, the Hopes. The christening of the aircraft carrier represented an opportunity of great magnitude. Their deaths would be simultaneous and captured live. News agencies all over the world would replay the killings for weeks. The American government would point fingers in every direction, as they always did in the aftermath of a crisis. And in the following months, Sam Fairing would come forward and take credit for avenging his Iraq. And that would begin his rise to power.

Jason Rodgers had nearly ruined their mission. Zanns gave him reluctant credit. He'd been implicated in the assassinations and escaped the attempt on his life. Though their plan to eliminate him had failed, he was hunted by local police, more concerned with avoiding capture and preserving his own life than spoiling her mission. He was a nonfactor now.

The glowing flames from the burning, sinking yacht reflected off the inside of the plane's cabin. Zanns smiled at Oliver. "Our mission is almost complete," she said wistfully.

She said a *du'a* for her two children. Jasmine's chances for survival were slim. But her mission was a holy one. Sam's escape, on the other hand, had been planned carefully. He must live to claim his birthright. Allah would reward them both with places in heaven, Jasmine sooner than later.

"You're right. It won't be long now," he said. Oliver turned southeast, toward the Atlantic Ocean and a rendezvous with a Liberian tanker somewhere off the North Carolina coast. From there, Delilah Hussein, a.k.a. Lily Zanns, would begin her new life, the second in twenty years. Oliver would be beside her, as a faithful servant and protector.

* * *

Jasmine Kader hunkered down in the rubber raft, out of the breeze. She floated a hundred yards offshore. The Raggy Island Wildlife Refuge, where the bridge met the southern shore of the James, was three and a half miles upriver.

The Secret Service would begin their final canvas well before dawn, securing the perimeter. By then, she would be in place, out of view long before the last sweep. The tower of the James River Bridge would not be manned by an agent. Helicopters would fly over the structure, looking for any potential long-range threats, and find nothing out of the ordinary.

Her nest was perfectly camouflaged. Like a true sniper, she would lie in wait for hours until the targets took their positions. The .50-caliber projectile would rip through fabric and flesh with amazingly destructive force.

An explosion rocked the stillness. The northwest horizon turned yellow for a moment, then darkened again. She could not see the flames, but knew it was her signal. Lily and Oliver were airborne. Time to move.

She shrugged off the chill and turned the fifteen-horsepower Mercury engine over. A small plane droned overhead. She caught glimpses of its silhouette against the sky, passing between clouds. Clad in black, a large dark drag bag at her feet, she negotiated the raft along the southern shoreline. Food, water, her sniper rifle, and her Mauser 7.65 mm loaded with a full eight-round magazine were the bag's only contents.

Kader had no illusions about her journey. It was a suicide mission.

* * *

Sam Fairing knelt on the prayer rug, forehead pressed against it, mumbling another short prayer. The Quran lay open on the floor in front of him as he flipped through appropriate passages. He chanted in Arabic, rocking himself with an intensity and elation he'd never felt before.

He would not show up for work again. Not that he cared. Billy Parks thought he was covering until Monday. Fairing's absence was permanent; his weekend trip to Canada was a lie.

He had enough food and drink for twice that amount of time. A stack of eight DVDs sat on the television, rented this morning to help pass the time. Fairing couldn't relax enough to watch them. A packed suitcase with a change of clothes sat by the front door of his seventeenth-floor condo of the south tower of the Windsor Towers complex. The fatal shot would not be taken from here. The angle was too high. It had, nonetheless, provided an excellent vista of the dry dock for the last three years. Using binoculars set on a tripod, Fairing had memorized every inch of the aircraft carrier and the dock.

The shot would be executed thirteen floors below, in the north-tower condo. Of course, Cooper did not own it. Whatever organization he worked for did. It had remained unoccupied for three years. Fairing had maintained it, checking it monthly. The last thirty days had been spent preparing it for Saturday's christening. The rifle had been dismantled after the last training session. Perfectly sighted and aligned, it now sat in the closet of Fairing's condo.

Fairing glanced at the red numerals of the digital clock on the nightstand. He rose, then reconsidered, turning on the television and turning up the volume. Let everyone think he was still here. He retrieved the Quran and placed it on top of the food and DVDs. Fairing moved through the living room, carrying his supplies in a large, brown paper bag from Keller's Food and Drug. Jason Rodgers once worked there. *Should have stayed put, Jason*, he thought. He picked up his suitcase and the grocery bag and exited, locking the door for the last time.

In the north tower, he passed through the ornate lobby and eschewed the elevator, opting for the stairs. It was harder lugging the suitcase, but there was less chance of being seen. He ascended the stairs slowly, lugging his bag of supplies and clunking the large, wheeled suitcase behind him.

The fourth-floor corridor, like all the others, was set at an obtuse angle. Each tower was shaped in a lazy V, like a boomerang. Tonight, the plush carpeting and the thickly textured wall coverings seemed brighter, more vibrant. The wall sconces glowed hotter. His senses always worked overtime the night before a kill.

The door, like all the units in the complex, was on the left, allowing the owners a view of the water. This particular unit was a double, spreading over 2,500 square feet. Directly opposite the front door, a large picture window framed the aircraft carrier in the flooded dry dock, awash in floodlights and final preparations.

A christening celebrated a ship's first float. The beginning of the vessel's journey of years on seas, both calm and turbulent. Tomorrow, Fairing's bullet would find its target during the high-water mark of the ceremony. The ceremony would be ruined, catapulted into panic and hysteria. The ship would be cursed by the last breaths of its namesake and his son. Sailors would consider it unlucky, a ship of death. The world would remember it as tragic history. Fairing gazed at the *Hope* as if seeing it for the first time. Tonight, the lights of the city and shipyard shone only for him.

The condo was empty. He set the large rifle case on the floor under the picture window and opened it. He smiled every time he set eyes on it. A .50 caliber with a bipod and thermal infrared scope. Beside the rifle, nestled in the foam, sat two boxes of specially prepared mercury-filled M33 rounds. The mercury would cause the projectiles to disintegrate on contact. It was the same technology that had killed Kennedy. Of course, only one or two rounds would be required. Farther down the hall, in the master bedroom, Fairing had set up a bed, a prayer rug angled east to west, and a television with cable. In the kitchen, he set the bag of food and DVDs on the small table. The front bedroom contained a large wooden platform constructed of smooth pine by his own hand to exacting specifications of height and angle. Beside it lay the tools and supplies used to construct it. Discarded pieces of wood, boxes of nails, a circular saw, a T-square, level, a miter box, sawhorses, and some duct tape. The platform was identical to the one at the Camp in North Carolina.

Returning to the master bedroom, he laid his suitcase on the bed and proceeded into the bathroom. A collection of toiletries sat on the vanity along with a pile of freshly folded towels. Fairing brushed his teeth, splashed water on his face, and lay down, pulling his lips into a wide smile.

He flipped on the television. News shows and movies raced by. Nothing interested him. His mind raced, cycling over the details he'd studied over a thousand times.

The schedule had been pushed up by twenty-four hours, at least for his mother. Zanns and Oliver hadn't been supposed to disappear until tomorrow. Rodgers had changed things slightly. Better to get out now, rather than risk capture, torture, and humiliation. Anxious and restless, Fairing moved to the hall and picked up the rifle case.

Slowly, with the careful, deliberate precision of a master craftsman, he began assembling the lethal instrument.

CHAPTER 71

Jason planned on sneaking into the mansion grounds and taking out Zanns himself. He didn't know what he would do or how he would do it. If he could cut off the head, perhaps, the entire operation would disintegrate. They were fanatics. He knew his chances were slim.

He parked the stolen Taurus in the deserted driveway. It was a simple task people took for granted every day. Nothing was simple anymore. He'd thought about parking down the road and sneaking back. But if he was spotted, someone might call the cops. Better to park in the driveway and pretend he belonged.

Before the engine stopped turning, it became apparent he would not be facing Lily Zanns tonight. The mansion was dark. The air was heavy with the promise of rain. The walls whispered Lily was gone. The place was a carcass of brick and wood rather than the glorious mansion Jason had experienced at the gala for Thomas.

He circled the mansion, hugging the exterior brick walls. If the alarm system was activated, he doubted it would capture his movement this close to the main house. At the rear, he peered into Zanns's study and saw the dark security panel. The system appeared to be inactive. A light near the french doors lit up the patio and most of the backyard. Jason moved back to the front, where the portico was in relative darkness.

He didn't bother with the enormous front door, assuming it was locked. Fully clothed now in tight-fitting jeans and a T-shirt, compliments of the young couple's suitcases in the stolen car, Jason stepped to a window along the portico. Using an elbow, he broke the glass pane, knocked an opening wide enough to reach in and unlock it. He paused, prepared to run if there was any sign he'd alerted a neighbor or someone lurking in the house. Eerie silence filled his ears. He pushed up the window and crawled in.

Jason moved cautiously through the house, keeping the lights off as he searched. He started near the foyer. He could see he was wrong about the door being locked. The molding and door jamb had been splintered, as if someone had kicked it in.

In the living room, his foot crunched something. He knelt and felt plaster dust and shards of glass on the carpet. Through the shadows, he saw two bullet holes in the ceiling. One of the recessed light fixtures had exploded. The remnants of a shattered vase rested on the carpet like discarded seashells.

Jason climbed the stairs to the second floor. Spacious bedrooms the size of his entire living room, with sitting areas and fireplaces, lined the wide hallway. The most elegant was the master bedroom. Large enough to play baseball in, it contained a bed of dark, ornately carved wood. Drawers, bathrooms, and closets revealed nothing unusual. The walk-in closet still held Zanns's expensive outfits. He found nothing that indicated where she might be going. If Lily Zanns had skipped town, she was leaving the dirty work to her cohorts while she turned tail and ran.

Ten minutes later, he was back downstairs. He searched the garage. The vehicles he'd seen before, the Mercedes and the Maserati, were missing.

He walked the area, taking in everything and seeing nothing remotely significant. In one corner, Jason noticed a change in the texture of the concrete. A square was outlined on the floor. When he approached the anomaly, Jason saw it was a hinged door made of thick oak with a large padlock looped through a hasp, securing it. There was some kind of open space below the garage. Jason located a crowbar on a workbench. Fifteen minutes later, dripping with sweat, he succeeded in separating the hasp from the wood, dislodging the lock along with it. Jason descended a steep set of wooden steps. He found a light switch and flipped it.

The room looked like a morgue. Two large, stainless-steel tables stood in the center. One wall was entirely consumed by an enormous refrigerator; another held stainless-steel countertops with two sinks. Laid out between the sinks in neat, precise order were what appeared to be medical and dental instruments. Angled mirrors, tiny metal picks, scalpels, and syringes. The pungent odor of antiseptics filled the room. Jason moved to the refrigerator, opening the heavy door. It was large enough to walk into and had pull-out drawers, just like in a morgue.

He stepped on something. It was soft and flattened under his weight. Jason reached down and brought it into the light.

A severed human finger.

He threw it down in disgust.

A search of the first floor left Jason empty-handed. In the office, he risked turning on the desk lamp, bathing the room in a yellowish glow. He rifled through drawers. Nothing.

A thought struck him as he looked over the desk and saw the phone. He needed to contact his brother. He remembered the electronic bugs he'd found in his own house. A call would be safer from here. This place probably wasn't being monitored, at least not by Zanns. Jason lifted the handset and heard a dial tone. He didn't remember his brother's cell number, but Peter's home number was etched into his brain. Jason dialed.

The line rang and rang. Was Peter on the phone, or was it off the hook? It rolled to voicemail.

Jason left a message. Then a more frightening thought struck him: had they found Peter? Was he injured or worse?

Concerns about Christine and Michael reared themselves as well. Jason hung up, pushing the thoughts from his mind. He continued scanning the spacious study. Photos of the aircraft carrier were still on the wall. He went over to the bookshelves, running his hand across the leather bindings as if they could communicate with him through the pads of his fingers. There was nothing here.

As he turned to leave, he spotted a tome lying flat on a shelf. It was Zanns's copy of the book she had given him his first day on the job, *The Essential Drucker*. Jason lifted it from the bookcase and ran his hand over the cover, hoping it would yield an insight.

It's amazing what turns and challenges life throws at you, he mused. The first time he'd opened his copy, his life had seemed to be heading down a new, exciting road. Since that day, it had all suddenly collapsed around him. He fanned the pages.

A piece of paper fell out, floating to the carpet. Jason picked it up and turned it over. It wasn't paper, but a faded, aging photograph, cracked and bent. Two people, a man and woman, stood arm in arm, smiling. Jason recognized the much-younger Lily Zanns immediately. The man was someone Jason recognized as well. Not because Jason knew him personally, but because his face was known all over the world. Infamous and reviled. A younger Saddam Hussein. The Butcher of Baghdad. His arm comfortably draped around Lily Zanns's shoulder, a sly, heartless smile creasing his face.

Jason's eyes widened and his jaw fell open.

Holy shit!

It took a minute to recover. With his heart still racing, Jason dialed Peter again, keeping his eyes glued to the image of Zanns and Saddam. Once more, the line was busy, rolling to voice mail.

Please let Peter be safe!

He left a message, then, remembering his pledge to get her to safety, he dialed Christine's house. The phone rang several times.

Answer! It, too, rolled to voice mail. Jason left a message, hoping Christine was screening calls. Five minutes later, he redialed with the same result. Had they gotten to her, too?

He prayed that Peter and Chrissie were still alive. The thought of both of them dead sent an icy chill down his back. *Don't do this! Focus on the task at hand!* Pushing panic aside, he calculated his options. Taking the wrinkled photograph, he limped from the mansion.

Chapter 72

"They're called the Simoon," Tom Johnson said.

Peter stood in his dark kitchen, peering out into his backyard. He held the cordless phone to his ear, his free hand was rooted on his hip. His concentration on his friend's words was absolute. The trees were deadly still, the atmosphere thick and humid. Peter knew from his years of outdoors duty that a storm was brewing.

The clicking on the line indicated an incoming call. Peter ignored it, riveted by his friend's words.

The guard on duty at the jail had informed Peter that his brother had been taken by ambulance to the hospital. The attorney he'd retained to represent Jason had followed Peter to the emergency room at Tidewater Regional Medical Center. A sinking feeling hit Peter when he saw the police cars surrounding the entrance and the dented fenders of a Buick Riviera and a police cruiser. He prayed it was all for someone else. His prayers went unanswered when they were told Jason had escaped after a scuffle. Peter could not determine if Jason was the one who'd initiated it.

When they were younger, Peter would physically threaten anyone who messed with his kid brother. He'd guided Jason safely through the bumpy road of adolescence. A man comfortable with the frenetic danger of firefights in Iraq, Peter felt an incredible sense of duty toward his younger sibling that was equaled by his sense of futility. In battle he could see his enemies and shoot them dead. Tonight, and every night since he'd been dragged into this mess, the enemy was in the shadows. Deadly, ruthless cowards that made protecting Jason difficult. Peter was not a betting man. But if these men were as well connected and powerful as it seemed they were, the odds were against them. Peter, Jason, Waterhouse, and Christine were short stacked, all-in, and facing a pair of bullets before the flop.

Peter had told his wife, Lisa, to get out. Don't go to your mother's, don't go to your sister's, don't use the cell phone, he'd told her. Find a hotel, pay with cash, and stay out of sight. He would call when it was safe. Maybe sometime this weekend.

It hadn't played out well. She'd asked why. *What you don't know, you can't tell,* he thought, as he told her not to ask. But as usual, she'd persisted. Peter, impatient and scared for his family, had screamed at her to leave. He loved his wife and kids more than anything, but he couldn't help overreacting in the midst of his stress. Hurt and confused, Lisa had piled the girls into the van and peeled away. But he felt better knowing they were safe.

"Simoon?" Peter replied.

"We don't know much about them. I called a CIA buddy, and he queried some ultrasecret databases. It's some secret organization that doesn't officially exist."

"What're they all about?"

"Saddam funded a small group of killers to carry out hits against enemies of Iraq. Apparently, they didn't get the memo that the Butcher of Baghdad was dead. No one knows who runs it or who's involved. My buddy ran a search of CIA communications intercepted in the last ten years to see if there was any mention of the word 'Simoon.' Nothing came up, no bank accounts, no paper trails. It was a dead end."

"So how do they know they exist?"

"There's an operative inside the Iraqi government who dealt with one of their agents. That's all he'd tell me."

"Well, they're in Newport News. We have two sightings of those tattoos on two different people. The art matches what we saw in Basra."

"No shit! Why?"

"They're trying to kill two more people."

"Two *more?*"

"Three people are already dead because they knew too much."

"Who are the targets?"

"I don't know. They used codenames. Torpedo and Thunderbolt."

A heavy silence hung on Johnson's end of the line.

"Tom, are you still there?"

"Yeah, I'm here. Did I just hear you right? Did you say Torpedo and Thunderbolt?"

"That's right."

"What kind of proof do you have?"

"We have a recorded conversation between the major players. They used prescriptions to signal dead drops. We witnessed one of the drops. They're going to use snipers. We just don't know who the targets are."

"I do."

"Don't keep me in suspense."

Movement beyond the swing set in the backyard caught Peter's eye. The lights were off in the kitchen. He was immersed in shadow, and could see into the darkness easily. A shadow quickly darted from one tree to another. Peter stepped away from the window.

"Torpedo and Thunderbolt are Secret Service codenames for President Jacob R. Hope and his son, Gary."

Peter's jaw fell open as the shadowy figure stopped under the large oak.

"You yanking my chain?"

"I shit you not, ole buddy. Are you sure about this?"

"As sure as the fact that you'll never scratch your toes again."

"I'll contact Woody Austin in the Presidential Protection Division. He's the top kick. And I'll have them get in touch with the agent in charge for the christening. Okay?"

Peter noticed a second figure, hunched against another tree.

"Pete, are you there?"

"Yeah, I'm here."

"You need to keep your head down on this one."

"Don't worry, I plan on it."

Peter hung up and watched as the figures executed another move, closing in. Thirty yards of ground separated them from the deck. He didn't have much time, and he'd forgotten all about the earlier, missed call.

"Not tonight," Peter whispered. "Not tonight, motherfuckers!"

* * *

It took as long to cross the last one hundred yards as it had to get from the bus stop to her current location. The bus had let her off a quarter mile from her house. The driver had eyed her with concern, as did the few passengers. She was soaked and matted. Luckily, she had a ten-dollar bill in her pocket. More than enough for the fare. She hadn't waited for her change.

Christine crouched under a magnolia tree. The police had had plenty of time to send a car to watch her place. She ducked behind a parked SUV and studied the quiet avenue.

The bend in the road made it impossible to see her house. She ducked between the Jensen's and Smith's. Neither property was fenced, and she melted easily into the woods beyond the backyards.

Christine thought about going to Mrs. Liggieri's, but quickly nixed that idea. The last thing she wanted to do was scare the old woman and implicate her by association. She'd probably drop dead on the spot.

She made her way to the decrepit garage in her own backyard, which served as a storage shed. Her house was dark. She hadn't been home since early this morning.

The moon ducked behind a patch of clouds. Christine moved into the open, shielded by the darkness. At the corner of the house, she peered through shrubs. The car was parked on the opposite curb and didn't belong. She'd never seen it before. Two men sat in the front seat. She couldn't identify the model, but its unimaginative design suggested an undercover police car.

Retreating slowly, she slipped to the deck and climbed the stairs. She slipped the key into the lock, opened the door a crack, and angled in. Dropping to all fours, she crawled through the kitchen and foyer and up the stairs to her bedroom. She finally stood and regarded herself in the mirror. She looked awful and felt worse. Matted hair, wet clothes, scratches, and lacerations on her face and hands.

Her mind kept coming back to Jason. Christine picked up the phone and tried his cell numbers and house phones, mashing the buttons as if added pressure would ensure an answer. Only voice mail answered her. "Jason, this Chrissie. I need your help. Please call me!"

Christine held the phone away from her ear, thinking. *Peter!* Maybe he would know where Jason was, or maybe Jason was with him. She found the number and dialed. It rang numerous times, but eventually the voice mail picked up.

Christine hung up, frustrated.

Click!

The sound was a familiar one. The front door latch had been disengaged. She heard it four or five times daily as she entered and left her house. A sound so ingrained in her memory, she didn't hear it even when she did. Christine had locked the door this morning. Of that she was certain. A single woman living in Newport News always locked her doors. Tonight, that click reverberated like a cannon shot along the dark walls.

No one else had a key to her house. She hadn't even given one to her father.

How could they be unlocking her front door? And more importantly, why? Police didn't sneak into people's houses. They knocked down doors if need be.

In the milliseconds it took for the sound waves to vibrate her eardrum and reach her brain, Christine processed these inconsistencies on a subconscious level. She sensed the danger like an insect trapped in a spider's web. Early recognition meant the difference between life and death. She peered out the window. The car across the street was empty. The men watching her house were gone. They were at her door.

These men were not here to arrest her. Were they here to kill her?

She pushed up a window, stuck one leg out, and ducked through, grabbing the sill with both hands and easing the other leg out. The window opened onto the shingled rooftop over the back porch. She crawled out onto it and quietly moved to the edge. With the deftness of a gymnast, she lowered herself over the eave and hung for a brief moment before dropping to the soft ground. Christine knelt, listened, then ran toward the empty car.

CHAPTER 73

These men outnumbered him two to one—assuming there were no others. At least he was aware of their presence; that gave him the advantage. An advantage he was going to exploit.

Peter removed two 9 mm pistols, a sawed-off shotgun, and a sniper rifle from the cabinet in the garage and left them in the kitchen. He went upstairs, turned on the bathroom light, left it on for a few moments, turned it off, and turned on the bedroom lights. He walked around, making sure his shadow was cast on the blinds. They were carrying handguns. A shot at a shadow through a window from the backyard was unlikely. He lay on the bed. Carefully, he slipped off the bed and onto the floor, crawled to the stairs, and hustled to the kitchen.

He grabbed the phone and dialed 911. When the operator came on, he said simply, "Two armed men are at my house. Send the police quickly." Peter gave the address and hung up.

Returning to the darkened kitchen, he leaned on the counter, peering through the scope of his sniper rifle. It took a moment, but he relocated one of the targets. There had been no movement for a full minute. He had to even the odds. He lowered the rifle, raised the window a few inches, and looked through the drapes with his naked eye.

There!

At the base of the middle tree in a copse of five loblolly pines, a dark silhouette stuck out like a cancer. He raised the rifle and eyed the scope. He could see the magnified profile of a face in the moonlight. The head moved back and forth slowly, as darkened eyes darted under the ridges of a thick brow. Peter zeroed in on the right temple. Using the mil-dots, he estimated the range at forty yards. The barrel of the weapon rested on the sill of the open window, but did not protrude through it. He cradled the stock against his right shoulder.

There was a slight breeze from his left. At this short distance, the effect on the trajectory of the round would be nonexistent. He sucked in a deep breath and let out half. As he stopped the exhalation, he gently squeezed. The report sounded like a bomb exploding. For a nanosecond, blinding whiteness overwhelmed the darkness.

The vapor trail of the projectile rose up in his view. It intersected with the two perpendicular lines on his mil-dot reticle. The round connected with the man's skull, snapping the head backward. The body disappeared from his scope.

One down. One to go. His odds had just doubled. Crouching below the kitchen counter, he grabbed the pistol and the shotgun. Peter sat on the kitchen floor, leaning against the cabinets, contemplating his next move. It was too much to expect the second man to simply go away. He rose up, facing the front door, when it opened with a crash.

The sound of splintering wood was followed quickly by three silenced shots zipping into the kitchen like angry hornets. The first and third shots missed. The second hit Peter above the right knee in the fleshy part of the thigh. He groaned, clutching his knee and dropping the shotgun. In one smooth motion, he withdrew the 9 mm. He pulled off three rounds from the pistol, missing with each one. The figure had moved into the house. Peter rolled onto his back, dragging himself under the dinette. Pain seared his leg. Blood seeped quickly from the wound, through his fingers, soaking his pants. The silhouetted figure in the doorway had disappeared into the living room to Peter's right.

Peter crawled awkwardly from under the table and struggled to his feet. His face contorted with pain, he leaned against the refrigerator.

Two doors led into the living room. One from the foyer, the other from the kitchen. Peter limped to the kitchen door to cut off the intruder. His leg was on fire. Gasping heavily, he tried to remain quiet and peered around the frame.

A floorboard creaked behind him.

Quickly, he spun toward the sound, bringing his gun up. Too late. The figure was already there. His long, silenced barrel aimed, center mass, at the former marine's chest. Peter Rodgers let out an audible exhale and waited for the bullet to rip through his body.

At that exact moment, the wall-mounted kitchen phone—right next to the killer's left ear—rang like a school bell. The assassin jumped at the unexpected noise, elevating the barrel of his weapon a few inches. Shots burped, missing Peter's head and puncturing the skin of the refrigerator. Peter brought the Glock up, firing in a wide arc as he dove to the floor.

The phone rang again.

The killer was jerked off his feet and thrown backward into the hallway. Dark, rich crimson oozed through his shirt from the craters left by the 9 mm rounds.

Peter Rodgers lay on the floor, gun still aimed at his target. The magazine was empty and the slide locked to the rear. Peter, nonetheless, silently squeezed the trigger for a few seconds more. As quickly as the battle had begun, it was over.

The phone on the kitchen wall rang eight more times. In the distance, wailing sirens approached. Peter dragged himself to the phone and grabbed the handset. Too late again. The caller had hung up before he could get there. The ID read "Pettigrew."

Christine Pettigrew.

Peter smiled and wondered what she would say when she found out she'd saved his life with an unanswered phone call. He chuckled, looked at his blood-soaked leg, and waited in silent agony for the emergency vehicles to arrive.

CHAPTER 74

Christine ran straight to the killers' generic vehicle. It was one of those crazy decisions made under an enormous amount of stress. She hoped they'd be careless enough to leave the keys in the ignition. Luckily, they'd left the doors unlocked.

She quietly slipped inside the driver's side.

If Christine had had any doubts about her intruders' unofficial nature, they were erased by the interior of the dark blue Lincoln. It was devoid of the standard-issue police equipment. There was no laptop, no hidden flashing light on the dashboard, and no nightstick. There wasn't even a two-way radio. It was your average, everyday vehicle, driven by two killers.

No keys dangled from the ignition. She reached down and groped through the darkness, hoping they were on the floor mat. Nothing.

A seizure of panic overtook her. She needed to get out of the car before the killers realized she wasn't in the house and returned. Christine slipped along the front seat and crawled out the passenger-side door, closing it gently. She peered through the glass at her darkened house,

368

trying to decide what to do. Christine could hear her breath wheezing in her chest. Her hand shook as she rested it on the car door.

A shadowy movement caught her eye. A tall, masculine figure was coming around the back of the house. And it was moving in her direction.

If she ran, she would be spotted. Christine crawled on all fours to the rear of the car. Veering left, she disappeared into the hedges lining the Taylors' property and lay flat on her stomach, paralyzed with fear. A second figure had joined the first. Christine could hear snippets of whispered conversation.

"Where the fuck did she go?"

"How the hell do I know? Must have slipped out the back. She can't be far. I'll check the street. You check the backyards."

Christine watched the second figure move off. The first man moved slowly, looking for movement, listening for the slightest sound. Through dim light, she saw a gun in his hand pressed against his thigh. A long, extended silencer was attached to the barrel. He was no more than six feet from where she lay.

Christine held her breath, afraid exhaling might give her away.

The minutes seemed to pass like hours. Finally, she forced herself to let out a slow, shallow exhalation. Beads of sweat had formed on every inch of her already-soaked skin. The man moved toward the other end of the car, away from her.

Christine rolled slowly into the yard beneath the dark shadows of a giant oak. She sidled against the base of the trunk on her stomach and wrapped an arm around it.

The two men returned to the car. More whispering.

"Are you shittin' me! She's a friggin' accountant. How the hell did she get away?"

"You go back into the house in case she comes back. I'll drive around and watch for her."

One of the men returned to Christine's house. She felt violated, knowing a stranger was waiting for her in there.

She remembered something Mrs. Liggieri had told her when she was helping with the arrangements for Daddy's funeral. When the car moved off, Christine snaked on her belly, east toward Liggieri's yard, staying in the shadows.

It was at least forty yards away. It took her fifteen minutes to traverse the distance.

Christine made it to the driveway and crawled around the car to the doorway. She ran her hands through the plants and flowers near the door and found what she was looking for. The small fake stone. Lifting it, Christine removed the key.

Staying on her knees, she opened the door and slipped inside. She hazarded a glance back toward her own house and saw no movement. She hated what she was about to do, but saw no other choice.

* * * *

Christine drove Mrs. Liggieri's Cadillac, her mind buzzing with questions. How did they know she was home? Had she done something to tip them off? Christine mentally retraced her steps, but was too frightened to think clearly.

She drove for ten minutes, turning onto Victory Boulevard, heading north toward Yorktown. With no route planned, she let her subconscious guide her like the needle of a compass pointing toward magnetic north. Her attempt to contact Jason and Peter had failed. She'd never bothered to get Walter's number, and didn't even know where he lived.

Why hadn't Jason answered? Where was he? Had killers gotten to him too?

Fifteen minutes later, she was a quarter mile from Big Bethel Road. She turned right, on automatic pilot. It felt familiar and friendly. She'd been here before, to discuss Lily Zanns and her plot. A mile later, she recognized the entrance to the Running Man subdivision in York County, Jason's neighborhood. Spurred by their abruptly interrupted love affair and the desire to find him, she'd been drawn to his house. Perhaps there would be a clue to Jason's whereabouts there. It was the only place she knew to go. And in any case, she wasn't leaving the area without Jason.

Until the moment she pulled into the neighborhood, Christine had not considered the danger. It hit her now like a falling meteor. She pulled the car to the shoulder. Care would be needed here. Killers might be watching his house as well. The last thing she needed to do now was stumble into a trap meant for Jason.

The car radio, which she'd left on, suddenly broke into her preoccupation and gave her an unwanted answer.

"Police in York County have reported that Jason Rodgers, a pharmacist at the Colonial Pharmacy in Newport News, escaped from custody three hours ago and is currently on the run. Rodgers is accused of stabbing his ex-girlfriend Sheila Boquist to death. He was being held in the regional jail in Williamsburg awaiting arraignment.

"Details are sketchy at this hour. Apparently, the prisoner was stabbed in a jailhouse scuffle. He was taken to Tidewater Regional Medical Center, where he managed to escape while being treated…"

Christine's gut clenched as the words sunk in.

Could he really have killed his ex-girlfriend? She didn't believe Jason was capable of murder.

She drove the remaining five blocks to Jason's street, cruising past the house slowly, looking for any signs of danger. She knew that, in her exhausted and petrified state, it would be easy to miss something. The house was dark. The street appeared grossly normal.

She circled back onto the main road and drove three blocks in the direction from which she'd just come to a deserted cul-de-sac. The well-to-do families, with the professional husbands and stay-at-home moms, were buttoned up for the night. Christine parked and picked her way through yards and bushes, approaching Jason's from the rear.

Fifteen minutes later, she peered through the darkness and shadows of the two-story house. With the front door out of the question, she reached the deck, tried the back door, and found it locked. She lifted the mat but found no key.

Five windows stretched across the first floor. She tried the two looking out over the deck. Locked. The third, a kitchen window, was off the deck and too high for her to reach. Moving on to the downstairs bedroom window, she spotted a black wire snaking out through the cracked-open window to a small, rectangular box attached to the side of the house. She'd seen these before. Satellite radio antenna.

It took four tries, but finally the window grudgingly moved high enough for her to slide through. She pulled the antenna in and shut the window firmly, locking it behind her.

* * *

From a quarter mile away, Jason could see the flashing blue lights. His mood and expectations sank. Jason slowed the Taurus and slid past the commotion. A draped body lay half in, half out of the door of Waterhouse's home.

Jason cursed to no one and everyone.

There was still no way of knowing whether or not Waterhouse had sent the evidence to John Palmer in Newport News. He wasn't turning himself in until he knew Palmer had received Waterhouse's e-mail with the file of the recording attached. And he wasn't about to walk up to these Poquoson police officers and ask them if he could check.

He circled out of the neighborhood. There was one other way to determine if Waterhouse had dispatched the evidence. It would have to be a quick in and out. As with his trip to Zanns's mansion, Jason felt he was tempting fate. But he couldn't walk into a police station as a fugitive without that recording to prove his innocence.

* * *

Blue moonlight, filtered through fast-moving, low-hanging clouds, speckled the deck and nimbly danced through the swaying branches and leaves. Jason surveyed the doors and windows, locked out of his own house. His keys were in a manila envelope somewhere in the York County jail, along with his other possessions. He didn't notice his satellite antenna was missing. He retrieved a broken brick from a pile of yard debris behind the shed. Seeing car headlights approaching in the distance, he smashed the brick into the glass of the back door as the car passed by with perfect timing, masking the noise.

Before meeting Chrissie for dinner at Maggie's Tavern, Jason had let Waterhouse sweep his home for any remaining bugs. Jason had rushed off, leaving the private investigator to his work. He prayed Waterhouse had been thorough.

He crept like a thief into his own living room. Instantly, he recognized something was amiss. He'd seen the familiar shadows play out thousands of times. But, tonight, the shadows were different. He could feel his eyebrows converge and his forehead wrinkle as he tried to assimilate.

The silhouetted form standing at the junction of the living room and kitchen caught his eye only when it began to move. Jason recoiled too late. A heavy object struck him just above the right ear with a hollow, metallic chime. White light filled Jason's field of vision, and he crashed to the floor.

CHAPTER 75

Lisa Rodgers's tanned complexion turned as white as the hospital walls when she laid eyes on her husband. He had borrowed a paramedic's cell phone in the ambulance and calmly explained the shooting as if he were discussing changing the oil in the Hummer or picking up a gallon of milk. Despite his warnings against using the cell phone, she'd answered. Peter knew his wife too well.

She was by his side in forty-five minutes, barely containing her growing panic. She didn't tell him where she had been hiding, and he didn't ask.

"What the hell is going on, honey? You and Jason have been sneaking around for days. Now you've been shot. I want an explanation."

Peter laid everything out, from Jason's arrest and escape, to Zanns's conversation about the presidents, to the attackers that had nearly killed him. He said he'd dispatched them easily, conveniently leaving out that he'd been a fraction of a second from having a 9 mm round rip through his chest.

She put a gentle hand on his heavily bandaged leg. The bullet had not severed any major blood vessels, passing only through well-toned muscle. The on-call surgeon had used twenty internal sutures and seven external sutures to close the wound right there in the emergency room. A heavy dose of pain medication and antibiotics had been prescribed. Lisa could tell by his fidgeting that his leg was beginning to ache.

"I need your cell phone," he said.

"Are you serious?" Lisa asked. "You called me to come back because you need my cell phone. That's it?"

Peter nodded. Lisa covered her mouth with a trembling hand. "No. I'm leaving, and you're coming with me."

"No! Just give me the phone!"

"Two men tried to kill you! If me and the girls had been home, we might be dead, too. I'm not leaving without you again. We have our children to think about!" She clamped her arms tightly across her chest.

"I would never have knowingly—"

She put a finger in the air, silencing him. "I know. But it's time to go."

"What about Jason?" said Peter. "He's in trouble."

"I love Jason too. But I have to put us—our family—first."

"What would you do if it was your sister?" Peter said, lifting a defiant chin.

"That's not fair, Peter."

"None of this fair, Lise. Jason is family. *My* family!"

Lisa sighed. Peter drilled her with an unrelenting stare.

"How do you expect to help your brother in this condition?"

"I can get the right people involved. If we can clear him, then he can stop running and come in."

"Then let me help you!" Lisa demanded.

"No, your place is with the kids. Leave the phone and go. Don't make me yell again. Now!"

Lisa shook her head in disgust, torn between returning to her children and remaining to watch over her wounded warrior. She could feel a tear tracing a path down her face. "Fine! I'm leaving," she pouted.

"Only because *your* daughters need at least one parent alive. But not because you asked me to."

"That's the right decision," Peter replied evenly.

Her features softened. She leaned in, giving him a long, tender kiss, "I love you."

"I love you, too." Peter paused, then said, "Leave the phone."

Lisa Rodgers fished it out of her purse as another tear snaked down her cheek. She crammed it into his open palm, spun on her heel, and left.

* * *

Peter watched the doorway for several long seconds after his wife had departed. Finally, he turned toward the muted television. A news program cut to a reporter, speaking to the camera, standing in front of a house Peter recognized. He increased the volume.

"...victim was a white male in his fifties. He was a private investigator. Police are not releasing his name until next of kin have been notified. He was shot outside his Poquoson home in the early evening hours yesterday..."

The camera panned, and he saw Waterhouse's red Chevy Blazer. A cold shudder coursed through his body. "I don't know how I'm gonna get you out of this one, brother," he said out loud. The image and the feeling of impotence spawned in him a desire to act.

Sitting on his ass or his hands—or any other body part—was not in his nature. His friend in Washington, Tom Johnson, had promised to get back to him. Had he already missed the call? There was no way for him to know.

Peter decided to attack it from the other end. Using Lisa's cell phone, he dialed information and got the nonemergency number for the Newport News Police Department.

"Police communications, Dispatcher Ridley." At three in the morning, the female voice was bored, unexcited.

"I need to speak with a Detective John Palmer, please. It's urgent."

"I'm sure Detective Palmer isn't in at this hour. Can I leave him a message?"

"Isn't there any way for you to get in touch with him?"

"What is this about, sir?"

"I have knowledge that someone is trying to kill the presidents!"

"The presidents? There's only one president, sir."

"I need to speak to Detective John Palmer. Now!"

"What is your name, sir?"

Peter gave it.

"Hold on, please," the dispatcher replied irritably, before the line rolled to the generic muzak.

* * *

Jason tried to shake the warbling from his ears along with the pain in his skull. Whatever had struck him felt like a wrecking ball. He tried to push himself up, but failed. Instead, he sank back to the floor and rolled onto his back.

As the pain and nausea waned, fear welled. He realized he was probably face to face with one of Zanns's assassins. Then the silhouetted figure spoke. The female voice, though nervous, tried to sound ominous. "Don't move! Or I'll hit you again!" The woman loomed over him, holding his DeMarini softball bat.

An intimacy coated the woman's words. It took a second, but Jason recognized the determined voice. "Chrissie?"

Several seconds passed. Jason sensed she was assessing, trying to assimilate the sound of her name, the voice that had spoken it. Jason saw the bat drop several inches as she said, "Jason?"

"Yeah, it's me."

The soft whoosh of clothing preceded Christine dropping to her knees. The bat clanked to the floor, and her arms went around his neck, squeezing him in a loving death grip. The warmth of her face against his felt like a blazing fire in a barren snowfield.

Jason returned her embrace with a weak one of his own, comforting her, stroking her matted hair. Finally, Christine pulled back. "I thought you were—"

"I'm fine." He rubbed the side of his head. "But I'm gonna have one helluva knot."

"I am so glad you're all right," she whispered. She helped him to his feet, pulled him close, and placed her lips on his. Christine cried as they kissed, her tears mixing with the sweat coating Jason's face. Her lips were soft and warm, inviting him to press against her. Jason complied. They released, and then embraced again. Jason wiped her cheek with a gentle caress of his thumb.

"Are you okay?" he asked.

"I'm better now," she replied in a low, soft whisper. Then she remembered the news report. "You're hurt!"

"Yeah, a little," he replied.

"Like hell. You were stabbed. Show me!"

He lifted the T-shirt he'd found in the suitcase of the Taurus. Even in the shadows, the wound looked bad. "Oh my God, Jason! That looks awful. You need a doctor!"

"That won't be happening anytime soon. I'd be back in custody the second I set foot in an emergency room."

"That needs to be treated. Where are your bandages?"

"Upstairs. How did you know I was stabbed?"

"It's all over the news."

She led him up the steps to the bathroom and was about to flip the light switch. "No lights!" Jason instructed.

He coached her on where to find the supplies. Christine gathered bandages and medicated ointment in the darkness. She helped him to the floor and told him to lie on his side. Setting the supplies on the floor beside him, she lit a small candle and placed it near the wound. Jason told her to smear the antibiotic goo onto a balled bandage. When she had done that, she turned to Jason. "Now what?"

"I want you to stuff the whole thing into the wound."

"That's a pretty deep wound. Won't that hurt?"

"It's going to hurt like a bitch. Do it on three!" This procedure was akin to repairing a broken levee by sticking your finger in it. But it was all he could do at the moment. The wound was leaking. The edges were already black and caked with dried blood. He was beginning to feel the burn of a fever, which meant it was probably already infected.

On three, Christine rammed the coated gauze into his wound with two fingers. The pressure she applied opened the wound, forcing the coated gauze into the puncture. Jason tensed and winced, fighting the intense pain. Beads of sweat appeared on his forehead, glistening in the candlelight. Christine held her hands away from him, waiting with rapt concern to see what happened. Jason breathed rapidly for several minutes, trying to blow away the mounting agony. Finally, the pain subsided. Christine covered the gauze-packed wound with another square of gauze, then, with difficulty, wrapped a bandage around Jason's trunk. When he relaxed, Christine hugged him again, careful to avoid his side.

Jason gently pushed her away and sat up. "I need to check my e-mail," he said.

Jason retrieved his laptop from the chest-high safe bolted to the floor of his bedroom closet . He rarely used the laptop, having little use for it at work. The desktop computer was gone, probably sitting in a police evidence locker. Christine watched from over his shoulder as he turned it on and logged into his e-mail account.

"There it is," he said. "Walter sent a copy of the recording to me, the detective in Newport News, and himself. Hopefully, they've taken steps." An exhausting relief washed over him.

"So what now?" Christine asked.

At that moment, the phone rang. Jason hobbled to the phone and checked the caller ID. It was his sister-in-law's cell number. What the hell was Peter's wife calling at this hour for? Then the realization struck him again that Peter might be hurt or in danger. "Shit," he whispered.

He pressed talk. "Lisa?"

"No, it's me."

Jason breathed again, hearing his brother's voice. "Pete, where are you? How did you know to call me here?"

"I called your cell. There was no answer. I was taking a shot in the dark. Hoping maybe you'd check your messages."

Peter explained about the attacks, his wounded leg, and Waterhouse's murder. "You have to come and get me out of here. I'm a sitting duck!"

"We're on our way!" Jason ended the call and turned to Christine.

"Peter's in the hospital. We're going to get him. We can't stay here any longer anyway. The cops are sure to be watching the house. Are you up for this?"

Christine met his gaze and smiled. "As long as I'm with you! Don't leave me again."

"Don't worry. It won't happen again."

Five minutes later, Jason had burned a copy of the recording onto a flash drive in his desk drawer. If things didn't go as planned, the Conversation was his get-out-of-jail-free card.

Jason faced Christine and smiled, caressed her cheek, and said, "Let's go get the bastards who killed your father before they can assassinate the presidents!"

"The presidents!" Christine looked dumfounded.

"I'll explain on the way."

At that moment, the front door burst open with a loud crash. A man silhouetted against the moonlight rushed through the opening, holding a pistol capped with a very long silencer.

CHAPTER 76

His face illuminated by the glow of his computer screen, Steven Cooper smiled as he scrolled down. His dubious role in this sordid affair was almost complete. He was already a delightfully rich man. When it was over, he planned on enjoying every delectable penny.

He had been the mouthpiece for the ultrasecret, nameless group headed by the unseen puppetmaster named Hammon. He'd posed as the businessman funneling funds to Zanns and her Simoon. The additional five million dollar fee he'd squeezed from Zanns was parked neatly in the designated accounts, every dime untraceable. The funds slithered through a maze of dummy ledgers around the world, ending up in the Caymans, Switzerland, and Indonesia.

Five million dollars!

He leaned back, hands clasped behind his head, satisfaction enveloping him. Retirement would be a welcome change, and it loomed right around the corner. He'd received Hammon's blessing to end his career after this operation was complete, on the condition that he left the country, never to return.

His job was simple. Cooper would operate Cyclops, enabling Sam Fairing and Jasmine Kader to take their shots. He'd slip quietly out of the Windsor Towers and into a life of complete anonymity. He had no beef with either of the doomed politicians. He was not a political man, preferring to avoid the nastiness that accompanied ideology. He was a grunt. He followed orders. And following orders had made him very wealthy.

The risk, however, was enormous. As the appointed hour ticked closer, the danger of the entire scheme was beginning to rear its head in his mind. They would be sitting on the fourth floor of an apartment building whose roof would be patrolled by countersnipers of the United States Secret Service. He'd have no more than fifteen minutes to escape after the shots were fired. The car was parked in the lot near the exit. Take the stairs, run through the lobby and across the parking lot to the car. His best time was eight minutes, his worst ten.

He'd bluffed Zanns, telling her he'd skip out if she didn't pay. But even if he'd had the balls to leave, he had little choice now. If he failed to complete his part, Hammon's henchmen—the same men currently hunting the pharmacist and his friends—would be retasked to kill him. Money and distance would not buy him safety. He held no desire to incur their emotionless wrath.

The oversized briefcase sat on the floor beside him. "Cyclops" was the only machine of its kind, and key to the mission's success. Zanns had paid dearly for it. Cooper was the only person with the know-how—and the pass codes—to operate it. He'd made sure of that. It made him indispensable and, he was quite certain, was keeping him alive. At the moment, he was a very valuable asset. His phone rang. Only one person had this number.

"They have a CD recording of Z and her team." It was Hammon's gravelly voice.

"I know," Cooper replied.

"What's on it?"

"Talk of the big event."

"Wonderful," Hammon replied sarcastically.

"Actually, it's good news. The pharmacist and his cohorts know of no other conspirators. The recording implicates Z and her people. We should obtain the file and leak it."

Hammon cleared his throat. Cooper could hear the familiar click of the pipe stem against teeth. "The private investigator is no longer a concern. Eurus and Ford dispatched him. Zephyr and Horn haven't reported in. We have to assume they've been compromised, probably taken out by the marine. Reports say he's been taken to the hospital. There's no word from Notus and Miller." Hammon's voice was heavy. "We'll get the pharmacist within minutes. The fool returned to his house and took a call there. Boreas and McCall are moving on him now."

Cooper swallowed. He spoke tentatively. Hammon was not a man accustomed to being told what to do. "Since Eurus and Ford are free, might I suggest sending them to the private investigator's home to find the recording or the device itself?"

"That place is crawling with police. I'll send them after the marine."

* * *

Christine screamed. Jason shoved her toward the back of the house, cutting her anguished cry short. Two quick shots buried themselves in the far wall. Jason ducked out of view.

Christine stumbled to a knee. Jason grabbed her by the waistband, yanking her to her feet.

"Go! Go! Go!" he shouted, shoving her toward the back door. "Get out!"

Jason squeezed against the wall, staying between the intruder and Christine. The long black cylinder of the silencer appeared around the corner, followed by the pistol.

Jason flung himself at the gun, grabbing the hand holding the weapon. He slammed it against the sharp corner of a counter top. The pistol clattered across the tile floor. Jason aimed an elbow at the man's nose. The face turned at the last instant, causing the blow to smash the cheek instead. The man staggered and fell, squeezing a handful of shirt, pulling Jason to the floor. "Christine! Get the—" Jason's voice was cut short by a chop to the throat.

* * *

Christine watched for a heartbeat until Jason's words broke her panicked trance. She darted to the weapon and picked it up. Shakily, she aimed at the two men rolling about, entangled in a frantic death struggle. Christine trained for a shot on the enemy combatant without hitting Jason.

At that instant, the glass of the back door shattered. A shower of sparkling glass blew inward. Another armed man crashed through. Head down, protecting his face, the gunman recovered and came up firing. As Christine turned, silenced rounds thumped around her.

Reflexively, she fired, ripping off five shots. The third shot struck the collarbone, twisting his body in midair. His weapon flailed, showering bullets in a wide arc as he crumpled to the carpet.

Christine stepped to the wounded man, leveling the weapon. Blood spurted from a large vessel near his clavicle. The pistol lay inches from his twitching fingers. His eyes were wide with the knowledge of his own impending death. Yet an ingrained instinct compelled him to finish his mission.

"Don't do it!" Christine shouted. In the background, the punches and gasps of Jason's struggle echoed through the darkened house.

In a final, desperate spasm, he raised the gun...

An eruption of red coincided with the dull report from the weapon in her hands. The man's neck exploded. In seconds, the amount of blood on the carpet tripled.

The noise of the struggle behind her had ceased, followed by heavy footfalls. Christine turned. Her field of vision went black, then white, as she was tackled and lifted into the air.

* * *

The front-door attacker had broken free after pummeling Jason in the face, stunning him. The man darted around the corner. Jason pursued a step behind and watched helplessly as he rammed into Christine, grabbing at the gun in her hands. They sailed over the back of the sofa. The man landed on top of her, crushing her into the coffee table, which splintered in loud, sickening cracks.

Jason launched himself over the couch, wrapping an arm around the killer's throat and pulling him off Christine. He squeezed desperately, crushing the windpipe and choking off the killer's air. He saw the man's ears grow several shades redder even in the moonlight. Jason could feel his own face burning. He had out-bruted Jason in the foyer, and Jason was making him pay by crushing his neck with every pound of pressure he possessed. A minute passed. The tension in his opponent slackened. Another thirty seconds, and it was gone completely. Jason held his position for fifteen seconds more. Slowly, he relaxed, and the killer flopped face-first onto the carpet.

Among the shattered glass, broken furniture, and human remains, Jason crawled desperately to Christine. She was not moving.

CHAPTER 77

Routine maintenance, my ass! Palmer thought. The server had been down for two hours, a regularly scheduled procedure he'd never needed to know about until now. It was close to four in the morning. The phone call from Peter Rodgers had come in an hour ago. His Blackberry hadn't been able to access his department e-mail account. The detective raced to the police administration building, hoping his desktop would allow him access. When that failed, he called IS and was given the bad news.

Peter Rodgers had been the fourth man in the room the day Jason Rodgers and Waterhouse had tried in vain to convince him that Thomas Pettigrew had been murdered. He recalled him as very quiet, with a permanent scowl and eyes that held a reckless quality.

The facts of this case were convoluted and bizarre. At this point, Palmer had a hard time knowing what to believe. Jason Rodgers was on the run, an escaped prisoner, accused of murdering his ex-girlfriend. He was the same man who'd claimed Thomas Pettigrew had been murdered by insurance scammers at the Colonial Pharmacy in Newport

386

News. Jason and Walter Waterhouse, an acquaintance of Palmer's, had also been present when one Douglas Winstead had his head blown off. Christine Pettigrew, Thomas's daughter, had fired a weapon inside Lily Zanns's home, trying to kill the woman. Now, only an hour ago, the brother had phoned, saying that Jason Rodgers was being framed and that President Hope and his father were in danger of assassination on Saturday during the christening.

Palmer recalled a phrase his father often used to describe such fucked-up situations. "Shitfire!" he said out loud.

The brother had said that Waterhouse had sent him an e-mail with a file attachment of the conversation between Zanns and her alleged coconspirators. It proved their intent to kill the presidents. It also contained a statement exonerating Jason Rodgers. What made the situation even more fucked up was a Secret Service bulletin that stated Jason Rodgers was not only wanted for the murder, but implicated in the assassination plot based on evidence found in his home.

Double shitfire!

As a cop, his first course of action should be to immediately call the Secret Service whenever he received a threat to the president, and let them handle it. They had a two-way flow of information with the department in preparation for the christening. The NNPD had assigned a detective to a task force created just for that purpose.

Palmer picked up the phone. He replaced the handset, deciding to wait to hear the recording for himself before making the call. He would confirm its existence and forward it to the task force liaison then. He was determined not to make the same mistake again.

Six years ago, a man had called in a threat to the president. Hope was in town for a commencement address. Without checking it out, Palmer had immediately called the Secret Service. Because the event was scheduled for the next day, agents had been dispatched to the home of an influential business executive in the middle of the night, waking his wife and kids and scaring the living shit out of them. The caller turned out to be a disgruntled employee bent on revenge for being fired.

The former employee had been prosecuted and eventually found guilty. But not before the police chief had had his ass chewed by the mayor. The executive was the largest contributor to the mayor's re-election campaign and a very good friend. The police chief in turn had lit Palmer up for forty-five, red-faced, spittle-spewing minutes. To this day, Palmer was still reminded of his mistake by some of the older veterans.

While he waited for the server to come back online, Palmer reviewed the daily intelligence report. The secret squirrels—that's what he called the guys from the Newport News Intelligence Division—distributed it daily. Homicide supervisor Sergeant Barry Waters had left it on his desk earlier that evening. It was a summary of all crimes in the area from neighboring localities, including Newport News.

Now, Palmer studied the report for any tidbit that might clue him into Jason Rodgers's activities in the last twenty-four hours. If the pharmacist was smart, he'd be in another state or country. That was probably not the case. Criminals were human, and humans, by nature, were creatures of habit. They had rituals. They relied on their local network of people. Palmer sensed Rodgers was not a career criminal, but if he was involved in the assassination plot, Palmer knew he could be wrong. He guessed the pharmacist would stay close to home. Nonetheless, an alert for Rodgers and his female friend, Christine Pettigrew, had been put out statewide and nationally. Fugitives usually committed more crimes to avoid capture. Rodgers would make a mistake. Then they'd find him.

Rodgers's escape from the regional jail was all over the news. Normally, he'd have let the sheriff's department up there handle it. But Rodgers was also an employee of the Colonial, which was in Newport News. He was connected to crimes revolving around the pharmacy, and, evidently, a threat to the presidents.

Were all these crimes coincidences? Palmer didn't think so. They all shared a common link. He just needed to find that small, exposed thread and pull until everything fell apart.

The report was arranged in alphabetical order by city. Chesapeake. Hampton. Newport News. Norfolk. Poquoson. Smithfield. Suffolk. Virginia Beach. Williamsburg. York County.

Chesapeake: an armed robbery of a convenience store, a hit-and-run accident.

Hampton: two shootings and two stolen vehicles, taken from driveways while owners slept. Palmer circled those listings. Those could be Rodgers trying to find wheels. He would have one of the junior detectives run it down.

In Newport News, the only listing of interest was a boat exploding on the James. Two charred bodies were found floating in the river. The fire department's boat was on the scene. There were no other details.

Norfolk, the largest urban area in Tidewater, had a list filling two-and-a-half pages. Armed robbery, carjacking (possibly Rodgers), several break-ins, and an apparent suicide, among others.

Poquoson was next. One crime was detailed. Palmer was so stunned by the name of the victim, he spilled the open bottle of water onto his report.

He cursed.

Walter Waterhouse. Gunshot wound to the head. Dead at the scene. If it had made the news, Palmer hadn't seen it. He looked at it twice, making sure he'd read it correctly.

He swore again as he blotted up the water with some tissues. Palmer put the paper down and absorbed the news. Waterhouse was somewhere between an acquaintance and a friend. The hairs on the back of his neck stood on end. He picked up the phone to dial the Poquoson Police Department. He stopped when he read the next item on the list.

Smithfield: a shooting in a residential neighborhood. Two men were killed after a B and E. The owner shot them dead. Palmer would have skipped it, but the name caught his eye.

Rodgers. Peter Rodgers.

Isn't that the same guy who called an hour ago?

Palmer drew a star next to the listing and wrote, *Call Smithfield PD*.

There was nothing in Virginia Beach. Pretty quiet for a resort city.

Palmer realized his right foot was bouncing up and down furiously. His nerves were frayed.

He picked up the phone a third time and dialed IS. "When am I getting my fuckin' e-mail back!" he shouted at the technician on the other end.

"Detective, we've run into a problem. We've lost the connectivity network-attached storage. You won't be able to access your e-mail until we get it back. It looks like it'll be down for at least another two hours."

"Bullshit! You gotta be kidding me!"

Palmer slammed the phone onto its cradle and released another string of curses. Barely able to focus, he scanned the remainder of the report.

Palmer read the only listing in Williamsburg. A young couple's green Ford Taurus had been carjacked. The young woman had been momentarily kidnapped. The perp was wearing only underwear and had a wound in his left side. Palmer leafed through a stack of papers and found the police report filed after Rodgers's escape from the hospital. He traced his index finger down the text, stopping at the lines he was looking for. Rodgers had a stab wound in his left side. He'd hijacked the ambulance wearing only his underwear and his flip flops. The ambulance had been found in the parking lot of President's Park in Williamsburg.

"That's him!" Palmer said out loud.

He called the regional jail, demanding to speak with one of the officers there. "Send Rodgers's mug shot over to Williamsburg PD," he instructed

The next call was to the Williamsburg PD. Palmer spoke to the detective handling carjacking and rapidly explained his hunch. The man said he would personally deliver the photo to the couple, who were still staying at the hotel in Williamsburg. Palmer gave the man his cell number and ended the call.

Through one more call to the Smithfield PD, Palmer learned Peter Rodgers had been wounded by fire from the assailants and was taken to a hospital in Suffolk, a fact the man had failed to mention when he'd phoned Palmer.

Palmer weighed his options, his knee banging the underside of the cubicle desk. Was it time to call the Secret Service? *No*, he told himself. This time he was going to get confirmation. If the server didn't come up in the next hour, Palmer promised himself he'd report the threat whether he had an e-mail or not. In the meantime, he'd drive over to Suffolk and have a talk with Peter Rodgers.

Palmer grabbed his jacket and waved down a rookie, David Bartlett, affectionately known as Opie because of his freckles, red hair, and aw-shucks attitude.

"Let's go!" he barked.

* * *

For a fleeting moment, Jason thought Christine might be dead. He placed a hand on her back, feeling for the heave of her chest. Silence. No movement.

"Oh God, no," he whispered as panic welled.

Then a shallow, weak expansion of her rib cage elevated his hand slightly. An eternity seemed to pass. Then a second breath was followed by a third.

She was alive.

Her neck had been whipped by the tackle and whipped again when she hit the coffee table. Fearing a neck injury, he lightly traversed her skull and neck with his fingers. No obvious fractures. But a warm, sticky, pinkish fluid caressed the pads of his fingers behind her ear at the base of her skull. When Jason pulled back her hair, he saw it had oozed from the ear canal. He'd taken enough emergency first-aid classes to know about concussions and cerebrospinal fluid. *Could be a skull fracture*, he thought. Putting his ear to her face, he felt slight, hesitant breaths against his cheek.

Shit!

Time was short. He needed to get her to a hospital. With the possibility of a neck or head injury, it was best not to move her. As much as he wanted to get Christine the medical help she needed, the situation wouldn't allow time for the detour.

Don't leave her again, he thought. *Don't leave her again!*

Unfortunately, it was exactly what he knew he must do. He stood on wobbly legs, ran to the phone, and dialed 911.

CHAPTER 78

The sirens approached.

Jason placed a hand on Christine's chest again to make sure she was still breathing, more to reassure himself than anything else. Her respirations were still shallow and slow. The pulse was weak but palpable.

It was time to go. Jason could do nothing more.

By the pitch of the sirens, the ambulance had rounded the entrance to his subdivision. He checked both bodies and fished out a set of keys.

He leaned over Christine, brushed her hair back, and gently kissed her forehead. Her words came back to him.

Don't leave me again!

He was abandoning her all over again. She was hurt badly, and he was leaving her. And worse, it was because of him, because he'd come back into her life, that Chrissie now lay mangled in his living room.

He left the front door open so the paramedics would know which house she was in. The killers had parked in the driveway. He started the killers' car and sped off. In his rearview mirror, he watched the ambulance pull into the driveway, lights circling. Jason prayed it would not be the last time he saw the only woman he'd ever really loved alive.

* * *

"Do you know that your brother escaped from the regional jail in Williamsburg last night?" Palmer asked in the hospital room. The ex-marine's left leg was elevated on three pillows, the knee heavily bandaged.

Palmer and a second, boyish detective had burst into his room minutes ago, flashing badges.

"Yeah. Unfortunately, it's all over the news." Peter lifted a thumb in the direction of the television.

"Has he tried to contact you?"

"No," Peter lied. *But I called him.*

"Do you know where he is?"

"No." It was the truth. Jason could be anywhere between his house and Peter's hospital room, ready to stumble into the arms of these cops while he was talking to them. "Jason didn't kill that woman."

"Then why did he run?"

"I don't know for sure. But I can guess."

"Go on."

"His life is in danger. *All* our lives are in danger. As I told you on the phone, he has important information about the christening. People are trying to kill the presidents. Didn't you get our e-mail?"

"Unfortunately, there are some kinks in our system."

"It has all the proof you need," Peter insisted.

Palmer rubbed his chin. "How did you come into possession of this recording?"

"We—"

"We, *meaning?*"

"Meaning Jason, me, and Walter Waterhouse. We planted a listening device aboard Zanns's yacht."

"I'll ignore the legal implications of planting a listening device on someone's private yacht for the moment," Palmer replied, fixing Peter with a hard stare. "I thought you and your crew were concerned about the murder of Thomas Pettigrew?"

"We were. It turned out to be more than fraud, more than murder."

"You mean all this stuff about insurance fraud is really a plot to kill the presidents?" His tone spoke volumes about how little Palmer believed Peter's words.

"Now you're getting the picture."

"And the Zanns woman is responsible?"

Peter nodded. "Yup! And her three accomplices. The pharmacist, Fairing, and a doctor—can't remember her name right now, Jasmine something-or-other—and Zanns's houseboy, Oliver. That's one of the reasons Jason escaped. They're trying to eliminate us." Peter pointed to his bandaged leg. "The recording proves it."

Palmer scribbled notes on a pad and asked the question again. "I can't help you unless you tell me the truth. You've been in contact with your brother, haven't you?"

Peter hesitated, and then decided to come clean. "Yes. I spoke with him this morning."

"Where is he?"

"At this moment, I don't know. And if I did, I wouldn't tell you."

* * *

Jason strained to hear what the detective and his brother were saying inside the hospital room. He fingered the flash drive in his pocket. Waterhouse had sent the e-mail. But Jason gathered that Palmer, for some reason, hadn't received it.

He'd raced to the hospital after leaving Christine. He'd spotted Detective Palmer and his red-headed sidekick walking through the entrance as he pulled into the parking lot. Jason gave the cops a three-minute head start and followed them in.

This was as good a time as any to turn himself in. He had the proof, and Palmer was only a few steps away. He inflated his lungs, about to confront Palmer with the recording. But a flash of movement caught his eye, freezing him in place.

* * *

"Can you identify the people who are trying to kill the presidents?" asked Palmer.

"No, but my brother can."

"Who tried to break into your house?" Palmer peered at Peter.

"They weren't trying to break in. They were trying to kill me, and probably my family. Their weapons had silencers."

* * *

Out of the corner of his eye, he saw the figure enter the far end of the hospital hallway, moving quickly.

Jason backed against the wall. The red-headed cop was on his cell asking about the e-mail server and roaming dangerously close to the doorway.

The man who'd entered the hallway wore a blue windbreaker and had a hand in his pocket, clutching something. The determined stride and the imperturbable stare made Jason's blood run cold. Instinctively, Jason glanced toward the opposite end of the corridor, where a second figure had entered and was also moving toward him. His hand, too, was hidden inside his windbreaker. Both men would be on him in seconds. Their eyes locked on Jason, silently signaling their lethal intent.

Trapped, his stomach went to his throat. The bulges in their jackets were visible now.

Number One pulled his hand from inside his pocket and removed the weapon. Number Two did the same.

Act now!

His choices were limited, his chances of survival slim. Jason quickstepped into his brother's hospital room.

CHAPTER 79

"*Gun! Gun!*" Jason shouted, pushing the half-open door to the wall.

The redhead gawked at Jason, then withdrew his Smith and Wesson from its holster. Palmer, the veteran, had his pistol out from under his armpit in milliseconds, his notepad fluttering to the floor. Jason stepped out of the doorway and what would be the line of fire, melting into the wall. He didn't have the presence of mind to slam the door shut.

Palmer leveled the pistol at Jason.

"They're coming down the hall!" Jason hollered.

"Freeze!" Palmer ordered. "Show me your hands—"

"Two men with guns. The hallway!" Jason yelled again, pointing.

Peter sat up straight in bed. "Jason! What the hell?"

"Get down!"

"Freeze! On your face! Now!" Palmer still had the gun on Jason.

"Guns! In the hall! Move!"

Palmer's eyes darted between his suspect and the doorway.

"Check it out!" he commanded Bartlett.

As Bartlett stepped into the opening, a round erupted out the back of his head. He folded like a discarded marionette. Palmer, Jason, and Peter recoiled. Jason slid to the floor. Peter dove under the bed. Palmer dropped to one knee and turned his weapon on the doorway.

A hand appeared around the doorframe, leveling a weapon. Palmer ripped off two rounds. The hand retreated into the corridor.

The second killer appeared from the opposite side of the doorframe, spraying the room. Palmer returned fire in rapid sequence, hitting him. Blood blossomed through the man's shirt. He spun and dropped, slamming face-first into floor.

"Get on the phone!" Palmer shouted.

Peter grabbed the telephone from his position on the floor and dialed the operator. He screamed into the handset for police and security in room three-fifteen.

A short silence ensued, followed by the echo of running footfalls. Palmer ran to the door, hazarded a look, and turned back to Jason and Peter. "Check him!" he commanded Jason, referring to the wounded detective. "Stay here!" Palmer disappeared down the corridor.

Jason checked the young man's pulse as he fought the urge to gag. Blood covered everything. The eyes were open, staring through Jason. The detective was dead.

Jason moved to Peter and pulled him off the floor. "Can you walk?" Jason asked.

"I think so."

"We're not staying. Let's go."

"Maybe we should wait for Palmer to get back."

"Peter," Jason replied, pointing to the dead cop. "These guys could kill Palmer, then come back and get us. You want to take that chance?"

They hopped over the body and headed in the opposite direction Palmer had run. Five seconds before hospital security arrived, they slipped into a utility room. Frantic yelling and screaming filled the corridor, mingling with running footsteps. Female voices hollered instructions. The overhead paging system called the trauma team to

Peter's former room. A crash cart rumbled by, pushed by two nurses and an attending physician.

Jason grabbed a set of green scrubs off a rack, and they took the stairs as fast as Peter's leg and Jason's wound allowed. In minutes, they were squealing out of the parking lot before anyone could give chase.

Chapter 80

Clay Broadhurst walked along the covered dais under the prow of the mighty ship. He stood at the podium in the exact spot where the presidents, Torpedo and his son Thunderbolt, would deliver their addresses in less than twenty-four hours. He surveyed the area, reviewing his mental checklist. Special guests would be seated facing the dais on two barges floating directly in front of the vessel, on the north side of the dry dock. The southern side held seating for the public. A short gangway led from the dais to the bottle-break stand against the gunmetal-gray steel of the ship's bow. Katherine Hope Morris, the former president's daughter and the ship's sponsor, would break the bottle of sparkling American wine against the metal bar jutting from the bow. A likeness of Hope outlined in red, white, and blue was mounted above the spot that would be showered.

Thirty yards to the north, a large white canvas had been stretched between two forty-foot poles. Seventy-five feet wide and thirty feet high, the fabric provided no special protection, other than obscuring the view of possible snipers from the north, specifically from the identical twin spires of the Windsor Towers. Those who would be witnessing the ceremony tomorrow were some of the most influential human beings on the planet, and they would all be congregated well within range of an expert marksman.

Shipyard workers were putting on the finishing touches, hanging red, white, and blue bunting, running sound cables and adjusting microphones, placing cameras, and arranging chairs. The slate-gray sky, crowded with dark, low-hanging clouds, forecast heavy rain and thunder. An impromptu covering had been placed over the stage, VIP seating, and podium to keep the politicos dry. As usual, it would be the common folk getting rained on.

Crowds would be funneled through metal detectors and searched. No bags, cameras, or video equipment would be allowed inside the yard. Plainclothes Secret Service agents would be scattered among the throng, looking for signs of trouble. Agents would never be more than a few feet from the president and the other dignitaries. Broadhurst had spent the last month making sure the three concentric layers of protection around the president were solid and impenetrable.

Broadhurst threw his head back, staring up at the gargantuan warship as ceremonial fabric fluttered in the breeze. He could not help but admire the handiwork of the shipyard employees, which had taken eight years to construct and had cost taxpayers billions. The wind blew in from the southwest, lugging with it nasty weather.

Broadhurst turned his collar up and studied the choppy river waters and the vertical drawbridge of James River Bridge beyond, looming out of the thickening haze.

Jacob R. Hope, president number 42, would arrive today and check in at the Williamsburg Inn. His son Gary, number 44 and current chief executive, would arrive aboard Air Force One in the morning, landing at Newport News–Williamsburg International Airport.

When Gary was elected, the Hopes joined a most exclusive club. They were the third pair of father-son presidents behind the Adamses and the Bushes. The Harrisons, William Henry and Benjamin, were grandfather and grandson. Since Jacob's election in 1980, the White house had been occupied by either a Bush or a Hope, alternating family names with each administration. Broadhurst had served for three years under George W. Bush and under the newly elected Gary Hope since his election last year.

The motorcade would travel along Jefferson Avenue and cross over to Warwick Boulevard. A full police escort would stop traffic and provide an uninterrupted journey. Jacob R. and Gary would meet up at the shipyard at a prechristening reception. Of course, only Broadhurst and a handful of agents knew these details.

He'd scrutinized every detail of the security plan with his detail this morning. Nothing had been omitted. The motorcade routes had been secured. Mailboxes were removed and manhole covers were welded shut along the route. Every building taller than three stories in the immediate area had been scanned and inspected. The church steeple nearby had been buttoned down, and an agent had been standing a lonely post. Residents of the Windsor Towers had been instructed to leave all windows closed for the twenty-four hours leading up to the christening. Agents scanned the building with powerful field glasses, making sure everyone was in compliance. Countersnipers had been positioned on the roofs of both buildings.

Jason Rodgers's mug shot flashed in Broadhurst's mind, haunting him. The man was at large, and that fact alone ate away at his gastric lining. But other troublesome facts had been uncovered by the background check and investigation into Rodgers's finances. Two large deposits from Cooper Venture Capital had been deposited to his account within a week of each other in the last month. The address of the company headquarters was fake, and they could find no listing of any business with such a name in any corporate directories. Specific details about the event, known only to a select few, had been found in Rodgers's home.

How the hell had Jason Rodgers, a pharmacist apparently lacking any ties to political or terror groups, gotten his hands on classified details of the christening? What his beef with Gary Hope or his father was, Broadhurst didn't know. But he wasn't going to let Rodgers or anyone bring harm to his charges. Agents from the field offices in Richmond, Norfolk, and Charlotte had been called in to bolster manpower.

Broadhurst had wanted to delay the christening for twenty-four hours until they could capture Rodgers. But that was not his call. Politics outside his control influenced this christening. President Hope and his father would have the final say. The elder President Hope was in his eighties and not getting any younger. The next step in the life of this vessel would be the commissioning ceremony, two years hence. Broadhurst suspected that they both wanted the ship commissioned while 42 was still alive and 44 was still in office. No other ship's namesake had ever been alive to witness either its christening or its commissioning.

Back in Washington, Special Agent Woody Austin had promised Broadhurst he would personally convey his concerns to the president. Since they'd spoke thirty-six hours ago, the director of the presidential protection division had not communicated with Broadhurst. Until he was told otherwise, the christening would go off as scheduled, bad weather, potential assassins, and all. Broadhurst pulled his overcoat tighter around him, the chill in his bones caused by something deeper than weather. As he walked along the gangway to the rear of the ship, his cell phone rang.

Broadhurst flipped open his phone. "Agent Broadhurst, this is Detective John Palmer with the Newport News Police Department. We need to talk. Now!"

CHAPTER 81

Peter's cell phone chirped. It was Tom Johnson. Peter let it go to voice mail, turned the phone off, and removed the battery. He removed Lisa's phone, redialing his friend's number as they sped out of Suffolk.

"Tom, it's Peter. What's up?"

Peter listened in silence for two minutes.

"Okay, thanks, Tom."

"What was that all about?" asked Jason.

"First, we go to the gun shop. Then we need to get in touch with the special agent in charge at the shipyard."

"Who was on the phone?" asked Jason.

"Tom Johnson. There's a mole inside the Secret Service or the White House. There may be others on-site at the shipyard. My instructions are to warn Special Agent Broadhurst. Deliver the message in person. No phones, no cells, no e-mails. All electronic communications may be compromised. Tom spoke with the director of the presidential protection division himself. A guy named Woody Austin."

Peter studied the passing scenery as he rubbed the scar over his eye. "Austin didn't tell Tom what was going on. But Tom guesses that Austin was blackmailed into helping to place the moles. I guess Austin had enough of the BS and asked Tom to contact Broadhurst through me. He figured Tom could be trusted, since he works in the counterfeit division and isn't close to what's going on. Austin told Tom that since I was one of the people who recorded Zanns's meeting, I was to deliver the message."

They pulled into the gun shop parking lot and parked around back. Jason waited in the car while Peter went inside.

Ten minutes later, Peter had loaded the trunk with two pistols, five boxes of ammo for each, and an AR-15, the civilian version of an M-16.

Jason merged into traffic and followed Route 258 back over the James River Bridge. "We need to get rid of this car," he said.

"Got any ideas?" asked Peter.

"I know a place we can get a car without having to steal one," Jason replied.

CHAPTER 82

"Are you sure you don't want me to go in there?" Jason asked as the car idled. He pulled the killer's Lincoln in front of the sliding doors of Keller's Food and Drug, his former employer.

"Can't risk it. You used to work here, remember? The last thing we need right now is someone recognizing you." Peter shot Jason a sideways glance. "Are you sure she'll help us?"

"I'm not sure about anything at this point. I burned a bridge, but I don't know who else to turn to. Barbara's a good technician, and I trust her. How far that trust will take us, I don't know. Just tell her that I'm out here and get her to come outside."

Peter eased out of the car, favoring his wounded leg. Jason found a parking spot with a view of the front door, sunk low in the seat, and kept the car running.

* * *

The line at the pharmacy counter was three-deep, served by a male pharmacist and his two helpers. Jason had briefed Peter on the way over. Lawrence Quigley would probably be on duty, and both technicians were female. Barbara Jensen, stout and round, weighed in at about two hundred eighty. Peter picked her out easily, as she stood with her head down studying something on the counter behind the wall of glass.

Customers in front of him picked up their prescriptions, paid their bills, and moved off. When it was his turn, he walked to the register. The black woman saw him and walked over. "May I help you?"

"Barbara Jensen, please?"

Hearing her name, Barbara Jensen shuffled over. The woman was massive, a wrecking ball draped in a gray lab coat. Her sad, circular, blue eyes peered at Peter from deep inside a spherical face capped with thin, gray hair.

"Can I help you?"

"Barbara, my name is Peter. I have a message from a friend I've been asked to deliver. Can I speak to you for just a moment?" Peter motioned with his head, indicating he wanted her to step out of the pharmacy.

The large technician met him in the health and beauty aisle. "What can I do for you?" she asked, glancing at his leg.

"My brother is Jason Rodgers."

Her eyes widened slowly. "My God!" she said loudly. "He's been all over the—"

Peter put a finger to his lips. "I know," he said, looking around nervously.

"Is he okay?"

"Yes—and no."

"Tell me he didn't kill that woman!" Jensen had sense enough to whisper the question.

"You can ask him yourself. He's outside. He—we—need your help."

Her girth swayed away from Peter, as if he had some extremely contagious disease.

"Everything you see on television is wrong. We're dealing with some really deep shit here. Just give Jason a few minutes, please," Peter pleaded.

Jensen studied Peter, peering into his concerned eyes. "No. Trouble's the last thing I need."

His voice quavered. *"Please!* It's a matter of life and death. Not just his life, but others' as well."

The woman put her fleshy hands on her hips in displeasure. "Let me tell you," she began. "Your brother left us—left me—high and dry when he quit a few weeks ago. I worked hard for him for four years. He didn't even have the decency to give proper notice, let alone ask me to come with him. Now I'm stuck here with this dimwit," she said, jerking her thumb toward the pharmacy.

"Please, he said we could count on you."

"I can't," she replied, shaking her head. "That's asking way too much."

* * *

Peter appeared in the sliding doors of the grocery store—alone. Jason's heart sank. He rammed the gearshift into drive and pulled to the entrance, whispering curses. Peter got in; Jason depressed the accelerator, and the stolen Lincoln began to move away. Jason braked, allowing a car to pass.

Out of the corner of his eye, Jason saw the doors opening again.

Peter placed a hand on Jason's arm. "Hold on!"

Jason turned his head. The brothers watched the nearly three-hundred-pound woman break out in a painfully hurried waddle. Barbara Jensen, out of breath, put her weight on the car door and leaned in the open window, looking to Peter first.

"I'm sorry. I didn't know how to react." She looked at Jason. "I owe you. I haven't forgotten the time you covered for me when my husband was dying. If it wasn't for you, Carl would've died alone. I just needed time to wrap my brain around all this."

She examined his bruised, battered face, and smiled. "Your looks have improved."

"Nice to see you, too," Jason replied.

"Oh, honey, you deserve a lot more than that black eye. But we'll save that for later."

"We need a place to get out of sight for a few hours."

"You mean hide?" she deadpanned.

"Whatever," Jason replied.

Barbara reached into her lab jacket and jangled a set of keys. Removing one, she handed it over. "You remember where I live?"

Jason nodded. "We'll ditch the car away from the store so it's not traced to you."

Jensen smiled. "I'll be home in a few hours. Help yourself to what's in the fridge. I'll make you something to eat when I get back. And I'm going to want a full explanation on how you managed to get yourself in such trouble. It's the least you can do after leaving me with numbnuts in there."

"Deal," Jason said, not sure he would ever be able to relay any of his story. "And Barbara, we also need to borrow your car."

Barbara frowned. "Boy, I guess you really *do* trust me. You're gonna owe me big time." She reached into her lab jacket one more time and handed over the whole key chain. "I'll catch a ride home with Carol."

"Oh, one more thing," Jason said sheepishly. "Can I use your cell phone?"

"You need me to change your diapers too?"

CHAPTER 83

Broadhurst and the driver exited the lead vehicle of the four-sedan convoy, jogging up the granite steps. Six more Secret Service agents materialized from the trailing two vehicles. They fanned out, moving alongside the enormous house, guns drawn. A final pair joined Broadhurst on the portico.

Preparations for tomorrow's christening were complete. Everything was taken care of, except, that is, for the unresolved issue of Jason Rodgers and now Lily Zanns. Detective John Palmer's phone call two hours ago had launched Broadhurst's anxiety into the ionosphere. The Newport News cop had quickly outlined the prescription scam, insurance fraud, and the alleged recording of Lily Zanns and her quartet of killers. Broadhurst's stomach began to fold in on itself as Palmer ticked off each item. The death of the previous owner, Thomas Pettigrew, the murders of a patient named Douglas Winstead and of a private investigator—they were all connected, Palmer said. His interview with Peter Rodgers had occurred three hours ago, and could not as yet be verified. Broadhurst told him to burn a copy of the recording of Zanns as soon as Palmer got his hands on it. The file was already out in cyberspace. The last thing he needed was for it to be replicated and distributed to all corners of the World Wide Web. Until he had evidence to the contrary, Broadhurst was treating the story as if it were gospel.

Broadhurst had dispatched a pair of agents to the Colonial, asking for Zanns and Fairing. A clerk had informed them neither was in, and he didn't know where they were. The pharmacist on duty, a man named Billy Parks, said Fairing had left for Canada for a weekend getaway. He hadn't been in touch with Zanns, and didn't know where she was. On Palmer's word, a sympathetic judge had issued four search warrants in under an hour.

Along with the squad of agents about to enter Zanns's mansion, Broadhurst had dispatched three other teams. One was knocking on the door of Sam Fairing's seventeenth-floor condo in the south Windsor Tower; a third team was at Dr. Jasmine Kader's home; and a fourth was at her medical office. The searches had been synchronized to commence simultaneously.

* * *

The window beside the door was broken and had been pushed open. Broadhurst pounded on the door. "Federal agents," he yelled. "Open up!"

When no one answered, Broadhurst lifted his radio. "We're going in."

The heavy oak door yielded to the heavy ram with one blow. The door frame had been previously splintered. Four agents rushed in, guns leveled, securing the first floor. The last two agents climbed the stairs to the second floor. The house appeared empty. They searched the grounds all the way to the water for an hour. A pier extended into the river, but the yacht and plane were missing. Broadhurst crumpled the search warrant, slammed it onto the grass, and marched back to the house.

As he was about to end the search, Broadhurst was summoned to the three-car garage. A stainless-steel room containing refrigerators, dental instruments, and medical-type tables had been discovered under a trapdoor. On the floor near one of the freezers was a severed human finger. Ninety minutes after entering, Broadhurst left with more questions than answers.

Back in the SUV, his cell phone rang. The agents had found Kader's home deserted. Her office staff said she had left for a vacation in Hilton Head. Two minutes later, the phone rang again. In Fairing's condo, the television was on, no one was home, and everything appeared to be in order. They'd found no evidence of weapons or documents indicating any type of plot.

He cursed under his breath. The phone rang a third time. Broadhurst did not recognize the number.

"Agent Broadhurst, my name is Peter Rodgers…"

Broadhurst stiffened. "Go on!"

"I have some information about tomorrow's christening."

"I'm listening."

"I've been instructed to discuss this in person. This line isn't secure."

"I don't have time for—where's your brother?"

"Somewhere safe for the moment."

"I need to talk to him."

"That can be negotiated. Now be quiet and listen. I was told by the director of the presidential protection division through an intermediary to contact you. We need to get off this line so I can give you the message."

"You're not in an ideal negotiating position, Mr. Rodgers!"

"I was told to use the code word 'Anaconda.'"

"Meet me in the lobby of the Omni in thirty minutes."

CHAPTER 84

Peter limped into the lobby of the Omni Hotel. A man dressed in a dark suit coat, neatly pressed white shirt, and dark sunglasses approached. He was three inches taller than the gun shop owner, broad-shouldered, with a square chin. His jaw muscles rippled with tension.

Peter put up a hand when Broadhurst was six feet away. "That's far enough," he said. "Are you Broadhurst?"

The agent nodded and flashed his badge.

"I want to let you know—" Peter lowered his voice so the smattering of guests and hotel staff did not hear him. "I have a weapon on me. But I have no intention of using it here."

Two large agents approached the former marine from behind, each grabbing an arm. They forced him to the nearest wall with surprising ease. One conducted a pat down and removed the gun from his waistband. The pistol disappeared inside a suit coat.

Noticing Peter's wounded leg, they then literally lifted him off his feet, carrying him to the elevator. On the fifth floor, Broadhurst slid a magnetic key into the door of the room. Inside, Broadhurst nodded to the bed. Peter was deposited on it as Broadhurst moved in.

"How did you know about Anaconda?"

"It was given to me by a friend. His name's Tom Johnson. He works counterfeit in the Secret Service."

"If he works counterfeit, he wouldn't have it."

Peter opened his mouth, but Broadhurst cut him off. "Where's your brother?"

"I don't think I like your attitude."

"I don't give a shit what you like or don't like! Your brother is a suspect in a murder. When the local cops searched his house, they found classified documents about the christening. He is considered a threat to the president. Where is he?"

"He's being framed. They murdered Jason's ex and set him up. It's the same group that's trying to kill the presidents."

"You and he are working together."

"Only to get out of this friggin' mess! You think we're trying to kill the president? So the first place I run to is you?"

"How do you know the code—Anaconda?"

Peter let out a long breath. "I told you. Tom Johnson. He works for the Secret Service in the counterfeit division. We were in the same unit in the corps during Persian Gulf One."

"How did *he* get it?"

"Someone gave it to him."

"Who?"

"Woody Austin. Director of the presidential protection division."

Broadhurst sighed and ran a hand through his hair.

Peter continued, "Austin told Johnson the entire security network of the service—electronic, wireless, landlines—is compromised. He wanted me to deliver this message in person."

"Why didn't he send an agent down here, or someone at the Richmond or Norfolk field offices?"

"I don't know. I was told he only trusts you. Evidently, the infiltration is significant."

Broadhurst studied Peter, weighing his credibility. "What proof do you have of the assassination plot?"

Peter explained about the recording of Zanns and her cohorts. Broadhurst cut him off. "We know about it. But until I hear for myself, it's just a fairytale. Where's your brother now?"

"I'm not saying for the moment. He wants to stop this thing. But he doesn't trust anyone, and I don't blame him. He has a copy of the recording on a flash drive."

"If you have it, why didn't you bring it?"

"We'll get to that."

The steel in Broadhurst's voice softened. "Can you talk him into coming in?"

"If I tell him it's safe, he'll come in. But we need a guarantee you won't just turn him over to York County. The guys up there want his head on a platter."

Broadhurst searched Peter's eyes. Peter sensed an internal battle raging inside the man. "If he's truly innocent, he's got nothing to worry about from the law."

Peter smirked. "Spare me the bullshit, will you! Jason's wanted by the locals. What are you going to do to protect him?"

Broadhurst's shoulders sagged. "Here's the deal," he began. "Your brother is still technically in custody. If he turns himself in, I'm required to hand him over to the locals. I don't have much choice. We'd have to interrogate him in jail."

"No can do, Agent," Peter spat. "You guarantee his safety until after the christening, or Jason stays in hiding and you deal with these assassins yourself. You see, my brother is the only one who can help you. He's the only one who can identify all the players."

Broadhurst studied the former marine. "I can just waltz over to the Colonial and enlist the help of one of Zanns's other employees."

"What about Jasmine, the doctor? Do they know what she looks like?" Peter paused, then answered his own question. "I don't think so!"

"What does your brother want?"

"Keep him, both of us for that matter, in your custody until this is over. We'll deal with the locals later. Jason will assist you however he can to stop Zanns. Then later, after you hear the recording, you help to clear his name."

"Can he identify Zanns and these other people?"

Peter nodded.

"And if I don't?" Broadhurst asked.

"We don't help you and the recording goes public."

"My ass will be in a sling if I don't turn your brother over immediately to the local cops."

Peter held his hands up as if to say, "Oh, well."

Broadhurst rubbed his chin. "I need to talk to this friend of yours in the counterfeit division."

CHAPTER 85

"Tell me what you know," Broadhurst demanded over the phone.

Tom Johnson spoke calmly, but with determined emphasis. "I contacted Woody Austin after Sarge—I mean, Peter—told me about the recording and the code names."

"Just like that? You took Peter Rodgers's word for it?"

"I served in Iraq and Kuwait with him, Agent. The man saved my ass on two occasions."

The statement hung there for a second before Johnson continued. "I told Austin there might be a problem. He already knew there was trouble. Don't ask me how, but he did. He asked me to meet him at Union Station, away from the Executive Office Building. His orders were to get in touch with you through Peter outside normal channels. He said the service had been compromised."

"How?"

"I don't know, and he wouldn't explain. I've met Austin on several occasions at a couple of functions. He didn't seem himself. He looked stressed."

"Go on."

"He told me to pass on Anaconda through Peter."

"It's the code we use to communicate a threat to the president."

"Austin said people were going to die. It was personal. The man was a wreck. I think he *was* under duress. He said so in so many words."

"So now you're a goddamned psychiatrist!"

There was no animosity in Johnson's response. "No, just a trained agent."

"I need to speak with Woody."

"No can do, Special Agent," said Johnson.

"Why not?"

"He was found dead outside his Watergate apartment this morning. Apparent suicide. Jumped off his balcony."

CHAPTER 86

Jason had been checking the parking lot every three minutes and was wearing a path into the already-threadbare carpet. He peeked through the drapes, not liking what he saw. A female police officer was taking way too much interest in the stolen Lincoln. She was back in the cruiser, talking into the radio.

Jason whispered several curses. They shouldn't have left the car parked so close to Jensen's apartment. It was a huge—and potentially crippling—oversight.

His mug shot was probably digitally flying to every police force in the area, maybe the state. Armed and dangerous, an alleged murderer, his capture would be priority one. It was only a matter of time before this officer called in for backup and they started knocking on doors. He figured he had fifteen, thirty minutes, tops.

The desire to run was overwhelming. Jason jogged to the rear of the apartment, opened the back door and took one step onto the patio.

Lurking in the reeds, halfway between the adjacent neighborhood and Jensen's apartment, was the killer from the hospital, still wearing his windbreaker. The man brought his weapon up for a shot.

* * *

"Where's your brother now?" Broadhurst asked as he escorted Peter to Barbara Jensen's Honda Accord.

After his conversation with Tom Johnson, Broadhurst had phoned a colleague in the Executive Office Building, where the Secret Service was headquartered, asking to speak with Woody Austin. The agent on the other end of the line confirmed that Woody Austin had apparently jumped to his death from his tenth-floor balcony.

"What about me and my brother?" Peter demanded. "We want protection."

"You've got it. Now, where is he?"

"He's at the apartments behind the mall," Peter replied.

"We'll take my car. Let's go!"

Broadhurst had received what little data the intelligence division had on the three people Peter Rodgers was accusing. Lily Zanns, Sam Fairing, and Jasmine Kader were ghosts. The search had turned up nothing except driver's license data, vehicle registration, and Social Security numbers. Zanns and Fairing had never filed a tax return. He had photographs of the three of them from the Virginia DMV, but they were of poor quality and relatively old. He couldn't even be sure it was actually them. The employees of the medical practice and the Colonial could identify them easily, but rounding up those people could take hours. Hours that Broadhurst didn't have. There was one person intimately familiar with all three, according to Peter Rodgers: his brother, Jason. Broadhurst punched the accelerator. The sedan lurched forward, fishtailing around a corner as Peter gave directions.

* * *

Jason's eyes never left the crouching man as he backpedaled and slammed the door shut. A round thudded into wood. He pulled the pistol from his waistband and rammed it through the window, smashing glass, making as much noise as possible. He aimed it at the killer. Alerted by the noise, the assassin saw the gun protruding through the jagged glass. He dropped into the cover of the tall grass. Jason held his fire. The report would attract the attention of the police officer out front. The assassin's progress had been halted for the moment. The killer would pause, knowing his quarry was armed. Jason backed deeper into the apartment, breathing heavily.

In addition to the killer waiting beyond the back door, no doubt equally dangerous accomplices lurked out front. Not to mention that the police officer would soon be joined by an army of cops who wanted him for murder, kidnapping, and auto theft. But if he were to surrender to the cops, Jason wasn't confident they could protect him. He'd already been in jail once and had nearly ended up on a cold slab. Surrendering, to either party, was out of the question.

His mind working frantically, he cycled through several options, discarding them as quickly as they revealed themselves. Then the rudiments of a plan took shape.

Before he and Jenny had saved enough money to buy the house in Running Man, Jason had lived in an apartment complex similar to this one. Like this one, their apartment was old and had been built long before fire codes had been updated. There were still a few in the area. The rents were cheap and the walls thin, not separated by concrete firewalls. The blaring music coming from the apartment next door sounded like it was *inside* Barbara Jensen's place.

The aging apartment and the loud music sparked an idea. Jason rummaged around the apartment, looking in closets and the bathroom, violating the sanctity of his former technician's domicile. He found what he needed under the kitchen sink.

CHAPTER 87

Officer Karen Nolo keyed her radio. "This is Nolo, requesting backup. I think I've found the vehicle the two men stole from the hospital."

Finding the missing pharmacist had become the police department's only priority, it seemed. Every available body was taking part in the manhunt. The radio crackled every few minutes with bursts of traffic. Throwing this much manpower at your average, run-of-the-mill killer was unusual. But the brass had insisted the man be found. *Something big is going down*, she thought. *The shit just keeps getting deeper.*

Finding the stolen car had been pure luck. She'd decided to cruise through the apartment complex, just a quick pass before heading for lunch, when she spotted the Lincoln. The Smithfield PD had sent out a bulletin on the make, model, and tag numbers. She had just run them through the system when she got a hit. The car, though stolen, had been rented from an agency at the airport.

"I'm going to knock on some doors and see if anyone knows anything about this vehicle."

422

"Roger that," came the reply from the dispatcher. "Be careful, Karen. This guy's dangerous. The report said there were two men in the car when it left the hospital."

Nolo alighted from the cruiser. Smoke hit her nostrils before the door thunked closed. A cloud of grayish white vapors filled a passageway between two apartment buildings.

Forgetting the stolen car, she ran toward the smoke. "Anybody in there! Open up! Police!" Nolo pounded on the door of the ground-floor unit.

Thin wisps roiled from under the door. She covered her mouth with a handkerchief, but still choked on fumes. Brief flashes of orange flame lit up a window. She thought she heard a banging noise coming from inside, but through the crackling and roar of the flames, she wasn't certain. She grabbed the knob and burned her hand on scalding metal.

She raced up the steps of the open-air hallway, shaking her blistering hand, and banged savagely on a second-floor apartment door. When no answered, she kicked it in. Empty. The floor was warm, the heat from downstairs radiating up. Nolo climbed the third and final flight to the highest apartment. A woman answered with a small child in her arms.

"Get out now! The place is on fire!"

* * *

Broadhurst pulled the black, government-issue SUV into the courtyard. The sight of smoke and flashing lights caused both men to lean forward.

"You've got to be shittin' me," Peter said, spotting the source of the smoke. "That's the apartment Jason's in."

The SUV skidded to a halt. Broadhurst sprinted toward the blaze, watching the safety of his presidents literally going up in smoke. Peter followed, limping badly.

A female police officer was banging on an upper-level apartment door and hollering. The agent covered his mouth with the crook of his elbow and tried to look in the first-floor apartment. He, too, was overwhelmed, and retreated. Peter caught up with him, trying to push past the special agent. Broadhurst grabbed Peter's arm. With his wounded leg, Peter was no match for the taller, stronger man. His progress was halted instantly. "Let me in there!" Peter demanded.

"It's no use," Broadhurst said, placing both arms on Peter's shoulders.

Peter ripped himself away, stumbled, and fell.

"Stay here!" Broadhurst helped him up and pushed him away from the blaze onto the grass.

Sirens closed in as the gathering crowd mushroomed. A shrill scream from an apartment pierced the air. Broadhurst ran in that direction. A woman, wet and wearing only a towel, raced out of her apartment. Broadhurst yelled, "Is there anyone else in there?" She screamed, too panicked to respond, and rushed past him into the courtyard, clutching only the towel.

Broadhurst entered her space, managing a quick look around. The blaze was in the next-door apartment, and tendrils of smoke seeped in from a large hole in the common wall. Flames licked through the opening, beginning to roar with force. With the danger mounting and convinced the naked woman's unit was empty, Broadhurst left.

He returned to the courtyard, looking for Peter Rodgers. He was gone. Turning to an onlooker, he asked, "Where did that man go? The one who was limping?"

"He ran into that apartment, man. That guy's got a death wish."

Broadhurst's eye followed the onlooker's pointing finger. Gigantic eruptions of flame and smoke exploded from the lower windows, blackening the upper floors, melting the siding. Columns of black roiled skyward. An acrid, bitter smell filled the air. The crowd of gawkers was growing.

The only two men who could help him sort out this mess were roasting inside the apartment.

CHAPTER 88

Broadhurst contemplated going in after them, but nixed that idea quickly. He was no good dead, either to the service or his president. At this point, he expected to recover two charred bodies.

"Look!" someone shouted. "Someone's coming out!"

Smoke steaming from his clothes, Peter staggered into the courtyard. He collapsed on the grass as Broadhurst reached him. Flames licked the back of his shirt. Broadhurst patted them out with his bare hands. The policewoman helped the special agent roll him over. Peter's hands and the edges of his face were burnt and blistered.

"Are you okay?" asked Nolo.

Peter coughed. A mouthful of smoke shot from his lungs. "Just peachy. He's not—in there."

"You didn't see a body?"

Peter shook his head.

"Where the hell is he?" Broadhurst asked.

* * *

Jason opened his eyes. He peered into a gray-black, crisscross pattern that wavered every few seconds in the breeze. Crooked lines and odd shapes jostled in the breeze. His mind gradually surfaced from the murky depths. The boughs of the elms and maples created a maze, bathed by the moonlight. When he'd lain down on the cold ground blanketed with pine needles, the sky had been awash in the golden glow of late afternoon. Now clouds blotted out the stars. Hours had evaporated.

He pushed himself to a sitting position. The gun, still clutched in his fingers, felt welded to his hand. Though he hadn't pulled the trigger, it had saved his life.

He sucked in a deep breath, exhaled, and spasmed into a barking cough. His whole body convulsed, trying to expel the inhaled poisons. With each paroxysm, his side burned and nausea waved over him.

After escaping the burning apartment, Jason had run until his lungs wanted to burst. He'd stopped in a clearing between the gravel company and the railroad tracks just beyond Jefferson Avenue.

Setting the fire had been his only option.

The large container of lighter fluid under the sink had been almost full. Jason had doused everything, emptying the can. The front and back doors, curtains, furniture. He'd ignited the fuel with the matchsticks lying beside the lighter fluid. The fire had caught and spread faster than he'd anticipated. The smoke and fumes had hugged the ceiling in less than a minute, nearly overwhelming him.

As the blaze intensified, he'd chunked a hole in the plaster of the wall shared with the adjoining apartment with a kitchen knife, pulling away pieces with his bare hands. He'd realized he should have gouged out the hole first, before starting the fire. That mistake had nearly cost him his life.

Beneath the plaster, only fire-rated plywood covered the studs. Jason found the seam between two sheets of plywood. Luckily, he'd been right about the apartment complex's construction. There was no concrete firewall between the units. He worked the board away from the stud, ripping an opening. Several kicks forced out the plywood on the other side of the wall. Finally, he'd created an opening large enough to crawl through. At that point, Barbara's apartment had been fully engulfed. He'd slid through the fourteen-inch opening between studs, pulling electrical wiring with him. The heat had suffocated him, smoke and flames licking at his Nikes.

The music was loud. That and the roar of the flames masked his break-in. The naked woman emerged from the bathroom as Jason darted for the front door. Soaking wet, singing, and gyrating to "Satisfaction," the well-endowed female had frozen when she spotted him before letting out a scream.

She'd covered her breasts with one arm and her womanhood with the other as Jason walked calmly past. "The place is on fire," he'd said. "You better get out." He opened the door and stepped into the breezeway, moments before the Secret Service agent he'd encountered at the shipyard appeared from around the corner.

Ducking behind the corner and belly-crawling along the cement patio, he rose up to all fours and made his way to the opposite corner. The killer was behind him, waiting in the reeds, apparently unaware of Jason's escape. Jason crouched low, moving through the grass behind the man. He circled into the parking lot of the Patrick Henry Mall and completed his escape.

In the clearing, Jason stood to his full height. The heavy cloud cover hinted at coming rain. Every part of his body ached. The wound in his side felt like a torch had been taken to it. Despite his injuries, Jason pondered a question: how had they tracked him to Barbara's apartment?

The killers had been one step behind him at every stage, at the hospital, his house, and now, the apartment. They'd tracked Christine and Peter as well.

He pulled Barbara's phone out of his pocket. Barbara wouldn't have given Jason up; even if she had, the police or the FBI would have shown up, not Zanns's assassins. Had they followed him to Keller's, then to the apartment? He doubted that, too. They had doubled back numerous times. They'd done nothing but drive to the apartment and collect their weapons. And Peter had made a call to the Secret Service agent.

Jason pounded a fist into his thigh. Phone calls! Of course!

His mind flashed to the attack at his house. Peter had called him on his home landline from Lisa's cell, minutes before the killers burst in. He'd also used his wife's phone to call Broadhurst. If they were tracking Peter, they'd be able to track his wife's cell, too. Most cell phones contained GPS chips. Peter had mentioned moles in the Secret Service. Hell, a camera had been put in his house. It wasn't a stretch to think they had access to their cell numbers.

Jason considered ditching the phone. He stopped, and instead he opened the back and removed the battery. He'd read somewhere that if the battery were removed, it couldn't be tracked. They probably didn't know Jason had Barbara Jensen's phone. But he wasn't taking any chances.

A second question again nagged him: how many were out there after him and the others? He did a quick tally. Peter had killed two men. He and Christine had left two more dead at his house. Two more men had followed him to the hospital, where one had died. His buddy was outside Barbara Jensen's apartment. That made for at least six killers.

That invited a third, final question: how big was this conspiracy?

He already could imagine the answer.

That fact nudged him to make a decision. It was time to come in. He'd try it again. Staying on the run would only lead to his death. The flash drive in his pocket was his ticket. Jason was counting on the fact that Peter had reached Broadhurst and filled him in on the plot. He prayed, too, that his brother had negotiated terms for his surrender that would keep him out of jail until he could prove his innocence. The rendezvous point had been agreed upon in case of trouble. Jason began the slow trudge in that direction.

* * *

Broadhurst flipped open the laptop and inserted the CD. John Palmer had delivered it a minute ago and was standing to the side. The computers had finally come back online forty minutes ago. Broadhurst, together with two other agents, listened without comment. Palmer and the detective remained silent, letting the voices on the recording speak for themselves.

Broadhurst felt a frown crease his face. Everything about the recording sounded legit, but he needed to ask Peter Rodgers the question anyway. "How do I know this recording isn't just a setup?"

Peter scoffed. "Two gunmen killed a detective from Newport News in my hospital room. Just ask Palmer here," Peter said, pointing to the detective. "They were there to kill me, too. Hours before that two other guys also tried to put my lights out. The same thing happened to my brother. Walter Waterhouse is dead. How much more friggin' proof do you need?"

Palmer added, "He's right. I can confirm the murder of the private investigator. The Poquoson PD has set up a crime scene."

"There's something very sophisticated about this whole thing."

"Ya think?" said Peter.

"According to your friend, this Simoon organization, if it exists, is of Middle Eastern origin. There are no countries or organizations in the Middle East other than the Israelis with the ability to do what they've done. Hell, if Austin's right, the whole Secret Service communications network is compromised. They may have the financial resources, but not the intelligence network or electronic hardware to cripple the Secret Service. The sophistication is just not there."

"You're a spy now?" Peter challenged.

"No, just a law enforcement official. My job is to protect the president and keep him out of danger, and that includes assessing threats. This operation is too complex to be the work of a single organization like the Simoon."

"You got all that from what I just told you."

"I've been in law enforcement for fifteen years. If it walks like a duck…"

"So cancel the event."

"I'd love to. That's not my call. Austin was supposed to talk to the president. Now's he's dead. I don't know if he even discussed it with him."

"When do the presidents arrive?" Peter asked.

"That's none of your business," Broadhurst barked.

CHAPTER 89

The stench of stale urine and rotting food hung in the littered alleyway. Jason crouched beside a blue dumpster. Cars entered and left the parking lot of the 7-Eleven at the corner of Oyster Point Road and Jefferson Avenue every few minutes. Jason had no idea how long the walk from the sand company to City Center would take. Stealth, not speed, was the priority. That meant using wooded cover along Jefferson Avenue, cutting through parking lots and side streets. From behind the convenience store, he walked quickly to the edge of the sidewalk on Jefferson, staying in the shadows. Instead of using the crosswalk, he walked a hundred yards south and crossed in front of a Plaza Azteca, timing his jaunt across both directions of the divided avenue so he wouldn't have to stop in the median.

* * *

"Are you sure?" Vince Mahoney, the director of the Secret Service, asked.

431

Mahoney had been Broadhurst's second call. The first had been to the former president, Jacob R. Hope, at the Williamsburg Inn. Broadhurst had explained the threat in roundabout terms to the chief of Hope's protection detail and then to the old man himself, hoping to convince him to cancel the christening of his own ship. After some pointed questions, Hope told him he had confidence in the service and that he wasn't getting any younger. The event would proceed as planned.

"Yes, sir," Broadhurst replied to Mahoney's question. "As sure as we can be... There's one other thing, sir. It seems we have moles inside the service. These folks are privy to information only known by a select few agents. I'm pursuing a witness who has knowledge of that fact. Apparently, they've been planning this for some time." Broadhurst explained about the discovery of documents in Jason Rodgers's home.

"You're just full of good news tonight." Mahoney hung up.

Peter, who had been escorted out of the room so Broadhurst could speak with Mahoney, was led back in, along with John Palmer.

"For the third and last time, where is your brother?"

"I don't know, I told you!"

Peter had tried to call Jason on his cell phone then on Barbara Jensen's phone. Both calls rolled to voice mail.

"That fire was deliberately set. You said there was no one else in the apartment when you left. So he must have started it. Why would he do that?"

"They—whoever *they* are—are out there trying to kill us. They must have caught up with him. Starting the fire was probably his only way out."

"How did they catch up with him? What did you do while you were there?"

"We unloaded the guns from the car and I called you from my wife's cell—" Peter stopped and snapped his fingers. He looked at the phone lying on the table. "Son of a bitch! They must have triangulated our position. I hope I didn't give him away."

"We don't know how close these guys are to finding him. Hopefully, your brother's smart enough to ditch the phone."

"The calls rolled immediately to voicemail. He's probably turned it off or taken the battery out."

"Any bright ideas on how we can find him?"

Peter thought for a moment and said, "I have a pretty good idea where he'll be at eleven o'clock tonight."

"Let's hope we find him before these terrorists do!"

CHAPTER 90

"He's probably hiding, waiting for us to show," said Peter.

Broadhurst steered past the Marriott Hotel, circling the fountains at City Center.

There was no sign of Jason. The Friday night revelers crowding the sidewalks weren't making spotting him any easier.

"We've circled three times already! You sure he'll remember where to meet you?" Broadhurst paused. "Or he's dead—"

Peter shot him a hard glance. "He knows where to meet me!"

Broadhurst pulled to the curb. "Now we wait," he said.

Fifteen minutes passed. The back door of the car opened. Jason slid into the rear seat and said, "You're late."

Both men jerked their heads around. Peter smiled at his brother. "Let's get out of here," Jason said.

"Jason," Peter said, "This is Special Agent Broadhurst of the Secret Service."

434

Broadhurst nodded at the pharmacist. Jason smiled stiffly, remembering their encounter at the shipyard, and said, "We've met. Now, can we get the hell out of here?"

* * *

The physician stood between Jason and Peter's beds, looking at his two patients. The service had used him before. He was well paid, didn't ask a lot of questions, and, most importantly, kept his mouth shut. Broadhurst was by the window, looking at the brothers, but not seeing them. His mind was focused on other matters. Three untainted agents from the Richmond field office were standing guard in the hall.

"You've torn the surface sutures in your knee," the doctor said to Peter. "Try not to move. I've sutured the wound back in place. The internal sutures are intact. There's minimal bleeding. Your lung function appears to be okay. You didn't inhale too much smoke. The burns are minor. The antibiotic cream will keep them from getting infected. You're one lucky SOB."

The physician turned toward Jason, frowning. "You, young man, however, are in much worse shape," he said.

Broadhurst winced when he looked at Jason. The civilian had endured a hell of a lot in the last forty-eight hours. Jason's cheek was swollen and red from the attack in his home. The left eye was almost closed, and looked like he'd gone through seven defenseless rounds with Mike Tyson. His nostrils were black and congealed with blood.

The doctor ran a light over both pupils and palpated the entire length of Jason's body one more time, checking for unseen injuries and assessing neurological function. Jason lay still, unable or unwilling to respond. The physician unwrapped the elastic bandage from around his waist and removed the blood-soaked gauze from the hole in his side. Jason jumped as the gauze tore away.

"This man needs surgery. I see signs of infection," the doctor announced after inspecting and probing the wound. "His kidney's probably been lacerated. Quite frankly, I'm amazed he's still conscious. Except for the wound in his side, nothing else is life threatening. But this wound needs to be treated."

"Not until I resolve some issues, Doc," Broadhurst countered.

"He needs to be in a hospital!" said Peter.

"My job is to protect POTUS. Your brother stays in my custody until I understand and secure the situation." Broadhurst turned to the physician and said, "Do what you can, Doc."

"I can give him IV antibiotics," the doctor said. "I'll make a call. Give me an hour and I can have them here."

"Do it," Broadhurst commanded.

The doctor left to order his drugs.

"You bastard! You heard the doctor. He needs surgery!" Peter persisted. "We're not helping you until you get him to a hospital!"

"Peter, that's enough," Jason mumbled through the side of his mouth. "I've come this far. I'm seeing it through. What do I need to do?"

"Start from the beginning."

Jason explained the series of events Peter had shared with Broadhurst earlier, but in much greater detail.

"The recording mentions shooting locations," said Broadhurst.

"Fairing lives in the Windsor Towers just north of the shipyard," Jason said. "His condo overlooks the dry dock. I think they're gonna take a shot from his apartment in the towers."

"We've been to his apartment. He's not there. I've got agents standing guard outside the door. The same with Zanns's estate. It seems they've all disappeared."

"Maybe they left town?" asked Peter.

"Until I question them or have them in custody, we go on the assumption that they're still a threat."

"Why not postpone the christening?" Jason asked, propping himself on his elbows.

"I've tried that. It's a no-go." The director of the Secret Service, Vince Mahoney, had already returned Broadhurst's call. Both presidential father and son had denied his request for a postponement.

"So what happens now?"

"I'm going back to the shipyard to finalize a few things. You two need to get some sleep. The agents outside the door will make sure you're not disturbed," said Broadhurst.

"Or that we leave?" Peter said. "Are we being detained?"

"Let's just say that you're guests of the Secret Service." Broadhurst smiled. "I'm certainly not convinced that recording isn't a fake. So you two will remain that way until I release you after the christening tomorrow. If you want to leave, you can. But I will make sure you have two agents attached to each of you at the hip to keep you safe, if you know what I mean." Broadhurst took a step toward the door, then stopped. "And there are two more agents in a car sitting beneath your window," he added with a slight smile.

Peter motioned toward the men outside the door. "How do you know they're not—"

"Moles?"

"Yeah."

"Because they're from our Richmond field office. They helicoptered in a few hours ago. They're untainted. If they're not, you'll be dead soon."

CHAPTER 91

Saturday, October 7

Capped by vaulted ceilings and adorned with Persian carpets and expensive tile, the Omni's lobby boasted a gourmet coffee bar and ornate sofas. The gray morning light filtered through the rain-dotted windows. The phalanx of agents engulfed Jason and Peter in a tight, fast-moving perimeter as they exited the elevator. Heads turned when they emerged. This was not the slow, casual movement normally seen in the lobby of a luxury hotel.

Two smaller agents led the way as Jason and Peter were marched toward the entryway. Each was taller than Jason, with wide shoulders and short, gelled crew cuts. The brothers were flanked by the larger third and fourth agents. Each man clutched a fistful of deltoid, ensuring they did not slow the human convoy.

A young boy pointed at Jason's grotesquely mutilated face as he and his brother limped along. "Look at that man, Mommy," he said. The embarrassed mother quickly shushed her son.

438

The damp morning air was thickened by the rain and clouds. Two large black SUVs pulled under the overhang. Doors flew open, and the agents shoved their charges inside.

Jason only had a moment to breathe in the sweet air before he was shoved inside the second SUV. The two doses of intravenous antibiotics had quelled his fever during the night, but Jason was far from out of the woods. Without further treatment, the infection would return, threatening sepsis and more bouts of agony.

Jason had promised Broadhurst early this morning he was not about to let the small matter of his health get in the way of stopping these killers. Jason was not the Secret Service's prisoner. He could leave anytime, with a gaggle of well-armed men following close enough to know when he farted. Though technically not a prisoner, Jason was held captive to a more sinister force: the knowledge that his failure to act could cost important lives.

If Lily Zanns and her terrorists had their way, Newport News would be two words uttered with contempt and disdain by the rest of the world for decades to come. Jason Rodgers was prepared to do whatever he could to prevent it.

CHAPTER 92

Fairing watched Steven Cooper standing before the expanse of the large picture window, punching keys on Cyclops's keyboard. The infidel represented everything Fairing hated about Americans. He was blond and cocky, contaminated with an air of superiority. He had no comprehension of sacrifice, much like his lazy countrymen. His type of cowardice refused to dirty its hands. To topple their sitting government, they, instead, paid people like Fairing and the Simoon to do it for them.

Lily had informed Fairing about Cooper's five-million-dollar blackmail. Ever since, the desire to shove the barrel of the sniper rifle down Cooper's throat and pull the trigger was a formidable one. He would see that urge fulfilled.

Fairing shifted his gaze through the window to the yardage beyond. The gray behemoth sat in the flooded dry dock, awash in red, white, and blue as rain slanted across her decks, waiting to be released from her landlocked captivity.

The condo's windows had been tinted a year ago to protect it from outside eyes, especially those of the well-trained Secret Service

440

countersnipers, who were most assuredly stationed on the rooftops. Two two-inch-diameter holes had been carved in the glass, one for Cyclops's laser beams, the second for Fairing's projectile. Fairing shifted his gaze back to Cooper, who had paused from assembling Cyclops. Lazy smoke wafted toward the ceiling from the cigarette dangling from his lips. "That thing better be ready, Cooper," Fairing warned.

"Don't worry. It'll be fine," Cooper snapped without looking up.

Fairing snarled as he noticed Cooper's trembling hands and the dollops of sweat coating his neck. Cooper would have dispatched him long ago, had he not been the only one who could operate Cyclops. Fairing ran his hand over the pistol under his shirt. The first round in the magazine had Cooper's name on it.

The Secret Service had stretched the large white canvas behind the dais to prevent exactly the sort of long-range sniper shot they were about to execute. By painting an infrared laser target on the white fabric, Cooper's machine would make such an audacious shot not only possible, but very doable for Fairing and Jasmine Kader. The infrared laser, visible only through special scopes mounted on their sniper rifles, would mark the exact points at which Fairing and Jasmine would place their rounds. The projectiles would pass through the canvas, following a precisely predetermined trajectory to the presidential targets, without Fairing or Kader ever having to lay eyes on them.

Every detail had been accounted for: the exact heights of the standing Jacob R. Hope and the seated son; the downward angle of the shots; wind speed and direction; gravity; rain; and the deflection effect of the canvas. All had been programmed into the laptop attached to Cyclops. A small anemometer had been placed by another accomplice at the dry dock. The device transmitted wind speed and direction to Cyclops. The software calculated the exact location through which each bullet would need to pass, and translated that into a target. The parameters and specifications had been worked out in minute detail. The data was updated continuously, and the location of the laser target adjusted for a center mass blow to the torsos of both men. They were counting on the fact that both men would be in their expected locations and would not move significantly when the shots were taken.

The Camp, their secret range, had been laid out as an exact replica of the dimensions and trajectory of the Windsor Towers to the dry dock, situated in the same cardinal direction on the compass to account for wind and sun.

Grudgingly, Fairing admired the ingenuity of the device. Cyclops was a marvel of digital engineering. Two thin cables snaked from the expensive laptop to twin high-intensity lasers housed in horizontal cylinders. Each was mounted on motorized swivels set atop two minitripods that had been screwed into the wooden platform Fairing was using. Hammon had paid a hi-tech guru very well; millions had changed hands for its construction. It was the only one of its kind and had been built for only one purpose, today's christening. All blueprints and prototypes had been destroyed. After its use today, Cyclops would disappear.

One laser was programmed for the trajectory of Fairing's shot on 42, the second for Kader's on 44. Only the two killers would be able to see the laser target. To Secret Service agents and everyone on the ground, everything would appear normal. Every few seconds, the motorized swivels would whir as the lasers readjusted themselves to the changing conditions.

Cooper would only activate the laser beam fifteen seconds before they planned to fire. Those were his terms. Fairing also had terms: after they had killed the infidel presidents, he intended to turn the gun on Cooper and blow his brains all over the wall.

As much as he wanted to, Fairing could not dwell on Cooper at the moment. A more serious issue loomed. The entire building had been put in lockdown. A Secret Service agent guarded the elevator and the stairwell forty feet from their door. He'd been there for nearly ninety minutes now.

Something had gone very wrong; Fairing's chances for escape had just decreased significantly. He wasn't supposed to die in this condo; he was supposed to emerge from this mission as a hero to retake his Iraq from the infidels. But that destiny depended on escaping from this building after successfully dispatching the two American presidents. After his shot had been taken, Fairing would shoot Cooper, then take the stairs to the basement. In one of the storage closets, he'd retrieve the Newport News police uniform and the large pair of wire cutters that had been placed there four months ago. He would don the uniform and walk to the fence surrounding the towers. Hidden by the bushes and shrubs, he would cut a gap in the fencing, then walk across the street to the beach parking lot and the Crown Victoria waiting there for him.

There was one small piece of good news. The Secret Service had four teams searching for them. Three were canvassing the south tower. The wrong tower. Fairing and Cooper were in the north tower. The Americans had incorrectly assumed they would take the shot from the closer tower.

Had Jason Rodgers made it to the proper authorities and told them of their plan? Did they know where Fairing and Cooper were? Were they about to appear at the door?

It was too late to turn and run; they were committed. Not that he would have. Fairing sucked in several deep breaths, and his heart began to pound as he absorbed the possibility of his own death. He was ready to die if that was Allah's will. But that commitment did not keep his palms from sweating.

Fairing had placed the call an hour ago. There were men who lived in the building and were available for such a contingency. They'd buy enough time for him and Jasmine to make their shots. Cooper wasn't yet aware of the threat. Fairing wouldn't tell him. He didn't need the coward panicking.

Cooper stubbed out his cigarette, finished assembling Cyclops, and lifted a pair of binoculars to his face. To calm his nerves, Fairing checked his watch and recited verse sixty from sura eight, his favorite:

Against them make ready your strength to the utmost of your power, including steeds of war, to strike terror into the hearts of the enemies of

Allah... Whatever ye spend in the cause of Allah shall be repaid unto you, and ye shall not be treated unjustly.

* * *

From under the lead-lined tarpaulin, Jasmine Kader peered through another pair of high-powered binoculars. She had been in place since yesterday evening, atop the north drawbridge tower of the James River Bridge, a mile south of her brother's location. She'd heard the thumping of the helicopter's rotors above her two hours ago. The passengers had, no doubt, been inspecting the top of the structure.

Penrose Gatling Shipbuilders occupied a five-mile stretch of rusted, corrugated-rooftop warehouses and more modern buildings. The older structures housed dirty-fingernailed laborers who molded cold steel into sleek warships. The newer edifices designed and produced the ultramodern electronic communications and navigational systems for submarines and aircraft carriers.

After deflating the raft with a knife and sending it to the murky bottom, Kader had swum the three miles from the Carrollton shore to the north tower of the bridge. With her weapon disassembled in a watertight black bag strapped to her back, she'd climbed to the flat roof and slithered under the custom-made covering that she and Oliver had put in place two months ago.

The covering consisted of three everyday, twenty-five-by-forty-foot blue tarps, stitched together by an expert sailmaker in the Caribbean a year ago. Kader had purchased the tarps at the local Home Depot and had flown them down with Oliver. Each ply was sewn together with lead-weighted strips ringing the perimeter and honeycombed throughout, ensuring the cloth would not ripple in the wind or be blown away. Sandwiched between the three tarps were two layers of waterproof Kevlar. Finally, it had been painted to exactly match the drab green drawbridge. Two months ago, in the small hours of the morning under a moonless sky, Kader and Oliver had ferried the covering to the drawbridge in the Zodiac. Kader had strapped the covering, which weighed over a hundred pounds, to her back, then had hoisted it to the top with the strength of a champion climber and laid it out.

Three weeks earlier, Kader had climbed the structure in the dark, slipped beneath the tarp, and stayed there for twenty-four hours. Oliver had flown over with the float plane as the sun broke above the trees. Kader took up her position, while Oliver observed and videotaped from the plane. He made two passes, communicating by radio with her. From the sky, Oliver could barely see what he was looking for. And he knew it was there. The Americans would never find her. The tower would not be manned by the countersniper teams. It was beyond the effective range of a long-range sniper, or so they thought. But they would still inspect the area and see nothing more than the top of the structure. All this information about security procedures had been gleaned from their informant in Washington.

As she peered through the binoculars, Kader saw exactly what she'd expected. Everything was laid out as in the diagrams ferried to them through the dead drops. Prescriptions to signal the drops, and the resultant prescription bags left in their place as confirmation, were an archaic and cumbersome method. But the dead drops had worked. Lily had been right about the American government's ability to intercept any kind of electronic communications. The mission's secrecy, though challenged by Pettigrew and Rodgers, had not been compromised. Only four people knew exactly how the information had been transferred: Lily, Sam, herself, and the mole. Steven Cooper knew that they were receiving information from someone in Washington. But he didn't know how or when the data was sent.

Because of the large white screen, Kader's view was obscured. But she knew there were two decorated barges secured to the dry dock, lined with chairs facing the podium on the dais.

Kader swung the binoculars left. The eastern side of the dry dock would be opened to the general public in a few hours. The crowds were gathering, waiting for their chance to enter the grounds, aware they were about to witness history. They would witness history, all right. It would be very different than advertised.

The drizzle was a minor inconvenience. The wind, though, concerned her. Steady at about ten knots with gusts to fifteen. At a distance of a mile and a quarter, a projectile could be carried off course by tens of feet. She would need all of her skill today. The shot had been practiced from this distance countless times in the strong North Carolina winds. Her skill would not let her down. Closing her eyes, she recited the same verse her brother was whispering as she unzipped the watertight bag and began assembling her rifle.

CHAPTER 93

The driver of the first SUV flashed his badge to the attendant in the guardhouse. The swinging gate lifted, and the two vehicles proceeded to the entrance of the south Windsor Tower. Clay Broadhurst and the driver jumped out of the second vehicle. The remaining doors opened on cue. Jason and Peter were ushered inside and encircled by eight agents. In the lobby, the men gathered to hear Broadhurst's instructions. "We're looking for two people. Sam Fairing and Jasmine Kader. According to our witness"—Broadhurst pointed at Jason—"they are dark-skinned and of Middle Eastern descent. Other than that, we don't know much about them. Jason Rodgers here knows what they look like. We're going to knock on every door in both buildings, if need be, and ask the residents to submit to a search. He'll identify them for us." The special agent in charge passed out copies of the driver's license photographs. "These are very poor likenesses, according to Mr. Rodgers here. If you run across anyone remotely similar, detain them and take them to the lobby."

"That's gonna take hours," one agent said. "There are hundreds of units."

"Two hundred and thirty, to be exact. I've obtained a listing of the condo units above the fourth floor that have a view of the dry dock area. These units provide the best vantage point. An agent is posted on every floor between the stairwells and elevators. The whole building is locked down. No one enters until further notice. If anyone currently in the building wishes to leave, they may. But they won't be allowed back in until after the christening. Additionally, there are two-man teams stationed in both lobbies. Countersnipers are situated on the rooftops. Agents with field glasses are scanning the face of the towers, observing windows. We'll find them."

"Where did all these agents come from?" another one asked.

"They're Secret Service, FBI, and ATF from various field offices. Under the Patriot Act, each agency is required to cooperate with the service in the event of an emergency threatening the president's life. Today qualifies. Understood?"

Everyone nodded. "What about those folks that don't answer the door or aren't home?"

"I'm getting to that," Broadhurst replied. He motioned to two men standing a few feet away wearing Windsor Tower uniforms. "These men are employees of the towers. The condo association provides access to the residences in the event of an emergency, leaking pipes and such. We'll gain access under that codicil. Each one of these men will be assigned to one of two teams of four agents. If no one answers, they'll open the door with their passkey—"

Jason lifted his hand to get Broadhurst's attention. "What is it?" the agent barked. Jason motioned for Broadhurst to join him for a private conversation. "Make it quick," Broadhurst commanded.

"Agent, let me and my brother help in the search. You can break the teams in pairs and have four teams. We can stay with you. It'll make things go a lot faster."

Broadhurst had no intention of allowing two civilians anywhere near this operation for a truckload of reasons. "Not on your life! I can't be responsible for two civilians—"

"Look at me," Jason interrupted. "How much worse can it get? Besides, we want to see this through. Time's not on your side."

Broadhurst cracked a quick grin. "You've got balls, son. And, unfortunately, you're right. Time *is* running out."

Broadhurst and Jason returned to the group. "Change of plans. We're breaking into four two-man teams. Take any suspicious persons to the function room in the lobby of each tower and hold them until I can bring the pharmacist to ID them."

Broadhurst broke the agents into three two-man teams. Two more Windsor Tower employees were rounded up. The passkeys were divvied up between each team, and an employee was assigned to each. Broadhurst distributed the condo assignments, and then turned to Jason and Peter. "You two are with me. Keep up. If you slow me down, I'll shoot you myself."

* * *

Broadhurst, Jason, Peter, and a short, stocky man named Bill in a towers uniform, who carried a large ring laden with keys, rode the elevator to the twelfth floor of the south tower. Awkward silence and tension suffocated them. Broadhurst fidgeted with his earpiece. He popped two Tums into his mouth, and chewed furiously.

The elevator chimed. The doors swung open. Broadhurst exited, followed by Jason and Peter, who struggled to keep pace. The uniformed employee brought up the rear. Broadhurst led them to the first unit at the south end of the boomerang-shaped hallway. A three-inch *A* was mounted on the door.

Broadhurst waited a moment to allow Peter to catch up, the irritation evident on his face. Peter gimped to Jason's side. The door rattled as the knuckles of his huge right hand connected with it.

* * *

A man dressed in a dark blue blazer, starched white button-down shirt and tan slacks, with a coiled earpiece snaking down his collar, approached the agent posted between the stairwell and the elevators on Fairing's floor. A confused expression spread across the second man's features.

"Broadhurst wants you on the thirteenth floor," the impostor said.

"I never heard anything about that." The man tapped his earpiece. The chatter had been constant all morning long. Frequent post changes were not uncommon to prevent boredom.

"Are you Four?" Each agent was identified by the number of the floor on which they were posted.

"Yeah, that's right."

"Well, I just heard him tell you he needs to you move to thirteen!"

"I better check." The authentic agent started to bring his wrist to his mouth.

The impostor swung his weapon into place and fired a silenced round into the man's chest. The assassin caught the man with one arm as he slumped. This was the lowest floor on which agents had been posted. The agents on the four floors above this one had been dispatched in the same way. Their bodies lay in the stairwells of each floor. The last thing this killer wanted was the cavalry coming to the rescue.

He dragged the body to a door and knocked three times. Steven Cooper opened up, saw the dead man, and his features twisted in shock and fear.

"Don't just stand there, help me," the impostor commanded.

CHAPTER 94

The seats of the floating barge were filled with minor dignitaries, members of the armed services, especially the navy, Hope Sr.'s former branch, special guests, and friends from Hope's World War Two days. The United State Fleet Forces Band belted out patriotic tunes and marches as the public filed onto the south side of the dry dock. Umbrellas and plastic ponchos dotted the crowd. The rain, unable to decide if it should fall as a pesky drizzle or a steady downpour, had lightened again.

* * *

As each team moved from apartment to apartment, messages crackled through Broadhurst's earpiece. Team Alpha One, in the north tower, had cleared floors sixteen and seventeen, and was moving down another flight. None of the occupants looked remotely like the people they were looking for.

451

The three others teams, including his, were in the south tower. The north tower, he reasoned, was farther away and a longer, more difficult, shot. With three teams canvassing it, the south tower would be completed faster. As teams were freed up, they would be reassigned to the north tower.

The two teams above Broadhurst's on the upper floors of the south tower had run into problems. Irate owners berated the agents when they identified themselves and told them what they wanted. They were disrupting the Saturday-morning routines of very staid, regimented folks. One elderly lady, who was going to be late for her bridge club, actually punched an agent weakly in the chest. Another yuppie couple late for an indoor tennis date threatened legal action. The agents apologized and allowed them to leave after searching their units.

"Alpha Dog, this is Alpha One in the north tower. We have a man here, about thirty-five, that fits the general description."

Alpha Dog was Broadhurst, Jason, and Peter. The other squads were alphas one, two and three. Broadhurst moved his wrist to his mouth. "It'll take me too long to get there with the pharmacist. Search the apartment. Have the agent on that floor escort him to the holding area in the lobby until the ceremony is over, or until we can get there. Over. Alpha Three, report in."

"This is Alpha Three. We've checked all our floors. Nothing close to a potential suspect," came the reply. "We're moving to the north tower."

"Roger that, Alpha Three. Start on the fourth floor in the north building and work your way up."

* * *

Ten minutes later, the conversation between Alpha Three and the men on one of the floors in the north tower filled Broadhurst's earpiece. He jabbed a hand in the air, stopping the others.

Why are there three agents on this floor? Broadhurst heard the Alpha Three leader asked. The agent had keyed his microphone and left it open.

I wasn't needed over at the shipyard. They asked me to come over and help.

The questioning agent paused. *Okay, we're going to check the units on this floor. Then we'll be out of your way.*

Roger that.

* * *

The two Alpha Three agents turned and headed toward the first unit. They had taken four steps when the first round struck the back of the leader's head. The second man looked at his partner, registered what had happened, and began to turn. He made it ninety degrees before another silenced round ripped through his right temple.

* * *

Broadhurst was about to reassign the extra agents on that floor, when his earpiece was filled with what sounded like muffled burps, followed by hushed, clipped words, not the clinical, detached responses of trained agents.

Drag them back to the apartment. Hurry. There's not much time, the first voice said.

Broadhurst heard a knock, followed by rustling and the sound of a door closing.

What the hell's going on out there? a second voice asked. There was a short pause followed by the same voice. *They're going to find us. It's time to leave.*

No one leaves until the mission is complete, a third voice said. Broadhurst could have sworn he heard the bolt of a rifle snap into place.

Being captured wasn't part of the plan.

There was always a good chance this was a suicide mission.
Screw this! I want out!

* * *

Fairing removed the Mauser 7.65 mm from his belt and walked to Cooper, placing the barrel between the man's eyes, dimpling the skin. "You can die now or you can finish your task and still have a chance to escape. Your choice."

Cooper swallowed hard. "Easy, Sam. Put that away. I'll take care of my end." Sweat erupted on his forehead. "I want them"—he motioned toward the phony agents—"stationed outside the apartment." Cooper moved in slow motion back to Cyclops.

"One of you stay in here. The other two monitor the hallway," Fairing ordered.

Fairing scowled at the "agent" who remained behind, then at Cooper. "Keep your eyes on him. If he tries to leave or does anything stupid, shoot him."

* * *

Broadhurst listened, angling his head with a rigid intensity.

You can die now or you can finish your task and still have a chance to escape. Your choice.

Easy, Sam. Put that away. I'll take care of my end. I want them stationed outside the apartment.

One of you stay in here. The other two monitor the hallway.

Keep your eyes on him. If he tries to leave or does anything stupid, shoot him.

Broadhurst pressed the fob deeper into his ear. He brought his arm to his mouth to speak, but stopped short.

A mike had been left open. Where was the conversation taking place? Was someone dead, or injured and unable to speak?

Peter and Jason caught the concerned look on Broadhurst's face. Broadhurst turned to Jason. "What was the name of the pharmacist involved in this thing?" he asked.

"Sam Fairing."

"Shit!" Broadhurst said. "It's happening right now." He thought for a second. "Where did I send them?"

"Who?" asked Jason.

"Son of a bitch! Where did I send Alpha Three? In all the confusion, I forgot where they went."

Jason smiled. "You told them to go to the north tower. They're on the fourth floor..."

Broadhurst smiled at Jason, nodding his approval. "Not bad for a pill pusher."

Broadhurst didn't know if the assassins were listening in. He couldn't risk tipping them off and losing the element of surprise. He didn't bark any orders over the air. He directed the Windsor employee to stay behind, but confiscated his rings of keys. He turned to Jason and Peter. "Let's go!"

CHAPTER 95

The fully assembled rifle rested on the wooden platform, its barrel supported by a bipod, an infrared scope mounted atop the body. A fifty-round box of mercury-filled ammo sat beside it, forty-nine more than Fairing needed. Between him and Jasmine, it would be two shots, two kills.

A knock came at the door. The "agent" opened it. "What is it?" Fairing asked.

"They can hear everything going on in here," one whispered.

"What? How?"

"Someone's got an open mike." The three impostors checked their radios and found them in order. "We can hear your conversations. Check the bodies."

Fairing noticed Cooper's ashen face. "Get back to your equipment," he ordered.

Cooper looked vacantly through the sniper. The flippant spy was face-to-face with his own mortality—and he was losing it.

"Cooper, get back to your equipment! Now!"

Cooper paused. The sound of the slide of Fairing's pistol snapping a round into the chamber got his attention.

Fairing marched toward the door, putting himself between Cooper and escape. "Get your filthy American ass back to your equipment! We have a plan," Fairing lied. "Everything is under control!"

"Everything's gone to shit! It's time to get out."

Fairing raised the pistol higher, aiming just above Cooper's eyebrows. "You filthy pig! If you don't get back there now, you'll die on this very spot. If you want to live, you'll get back there and complete your mission."

* * *

Rain, slanted by the heavy winds, pelted the roof of the drawbridge. Through her binoculars, she could see only ten of twenty rows were filled. Patriotism, for most, did not constitute standing in the rain. For those hearty enough to brave the storm, their patience was as long as their clothing was wet.

Jasmine listened to the ceremony commence through her earpiece. A woman's voice came over the sound system.

Welcome to the christening ceremony for the aircraft carrier Jacob R. Hope, CVN-81. Please stand as the platform party takes their place on the dais…

One by one, admirals, congressmen, the prospective captain of the ship, matrons of honor, and minor dignitaries were introduced. Jasmine imagined them taking their seats in the rows along the dais. They were followed by major dignitaries seated in front: Supreme Court justices, the governor of Virginia, the two Virginian senators, the secretary of defense, and the top executives of Penrose Gatling Shipbuilders. The CEO escorted the ship's sponsor, Katherine Hope Morris.

The former president, the ship's namesake, and the former first lady, Margaret, were announced and walked to their seats accompanied by a majestic presidential tune. Jasmine knew exactly where they would be seated.

The voice announced the president and the first lady. "Hail to the Chief" erupted in an orchestral flurry. Kader watched through her scope as Gary Hope and First Lady Linda Hope strolled along the gangway until they disappeared behind the large white canvas and the speaker's platform.

The color guard of the Command Navy Region Mid-Atlantic soft-stepped into position before posting the colors. She heard the scraping of chairs as everyone rose in unison. The American national anthem burst into her earphone. Captain John Wilson, the executive director of the Armed Forces Chaplains Board, delivered the invocation.

We join our hearts together in prayer. All-powerful and all-merciful God...

* * *

Fairing adjusted his position in the tall captain's chair, the rifle nestled on his shoulder. The speakers on the kitchen counter carried the words and sounds of the ceremony. His sister was hearing the same words from her perch on the bridge tower. That knowledge comforted him. He checked his watch, which had been synchronized with the other conspirators'. The jamming of the Secret Service communications would commence in five minutes.

The president of Penrose Gatling Shipbuilders began the procession of speakers.

Good morning! Mr. President and Mrs. Hope, Mr. President and Mrs. Jacob R. Hope, Mrs. Morris, Governor, Senators, and all our distinguished platform guests—to the entire Hope family and many friends, and to everyone here today—on behalf of the thirty thousand shipbuilders of Penrose Gatling Shipbuilders, we welcome you to the birthplace of America's nuclear-powered aircraft carriers!

This is a historic day to be a shipbuilder, as we christen the Jacob R. Hope. We have many special guests…

* * *

Jason watched Broadhurst pace back and forth, checking his wristwatch so many times that Jason lost count.

Broadhurst rationalized out loud, though not to Jason and Peter. "I don't know how they expect to hit their targets with that canvas in place. The view is blocked. But they've obviously planned with a great deal of forethought, so they've got to have something up their sleeves. The recording mentioned something called 'Cyclops.' I have no idea what that is."

Broadhurst checked his watch again and cursed.

Jason frowned. "What are we waiting for?"

"I'm waiting on trained backup, asshole!" Broadhurst did not like the idea of assaulting the condo with two civilians. Time was running out, along with his patience. "I'm giving these guys three minutes to get here. Then we go to plan B."

Jason had listened with great interest as Broadhurst, as innocuously as possible, instructed Alpha One to meet him in the lobby of the north tower. Hopefully, the baddies hadn't understood the meaning of the coded radio message, and they'd retained the element of surprise. The two Alpha One agents were his most experienced and trusted. They had some ground to cover, but they should have reached the lobby by now. "With them, we can take down these pricks," Broadhurst announced. The agent put his sleeve mike to his mouth, then tapped his ear piece. "You've got to be shittin' me," Broadhurst said, ripping the cord from his ear. He reached into his jacket and fiddled with the small radio clipped to his belt. "Communications just went down."

Jason frowned again. "What the hell are we waiting for? If these guys are in position up there, we need to move now."

Broadhurst hesitated, looking at Jason like he wanted to crack him in the jaw. He grabbed the pharmacist by the shirt with both hands and almost lifted him off the ground. "Listen to me, dipshit," he barked, his mouth an inch from Jason's nose. "*I* decide when we move. Got that? Who the hell do you think you are?"

Broadhurst was two inches taller and twenty pounds heavier than Jason. But Jason slipped both arms between the Secret Service agent's and thrust them upward. Jason's shirt ripped, and Broadhurst was left holding shredded fabric. Jason put both hands on the man's chest and shoved him backward into his brother, who was stepping in to mediate. Peter broke Broadhurst's backward momentum with his outstretched hands.

Jason jabbed a finger in the agent's face. "I've been stabbed, shot at, and arrested for murder. These bastards almost killed me and the people close to me. Three people are dead. I'll be damned if I'm gonna stand around waiting for your guys while they're up there getting ready to kill the presidents! Now, let's *move!*"

Broadhurst shrugged off Peter and cast him a sideways glance.

Peter shrugged. "We're out of options," he said.

Broadhurst tried the radio again and frowned. "This thing's still out."

He looked at Jason, then Peter, then back to Jason, contemplating his predicament. "Okay, we're heading up. But if you let me down, Rodgers, you'll wish those bastards had killed you!"

"I need a weapon," said Jason.

Broadhurst reached into his jacket and handed Jason his Sig Sauer P229. He reached into the other side and pulled out a second pistol. He turned to Peter and said, "You'll stay here and wait for Alpha One."

Peter opened his mouth to object, but Broadhurst cut him off. "With that leg of yours, you're no use to me. I can't be responsible for you. Since communications are down, I need you to talk to them when they show. Bring them to the fourth-floor stairwell. End of discussion."

Broadhurst pointed at Jason. "Keep up!"

CHAPTER 96

Fairing studied the white field of the canvas through the infrared scope. The rifle barrel did not extend through the opening in the tinted window, because Secret Service agents would be watching for just such an indicator of trouble. The shades were drawn as low as possible, stopping above the two two-inch circles cut into the glass. Through one, his deadly projectile would fly. Through the second, Cooper's invisible laser beams were lighting up the canvas screen.

He took several deep breaths. The words coming through the sound system relaxed his frayed nerves.

Penrose's president was at the podium concluding his remarks.

For more than a century, the ships built here, like their builders, have rendered faithful service. Some of those ships serve today. Some met glorious ends in faraway seas, in defense of our way of life. Wood has given way to iron, and iron to steel. We progressed from coal-powered vessels to nuclear energy. But every vessel is a monument to our nation's values.

Our first guest speaker is the seventieth governor of the Commonwealth of Virginia...

The governor of Virginia began the procession of speakers, addressing the soaked throng for nearly two minutes. He then introduced the chairman and CEO of Penrose Gatling Corporation. The junior senator from Virginia followed the chairman, and he introduced the next speaker three minutes later. The chief of naval operations took the podium. With the rain slanting in sheets, the admiral boomed platitudes over the loud speakers.

Senator Austin, thank you for that warm and kind introduction. President Hope and Mrs. Hope, thank you for being here. You honor us with your presence, and we greatly appreciate your leadership at this time in our nation's history. And Mr. President, Mrs. Jacob R. Hope, thank you as well for sharing with us, not only this day, but your great name...

* * *

Jason and Broadhurst silently arrived on the fourth-floor stairwell landing.

"Stay here until I get back," Broadhurst whispered.

"You can't do this alone," Jason replied.

"I'm going to the upper floors to get help. Stay here and don't make a sound. If I can recruit their help, you'll be relieved."

* * *

Ten minutes later, Broadhurst returned. His features were ashen. "There are dead agents in the stairwells above us." Broadhurst expelled an agitated breath. "Look's like we're the only party crashers." He shot Jason a concerned look.

"Don't look so worried. I know how to use this," said Jason.

He waited and watched as Broadhurst inched to the stairwell door, his back scraping painted concrete. He silently cracked it and peeked out. Slowly, he pulled it open, swiveling and propping it open with his back. His weapon, clutched with both hands, pointed at the floor. Broadhurst stuck his head partially around the doorframe to take in the hallway. Broadhurst held up a finger. One person.

After quietly closing the door, he returned to Jason's side.

"What did you see?" asked Jason.

Before Broadhurst could respond, Jason saw the door move, opening slightly. A silenced pistol appeared through the narrow gap. Jason was about to yell a warning when burps erupted.

The fusillade lasted less than two seconds. The first shot hit Broadhurst in the back, exiting through the front shoulder, spinning him. He groaned, dropping to the stairs. Jason pushed him out of the way as he tried to merge with the wall. Shots two and three missed, whizzing past him. He lifted his weapon and answered with three shots toward the hand holding the gun. All three missed, splintering wood. The hand and the weapon disappeared behind the closing door.

* * *

The senior senator from Virginia took the podium after the admiral. He droned on for more than five minutes. After being politely reminded, he ended his speech and introduced the secretary of the navy, who kept his remarks succinct. Next was the secretary of defense, who began,

It's a real privilege, a high honor, to be able to say a word about this mighty ship and the man whose name will proudly carry it across the high seas into victory...

* * *

Fairing jerked at the sound of the shots that seemed to emanate from the walls. His accomplices carried silencers, so their shots were muffled. The loud reports had to have come from the weapons of their adversaries. The *real* Secret Service. Fairing swallowed and focused on his weapon. "Just a few more minutes," he whispered. "Just give me a few more minutes."

The "agent" posted inside stepped from the unit, crouched and weapon leveled, to check out the reports.

Fairing kept his eyes glued to the scope and the luminescent green image. Without looking up, he picked up the Mauser resting at his elbow and pointed at the now-quaking Cooper. "You move, you die!"

CHAPTER 97

The president of the United States pumped the secretary of defense's hand and replaced him behind the podium emblazoned with the presidential seal.

Thank you all. Mr. Secretary, thank you very much. Linda and I are honored to be here, to honor our dad. Appreciate your coming. Mom, good to see you. We've come a long way from the early days in Tennessee. I know you'll join me in saying to my father, President Hope, "Your ship is about to sail..."

* * *

The bogus agent, sweat coating his face, managed a quick swipe with his sleeve to dry his forehead. He lay on his belly, eyes and gun focused on the white stairwell door, marveling at his good fortune and the poor marksmanship of the man behind the door. Three shots, all fired at close range, had missed.

465

He didn't know how many others had amassed on the other side of the door. He'd only seen two men. One was wounded. If they burst through the door, they'd be caught in a lethal crossfire between two crack shots. His buddy was prone on the carpet beyond the stairwell, as was the third man, who had just exited the condo. The hallway outside the stairwell door was a perfect killing zone.

A door opened behind the shooter. He hazarded a quick glance. A man and woman stood outside their open condo door, trying to locate the source of the noise.

"Get back inside and do not come out!" he yelled, turning back to the stairwell door. "There's a man with a gun!"

The frightened pair exchanged bewildered looks. Another door opened. A woman's head popped into view.

"Move! Everyone back inside! Now!"

The residents quickly returned to the safety of their condos. Door latches caught, and the sounds of dead bolts being engaged sounded like thunderclaps in the corridor.

* * *

Blood seeped from Broadhurst's chest wound. The bullet had entered Broadhurst's back and exited the front through a half-dollar-sized hole. His pressed white shirt was quickly turning crimson.

He wheezed, bubbles of red-tinted saliva gurgled from his lips. Broadhurst tried to key his mike. Jason guessed he was trying to order the presidents to be taken to safety. Broadhurst checked the unit with his left hand. It trembled as if he had Parkinson's disease, moving haltingly, a heartbeat too slow. His eyelids wavered as he teetered on the edge of consciousness. *Radio must still be out*, Jason thought.

Broadhurst motioned for Jason to lean closer. His mouth formed words, but no sound came forth.

"What?" asked Jason.

A pained whisper slipped from Broadhurst's lips. "Communications...still down...Save...POTUS!"

Then the man's eyes rolled back in his head.

Jason put a bloody hand to the agent's neck. The pulse was barely palpable and coming in unsteady intervals.

Shit!

This man was going to die without serious—and immediate—medical intervention, Jason knew. His pharmacy training and practice had imbued him with basic medical skills, but traumas of this magnitude were not part of that training. Even soldiers like his brother had more skill in dealing with such wounds than he did.

Jason quickly weighed the options. If he stayed and attended to Broadhurst, there was a good chance that two presidents would die. If he left the agent, Broadhurst was doomed.

Jason compromised. He pulled off Broadhurst's shoes and removed both his socks, balling them tightly. With a grimace, he rammed one sock as far as he could into the gaping exit wound. He removed his suit coat and, rolling Broadhurst back over, did the same to the entry wound. He prayed the pressure would stem the colossal bleeding. It wasn't much, but it was the best he could do. It was the agent's only chance. The man's life was being measured in minutes.

Ignoring the guilt of leaving a dying man, Jason picked up Broadhurst's weapon, jammed it into his waistband beside the one already there, and vaulted the steps to the door.

CHAPTER 98

With his back against the wall, Jason pulled the door open an inch.

A bullet whizzed past his head like an angry hornet. Jason shrank back, releasing the door.

Shit! Shit!

He had glimpsed the man lying on the carpet, his weapon trained on the exit. If he stepped out, Jason would be riddled with bullets. All they had to do now was wait him out while Fairing and Kader lined up their shots. Jason frantically scanned the landing, trying to think of a way to open the door without getting shredded.

He needed a diversion. Jason moved back to Broadhurst and picked up one of his shoes.

* * *

President Gary Hope concluded his remarks and introduced his father to the citizens of southeastern Virginia.

On this fine day, the children of Jacob R. Hope bless their father's name. The United States Navy honors his name. May God watch over all the sailors stationed aboard her, all those who fly from her deck, and all those who pray for their safe return. I'm honored to bring to you the forty-second president, my father, Jacob R. Hope.

Jacob Hope, the octogenarian, walked haltingly across the dais.

Thank you, Mr. President, for that kind and wonderfully generous introduction. This is any aviator's dream come true. I first want to congratulate every man and woman who has made this vessel into the mighty war ship you see today...

* * *

The shot bisected the narrow opening. The fraudulent agent could put a hole in a quarter from fifty yards. His marksmanship was unparalleled. But he didn't know if he'd hit whoever had cracked the door. He flexed his fingers, his eyes never leaving the door. Ninety seconds had passed since he'd fired.

The door cracked again. The impostor held his fire for a brief moment, seeing nothing through the narrow slit. He pointed the weapon where he guessed a man's waist would be. An eternity passed. The door opened wider. Then, from above, something began to fall. He lifted his eyes. An object fell over the top of the door. In that split-second distraction, a weapon moved around the door. He tore his eyes away from the falling object a fraction too late. A muzzle flashed from inside the stairwell.

The explosion ripped through the impostor's brain, accompanied by a blinding whiteness before everything instantly went black. The black shoe bounced twice and came to rest on its polished side.

* * *

Jason pressed against the doorframe and pivoted, letting the door rest against his back as Broadhurst had done earlier. He peered down the hall that angled to his right. All he could see was decorative wallpaper. This section of the corridor was empty except for the "agent" he'd just killed. Blood splattered the walls, not from the man he'd just dispatched, but from other victims. He crept to the bend near the elevators, hazarding another glance. Two silenced shots thudded into the wall behind him. Two more men lay on their stomachs at the far end of the corridor, several feet from each other.

The pain in his flank, temporarily blocked by his adrenaline, throbbed with each heartbeat. Moving the gun to his left hand, he sucked in four quick breaths and stuck the Sig around the angle, firing four rapid shots without looking.

He peeked again. All four shots had missed, but the two exposed men scrambled for cover, crawling to a condo doorway. Jason fired two more shots at the legs of the second man. The second shot pierced the man's left leg below the knee. A howl echoed through the corridor as the bloodied limb disappeared through the open door.

A second later, return fire erupted from the condo. Jason hugged the wall, pressed the magazine release, and the near-empty clip fell into his hands. Two rounds left. He dropped the weapon and removed the second pistol from his back.

The elevator door opened with a loud, ominous chime.

Jason belly-crawled to within a few feet of the elevator, keeping the weapon trained on the door where the leg had disappeared. A head and pistol popped out of the open car. Jason recognized the agent. He was one of the men from Alpha One, the team they'd been waiting for. Jason held up a hand, hoping a bullet wouldn't disintegrate it, and pointed down the hallway.

"They're in that apartment! Follow me! Where's your partner?"

"Dealing with what we thought was another threat. He stayed behind. It's just us."

Jason and his new ally crept to within two feet of the door.

"We need to get in there," the agent whispered.

"How?"

"By kicking it in."

CHAPTER 99

Jason faced the closed door, lying on his belly, the pistol trained on the grainy oak. He sucked in a deep breath through a desert-dry throat, waiting for the hell that lay beyond.

"On the count of three," the agent whispered, standing by Jason's left shoulder. "I'll kick it in. Shoot anything that moves."

The agent rose to full height with a foot on either side of Jason's shoulders.

"Ready...one...two..."

* * *

Fairing, oblivious to the commotion around him, adjusted his scope. His concentration was absolute.

Cooper, on the other hand, was a total wreck. Vomit welled in the back of his throat as he watched the leg wound pump a small lake of blood over the carpet. He puffed his cheeks, suppressing the nausea. A streak of crimson trailed the wounded man to where

472

he writhed on the floor. The second agent applied a makeshift tourniquet with a cloth.

Cooper shifted his gaze toward the door, unable to take in the sight any longer.

Escape was a memory now. They were trapped. The gunfire beyond the condo walls told him his only means of escape was the open balcony. It was an option he was weighing heavily.

The tinny voice of the elder President Hope came through the speakers. Cyclops was programmed and ready. All Cooper needed to do was press a button, and the infrared laser target would be invisibly projected through the circular hole in the window and paint a twelve-inch reticle on the white canvas a mile away.

"Now, Cooper!" Fairing commanded.

Cooper lowered a quaking finger to the enter button on the keyboard. An inch lay between Cooper's index finger and world-wide catastrophe.

At that instant, the door burst open. Two men filled the doorway. The one standing had just kicked in the door. The other was on the floor, pointing a gun…

* * *

The elder President Hope talked about the days leading up to his enlistment in the navy. He was proud of each and every one of the kids who had served, he said. After America was savagely invaded at Pearl Harbor, a wave of young men and women had been anxious to serve, totally unified against all threats to freedom. He went on to explain that America had been an "innocent nation" of merchants, and had instantly become a major industrial producer of armaments.

CHAPTER 100

The Secret Service agent's foot connected with the door, splintering the frame and continuing through. As he kicked, the business end of his weapon tilted toward the ceiling, leaving him totally exposed and unprotected.

Jason scanned the apartment instantly. Four men were huddled in the condo. To the right, the man with the leg wound sat bleeding against one wall. A buddy kneeling over him. Steven Cooper stood in the middle of the group with his hand poised over a keyboard wired to an electronic gizmo. The fourth man was farther away, near a window, sitting in a tall chair behind a wooden platform, manipulating a mammoth rifle with an equally massive scope. Jason immediately recognized Sam Fairing's diminutive form.

The immediate threat came from the man kneeling over the wounded man. Jason ripped off five rounds as the man fired in the same instant. Two rounds tore into the Secret Service agent above Jason. He lurched backward, landed heavily on Jason's right leg, and bounced, unconscious or dead. Jason heard a loud pop as pain ripped through his lower leg.

Jason's shots riddled the kneeling man, two in the left arm causing the weapon to sail away, two more in the lower abdomen, and the final, fatal shot piercing the small depression at the base of the neck. A fountain of red spewed like a geyser from the jugular.

Jason retrained the gun on the wounded man, who had managed to grab a pistol. Jason pumped four rounds into his chest. The wounded man squeezed off only one. It missed.

Out of the corner of his eye, Jason saw Fairing disappear when the shooting began, retreating down a hallway to the left. Steven Cooper stood paralyzed a few feet to the right of the dead shooters. Jason turned the gun on the tall, lanky man. Before he could fire, Cooper dropped his weapon and raised his hands.

Jason crawled into the apartment and rose to his feet with difficulty. His knee was swelling and hurt like hell.

"On the floor, asshole," Jason commanded Cooper, scanning for Fairing but seeing nothing.

"Don't shoot!" Cooper pleaded. He dropped to his knees and lay facedown with his hands clasped behind his head. Jason picked up Cooper's gun and surveyed the carnage.

Four bullet-riddled bodies. Pools of expanding blood, the smell of cordite. The sniper rifle aimed out the window. A handgun abandoned on the platform, next to a laptop connected to some sort of machine.

Anger rose in Jason like a tsunami. The events of the last weeks swarmed him like agitated, malevolent ghosts. He bent over Cooper with a trembling hand and placed the barrel of the gun against the back of his head.

"You scumbag!" he seethed.

CHAPTER 101

Consumed by monumental ire and focused on Cooper, Jason did not see Fairing until it was too late. Jason looked up at the last instant. Fairing's clothing and skin filled Jason's field of vision as the pharmacist-assassin struck him hard. The gun flew out of Jason's hand, bouncing into a corner. The men landed in a heap with Fairing on top, struggling in a swirl of sweat and murderous desperation. Fairing drove a fist at his face. Jason dodged. The fist slammed the hard, carpeted floor. Jason countered with a quick but powerful elbow to the cheek.

Fairing, dazed by Jason's blow, blinked rapidly as he recovered. Jason seized a fistful of hair, holding the assassin's head in place as he connected with two rapid punches, snapping the nose. He pushed Fairing away. Blood poured from the assassin's nostrils. Jason scrambled to his feet, ignoring the pain seizing his leg and body. He assumed a fighting stance and began bouncing rapidly. His hands were near his face, balled into fists.

Fairing was dripping crimson droplets on the white carpet before Jason. His head was lowered, his shoulders sagged. Jason thought it was over. Fairing was giving up. But panic seized him when Fairing wrapped his fingers around the pistol that had been knocked from Jason's hands.

Jason was about to launch himself at Fairing, but the gun was already leveled. The round, black opening of the barrel stared into Jason's soul. It was too late. His intestines seized. His lungs deflated in a long, slow breath…

CHAPTER 102

A smile expanded slowly across Fairing's face as his finger curled around the trigger.

A shuffling noise came from Jason's left. Fairing reacted, shifting his gaze.

"Gun!" Jason yelled as Peter's limping form filled the door. He launched into a spinning round kick, connecting with Fairing's hand and knocking the gun barrel aside. Fairing maintained his grip on the weapon. It discharged. Out of the corner of his eye, Jason saw Peter go down. Fairing drove a blow into Jason's midsection and violently shoved him away.

Jason lunged again, when another loud boom rocked the room. The shot came from Peter's position. Fairing's body jerked as Jason grabbed hold of his shirt. A large rosette of blood expanded over Fairing's upper thigh. Fairing, undaunted, pummeled Jason's face. Jason blocked the punches and landed three of his own. Fairing's small but powerful fingers wrapped around Jason's throat, squeezing it closed. Jason, struggling for air, extended his right fore and middle fingers in a modified spearfinger attack. It looked like a kind of Boy Scout salute as Jason sank the tips into Fairing's right eye. The soft, gelatinous eyeball yielded as he buried the digits to the first knuckle.

Fairing screamed, releasing his choke hold. He rolled onto his side in agony. Jason grabbed the weapon, which had fallen to the floor, and kicked Fairing once in the head for good measure. He rolled and gyrated, screaming. Jason watched him for a few seconds.

Satisfied Fairing was temporarily out of commission, Jason went to Peter. His brother clutched the tissue over his right clavicle as blood seeped through his fingers.

"Thanks for showing up," Jason said.

Peter gave a pained nod.

"Where'd you get the gun?"

"Took it off the dead guy in the hallway. I'm getting tired of saving your ass, little brother."

Jason scoffed. "Hell, this was nothing compared to saving me from Greg the Goon in fifth grade." He motioned toward Peter's shoulder wound. "Is it serious?"

"I don't think so," Peter replied, wincing. "Like they say in the movies, it's a flesh wound."

CHAPTER 103

The elder Hope described how he'd gone off to war, taking off from the deck of the aircraft carrier *San Jose*. As an officer, he recalled having to read the outgoing mail, censoring the correspondence of his shipmates. "I learned a lot about the strong souls of those kids." The former president paused, bowing his head, choking back tears.

* * *

The words of the former president were partially obscured by static through the earpiece. The electrical storm was interfering with the signal. Jasmine Kader studied the canvas through the same model scope her brother used, waiting for the laser target to appear. The crosshairs rested on the spot where the laser target should be. She ran her finger along the trigger housing. *That idiot's late!*

The safety was off. One round was in the chamber, with another waiting in the magazine. She had sighted, balanced, and honed the

480

settings and aspects of the rifle so many times it felt like an extension of her own body.

Jasmine's upper torso was exposed, pelted by large raindrops. Her legs were covered by the tarp. She'd discovered as she'd maneuvered the rifle under the tarp that its heavy lead hampered her ability to adjust the barrel. A problem that hadn't been anticipated. After the current president had finished speaking, she'd carefully and slowly peeled back the covering, exposing her body to the elements.

Lightning flashes lit up the sky. The wind and rain were more treacherous. Droplets had formed on the hooded end of the scope and were affecting her line of sight.

Cursing out loud in Arabic, she spun on her belly and retreated back under the tarp. The heavy wind gusted. The rain popped the rooftop like small-arms fire. She extracted the towel from her bag.

* * *

Jason, realizing that his brother was in no immediate danger, stepped over the writhing Fairing. Blood and eyeball goo seeped through the dark skin of Fairing's fingers. The large hole in his trouser seeped blood, darkening the fabric. Jason quickly picked up one handgun from the floor and the other from the platform. He tossed them both to Peter, who leveled one in the direction of both Cooper and Fairing.

"I'm gonna find something to tie them up with. If they move, shoot them," said Jason.

"I'd love to," Peter replied.

Jason frantically searched the apartment. Thirty seconds later, he returned with some duct tape he'd found in one of the bedrooms near the tools used to make the platform. He ripped the cord running from the laptop to the wall and bound Cooper's hands behind his back with the cord, and his feet and knees with the duct tape.

He next bound Fairing. He needed Peter's help to restrain the writhing man. When they pulled his hands away from his face, there was a gaping hole where his eye had once been. Jason dragged the two bound men to opposite corners of the room.

"Don't fucking move," Jason commanded the cowering Cooper.

"They were close," Jason said, surveying the sight through the window.

"Too damn close," Peter replied.

"You!" Fairing called to Jason. "You think you've won. You have not won. Allah will rain the curse of hell upon you and your family!"

"I don't think so, Sam. You're done," Jason replied calmly.

Fairing's smile widened. "Your presidents are still dead men."

Remembering, Jason's eyes found Peter's. Jason shouted, "There's still another shooter! Jasmine's out there!"

"Where is she, Sam?" Jason demanded.

Fairing smiled confidently. "Allahu Akbar!"

Jason noticed Fairing's eye shift as he spoke the words. It focused for a brief moment over Jason's shoulder and out the picture window.

Jason knelt down and grabbed Fairing by the shirt. "Where is she?"

Fairing spit in Jason's face. Jason wiped it away with a sleeve and slammed Fairing in the face with a fist.

Jason looked again in the direction Fairing's eye had shifted. He saw the James River Bridge in the gray distance.

Peter was on his feet now, clutching his shoulder through a bloodied hand. He saw his brother's mind working. "What is it?"

"The recording," Jason began, "said Jasmine would be on the *other* north tower looking at traffic below. We didn't pay attention to that detail before. We all just assumed it meant this north tower. There's another one. Right there!" Peter pointed out the large window toward the James River Bridge.

Jason turned back to the one-eyed assassin. "Isn't that right, Sam?" Then he turned back to Peter. "I bet she's on that tower!"

Jason grabbed Fairing's sniper rifle from the platform. He lugged it back to the window and lifted it to his eye, scanning the bridge in the distance.

"If I were her, I'd be right there!" Peter pointed through the bay window overlooking the balcony and the river to the northern tower of the span.

Jason zeroed in. "There's someone on the nearer tower," he said. "It's hard to see, but there's someone there. That's her!"

Now that they knew what they were looking for, both men saw the figure with the naked eye, jutting from the rooftop like a tiny bump. "There's a gun! She looks like she's wiping off a weapon," said Jason. Through the high-powered scope, he could see the female form. "She looks like she's gonna take a shot."

A bolt of lightning cracked nearby, so close that the white streak was simultaneous with the ear-shattering thunder. Both Peter and Jason flinched.

"Damn, that was close," said Peter.

"I estimate we're about three quarters of a mile from the drawbridge," said Peter. He turned to his brother. "Jason, you can do this."

"Me?" Jason asked.

"Yeah. You've practiced this. I can't do it. Not with this shoulder."

Jason thought a moment. "You're right. It's our only option. Help me move this platform." They limped back to Fairing's platform.

* * *

The laser target still had not appeared. She was going to take the shot anyway. She had a good idea where the bullet needed to hit. She wasn't leaving here without firing her weapon. Chances were good she'd hit someone important.

The elder president was concluding his speech.

Now or never!

She readjusted her eyes on the scope, pulling back slowly on the trigger.

* * *

President Hope expressed his gratitude and overwhelming pride. He couldn't wait to see the massive vessel go to sea and asked permission of the commander in chief to be on board—an ear-splitting crack of thunder interrupted the former president. As it died off, he thanked the American people for the opportunity to serve this nation.

* * *

The injured brothers dragged Fairing's heavy platform and placed it before the now-open window with a clear line of sight to the James River Bridge.

A series of power lines paralleled the bridge fifty yards to the north. Peter used the landmarks to gauge the distance. Peter began talking out loud, ticking off vital statistics for his brother. "There are three high-voltage stanchions between the shoreline and the one closest to the tower. They're about two thousand feet apart. I estimate the distance to the target to be a tad over a mile.

"We're on the fourth floor. That puts us about forty feet in the air. I guess the top of that drawbridge to be about a hundred and fifty feet over the water. That means the roof is about a hundred and ten feet higher than we are. At a range of a mile, you'll need to aim a smidge low to avoid missing high."

Jason adjusted his scope.

"By the slant of the rain," Peter said, "I estimate the wind to be about ten miles per hour crossing from your right. Adjust your windage turret forty-four clicks."

Jason made his adjustments. The sound of the rain and wind pummeling the windows lent the scene an eerie backdrop.

Jason sucked in a lungful of air, released half of it. He smoothly pulled back on the trigger. At that precise moment, a white burst of lightning illuminated the sky. The thunderclap accompanying it was simultaneous with the flash. The projectile streaked toward Jasmine Kader at 2,800 feet per second.

The report of the weapon, enveloped by the thunder, was almost inaudible. The gun bucked against Jason's shoulder. A plume of white smoke seeped from the barrel of the .50 caliber. The acrid smell of cordite briefly filled their nostrils, then the smoke was sucked out into the rain.

Through the scope, Jason tracked the vapor trail of the projectile slicing the heavy air. Just under two seconds later, the projectile penetrated the side of Jasmine's head, exiting her skull in a plume of bone, brains, and blood. It passed through so quickly, she did not move, but instead lay without ever flinching.

Peter grabbed the rifle and checked the target. He turned to Jason and said, as if he were talking about a nine iron to the eighteenth green, "Nice shot!"

Peter dropped the weapon, and it clattered to the carpet. He pushed his brother in celebration, wrapping a beefy arm around Jason's neck. A wide, relieved grin involuntarily spread across Jason's face.

CHAPTER 104

Katherine Hope Morris took the podium, her voice cracking as she read from her notes in a short, glowing tribute to her father.

Mrs. Morris concluded her remarks and joined her brother, President Gary Hope, her father, and the Penrose executive on the bottle-break stand in front of the bow of the mighty vessel. The executive handed her a large bottle of American sparkling wine, encased in slotted aluminum and covered with a crocheted cotton sleeve, festooned with red, white, and blue streamers. She spoke the words that have been spoken for centuries. "I christen thee United States ship *Jacob R. Hope*. May God bless all who sail her!"

With a two-handed swing, Mrs. Morris smashed the bottle against the stainless-steel railing protruding from the bow. White spray foamed, and the Fleet Forces Band dove into "Anchors Away." The throng broke into cheers and rhythmic clapping. The four stood for photos before making their way back to the stage.

Sean Murphy, the famed Irish tenor and a good friend of the elder president, sang "God Bless America."

486

While the storm clouds gather far across the sea,
Let us swear allegiance to a land that's free,
Let us all be grateful for a land so fair,
As we raise our voices in a solemn prayer.
God Bless America…

* * *

Jason checked the two prisoners. Cooper was slumped in his corner, whimpering like a schoolgirl. Fairing, on the other hand, was apoplectic, struggling against his restraints, making low, menacing sounds. He leered at Cooper, mumbled something in Arabic, then shifted his good eye toward the brothers, locking eyes with Jason. He continued mumbling inaudible and unrecognizable epithets at the pharmacist.

"What did you say?" Jason asked.

"Those pigs deserved to die," Fairing snarled. "They destroyed my country. May Allah commend you to hell!" Fairing spat at Jason's face again, but the wad missed and landed on his shirt.

A slow, triumphant smile stretched Jason's lips. He leaned a little closer as Peter put a hand on his shoulders to stop him. "Sorry about your bad luck, asshole!"

Jason launched a front kick. Fairing's head banged into the wall. He slumped, unconscious.

A team of federal agents burst through the open door, guns drawn. "Freeze!"

Jason and Peter raised their hands in surrender. "Easy, guys." Jason cocked a head in Fairing's direction. "They're the ones you want."

"On the floor! Now!"

The brothers lay on the floor as agents surrounded them. As their hands were being secured with plasticuffs, Jason looked at his brother. "That's another seafood dinner for me."

Peter shook his head, dug deep into his marine corps repertoire, and released a string of vile curses. Then his face lit up in a wide smile. "Gladly," he whispered.

EPILOGUE

Monday, December 11

The Monday-morning prescription rush was in full fury. Refills called overnight and early morning were queued on the terminal, waiting to be billed to insurers, and the laser printer ejected labels at breakneck speed. The phone chirped every few minutes as doctor's offices called in antibiotics and cough syrups for their early appointments. The winter cold and flu season had hit full stride. Kevin Mitchell and Billy Parks scurried about. The counter was cluttered with prescriptions and pill bottles.

Most of Jason's physical injuries had mended. The scar on his flank, the only visible reminder of his gargantuan struggle, ached when the clouds rolled in and the air grew heavy. Luckily, it could be hidden under clothing. He still limped, the torn ACL in his left knee caused by the falling agent in the hallway. Surgery to repair it was scheduled for next week. It hurt and throbbed, but Jason was thankful he was still around and able to feel pain.

He stood back with his arms folded across his chest, taking his work environment in with a renewed sense of wonder. A retail pharmacist's work would always be, at times, stress-filled and frustrating, he realized. Sick, suffering patients wanted their meds quickly and with as little fuss as possible. But insurance companies, laws, regulations, and the bottom line sometimes made things difficult for everyone. It was the nature of the beast.

He would never again complain about the workload or the demanding patients. He'd been through enough in the last eight weeks to keep an army of psychiatrists busy for a decade. The relative boredom was a welcome change.

As he fingered the object in his pocket, Jason let his mind wander to what had transpired in the preceding two months.

* * *

Jason and Peter rapidly explained what had happened after the unfamiliar Secret Service agents had raided the condominium on the fourth floor of the north tower. Jason demanded that Broadhurst be attended to, if he was in fact still alive. An agent was sent to look for the fallen man. Agents debriefed the two men in separate bedrooms. After twenty minutes, someone in a dark suit appeared and examined Jason's stab wound and injured knee with what seemed to be advanced medical training. The stab wound was extremely serious and showed signs of infection. The interrogation was cut short, and Jason was rushed to the same Tidewater Regional Medical Center emergency room from which he'd escaped. As he was carried out on a stretcher, Jason noticed that Fairing and Cooper were no longer in the condo's living room. Peter later told him he'd seen them rushed out under heavy guard as Peter was being escorted to one of the bedrooms.

Surgeons removed the festering, necrotic kidney from Jason's flank that afternoon. The three days in intensive care battling sepsis had been touch and go. Only with a host of powerful intravenous antibiotics and other pharmaceuticals had he been able to fight off the near-fatal infection and intense pain.

A Secret Service agent and a Newport News police officer had been posted outside his ICU cubicle twenty-four hours a day. He was, after all, wanted for the murder of Sheila Boquist and for several other felonies. Jason was transferred to a step-down unit and a more conventional room after a week. Detective John Palmer and York County investigator Calvin Baxter appeared an hour after the nurses departed, wasting no time in asking pointed questions and laying out incriminating facts. Of course, Jason denied being anywhere near Sheila's house at the time she was murdered.

Palmer had a knowing, sympathetic look in his eyes as Baxter tossed about questions. It said, *I know what happened in the towers, but there's nothing I can say or do.* Palmer had heard the Conversation, and he knew Jason was innocent. Baxter was—and would remain—in the dark. Jasmine Kader was dead. Sam Fairing and Steven Cooper were in custody and had not been seen or heard from since. Lily and Oliver were dead, killed in a suspicious explosion aboard *Vengeance.* Everyone who could exonerate Jason was gone or had been sworn to silence. And the United States government was not about to offer up the audio to clear Jason's name.

Jason glared at Palmer, silently demanding, *Get me out of this. You know what happened.*

He was on the verge of requesting an attorney when a man in a dark suit appeared in the door, flashing a badge. It was Secret Service agent Stanley Limbert, who'd been the first agent through the door after Jason had killed Jasmine Kader. He'd taken charge during the hectic aftermath.

He motioned for the two detectives to meet him in the hallway. Snippets of heated conversation were audible. Three minutes later, Baxter and Palmer re-entered and told Jason that he was no longer a suspect. Baxter was now holding a pair of men's shoes suspended in a large plastic evidence bag, which Jason guessed Limbert had given to him. The detectives departed.

"Who killed Sheila?" Jason demanded of Limbert.

"Jason, I'm not at liberty to say how you've been cleared. Just know that your innocence is undisputed."

Limbert asked briefly about Jason's injuries, then began his own interrogation. "We have Waterhouse's digital recorder and the flash drive. Are there any more copies of the conversation between Zanns and her Simoon team?"

"No," Jason lied. "Those are the only copies I'm aware of."

Christine still had the copy Jason had brought to her house in the early hours of the morning. She'd agreed to keep its existence quiet, and it was now sitting in a safety deposit box in a local bank. He hadn't checked yet. But the e-mail he'd received from Waterhouse was probably still in his inbox. It might prove valuable, should the government pursue charges. Pettigrew's files were still locked in the safe in Peter's Gun Shop.

The agent studied him. Apparently satisfied, he changed the subject. "Your silence, along with that of your cohorts, is not only expected, Jason, it is, quite frankly, required. If you speak to anyone about any of what went on during the christening, your life will become very uncomfortable. We've managed to keep a lid on what happened so far."

"Eventually, people will talk," Jason interrupted, "and the facts will leak out. The events will become the stuff of legend and conjecture. I can't be held responsible for that."

Limbert scowled and shrugged. "Just keep your mouth shut!"

Jason remembered that Limbert had forbidden emergency technicians to enter Fairing's condo on the fourth floor. Only the agents, Jason, Peter, Fairing, and Cooper knew what had almost happened in Fairing's condo. Jason was certain Detective John Palmer had been leaned on heavily—most likely threatened, as Jason was being now. Not one mention in the papers or on TV had been made about an assassination attempt. There had been an article below the fold about the towers being locked down because of a shooting of a resident on the fourth floor. The story was quickly relegated to the local section, then disappeared.

"I want something in return for my silence," Jason said.

"And what is that?"

"I want my name cleared. The public thinks I'm an escaped murderer. I want an article printed on the front page of the *Gazette* declaring I'm no longer a suspect."

Limbert tugged an earlobe. "Fair enough. We can make that happen. We've arranged to drop the charges for the crimes you committed while on the run as well."

After Limbert's visit, Jason closed his eyes, sighed, and began to shake uncontrollably. The mental and emotional scars would last three lifetimes. Three weeks passed before he could sleep through the night, and even then he needed heavy doses of alprazolam and antidepressants to do it. But the sedated sleep could not be called refreshing.

* * *

"I can't find the end-of-week report," the female voice announced from the back hall. The click-clack of heels preceded her appearance. Christine strode through the doorway on a mission. She saw him, and her eyes sparkled.

"Good morning, handsome," she said, batting her eyes at Jason as she ran a finger provocatively along his arm. "Think you could help me find it?"

Jason whispered his response, "Why, Ms. Pettigrew, I do believe you're tempting me with the promise of sexual favors in return for my help."

"You're damned right I am," she replied. "I told you, I only use my powers for good." Christine planted a soft, wet kiss on Jason's lips that lingered a moment longer than it should have.

"After a kiss like that, I'll help you find the lost city of Atlantis," said Jason. "How's your headache?"

Christine shrugged. "It's better. Imitrex is a wonder drug." They walked back into Thomas's old office.

A CT scan had revealed a tiny skull fracture caused by the attack in Jason's living room. Cerebrospinal fluid had seeped from her ear canal. Though it was healing nicely, the doctors also diagnosed a severe concussion. In the office, Jason walked to a bookcase sagging under the weight of reams of papers, and pulled out the report.

"You're my hero," Christine said, taking the report. She clasped her hands behind his neck and gave him another deep, languid kiss. Jason closed his eyes, and his mind flashed to Christine's petite hand wrapped around his weak fingers in the hospital.

"I wish I could've been your hero for the last thirteen years," he whispered. "I need to make up for lost time."

"You'll have that chance, baby."

"When are we meeting the lawyer?" he asked.

"Wednesday. This will be a bear," she said. "I hope it works."

Technically, the Colonial had no owner. Billy Parks had stepped up to the plate and kept the place running while both Christine and Jason recuperated. Since no heirs to Zanns could be located, Christine—at Jason's urging—hired a lawyer and began proceedings to have the Colonial's ownership revert back to her father's estate and ultimately to her. The byzantine legal process was long and difficult. But a renewed sense of purpose and duty to her father motivated Christine. She owed him that much, she'd told Jason.

"It'll work," Jason replied. "Your father would be proud of you."

"This place was his life, even after he sold it," she said with resignation.

Jason removed the shiny object from his pocket. He took her hand in his and gently slipped the Heart Stone into her palm. Christine looked at the shiny, red, heart-shaped rock she had given Jason thirteen years ago.

"Oh my God," she whispered. "Jason, you kept it. After all these years, you still have it."

Jason lifted her chin with a finger. "Yes, I do. I've never stopped loving you, Chrissie. You gave this to me because you loved me." Jason closed her fingers around it. "I'm giving it back to you because…I love you. More than you'll ever know. I'm not letting you go. Ever again."

She flung her arms around Jason's neck, squeezed him tight, and gave him another long kiss. Christine pulled away, ran a hand gently over Jason's cheek, and locked eyes with his. She whispered, "I love you."

Ten seconds later, Rachel, the purple-haired cashier, appeared in the office door. She coughed loudly and knocked twice on the frame. "You have a visitor," she said.

The man looked smaller, more fragile. The skin hung over the cheekbones, its fullness gone. Despite the gaunt appearance, it was a face Jason would always recognize. Clay Broadhurst, his arm in a sling, smiled across the pharmacy counter at Jason and Christine. Broadhurst lying on his back in the stairwell, gurgling, "Save POTUS!" was a memory that would haunt Jason until the day he died.

"Can I have a word?"

They crammed into the small space of the office. Broadhurst was given the seat across from the dented metal desk. Christine sat in her father's chair, while Jason leaned against a file cabinet.

Broadhurst held Jason's gaze as the agent tried to get comfortable. Finally, he spoke. "Thank you," the agent whispered. "Thank you for what you did."

"I abandoned you," Jason replied. He'd been certain his decision at the time was a death sentence for Broadhurst. The agent who had kicked the door in as Jason lay on the floor had, in fact, died. Along with at least six others.

"I was thanking you for saving the presidents."

Jason simply nodded, while Christine smiled proudly.

Broadhurst continued. "I apologize, but the need for secrecy precluded my visit before today. People have been working very hard behind the scenes to—"

"To cover up the attempted assassination," Jason interrupted.

Broadhurst smiled wryly. "I can't argue that point. But it's in everyone's best interest that this episode not be made public. Your government is very grateful."

"Why are you here, Agent Broadhurst?"

"I need both of you to come with me."

* * *

The SUV pulled alongside its twin on the tarmac at Newport News–Williamsburg International airport. A Gulfstream jet waited in the morning chill, its cabin door open. Christine and Jason climbed aboard, followed by Broadhurst. Another agent emerged from the sister vehicle escorting Peter. Five minutes later, the jet engines roared as the aircraft sped along the runway and the plane lifted off.

"Where are we going?" asked Jason.

Broadhurst offered only a vague response. "We're heading north."

Jason popped a Coke and blurted the question he'd been longing to ask for two months—and which he'd thought might always go unanswered. "What happened to Fairing and Cooper?"

Broadhurst stared coolly. "That's as good a place to start as any," he said. "What I'm about to tell you is highly confidential, top secret in fact. I shouldn't tell you this. It could cost me my job." He scratched his cheek and looked at his patent leather shoes. "If you speak about this to anyone, the United States will prosecute to the fullest extent—and discredit all of you with extreme severity." He looked at each of them in turn. "Fairing and Cooper have been detained in a location to which even I am not privy. They will never stand trial—"

"So they'll never be brought to justice?" asked Peter.

"I didn't say that."

"Why were they trying to kill the presidents?"

"Under 'extreme' interrogation, Fairing revealed that he, Zanns, Oliver, and Jasmine Kader were part of an ultrasecret group known as—"

"The Simoon," Jason said.

"That's right. The word means 'poison wind.' In the Middle East, a simoon is a deadly sandstorm that rises up with little warning. They wanted revenge for the Gulf wars."

Jason removed the photograph from his wallet. It was the one of Lily Zanns and a much-younger Saddam Hussein he'd taken from the mansion. It had not left his person since he'd emerged from surgery. He showed it to Christine and Peter, then handed it to Broadhurst. "Does this help explain things?" asked Jason.

"Lily knows Saddam Hussein?" asked Christine.

"By the pose and looks on their faces," Broadhurst said, "it seems she knows him very well." He shook his head. "Why haven't I seen this photo before?"

"I was in surgery shortly after the assassination attempt. Things happened fast."

Jason removed a chain from around his neck and handed it over as well. On it hung the tiny camera he'd found in his house. "My house was bugged. Maybe this can help you find the other group."

"The other group?" Broadhurst asked. His shifty glance told Jason the agent knew more than he was letting on.

"Why were the Simoon trying to kill the presidents?" Christine persisted.

"According to Fairing," Broadhurst replied, "the Simoon were bent on revenge for the Gulf Wars. By the way, Fairing's not his real name. It's Sharif al-Faisal Hussein. Dr. Jasmine Kader was Jazan Hussein. They're Lily Zanns's children. Her real name was Delilah Hussein. She and Saddam were apparently never married, but she took his name. Sam, or Sharif, was destined to use the assassinations as a springboard to notoriety. It was planned that he would someday take Iraq back from what they consider to be their Western colonizers."

Peter said, "You told me in the middle of all this that Zanns's team had help. They had money, but not the technological ability to carry this out. 'They needed help,' you said."

Broadhurst gave them his best poker face. "I can't say anything about that."

"I'm right, aren't I?" Peter persisted.

"We all risked our lives. We deserve to know," Jason demanded.

Broadhurst leaned forward. "I don't give an airborne copulation what you deserve. This is a matter of national security. I've already told you too much."

Jason leaned forward, inches from Broadhurst's face. "Steven Cooper is an American, isn't he? He works for someone inside our government. Is he CIA?"

Broadhurst remained stone-faced.

Jason persisted. "Where did this secret American group come from? Who are they part of?"

Broadhurst put his palms up. "I can't tell you that."

"Who is Hammon?"

"I'm not going there, Jason! Give it up!"

Jason smirked in disbelief.

Perhaps Broadhurst felt he owed Jason. He relented somewhat. "Okay, okay. Let's assume, for the sake of argument, there's another group. If there were, it would explain a lot."

"How did they come to use the Colonial as a cover?" asked Peter.

"The Colonial had been targeted years earlier. Thirteen years, in fact. This group needed a front for money laundering. The Colonial was supposed to have been that cover. At the last minute, the plan was discarded."

Jason, Christine, and Peter exchanged glances.

Broadhurst continued, "Fairing and Cooper revealed some very interesting information about you, Jason. Information that goes back thirteen years."

"Oh yeah?" Jason's skin began to crawl.

"Yes," he said. "Before I go there, let me tell you something you already know. You were framed for the murder of Sheila Boquist."

"And?" Jason replied.

"Fairing and Kader killed her. They planted the wine glass, the knife, and the classified documents about the christening. The only reason we were able to connect Fairing to the murder was the bloody footprint he left in the house. Traces of blood found on his shoe soles matched Sheila's. We passed that on to the police, and that's why the charges were dropped. The locals in York County have closed the file on your girlfriend's murder."

"She was my ex-girlfriend," he corrected, glancing at Christine. "And she didn't deserve to die."

Broadhurst continued, "Back to what happened thirteen years ago. During your first stint at the Colonial, your employment ended rather suddenly. Why was that, Jason?"

Christine frowned. Peter looked at his brother, confused. Jason had not confided in his brother about that part of his past. Peter had been stationed in Hawaii at the Kaneohe Naval Air Station at the time.

"I was told to resign or be fired. If I stayed on, I would've lost my license to practice."

"Why?"

"Because, supposedly, I made a medication error that resulted in the death of an elderly patient. What the hell does this have to do with anything?"

Broadhurst smiled like the cat that swallowed a very fat canary. "You were set up then as well."

"What?"

"You were set up by the secret group that doesn't exist. Thomas Pettigrew had begun to experience financial problems as the big pharmacy chains took hold. He was targeted for ruin. Every employee at the Colonial was profiled, researched, and infiltrated. A series of unfortunate events were planned that would lead to the Colonial's downfall. Then our secret group would swoop in, buy the pharmacy, and save it, only to use it for their purposes. You were targeted for removal because you were considered a liability, someone who would get in the way, ask too many questions. So they set you up long before

Lily Zanns ever came into the picture. The medication error wasn't supposed to kill the woman, just be serious enough to get you fired."

"You mean…"

"Cooper knows the name, the place, and the drug involved. He knew details to which he couldn't possibly have been privy. The players posed as lawyers and put pressure on Pettigrew to fire you. The old man resisted at first. We don't know why. It may have had something to do with your relationship with Ms. Pettigrew here. More pressure was applied. He left the decision up to you."

The hum of the jet engines filled the silence.

"Daddy changed after that," Christine offered. "That must have been the catalyst for his obsession with conspiracies. He went downhill after you were gone."

Jason placed a hand on her arm, but directed his question to Broadhurst. "How did they convince the family to drop the suit?"

Broadhurst rubbed his chin. "According to Cooper—or whatever his name is—"

"You don't know his real name?" asked Peter.

"We do, but I'm not going to reveal that. Cooper told us the family was given a large sum of money. They accepted it, and the matter was dropped. You left the Colonial and went on your merry way."

"Merry way, my ass!" Jason spat.

Peter asked, "So why, after thirteen years, did they decide to use the Colonial again?"

"From what we can gather—Cooper's a little fuzzy on this—a man named Hammon kept tabs on the Colonial. Since both presidents would be attending the christening in Newport News, the Colonial was the perfect cover. Thomas Pettigrew managed to get into financial trouble on his own. They hired Zanns and her conspirators to kill the presidents. She swooped in to purchase the pharmacy three years ago. It had been in the works for that long."

"If they thought I was a liability the first time, why did she hire me the second time?" Jason asked.

"That was *her* mistake. She didn't know about the previous operation. You happened along at the right time, she needed a scapegoat. It was supposed to have been Thomas Pettigrew. You became the new fall guy."

Jason shook his head. "You know, it just occurred to me. Lily—or Delilah—hired me to be the vice-president so she could keep tabs on me while she set me up. She put me to work cleaning out the back room. If she hadn't, I never would've found that missing prescription with Thomas's note on the back. In a way, she brought herself down."

"Thomas," Peter added, "also helped. His files and his death led you back to the Colonial."

Jason asked one more question. "We know he was killed. They admitted it on the recording. How did they make it look like an accident?"

"As best we can piece it together," Broadhurst explained, "Thomas discovered the irregularities with the prescriptions. He installed the cameras, ran his reports, and followed Fairing the night of the second-to-last drop. He was spotted. Fairing said he was shot as he ran away. Jasmine Kader—who is a real physician—sutured the wound. Then someone forced him to drink whiskey, drove him to Smithfield, set the accelerator somehow, and rammed the car into a tree. The rest is…" Broadhurst's voice trailed off.

"Who actually killed Thomas?" asked Jason.

"Thomas's GPS never registered any more movement after Fairing returned to the towers that night. So we don't think Fairing did it."

"It was that secret organization that doesn't exist again, right?" asked Jason.

"You got it," Broadhurst replied.

"How did Dad learn about the Simoon?" Christine asked.

"We may never know the answer to that question. Perhaps he saw the tattoos on the arms, the way Jason did."

Jason asked, "Why use Winstead? Why not just call in a prescription over the phone?"

"They wanted to make the scenario look as normal as possible. It certainly wasn't infallible," Broadhurst replied.

"Another thing that bothers me," Jason interrupted, "is that they never had anyone sign the signature logs. They could've easily forged a signature to make it look like they'd dispensed the medication. Did Fairing give you any idea why they missed that?"

"We showed him the documents and reports Pettigrew had gathered, along with the video of Fairing in the Colonial picking up the empty prescription bag. He seemed quite embarrassed by the fact that they'd been so sloppy. He muttered something Arabic. My guess is they simply missed it."

Jason nodded slowly. "They'd planned this thing for three years, and something as simple as forgetting to forge a signature helped bring it all down?"

"Sometimes the smallest details can cause the biggest problem," Peter chimed in.

"Getting back to Winstead," Broadhurst began again, "Fairing mentioned that he was being paid very well to deliver the prescriptions. We checked his accounts and his house, but came up with nothing. An empty cubbyhole was found in his house in the living-room floor. Any of you happen to know what happened to the money?"

Jason looked nervously about the cabin. The money was lying safely wrapped in a plastic bag stuffed inside a half-full bag of grass seed in his shed. He would make certain it would wind up helping Winstead's daughter, Charlie, in Georgia.

The mention of the money sparked a myriad of memories. Thomas, Winstead, and the attempts on each of their lives. Being framed for murder. There was still a deputy somewhere in Williamsburg who'd been part of the attempt on his life in jail. He felt no sense of urgency, but at some point, Jason knew he would be paying the man a visit.

The pilot's voice came over the intercom. They were beginning their descent.

* * *

They disembarked, bundled against a stiff winter breeze.

"Where are we?" Jason asked as they walked toward another black SUV.

"Andrews Air Force Base," Broadhurst replied.

Thirty minutes later, the vehicle pulled to a gate in a wrought-iron fence. Jason, Peter, and Christine peered at the world's most famous residence through the safety glass of the vehicle. The driver radioed that they had arrived. "Bring him to the door," he instructed.

"Holy shit," Peter muttered.

Broadhurst smiled at the driver, but said nothing.

Jason said, "Why are we pulling up to the White House?"

Christine squeezed his hand in anticipation.

The vehicle circled up the drive, stopping under the tall portico overlooking the south lawn. Three suited men were standing outside near the curb. Two were dressed in dark suits. The third was shorter.

"Is that who I think it is?" Jason asked.

Broadhurst smiled. "It is."

Standing on the curb, waiting for Jason, Peter, and Christine, was President Gary Hope.

Broadhurst turned toward the stunned faces of his three passengers in the backseat and smiled. "Someone would like to thank you!"